"Amii Lorin always gives her readers something special!"

—*Romantic Times*

WHILE THE FIRE RAGES
Amii Lorin

Author of Five Million Books in Print!

Winner of Two *Romantic Times* Reviewers' Choice Awards!

As ambitious as she was beautiful, Jo Lawrence ran the Renninger Corporation's multimillion-dollar hotel business with skill and ease. But when her boss died and his moody brother took charge, Jo's busy world was turned upside down. Jo knew she was falling in love with Brett Renninger from the start, but Brett's odd behavior and short temper made her wonder if their relationship could survive the transition from the boardroom to the bedroom.

AMII LORIN

WHILE THE FIRE RAGES

LEISURE BOOKS NEW YORK CITY

A LEISURE BOOK®

December 1992

Published by

Dorchester Publishing Co., Inc.
276 Fifth Avenue
New York, NY 10001

Printed in the United States of America.

For Vivian Stephens,
who started it all for me,
with deep respect, appreciation, and gratitude.

WHILE THE FIRE RAGES

CHAPTER ONE

Brett Renninger stood at the wide window staring at the wind-tossed, grayish-green sea. The Atlantic flung its waves with uncaring force against the shoreline bordering Ocean City, New Jersey. The wide window covered most of the wall in what was now an office but had been the living room of Brett's brother Wolf's apartment. The personal quarters he kept in one of many Renninger hotels.

Wolf.

Brett sighed, deeply, soundlessly. It was over three weeks now, three long, tension-filled weeks. He had been the logical choice to take over, but even had he not been, he'd have volunteered. Of course, he had not had to volunteer—he'd been summarily drafted.

Had anyone asked him if he could metaphorically fill Wolf's shoes one week, one day, ten minutes before the call came, Brett would have answered promptly, emphatically: No way!

That phone call. Brett's lips twisted. The memory of it was vividly clear and fresh. Perhaps it always would be.

As his hands had been employed with a bottle and a corkscrew when the phone rang in his Atlanta apartment, he had nodded his assent when the lovely young thing sitting close to him on the long, velvet couch asked sweetly, "Would you like me to answer that, Brett, honey?"

Brett could even remember the assessing glance he'd swept over the curvacious blonde as she rose languidly, experience again the curl of desire he'd felt watching her glide across the plush carpeting to where the phone rested on his desk. He'd returned his attention to the business in hand as the blonde murmured a husky hello, only to slice a frowning glance at the slim gold watch on his wrist when she said softly, "Brett, honey, it's a Mrs. Renninger. Your mother?"

He had returned to Atlanta late that afternoon, after a three-week-long trip to New Mexico to iron out the final details concerning the company's plans for the erection of a tri-complex condominium unit. In the seconds required to set aside the bottle and walk to his desk, he'd chided himself for ever entertaining the belief that his mother would wait until he was in his office the following morning for her regulation briefing on his trip. Not on the outcome, of course, for that was—at least in his mother's mind—a foregone conclusion. Thus he'd deliberately laced his tone with rueful amusement and dispensed with the usual greeting.

"Yes, sir?" he'd drawled insolently, fully expecting to hear his mother's appreciative chuckle ripple along the line from Miami. The tightly controlled tone of his mother's voice washed the amusement from his face.

"Wolf has been injured in an accident, Brett. He's in a hospital in Boston."

Brett could still feel the shock of his mother's opening statement, could hear the echo of his own exclaimed, "What?"

"Micki called me less then ten minutes ago," she'd supplied tensely. "I have no details, as the child was practically incoherent but"—the choking pause that followed instilled cold fear in

12

Brett—"I—she—Brett, she said the doctors aren't sure if they can save him."

Standing at the window, staring sightlessly at the roiling sea, Brett shivered with the memory of the never-before-heard stark terror in his mother's voice. In truth, the emotion that had momentarily gripped him had come damned close to a like terror.

His big brother, Wolf?

Thankfully, the need for action had sent the destructive emotion into retreat almost immediately.

"I'll leave at once, Mother," he'd begun with forced calm.

"I'm going with you, I've called Eric," she said, referring to her third son. "He's having the Lear readied. We'll be in Atlanta within two hours."

"I'll be waiting."

Never would he forget that early-morning flight north: his mother's colorless face—for the very first time revealing every one of its sixty-five years; Eric's handsomeness, strangely enhanced by his rigidly controlled expression; his own thoughts of Wolf. Wolf—the hero of his boyhood, the—

The rustle of papers from behind him scattered the memory. Turning slowly, Brett ran a contemplative gaze over the gleaming dark head bent over Wolf's large, rectangular desk.

The super-efficient assistant. Brett's assessment was not complimentary. Lids narrowing over eyes chilled to a steely gray by his thoughts, he inventoried the woman's exterior.

Even seated, her height was obvious. Somewhere between five feet nine and ten, he estimated—correctly. Slender—almost too slender, her fine bone structure lending an appearance of fragility.

Brett had to suppress a snort of disdain. A confection spun of pure steel, he condemned scathingly, his glance raking her delicate facial features, the pink-tinged ivory skin that covered them, the beautifully sculpted lips that hid perfect white teeth.

13

Thick, long hair in a rich, dark brown adorned her classically shaped head. Brett knew that when, eventually, she raised her eyes from her work, she would gaze at him from gold-flecked hazel eyes surrounded by lashes as dark and full as her hair, and so long as to appear artificial.

Brett had committed the vitals to memory: JoAnne Lawrence; age twenty-eight; unmarried; degree in business management, a certificate in hotel management. She had gone to work for the Renninger Corporation on completion of training, first as an assistant manager, then manager of a Renninger hotel in Pittsburg, Pennsylvania. Three years earlier she had been hired as the assistant to the assistant to the East Coast manager of Renninger Corporation—Madam President's firstborn, Wolfgang. She had secured the coveted position of first assistant fifteen months before when Wolf's righthand man, wanting a change, asked for and was granted a transfer to the newly open Hawaii region.

His face free of expression, Brett stared at the shining crown of her head. Oh, yes, he knew quite a bit about Ms. JoAnne Lawrence—usually referred to as Jo. He had made it his business to know. Neither idle curiosity nor personal interest had motivated his research. His interest in her had been aroused in a hotel lounge in Boston late one night nearly three weeks ago by the stricken face and anguished voice of his sister-in-law, Wolf's wife, Micki.

"He was with a woman, Brett," Micki had blurted suddenly. "Probably his assistant, Jo."

At first, Brett had given little credence to her outburst. The waiting, nerve-shattering days following Wolf's accident had left them all on edge. Micki was distraught and very close to exhaustion. Hurting for her, feeling protective, he had tried to soothe what he thought were her irrational fears.

"Honey, if this Jo whoever is his assistant, his being with her would be the normal order of business."

14

"Not if he was trying to conceal it, and from all indications, he was."

"What indications?" Brett had deliberately injected a chiding note into his tone.

"I know how you feel about Wolf, Brett, but, please, don't patronize me." Micki had blinked furiously against the tears shimmering in her eyes.

Brett was very fond of Micki. In fact, he rather envied Wolf. His brothers, at least, had been extremely lucky in their chosen life mates. Seeing Micki so near the breaking point alarmed him.

"I'm sorry." Reaching across the dimly lighted table, he'd clasped her hand with his. "Okay. Tell me what these indications are."

"I had a commiserating call from a friend at home today," she'd begun haltingly. "She'd read of Wolf's accident in the paper. I was thanking her for her concern when she interrupted with 'and to think I saw you only hours before it happened. I called to you but you were already in the car. But, of course, Wolf told you he saw me'—I was stunned."

"And that's it?" he'd asked incredulously.

"No." Micki shook her head impatiently. "I was confused. I told my friend Wolf hadn't mentioned seeing her. Then I asked her where she'd seen him. She said right in front of the hotel, *this* hotel. She added that Wolf seemed distracted and in a hurry, and that he hadn't even acknowledged her greeting."

"But, honey, I fail to see any indication of a clandestine meeting in that!" Brett, fully aware of Micki's utter weariness, had tried to reason with her. "It sounds to me like the work of a malicious woman whose nose had been put out of joint because a man, an *important* man, did not give her the recognition she probably thinks she deserves."

Micki had been shaking her head in denial before he'd finished his rationalization. "No, Brett, not this woman. She is one of our best friends. In fact, I'm sure you know her. Cindy Grant? She and her husband, Benny, are the cub's godparents."

Now, as he had three weeks ago, Brett smiled gently at the reference to Wolf's son, dubbed "the cub." Now the smile was as fleeting as it had been that night.

"Okay, there was no malicious intent on Cindy's part." He'd sighed. "But I still cannot believe you think this sketchy information enough evidence to bear out a conviction. *If* the woman in the car was his assistant, she had every right to be there."

"Oh, it was her." Micki's bitter tone had been a shock simply because Brett had never heard the like of it from her before. "I checked. She was registered." Her lips twisted. "Her room was on the floor above his."

Considering what she'd been through the preceding days, Brett had stifled his growing impatience. "Honey, she's his assistant. There's nothing at all unusual ab—"

"No. Not as a rule," she'd interrupted harshly. "She travels with him quite often. And, like a fool, I'd believed quite innocently."

Brett had felt heartsick at the pain in her voice, the anguish in her usually so-bright blue eyes. He knew only too well what she was going through. Perhaps that was why she'd confided in him and not Eric. She'd sought a fellow sufferer. Still, unconvinced, he'd objected.

"Micki, there is no proof."

"Wolf told me, before he left, that she would not be going with him." Micki's response had had the measured sound of a death knell. "He offered the information. I had not asked. I think I have a very good case, Brett," she'd gone on in a whisper, her voice reedy with weariness. "By the way, her name is Jo Lawrence. She's beautiful."

Beautiful?
Hardly.
At that moment it seemed the vibrations from Brett's intense stare penetrated the concentration Jo Lawrence was applying to her work. Lifting her head, she met his stare with thought-

16

clouded hazel eyes, one perfectly shaped, dark brow arching questioningly.

"Is something wrong, Mr. Renninger?"

Everything's wrong, Ms. Lawrence.

"No." The tiny frown that briefly marred her smooth brow told him his attempted smile had been cynical. "I was just thinking."

"I see."

Her eyes drifted to the window to gaze out at the wind-ruffled, white-capped waves. Sitting up straight, she raised a slim hand to massage the back of her neck.

Beautiful?

In sudden decision, Brett strode to the door, taking his tweed jacket from the back of a chair as he passed it.

"I'm going to run out to the house," he said, referring to the home Wolf and Micki owned a short distance away. He tossed the toneless statement over his shoulder without looking at her again. "If you need me for anything, call me—or put it on hold till I get back." He was very careful not to slam the door behind him.

The silver Porsche 928S gleamed dully in the watery, late-afternoon sunlight. As Brett pushed through the wide, double-glass entrance doors, his eyes caressed the sleek lines of the powerful machine, parked in the no-parking section in the motel forecourt. He'd made sure the car was driven up from Atlanta for him as soon as possible and was happy now that it was at his disposal. It didn't really matter where he parked the car since, as the motel was closed for the season, the large lot was empty.

Standing beside the car, the wind sweeping back his gold-streaked, ash-blond hair, Brett breathed in deeply, filling his lungs with the crisp, sea-scented air. A raucous, mournful cry drew his attention, and, tilting his head back, he followed the gliding flight pattern of a lone sea gull. The bird's solitary passage struck a responsive chord in him.

For what seemed a very long time now, he'd known a like, if

earthbound, solitude. Even when in the company of others—others, in his case, being female—his soul had emitted a silent, lonely cry.

"Damn all women."

Even as he muttered the oath Brett knew he didn't mean it. There were women and then there were women. Most assuredly he would never damn Micki or his brother Eric's lovely lady-wife. But there were others, like his former playmate—in no way had she ever been a real *wife* to him—and the woman whose presence he'd escaped moments ago.

What in blazing hell were you thinking of?

The admonition was not self-directed. In his mind he flung the question at possibly the one and only man he'd hesitate in verbalizing it to: his brother, the formidable Wolfgang.

Damn you, Wolf, you had it all! Brett, folding his long length behind the wheel, mentally chastized the idol who had suddenly developed feet of clay. You had Micki, and two beautiful children, and the good life, and you risked it all—and for what?

Brett shook his head in wonder as he inserted the key into the ignition. With his inner eye he envisioned the object of his censure: whole, that slashing grin softening the chiseled planes of his face, his eyes glittering silver, the formally lone Wolf.

Do you love her, big brother? Or were you merely playing king stud?

Twisting the key with unnecessary force, Brett growled, "Get it in gear!" He was not referring to the car, which had quickly purred to life without a complaint.

Driving along the nearly deserted streets instilled in Brett a vaguely eerie sensation. It was as if the warning had gone out to evacuate and everybody had heard it but him.

Brett smiled at the whimisical thought. Actually, he rather liked the desolate look of the summer resort town in mid-October. He did not like the oddly abandoned look of his brother's large white-brick ranch house.

Separating the proper key from the others on his gold ring,

18

Brett loped along the flagstone walk to the wide door. Before he had a chance to put the key to use the door was opened by Wolf's housekeeper.

"Well, hello, Mrs. Jorgeson." Brett's smile was easy; he liked *this* woman. "I didn't expect to see you here today."

"Good afternoon, Mr. Renninger." Gertrude Jorgeson's return smile revealed a mutual regard. "I'm putting up the last of the tomatoes."

"In what way?" Brett's frown conveyed his ignorance of the hows and whys of putting up anything.

"Into sauce and stewed tomatoes." Gertrude smiled through eyes grown wise from sixty-one years of observing life. "Your brother and your sister-in-law love stewed tomatoes."

"I see." Brett's tone was noncommittal. He personally hated stewed tomatoes. "Well, I won't get in your way. I'll be in Wolf's study."

"All right, sir." Gertrude smiled again. "Would you like a cup of coffee?"

"No. Thank you." Brett grinned. "I think I'll help myself to the Scotch."

"As you like." The small, well-rounded woman turned back toward the kitchen. "Call me if there is anything I can help you with."

In the study, Brett went directly to the liquor cabinet set into one wall between well-stocked bookshelves. After measuring a good two inches of the expensive whisky into a short, squat glass, he splashed in a token amount of seltzer water, then, sipping at the liquid appreciatively, he glanced around the comfortable room.

The earth-tone colors, the functional yet luxurious furnishings, the oversized desk, stamped the room as Wolf's domain. However, there were small signs indicating the domain had been invaded.

A smile softened Brett's finely molded lips as his eyes paused on a large, brazenly red fire engine parked neatly in one corner.

19

He had witnessed his nephew tearing through the house on the riding toy with the same panache Wolf displayed behind the wheel of his equally brazen red Ferrari.

His thought banished the soft smile. The Ferrari was gone, totally demolished in the accident. It was several seconds before a twinge of pain in his jaw brought Brett out of his reverie to the realization of his tightly clenched teeth.

Damn, it was only a car! A car can be replaced. He would gladly write out his own personal check for a half dozen Ferraris if only Wolf . . .

Literally shaking himself out of his introspection, Brett moved purposefully to the desk. It had grown completely dark beyond the window behind him before he pushed the padded leather covered chair back and stood up.

The plot sickens.

Raking long, bony fingers through thick strands of slightly wavy hair, he grimaced sourly at the innocent-looking envelope on the desktop. The tightness in his stomach bore out his appraisal of the play unfolding in his mind.

Raising eyes gone steely gray with anger, Brett ran his gaze slowly around the room, seeing everything, seeing nothing, the document neatly folded inside the long, buff-colored envelope imprinted on his inner vision.

Does she love him?

Damn it! Whether or not Jo Lawrence was in love with Wolf should not be his uppermost consideration! Micki was the one who would suffer from this. *If* she found out.

Lids narrowing over eyes now icy with calculation, he sliced his gaze back to the desk. He had discovered the damned thing inside the locked top drawer of the desk, which, as he was in possession of Wolf's keyring, he'd opened without the slightest compunction.

As expected, he'd found everything pertaining to the company in perfect order. It was that one long envelope that had shaken him.

It was his job to make sure Micki did not find out.

"Damn!"

His very long, deceptively lean looking frame taut with frustration and anger, Brett snatched the empty whisky glass and walked out of the room with his habitual long stride.

Well trained to neatness by a caring mother, he rinsed the glass under steaming hot water and placed it in the draining rack beside the sink, his mind examining the ways in which to handle this new, unsavory development.

I ought to strangle the bitch.

Impractical, but effective. A wry smile shadowed his perfectly shaped lips as he strode back into his brother's study, his eyes, cold as the North Atlantic, fastening on the cause of his anger.

Crossing to the desk, he extended a hand to pluck the envelope up, then, turning abruptly, he walked out of the room. After activating the computerized alarm system to secure the house for the night, he left the house and loped to the low sports car shimmering like liquid silver in the moonlight.

The weightless document lay heavy in Brett's breast pocket as he backed the vehicle out of the driveway. Instead of making the turn that would take him back to the center of town, he spun the leather-covered wheel and headed toward the bay.

Now, in early evening, the streets were even more deserted than they'd been when he left the motel. The uncanny sensation of being the only living being in a dark, abandoned ghost town was even more pronounced.

Parking at the base of a street that dead-ended at the bay, Brett uncoiled his considerable length from behind the wheel and strolled to stand on the wide, oily-looking wood pilings.

The moonlight struck a glittering path across the ever-shifting water, dancing in time to the muted swish as wavelets wound themselves around the spindly legs supporting long, narrow docking piers. Empty now, the berthing slips had a forsaken look that would vanish with the return of spring and the water craft of all sizes, both motorized and those with the tall masts.

To the lone man, standing with hands thrust deep into the pockets of hand-tailored slacks, the scene was more conducive to contemplation than depression.

Because of the frantic mental state his sister-in-law had been in, Brett had found it relatively easy to convince Micki of Wolf's fidelity.

Without shame or misgiving, he had lied through his teeth.

The memory was strong, fanning the anger seething in him to a full, outraged blaze.

"I must know," Micki had whispered brokenly. "Brett, please, you must find out if it's true."

Suspicion aroused is not guilt proven. Brett would have preferred living with the doubt.

"To what purpose now, honey?" he'd soothed, attempting to dissuade her, knowing too well the hell in facing the truth. "You've been through so much, and you've got to get through a lot more. Why put yourself through the agony of—"

"You don't understand," she'd interrupted fiercely, grasping his hand tightly. "I don't want to know for myself." Her lids dropped over eyes sparkling like blue jewels from their glaze of tears, and she swallowed with obvious difficulty. "I'd just as soon *not* know, but you have got to go to New York and find out if it's true."

"You're right, I don't understand," Brett exploded, if softly. "If you would rather not know, then why . . . ?"

"For *him!*" Again she'd not let him finish. "I think—I thought I knew him, and the man I thought I knew would not enter lightly into infidelity. He must love her very much."

Brett had actually felt the pain that had scored her face. In that instant the rage had been born deep inside him.

"Go to New York, Brett." Micki's eyes pleaded as effectively as her quivering voice. "And, if you find it's true, bring her back with you."

"What!" Mindful of the other patrons scattered around the

dimly lighted lounge, Brett had managed to keep his tone low, but it was all the more intense for the incredulity lacing it.

"If"—a spasm fleetingly distorted her lovely features and she bit her lips before correcting herself harshly—"*when* he comes around, he will need the strength of the woman he loves."

Her slender hand grasping his tightened, oval nails digging into his palm. Brett felt the pain, not in his hand but in his heart. The rage spread fiery fingers into his mind with her next impassioned words.

"I hate it, Brett. I hate the very thought of it." Two tears escaped their blinking bounds to slide slowly down her cheeks. "But I want him to live. Oh, dear God, I want him to live, and I will use anyone, suffer *anything*, if it will help him." Staring directly into his eyes, she'd begged, "Don't think of me, Brett, think of him. Go to New York."

Of course he'd given in to her. How could he not? The affection and respect he'd felt for her from the beginning blossomed into pure filial love. He would do anything, perform any task she charged him with.

After escorting her to her room, he had gone to his own long enough to pick up a few things. One of those things was the phone, over which he informed his mother of his intentions—but not his motives. Another of those things was Wolf's briefcase, which he'd taken possession of on arrival but not as yet opened.

During the short flight from Boston to New York, he'd perused the contents of Wolf's case. Most of the papers inside were directly related to the reason Wolf had gone to Boston in the first place—that of the feasibility of renovating a rather run-down, old hotel into modern condominiums and the company's acquisition of same if the resultant figures proved out that feasibility.

One slim folder stood out glaringly in its difference.

The data confined between the covers of the cream-colored folder had come from the personnel manager directly to Wolf. One quick glance over the four sheets of pristine white paper and

Brett had a crawling suspicion he was closer to knowing the answer to Micki's question.

During the cab ride from Kennedy to Wolf's spacious apartment with its panoramic view of Central Park, Brett came very close to hating the formerly adored one.

It had been a long day. In truth, it had been three very long days, each one riddled with fear as Brett, his mother, Eric, and Micki, so brave, so vulnerable, waited, waited, waited.

Brett had been tired, and disillusioned, and bitter, yet, before dropping onto Wolf's over-oversized bed, he had more thoroughly studied the four sheets of paper. Each paper contained a detailed account of the professional performance of four company employees—three men and one woman.

The information had been gathered, at Wolf's request, for the purpose of choosing a replacement for a retiring senior executive of the East Coast branch of Renninger Corporation.

The lone female under consideration for the coveted position was JoAnne Lawrence.

Brett's last thought before falling asleep had been: I just might throw up.

The following morning, feeling charged with restless energy after days spent in the confines of hospital waiting rooms and corridors, Brett politely declined the apartment doorman's respectful offer of a cab.

Had he wanted to ride, there would have been no need to do it in the back of a world-famous—infamous?—New York City cab. All that would have been required were a few words spoken into a telephone and a limousine, plush, comfortable, fitted out to the nines, would have been waiting at the curb for him. When the occasion warranted, Brett was not averse to using his name, position, power, or wealth. This particular morning, Mr. Renninger chose to walk.

His brother's briefcase firmly in hand, he strode off, appearing, at least to the casual glance, much like hundreds of other young executives en route to the city's amalgam of offices. The more

24

discerning eye would have noted the supple leather of handmade shoes, the fine material of perfectly tailored, vested, chocolate-brown suit, the real silk of muted shrimp-toned shirt. The discerning female eye would appreciate the long, well-knit torso, the thick crop of sun-streaked, loose waves caressing a beautifully sculpted head, features so sharply etched as to appear austere in their masculine beauty, lips that promised heaven in their pleasure, hell in their disfavor. At the moment the tightness of those lips proclaimed extreme disfavor with someone.

Brett's strides ate up the sidewalk. Seeming so self-absorbed as to be aware of nothing around him, he was, in fact, fully conscious of everything within the radius of his near-perfect vision. Eyes dull steel, flat in contemplation of what may lay at destination's end, he strode on, his mind alive with his sister-in-law's charge:

"Go to New York, Brett, and, if you find it's true, bring her back with you."

Now, as he approached the tall glass-and-steel building that housed the offices of East Coast Region—Renninger Corporation, his mind repeated the same silent reply as the night before.

No way in hell!

Stepping out of the elevator at the twenty-third floor, Brett walked briskly down the carpeted hall to the office of the personnel manager. When he walked out of the office, fifteen minutes later, the retiring senior executive's replacement had been chosen. The choice was not a female.

From personnel, Brett took the elevator up three more floors. His body taut with purpose, he strode to a solid, unmarked door, twisted the handle, and, eyes narrowing with intent, stepped inside.

"May I help you?"

The query was directed at him from a frowning young woman seated behind the latest model in typewriters. Her confused expression made a demand: Who the devil are you? And how did you get up here unannounced?

A sardonic smile teased Brett's tightly compressed mouth. It *had* been a long time since his last foray into New York.

"Is Ms. Lawrence in?" Brett asked quietly, the smile tugging harder at his lips as he observed the confusion deepen in the young woman's eyes. Her expressive face telegraphed her mental self-questioning: Should I know this man? Is he someone important?

"Yes, sir." The secretary nodded. "But she is very busy. She left orders not to be disturbed."

"She'll see me." His cool, deliberately arrogant tone brought out the excellent secretarial school training instilled in the young woman who, at any other time, Brett would have found more than passably attractive.

"Really?" she replied with matching coolness. "I doubt it. She *is* very busy."

This pretty ball of fluff was actually giving him the brushoff! So much for one's self-image of intimidating authority!

Play time's over, honey.

"Press the little switch down on your intercom," he instructed patiently, "and inform *your* boss that *her* boss is waiting."

"Her boss?" The girl's brows drew together. "I don't understand."

Brett sighed. Of course she didn't understand. How could she? Hanging on to his patience, he smiled benignly.

"Tell Ms. Lawrence Brett Renninger wishes to see her."

"Oh my God!" The woman's eyes swallowed half her face.

"Exactly."

Wide brown eyes staring at him beseechingly, the girl's trembling fingers groped for the intercom. Before she could press the correct button, a door three feet to her right was thrust open and a melodious but impatient voice demanded:

"Reni! Who are you socializing with? I need that report you're working on."

"Ms. Lawrence, I . . . I . . . he . . ."

The attempted explanation died on her lips as JoAnne Lawrence followed her voice into the room.

At first sight of her something that had died inside Brett made its first faint stirrings toward resurrection.

Beautiful?

Brett was hard put not to laugh aloud. As a descriptive adjective, beautiful, in regards to the tall woman glaring at him, seemed woefully inadequate.

"Who are you? And what are you doing in here?"

Brett had been thankful for her imperious tone; it reminded him of exactly who this woman was.

"Oh, Ms. Lawrence," Reni squeaked fearfully, "he's . . . he's . . ."

"Reni! Will you please finish that report!" JoAnne's eyes sliced a quelling glance to Reni, then shot back to him. "Answer me!"

"With pleasure." Brett felt a curl of satisfaction when her impossibly long lashes flickered at his too-smooth, too-soft tone. Experiencing a sensation quite like joy, he let her have it with both barrels.

"Brett Renninger," he introduced himself silkily, feeling the curl of satisfaction spreading at the stillness that gripped her. "And I am here in the capacity of your employer for the duration."

In retrospect, Brett had to admit her aplomb was magnificient. There was a split second of appalled hesitation, then she stepped toward him gracefully, slim right hand extended.

"I'm sorry, sir," she apologized in a soft, clear voice.

A cool breeze skipped across the water, ruffling its inky-dark surface. Brett shivered inside the insufficient protection of the tweed sport coat. Chilled out of his reverie, he moved his shoulders in a tension-relieving shrug, a vague hollowness inside bringing awareness of how long it had been since he'd eaten.

At least he attributed the empty feeling to hunger.

Turning abruptly, he frowned as his ear caught the faint

crackle of the envelope nestled inside his breast pocket. The hole in his middle grew to a mini chasm.

Cold all over, Brett strode to the low-slung car, repressing a shudder as he slid behind the wheel. Punishing the ignition once again for his own conflicting emotions, he slammed his palm against the gear stick and backed the car the length of the street.

It had been so ridiculously easy to reassure Micki of Wolf's fidelity.

Cruising along the deserted street, a grimace broke the tight line of Brett's lips. He had simply relayed almost verbatim JoAnne's—rehearsed?—response to his interrogation in her office that morning.

Yes, she had been with Wolf in Boston.

No, the original arrangements had not been for her to accompany him.

Wolf had called her late in the afternoon the day after his arrival in Boston.

"I don't like the setup." JoAnne had quoted Wolf. "I think they believe they're dealing with a lightweight here. They should know better. But then, so should I. I failed to run a routine check. Get research on it now. I want a full report by tomorrow noon, hand delivered, by you."

Yes, she had delivered the report to him the following afternoon. They had gone over it together during dinner.

Yes, he had booked a room for her at the hotel but, as she had scheduled a meeting with his staff for the following morning, he drove her to the airport sometime around eleven that night. She had flown back to New York on the same company plane that had carried her to Boston.

Yes, he must have been on the way back to the hotel when the accident occurred.

Micki had gratefully, tearfully swallowed it whole; hook, line, and sinker.

Brett was a different type of fish. Keeping his own council, he had decided to search out the true depth of JoAnne's seemingly still waters.

Depth indeed!

Brett's entire body felt icy except for that one rectangular spot on his chest. The envelope crackled again as he mounted the steps in the silent motel.

I really ought to strangle the bitch.

Unlocking the apartment door, he strode angrily inside and stopped dead. Assuming she'd have gone to her own room by now, he had not expected to find her waiting for him. Brett voiced the first thought that came to his mind.

"Trouble?"

"No." Her sleek, dark hair moved sharply in the negative. "I just now decided to call it a day." An odd, sad smile brushed her soft, moist lips. "Possibly because I also just realized I haven't eaten since breakfast."

Brett shelved the idea of strangling her; very likely because he knew, subconsciously, that if he touched her, the strangling would come after he'd done a lot of other things to her first.

Instead, he took her out to dinner.

CHAPTER TWO

Absently unaware of the sensuousness of her actions, Jo toyed with her tulip-shaped wineglass, the fingers of her left hand caressing the stem with long, evocative strokes, the tip of her right forefinger slowly circling the rim.

Oblivious to the gray gaze following her finger play, she sighed with the unwilling realization that for the last several hours her thought pattern had mirrored the movement of her fingertips—round and round.

Why does he dislike me so?

After three weeks of regular repetition, the question was a familiar, if painful, refrain. She had repeatedly scoured her mind for reasons for his antipathy, and she came up blank time after time. Other than that first regretful morning in her office, she had scrupulously shown him all due respect. Surely the man had more intelligence than to carry a grudge for so slight an infraction! He *had* barged unannounced into her office! Her reaction to his sudden appearance had been completely normal.

Yet, since that first morning, uncomfortable waves of tension simmered between them whenever they were in the same room together, regardless of the number of feet that measured the distance between them.

It was more than unnerving; it was disheartening, because her initial reaction to him had been very positive, deeply favorable. In effect, Jo didn't even have to *be* in the same room with him to reexperience her initial reaction; all she had to do was *think* of him and tiny little physical devils began a game of touch and run with her libido. It was enough to make a fully mature, intelligent, reasonably level-headed woman weep with longing!

Though Jo was unconscious of the yearning sigh that whispered through her lips, Brett, very obviously, was not.

"Tired?"

Blinking herself out of the fruitless introspection, Jo donned a mask of nonchalance before raising her eyes to his.

"Yes." Her reply was blunt for two reasons; first, it was nothing but the plain truth; second, his taunting tone had instilled a chill. Was it her imagination, or did he continually use that exact tone with her for some reason she was too dim to decipher? Keeping a rigid harness on her own tongue—which did itch to lash a bit—she added tonelessly, "It's been a long three weeks."

For some obscure reason her statement seemed to anger him. Jo's carefully constructed mask slipped to reveal bafflement when Brett stiffened abruptly.

"I imagine it has been," he drawled icily. "Time has a tendency to drag when you're missing someone."

Jo's bafflement retreated at the advance of sheer incredulity. What the deuce was he talking about? Missing someone? Whoever could he . . . good grief, he couldn't possibly be referring to Gary? How had he even heard of that ill-fated involvement? Though she wasn't aware of any gossip about her breakup with Gary Devlin, there was always the chance he had heard through the company grapevine. This man would surely demand to know all there was to know about an assistant he had no voice in choosing. All there was to know officially, and unofficially. But why would he think she was missing Gary? It was almost a year and a half since . . .

"If you're ready to leave?"

Brett's cold query put an end to her conjecturing. Employing fierce determination to keep her eyebrows from joining in a frown, Jo let a cool nod suffice for an answer. Inside, she seethed to tell him to go take a flying leap into the bay. Who the hell was he to think he could speak so condescendingly to her!

Inside the sports car, Jo sat rigidly erect, staring out the windshield all the way back to the motel.

Did he *have* to smell so damned good? Jo blessed the darkness that concealed the rush of heat to her face at the unexpected thought.

Slowly, very carefully, she inhaled, drawing the mingled scent of pure male and expensive aftershave into her senses.

I wonder what he tastes like? The heat in her cheeks intensified at the reflection. Jo shifted against the supple leather covering the bucket seat, becoming more uncomfortable from the heat uncoiling inside than the warmth singeing her outermost layer of skin.

Eyes forced ruthlessly forward, she forbade her sight the pleasure of examining his breath-robbing, austerely handsome face, the contemplation of the possible ecstasy his beautiful mouth could wreak on hers.

What does he look like stripped to the buff? That consideration cut her breath off in her throat.

I am going totally mad!

Thankfully, at that moment Brett drove the car onto the motel parking lot and her musings were shifted to the edge of consciousness. The ensuing opening and closing of car doors were the only sounds that broke the silence from the time they left the car until they came to an awkward halt at the door to her room.

For one pulse-shattering, brief instant, Jo fancifully imagined she saw a flame leap in the remote grayness of the eyes studying her face. Then, with a brusquely muttered good night, he spun and strode to the door of Wolf's former lair.

Stepping quickly into the pitch-black room, Jo closed and locked the door, then sagged back against its solid support. After gulping in numerous deep, calming breaths, she pushed her limp body erect, her hand groping for the wall switch.

For one infinitesimal moment there she had actually thought he might kiss her. What would she have done if he had? Jo frowned as she mentally ticked off her possible responses. Would she have chastized him in a scathing, acidic tone? Or, would she, perhaps, have laughed it off as of little meaning? Or, would she, much less likely, have allowed her palm to meet his cheek with resounding force?

Who are you trying to kid? she asked herself wearily. After three weeks of wondering, hoping, longing, you know exactly how you would have responded: You would have wrapped yourself around him like a wet bath towel!

The thought conjured the image and an anticipatory shiver feathered her skin, raising tiny goose bumps on her arms and thighs. Her physical response to the mere idea of being crushed to Brett's hard, lean body no longer had the power to shock her, although it certainly had the first time it had occurred.

Performing the routine before-bed ritual of cleansing her skin and brushing her teeth, Jo's thoughts backtracked to the first time she'd felt that hot-cold reaction to him.

It had certainly not happened that first morning, when he'd presented himself to her. She'd been much too flustered and embarrassed then to notice much of anything other than the fact that the Renninger brothers bore very little resemblance, physically or in personality.

Actually, he'd been in her office a very short time, during which he'd fired questions at her in a taut, angry tone that she'd later attributed to anxiety over Wolf's accident.

Somewhat proud of herself for the appearance of composure she'd maintained, she had answered his questions clearly and concisely. It was when it became obvious that he was about to make an abrupt departure that Jo, voicing a query of her own, received the impression of his dislike of her. Confused, wondering why he should dislike her when he didn't even know her, she had nevertheless repeated her question when he hesitated over answering.

"How *is* Wolf doing?"

"He is still on the critical list," he'd finally, begrudgingly answered, confusing her all the more by his apparent unwillingness to discuss his brother's condition. "I'm leaving now to fly back to Boston," he'd gone on coldly, long fingers curling around the doorknob, giving the impression he couldn't get out fast enough. "If there are any questions"—he'd paused, tone hardening—"pertaining to business, call the hotel and leave a message. I'll get back to you."

Stunned by both his tone and his attitude, frowning in perplexity, Jo had mutely watched as he opened the door then closed it again before turning to pin her with an icy, narrow-eyed stare.

"By the way," he'd almost purred, "I've tapped Bob Harley for the executive slot opening soon." The silky satisfaction in his voice went through her like the sound of a nail being scraped the length of a blackboard. "Sorry about that."

With a twist of his lips that was more a sneer than a smile, he strode from her office, leaving her staring after him in total bewilderment.

Four days later he was back.

Those four days had been rather trying for Jo—what with holding down the fort, so to speak, and worrying about Wolf, she'd been getting a teensy bit short-tempered.

In truth, Jo almost adored Wolfgang Renninger. In her admittedly prejudiced opinion he was kind, considerate, oftimes droll, and a dynamic businessman. Her liking for him had been spontaneous, her respect endless. Strangely, she had never felt even the mildest tug of physical attraction toward him. Wolf was employer, friend, and, during a few weak moments Jo had experienced, confidant.

Brett was a whole new ball game.

Added to the business responsibilities she'd shouldered—she'd be damned if she'd call and leave *messages* for *him*—and her concern for Wolf, Jo had further strained her nerves by repeatedly reviewing that scene in the office.

Why had Brett been so very tense, so very hostile?

Why had he seemed so smugly satisfied about informing her of Bob Harley's promotion? In Jo's opinion Bob was the logical choice for the job!

Why did he dislike her?

It was the last of the constantly revolving trio of questions that bothered her most of all, simply because, she assured herself, she had done nothing to warrant his disdain.

She had had no prior warning of his imminent return. Arriving at the office before her secretary that Tuesday morning, she had no sooner pulled her chair to her desk when the phone rang, the blinking button on the white instrument indicating an inner office line. Her response had been as it always was.

"Jo Lawrence."

"I want to see you, now, in Wolf's . . . my . . . office."

That was it. No time wasted on mundane pleasantries such as good morning, merely, in effect, get in here.

Staring at the receiver in her hand, Jo had rationalized the sudden burst of adrenaline rushing through her as her body gearing for a verbal confrontation, *not* in expectancy of the sight of him.

HA!

With all her assumed coolness intact, she had walked briskly into Wolf's . . . Brett's . . . office, taken one look at him, and, metaphorically at least, begun melting.

It simply was not fair for one man to look that damn good! The image this man projected did not sneak up on one; to the contrary, his persona immediately ensnared, jolting emotions,

35

tangling thoughts, luring the unwary to further investigate his seeming quintessence.

After four days of grappling with the fact of his apparent disdain, Jo was nothing if not wary. Lashes lowered over hazel eyes too bright with feminine interest, she viewed the splendor of his male form.

He stood so very straight, his bearing almost military, and so very tall, taller even than Wolf's six feet. His thick, silky-looking, fair hair was cut short at the sides and back. The hint of a wave in the sweep in front was an invitation to eager, feminine fingers. The shortness of his hair revealed the perfect sculpting of his head, his wide brow, straight nose, high cheekbones, and firm jawline lending an overall effect of a mastersculptor's finest work of art. The very spare but sinewy flesh that covered his long frame enhanced the illusion of an elite warrior of a bygone era.

That magnificent human form should never be adorned in anything more than the merest wisp of draping over the hips.

The thought conjured the image. Her composure threatened by her own reflective imaginings, Jo had blurted the first unrelated subject her scrambled mind was successful in latching onto.

"Wolf?"

Jo was much too busy being amazed at the picture of aloof composure her cool tone had drawn for him to notice the glittery sheen that came into his eyes.

"He'll live."

Her amazement did not extend to missing the frost that rimmed his voice, but she ignored it in the relief that swept through her entire being; not until that moment had she allowed herself to face the very real possibility that Wolf might actually die. Her sigh was more eloquent of her feelings than any amount of words could have been.

The glitter in the gray eyes intensified, embuing a molten steel quality. If his expression of cold hauteur was assumed to intimidate, it worked admirably.

"But," he finally continued with icy deliberation, "if you are eagerly looking forward to seeing me dispatched back to Atlanta before long, forget it. Wolf will be a long time in mending."

"His injuries were extensive?" With an unconsciously beguiling sweep of her incredibly thick long lashes, Jo forced herself to meet his direct stare, praying he could not hear the *ba-bump* kick her heart telegraphed.

"Yes." Brett's clipped reply indicated he would not elaborate, thus it surprised Jo when he did. "The point of impact was at the door on the left." At Jo's horror-widened eyes, he nodded once, sharply. "Quite." His lips twisted briefly, as if in memory of a painful sight. "There is hardly an inch on Wolf's left side that is not contused, lacerated, or fractured; not to mention concussed. When I left him this morning he resembled a mummy more than a man." The cloudy haze that had momentarily dulled his eyes dissipated. Once again he staked her with that glittering stare. "As stated, the mending will take a long time." His lids narrowed menacingly, causing a twist of alarm in Jo's midsection. "Had that drunken bastard who ran into Wolf's car not have died in his self-created hell, I'd have sent him there with my own hands."

Jo did not doubt his word for a second. In that instant, Brett looked frighteningly capable of perpetrating a man's demise without weaponry. Appalled by the quiet fierceness of him, feeling herself pale under the steely rapier points flashing from his eyes, Jo slowly collapsed onto the tweed-covered chair to the side of his desk.

Pray God I never incite this man's wrath! Holding her breath, fighting to control the series of shudders quaking through her, Jo gripped the slender arms of the chair, unmindful of her whitening knuckles.

"Okay. Business as usual."

Smothering a gasp, Jo started at his abrupt change in tone and facial expression. Oh, he still looked haughty, but the mien of murderous intent had vanished. Taking command of Wolf's high-backed chair, Brett drew it to the large pine desk, then, settling back comfortably, he arched one pale, aristocratic brow at her.

"Any more questions?"

Jo ground her teeth at his patronizing tone, cautioning herself against incurring his wrath before their interview was over. She truly did not care to leave his office the victim of his displeasure. The very idea of the scene injected steel into her backbone—very cool steel that manifested itself in her voice.

"Yes . . . sir. Several." The tiny but telling pause over the term of respect was noted by a flicker in his attentive expression. Undaunted by a slight tightening at the edges of his lips, Jo led off with query one.

"Does the prognosis call for complete recovery?"

"At this point, yes."

"How long will he be confined to the hospital?"

"The word this morning was at least three, possibly four, weeks."

Four weeks! Jo swallowed her dismay at the thought of having to work side by side with this man for the better part of a month.

"May I see him?" She was further dismayed by the pleading note threading her voice.

"No."

Jo's eyes widened at his icily emphatic denial. What possible reason could he have for refusing her visitation rights to her boss? Or did he believe himself above the need for reasons? Her loss of control was evidenced by the angry outcry.

"But why?"

"The idea, *Ms.* Lawrence, is recuperation. You represent something altogether different."

Anger drowned in a flood of confusion. Had Brett really sneered that last assertion? Could he consider her role of assistant so unimportant as to be sneered at? Jo figuratively shook the consideration away. She knew he employed several assistants himself; he could not help but be aware of the responsibilities entailed. But then, damn it, why *had* he sneered at her?

Jetting her mind free of the quagmire of her own thoughts, Jo faced him boldly.

"You will be . . . filling in . . . for him the entire three or four weeks?"

"In every way required."

For some unfathomable reason, Jo was grateful for the ignorance she felt at not understanding the cause of his sardonic tone and matching smile. Thankfully, she was given no time to ponder either.

"Actually, I will very probably be in residence in this office a great deal longer than three or four weeks."

"But you just said—"

"I *said*," Brett interrupted smoothly, "Wolf will be hospitalized for that length of time. Plans have already been made for him to complete his recuperation at our mother's horse farm in Florida."

Jo opened her mouth to ask the obvious. Brett anticipated her.

"Anywhere from four to six months."

Uh-huh. You bet. Why not?

Rapid fire, the seemingly unrelated terms sprang pell-mell into Jo's thoroughly rattled brain. I am not really hearing what I think I'm hearing, she assured herself a trifle wildly. He did not actually raise the possibility of six months—did he? I'll kill myself!

Had she been, at that moment, presented with a mirror, Jo would have been shocked. Inside, she felt somewhat like a quivering mass of mush. Outwardly she appeared unruffled and unaffected by the news she'd received.

Transmitting an order to her hands to release their death grip on the innocent chair arms, she laced her tension-numbed fingers together demurely in her lap. Between evenly spaced breaths, she managed to calmly ask the question whose answer would see her retained or deposed.

"You will be bringing Richard Colby to New York?"

Over the previous three years, Jo had heard much, all of it

good, of Richard Colby, redoubtable right arm to the head of the mid-Atlantic Coast region. Her assumption that Brett would want his right arm with him now was natural, if unsettling.

"Not likely." Brett's disclaimer startled Jo; had she really detected a hint of amusement in his tone? His dry smile answered her silent question. "Richard hates New York." Brett's voice was every bit as dry as his smile and held a very deliberate drawl. "He hates the pace. He hates the weather. And, more than the preceding, he hates the hard, Yank-ee twang."

Oh help!

Staring at him in bemusement, Jo felt the melting process begin all over again. His soft, drawling tone turned her rigidly stiff spine to the consistency of soft wax. Glory, but he is beautiful! His face is beautiful. His body is beautiful. His voice is beautiful. He is probably magnificently beautiful in bed as well.

Lost in her own suddenly erotic imaginings, Jo was sublimely unaware of the seconds sliding into minutes. What she *was* suddenly aware of was a longing to experience the magnificence of his beautiful body.

"Ms. Lawrence?"

Jo blinked herself back to reality. Though Brett's voice had lost the long drawl, its softness enticed a shivering response through the entire length of her body.

"Have I wakened you?" Brett's taunt was a mild reprimand for her inattentiveness.

Yes, damn you! Jo silently acknowledged the taunt for a much more earthy reason. You've awakened me inside, where I live, and I don't particularly like it, especially since it's so very obvious *you* don't particularly like me.

"No, sir." Jo's independent spirit cringed at the self-satisfied smile he flaunted in reaction to her unhesitating use of the respectful term.

"I'm relieved." His tone was a blatant denial of his assertion. "I'm certain that having a woman as lovely as you fall asleep while I'm speaking would do irreparable damage to my ego."

How very droll. How very sophisticated. How very deceitful. Positive her eyes were flashing her mental accusations at him, Jo lowered her lashes in concealment.

"Is your ego so very delicate?" she ventured softly, hating the surge of excitement that pulsed through her veins. What would it be like, she asked herself, to possess the power to damage this man's ego? You'll never know, her self answered with discouraging swiftness.

"No." Brett's reply was equally swift, equally discouraging, and amused in the bargain. "I'd say my ego is about as delicate as an enraged Brahma bull."

Well, now that I've been firmly put in my place, where do we go from here? Jo wondered bleakly. Apparently Brett's train of thought was running along the same track, only he knew the name of the next station was: Business first, always.

"Now." He sat forward in his chair and placed his palms flat on the desk. "If there are no further questions?"

Feeling anything but the highly efficient assistant she knew herself to be, Jo shook her head mutely.

Sliding between the cold sheets on the unfamiliar motel room bed, Jo sighed with the realization of the number of times she'd shaken her head mutely over the previous three weeks.

God! Had it really only been three weeks? It seemed like years, decades, a millennium! And every second of it filled to bursting with *him*.

Jo had no idea why it had happened. She had no idea how it had happened. She only knew most assuredly that it *had* happened. Against all reason or sense of self-protection, she was stupidly, hopelessly, mushily in love with Brett Renninger.

Balling the covers into a comforting bunch under her chin, Jo rolled onto her side, drawing her knees up almost to her chest. Then she did something she would have been mortified to have Brett witness: She cried long into the night.

Habits formed, good or bad, are not easily set aside. With less than four hours sleep, and that not very restful, Jo woke at her usual early hour. Filled with periodic spells of weeping and tossing, the long night had produced little comfort. As Jo lay staring through the large, square window at a brilliant blue Indian summer sky, her tired mind held on to the two concretes it had formed while blackness painted the window.

For good or ill, and very probably forever, she loved Brett Renninger—that was concrete number one. Concrete number two was wrapped around the fact that, at all costs, she had to diligently work at preventing Brett form discovering concrete number one.

How this feat was to be accomplished when the mere thought of Brett's existence on the earth was enough to activate the inner melting process, had been the major cause of Jo's sleeplessness. The thought had occurred of secrecy through distance. All she had to do to remove herself from temptation was resign her position as his assistant; she'd have as soon resigned her soul to purgatory.

As daylight seemed to have little effect in diverting her endlessly circling thoughts, Jo pushed back the covers, deciding she might as well face the morning—and her own haggard reflection in the mirror.

Thirty-five minutes later, securely hidden behind the magic of expertly applied cosmetics and a neatly tailored, pearl-gray suit with a complementing heather-blue blouse, Jo walked briskly into the apartment-cum-office and came to a disbelieving halt, incredulous at the sight her sweeping gaze encountered.

Attired for the work day in navy suit pants, matching vest, crisp white shirt, and a red-on-gray diagonally striped tie, Brett presented to her widened eyes the picture of domesticity as he turned to greet her from his position at the range in the compact kitchen.

"Good morning, JoAnne. Pull a stool up to the counter, breakfast is almost ready."

The counter was atop a room divider that separated the living-room area from the kitchen. Shelves lined with books, both hardcover and paper, faced the living room. On the kitchen side, three stools, fashioned of cane, with padded seats, filled the space under the Formica counter.

"Breakfast?"

Jo heard the blank confusion her voice conveyed to him and, hearing it, strove to correct the impression of early-morning dullness.

"You're cooking breakfast? For me?"

She had to repress a wince at the expression of boredom that flirted with his features. True, the voice now held alertness; it was the question that, being obvious, was therefore stupid.

"I could hardly fix breakfast for myself alone"—Brett assumed the exaggerated drawl—"and still call myself a Southern gentleman, now could I?"

I could hardly smack your too-superior-looking face, Jo retorted bitterly, if silently, and still call myself *any* kind of rational woman, could I? The temptation to put thought into action was so strong Jo curled her slender fingers into her palms and held them rigidly at her sides, her body tightening with her determination not to respond to his taunt.

Brett's expression of boredom gave way to amusement as his sharp-eyed gaze swept over Jo's stiffening form. For some reason she could not begin to understand, he seemed to derive great satisfaction from knowing he had the power to rattle her composure.

A derisive half smile curving his far too attractive mouth, Brett swung back to the compact stove to dish up bacon and eggs.

"As is obvious"—a jerk of his head indicated the two place settings, complete with small glasses of orange juice and tall glasses of iced water, on the countertop—"everything is ready." Two steaming plates in hand, he turned to her. "If you will seat yourself, Ms. Lawrence, I will serve." His smile grew openly mocking. "You will then be among a small, select group of women who have the right to claim they have been waited upon by Brett Renninger."

What is he trying to do? Holding his glittering gray stare with assumed carelessness, Jo walked slowly into the small kitchen. And why is he trying to do it? The questions teased her mind repeatedly as she slid her trim, rounded bottom onto the thickly padded seat. Had she lost all perceptiveness entirely, or was his mockery self-directed?

The Brett Renninger? Mocking himself? Sure—with the first frost to paint the nether reaches of hell! Why mock himself when he had a much more likely target in the form of his unwanted, unwelcome, uncared-for assistant?

"My meager efforts do not appeal?"

The vocal nudge came from beside her, one stool removed. Blinking, Jo focused first on the bit of gray visible through narrowed lids, then, shifting her glance, to the golden toast, creamy scrambled eggs, and perfectly crisped bacon on her plate. When had he poured the coffee? This as her gaze was caught by the aromatic, dark brew in a cup near her right hand.

"No . . . I mean, yes, of course . . . I'm sorry, I . . . " Darn! Why wouldn't her mouth work this morning?

"How fascinating." The drawl was more pronounced now. "Are you always this articulate first thing in the morning?" Brett arched one beautifully shaped blond brow.

Why did I have to fall for this stiletto-tongued, twentieth-century Adonis? Jo wondered, staring helplessly into a pair of gray eyes that danced with amusement at her expense. She had amused Gary at the beginning too. Perhaps it's true—the psychological thesis claiming women keep seeking out the same type of man. A vision of another Adonis, one with tanned skin, blue eyes, and dark hair, formed in her mind.

"Ah ha! I've solved the mystery!" Jo blinked at the sharp click of Brett's snapping fingers. "You're a somnambulist and not really aware of being here at all."

44

"How fascinating." Jo managed a fair imitation of his drawl. "Are you always this brilliant first thing in the morning?"

"I'm always this brilliant, period," Brett retorted dryly.

"Modest too!" Jo simpered, oversweetly. Turning away with slow deliberation, she picked up her fork and stabbed at her eggs—prudently denying the urge to sink the long prongs elsewhere. Much too aware of his sudden stillness, she conveyed the utensil to her mouth, chewing consideringly before offering, sincerely, "Very good; creamy. Mine always come out too dry." She sampled the bacon. "Perfectly cooked." The coffee came under her serious consideration. "Nectar," she concluded after one delicious sip. "You could very easily spoil a working woman with a passion for breakfast."

"And you have such a passion?"

His quiet tone and steady regard should have warned her. It didn't. She walked right into it.

"Yes," she admitted, "I'm a so-so cook who's a breakfast freak."

"I always fix my own breakfast when I'm at home." Brett ran a cool gaze over her before returning to her face to pin her with gray eyes that suddenly flared to glittering brilliance. "I would gladly perform the service *for* you"—a tiny pause—"in exchange for an even more basic service *from* you."

Jo's forkful of eggs hung suspended in midair. Was she pushed? Or had she jumped? Jo was uncertain of what method had brought it about, but she felt sure she had finally gone over the edge. She must have, it was the only reasonable explanation for this sensation of free-falling through space. As if it could anchor her to the stool, Jo gripped the handle of the fork and scoured her mind for a suitably scathing put-down. She couldn't find any—which was just as well, for she felt positive she'd misinterpreted his remark.

"I beg your pardon?" She certainly hadn't had to force the note of confusion into her tone; Jo was thoroughly confused.

"Is that a no?"

Jo blinked herself free of his impaling stare. He was serious! Incredible as it seemed, Brett Renninger, in his own peculiar fashion, had actually invited her—*her!*—into his bed!

Too damned much!

The temptation to thankfully, humbly, submissively accept his oddly offered proposition was so strong Jo's teeth ached—understandably, as they were locked together in a death clamp. Her answer required every ounce of willpower she possessed.

"Yes."

"Yes, that is a no?" Brett drawled mockingly. "Or, yes, you'll buy the first meal of the day"—a smile flirted with his lips—"with the last act of the evening?"

Cancel all doubt.

She had not slipped over reason's edge.

She had not misinterpreted him.

She had not passed go.

She had not collected two hundred dollars.

She *had* been propositioned.

The only doubt remaining had to do with her ability to refuse him.

"Yes, that is a no." Had she actually replied in that oh-so-cool, touch-me-not tone? Had she actually declined, when she was on fire and he was the only extinguisher? Was she, in fact, completely out of her mind? Hadn't she wept and writhed through most of the previous night in an agony of need for his touch, his possession?

The questions trembled, rapid fire, through Jo's mind while she strove to maintain a modicum of composure. She wanted him—yes, but not like this! Not at the casually proposed offer of breakfast. Breakfast, for heaven's sake!

The rotten bastard! Jo shocked herself with the silent accusation. But she loved him, she excused herself. While he, *he* has the unmitigated gall to suggest he share my bed—for the paltry sum of filling my stomach!

Jo was forced to lower her fork to the table as a shudder shook her slender frame. Brett obviously saw and misinterpreted her movement.

"Have I shocked your sensitive little soul?" he taunted softly. With a minimum of expanded energy, he slid from his stool to the one beside her. As he leaned still closer Jo felt his warm breath caress her ear. "I can guarantee satisfaction with both performances—in the kitchen and the bedroom."

Jo, teetering on the edge of capitulation, and desperate because of it, steeled herself against the entreaty in his soft tone. When the much yearned for male lips brushed her ear, she jerked away frantically.

"Stop it!" Jo did not have to fabricate the angry tone; she *was* angry! All of a sudden she was explosively angry. The only explanation for his behavior that made any kind of sense was that she'd betrayed herself, her true feelings, to him. Positive he was merely tormenting her for having the temerity to fall in love with a Renninger, Jo lashed out at him defensively. "No, *sir*, you have not shocked my sensitve little soul. I've been propositioned before." With cold deliberation, she injected a sneer onto her lips, venom into her tone. "And one does not take note of an amateur when one has been approached by an expert."

Jo hadn't the vaguest idea what she was saying, yet, whatever it was, it worked. Brett, his expression suddenly blank, went stiff all over. Moving slowly, he straightened, then stood up and carried his barely touched meal to the sink. The sound of the food being scraped into the disposal was loud and abrasive.

"An expert!" Brett's soft, considering statement was not aimed at her. Still, made fearful by his stillness as he stood beside the sink, she raised challenging eyes to his.

"An expert," he repeated even more softly. "Of course."

The challenge in Jo's eyes was replaced by bafflement. Something in his tone conveyed acceptance—of some truth or other. But what? *She* had no idea what she was even talking about; how could he?

47

"Brett?" Jo didn't have an inkling of what to say to him. All she knew was she had to break through his strange stillness.

"Never mind." Moving abruptly, Brett strode from the kitchen. "Let's get this work cleaned up so we can get out of here."

Following his example, Jo scraped her own plate, then stacked their dishes in the dishwasher. As she absently performed the light kitchen duty, Jo told herself she absolutely had to get more sleep. She was beginning to talk off the top of her head, which, in itself, was bad enough. But, it would appear, she was also beginning to believe Brett fully understood her gibberish, and that was scary.

CHAPTER THREE

You are without doubt the most blundering of blundering fools on the entire East Coast.

Brett was, again, taking up space in front of the wide window. It was now some two hours since he'd stormed—childishly, he admitted to himself ruefully—out of the kitchen.

What devil had possessed him, prompting him to issue such an idiotic proposition? He didn't even like the woman, let alone desire her!

So your mind says, now convince your body!

Like or dislike, the cold fact was that he desired her with an intensity the like of which he'd never experienced before, and he'd known some raging passions.

I probably should simply fire her and have done with it.

The tip of Brett's tongue slid along the edge of his bottom teeth, and his unseeing eyes stared at the sun-sparkled Atlantic whitecaps.

If not firing then, at the very least, making her life pure misery was in order.

Damn!

Moving restlessly, Brett shoved his itching hands deep into the slash pockets in his slacks, a wry, self-derisive smile curving his lips. He knew the itch in his palms was not caused by the need to inflict violence; the itch came from the need to caress her soft, pale skin.

God, he wanted her, wanted her as he'd never wanted another woman.

This is sick!

Brett's shoulders moved, as if trying to dislodge an unwelcome rider on his back. His purpose had been so clearcut at the beginning. What the hell had happened to confuse the issue? Not to mention him?

Even though it *had* been ridiculously easy to reassure his sister-in-law concerning his brother's fidelity, Brett's own newly aroused suspicions were not mollified.

In relating to Micki Jo's reasons for being in Boston on the day of Wolf's accident, Brett had injected a businesslike briskness into his tone. Couched in that manner, Jo's explanation sounded plausible. Micki had, gratefully, swallowed it whole. But, then, Micki had not been there to witness the face of fear Jo had worn regarding the accident. Nor had Micki been in the New York office several days later to see, firsthand, Jo's face whiten on hearing the full extent of Wolf's injuries.

Brett had been there. He had kept a sharp eye out for her slightest reaction to his news, only to find a sharp eye had not been necessary; Jo's dismay had been obvious.

Now, three weeks later, Brett realized it had been at the moment she'd displayed the most pain that he'd decided Micki's fears were based on fact and Jo was, indeed, Wolf's mistress.

Again Brett's tongue snaked across his teeth. It was also at that exact moment, he finally acknowledged, that he'd felt the first lick of physical desire for her.

That moment had occurred after his detailed account of Wolf's injuries. Jo had gone deathly pale, then had nearly fallen into the chair by Wolf's desk, hand groping at the chair arm for support. It was when she'd lowered her lashes in pain that he'd allowed his gaze to leave her face to roam freely over her slender body. It was then he'd suffered the first stirring of need for her.

The question of whether he wanted Jo because she *was*, or had been, Wolf's reared its nasty little head. Instantly, Brett assured himself that their past relationship had nothing to do with his present yearnings. Hard on the heels of that self-assurance came the fervent hope that he was not lying to himself.

Brett was well aware of the depth of feeling he held for his older brother. He had idolized Wolf for as long as he could remember, had always tried to emulate him. But to carry his hero worship to the point of wanting to possess Wolf's mistress was not only ludicrous, it was downright unhealthy.

The fact remained that Jo had belonged to Wolf; in his own mind Brett was now certain of that. He had uncovered just too damned many incriminating signs during the previous three weeks for their liaison to be strictly business. One of those signs now lay snugly in a long envelope inside his breast pocket, crackling faintly every time he moved. Brett had even had the fanciful idea that the blasted envelope was laughing at him every time it crackled.

You are sick!

The self-admonition was silently issued in an attempt to quell the strong urge gripping him to turn and feast his eyes on Jo's tall, delicately formed body.

Feast his eyes, hell! He wanted, longed, ached to feast his mouth, tongue, hands, and body on top of hers.

Again his tongue flicked at his teeth, barely withdrawing in time to prevent being lacerated by his descending hard upper teeth. Will you knock it off? She belongs to him! His hard white molars clamped together in frustration and self-disgust.

She belongs to him.

Without conscious thought, Brett's spine straightened and his shoulders squared. Face it, chum, he advised himself reluctantly. When Wolf comes back, should he so choose, it will be to take over Jo as well as the region.

51

Hot rebellion, more fierce than he'd felt throughout his rebellious teenage years, seared Brett's emotions. In an effort at maintaining control, he breathed in, slowly, deeply repeating the same phrase over and over in his mind: You're out of line here, she is his.

His ploy at self-chastisement was a total failure, for the rebel in his mind chanted back: He can no longer have her, I will make her mine.

Back and forth, the battle raged between control and rebellion, rendering him temporarily motionless while both vied for supremacy. The deciding factor came not from within but from without.

"Brett, I'm sorry to bother you." Jo's voice was entirely free of facetiousness. She genuinely sounded sorry about having to intrude on his thoughts; she also sounded genuinely confused. "There's something here I don't quite understand."

His given name, coming voluntarily from her soft lips, whipped Brett around as if he were attached to a string she held tightly in her slim fingers. Brett breathed a sigh of relief on realizing Jo had not witnessed his humiliatingly swift snap to obedience. Gleaming head bent, Jo scowled in consternation at the folder in her hands.

"Concerning what?" Strolling slowly—to make up for his earlier quickness?—to the desk, Brett held out one hand for the source of her confusion.

"The Vermont project." Unaware of his outstretched hand, Jo pursed her lips at the printed words under her perusal. "I thought Wolf had decided to scrap the idea of yet another condominium complex aimed at the skiing set, but, from the info here, he must have continued the preliminary investigation on his own."

Halting at the side of the desk, Brett leaned toward her. For a fleeting half instant he hesitated, fighting the impulse to slide his hand under her chin, tilt her head up, and taste her pursing lips with his own. The effort required to bypass her head and pluck the folder from her hands was evidenced by the barely discernable tremor in his fingers.

Jo had the good sense to remain quiet while he studied the folder's contents. Gradually, the tension eased out of Brett as his eyes skimmed the neatly typed lines on each successive sheet of paper contained within the folder's cream-colored covers.

Yes. Yes. A tiny smile played over Brett's lips in appreciation of the thorough investigative job Wolf had done on the proposed project. Before he came to the final sheet, Brett fully agreed with his brother's conclusions. The location was good. Wolf's figures, if accurate—and Brett knew they would be—were well within reason for a complex of this size. The time for action was now if the groundwork was to be completed and excavation begun by late spring.

Behind the typed sheets were several handwritten pages. Brett's smile grew on recognition of Wolf's slashing, straight-line penmanship. In a bold hand, Wolf had outlined a comprehensive, detailed directive on exactly how the official prospectus should be blocked out.

Impressive bit of work, old son, Brett silently congratulated his elder sibling, then he mentally telegraphed a promise: You very obviously wanted this. I'm going to get it for you. It may not be much in exchange for your oh-so-exquisite plaything here, but thems the breaks, bro.

Raising his head, Brett focused his attention on the hazel-eyed plaything sitting very quietly, very patiently at Wolf's desk. Gazing into the amber-flecked depths, Brett reiterated what he'd known for a very long time. One could never fault Wolf's taste in women. It seemed his taste in assistants was faultless as well, for Jo Lawrence was every bit as efficient at her work as his own paragon, Richard Colby. And that was a compliment Brett had bestowed on no other.

"You're staring, Brett."

Jo's tone conveyed enlightenment, not censure. Smiling wryly,

Brett brought the cream covers together with a businesslike snap before handing the folder to her.

"Slide this into your briefcase," he ordered as he started to turn away from the desk.

"We're going to pursue it?"

"We're going to pursue it," he repeated, tilting his head back to her. "Can we wrap it up here soon?" he went on, deliberately stifling any attempt she might have made at questioning him further. "I'd like to be on the road by lunchtime, and I want to stop by the house on our way out."

"This apparently not-to-be-discussed report was the last of it." Jo held up the folder. "Are you positive you feel safe leaving it in my care?" Her tone betrayed her slightly out-of-joint, but adorable, nose.

"Simmer down, Ms. Assistant." Brett sighed. "We will discuss the thing, probably to your screaming point, after we're back in the city." Stepping back, he indicated she was free to leave the desk without fear of having to get too close to him. "Are you packed?"

"Yes."

"Good." Brett ran a quick glance over her and took another step back, advising himself not to tempt fate or his own swiftly dissolving control. "So am I. Let's get this place in order and get out of here."

Working together, the apartment was quickly restored to the neat condition they had found it to be in on their arrival two days previously. It was when Brett strode into the hall toward the bedroom to collect his suitcase that he felt the now-familiar tightening in his stomach muscles. The juices inside that particular organ began to roil much like the gray-green waves pounding against the shoreline.

Brett didn't see the waves, or the shoreline; he didn't even see the long wide window that took up most of one of the bedroom's walls. A grimace twisting his lips reflected his inner image. His eyes, a moody dark gray, were fastened on the oversized bed. The

54

figures his actively churning imagination projected onto that bed were the cause of sudden nausea.

Within the luxury of that rich man's couch, Wolf had consummated his marriage to Micki. Brett knew that. What he didn't know and what had tormented him throughout most of last night was whether Wolf had also consummated his liaison with Jo Lawrence there as well.

God damn!

Standing perfectly still, his long body rigid with tension, Brett was not even aware of the fingers of his right hand curling into his palm; was not conscious of the urge that sent that hand hurtling out to make painful contact with the solid wood that framed the doorway. Consciousness came with the tongue of fire that shot from his knuckles to the base of his skull.

Eyes mirroring disbelief, Brett stared at the abraded skin covering his fingers. Although the door frame had been the recipient of his lashing blow, Wolf's face had been his mental target.

Wolf?

As he stared at his still-balled hand Brett's expression changed from disbelief to incredulity. Good God! Was he cracking up completely? He had never ever felt anything but near adulation for Wolf. Now, because of a woman . . . a shudder rippled through him. With a concentrated effort Brett uncurled his fingers.

Brett felt the sickness roil again as against his will his gaze drifted back to the opulent bed. Did he want Jo because of *who* she was, or because of *what* she was to Wolf?

Moving with an unusual jerky swiftness, Brett clutched the handles of his supple leather case and swung out of the room. There were connotations here he didn't want to examine at the moment. Later, when he was back in New York, and alone, he'd pick his mental and emotional feelings to pieces.

Jo stood patiently waiting for him in the hall, her tall, sleek body an invitation, her cool, aloof expression a denial of same.

Nodding curtly for her to precede him, he scooped up her

cream-toned suitcase, thankful for the necessity of bending over and thereby concealing the evidence of the need growing even greater within.

Following her smoothly swaying, ultra-slim hips along the corridor and down the open stairs to the first level, Brett wondered what had happened to his hard-won, tightly reined control. He had not touched his wife, Sondra, once during the last six months of the farce they'd called their marriage. And his celibacy had been by choice, not by Sondra's rejection.

His eyes caressing the enticing symmetry of Jo's tush, Brett's lip lifted in a sneer in memory of Sondra's professed willingness to, in her own words, share her wealth.

"Brett?"

The voice was not the soft, languid drawl that had captivated him five years ago but the businesslike clip of a motivated woman who had worked her way up from assistant hotel manager to assistant everything. With a mental shake, Brett banished the memory of his former wife—at least temporarily.

A frown on her more-than-merely-beautiful face, Jo held the heavy glass door for his passage.

"You have the look of a man who has forgotten something," Jo murmured as he strode by her. "Have you?"

I wish to hell I could forget *everything*, Brett thought savagely. Most particularly you! He let a sharp movement of his head answer in the negative.

After a last-minute check on Wolf's house, during which Jo remained in the car—because of an aversion to entering the home Wolf shared with Micki? Brett wondered—he headed the sports car toward New York.

To Brett the drive seemed exceptionally long and rife with tension. Being confined in such a small area with a woman— upon whose bones he ached to bounce—was not exactly conducive to tranquil travel. The fact that said woman smelled intoxicating, not of perfume but of pure, sweet female tormented him to the brink of squirming in the bucket seat.

I've got to have her, and it's got to be soon. The stark realization followed the silent sigh that slipped the barrier of his lips as Brett joined his car in jockeying for position in the melee laughingly referred to as New York traffic.

Jo's apartment, located in a fashionable if not exclusive section of the city, was relatively easy to find. Drawing the car to a halt in front of the high-rise, Brett stepped out of the low car and smiled sardonically at the doorman who moved with alacrity to assist Jo in alighting.

With a word to the obsequious man to stand by the Porsche, Brett again suffered the discomfort of trailing the delicate figure he lusted after. Confinement in the elevator proved almost as unnerving as confinement in the Porsche. Finally, after a long trek along the hall on the ninth floor, Jo came to a halt before an unmarked door. She had her key in hand. A long, oddly shaped key, the sight of which glued Brett's teeth together. He recognized that key. Was he not in possession of one exactly like it? Was it not, at that very moment, inside his pocket, nestled among the other keys on Wolf's gold ring?

He did.

It was.

God damn.

The emotions that welled to congregate in Brett's throat burned with a bitter sting. Fury, disappointment, disgust merged into a choking mass. Yet, overall, frustration reigned, prompting him to snatch the key from Jo impatiently when she hesitated at inserting it into the lock.

A quick, vicious turn of the key and the door swung open. Stepping back, Brett frowned a silent order for Jo to enter her apartment, knowing he had to get her inside as quickly as possible and get himself out of there.

Jo murmured, "Thank you."

Brett murmured, "You're welcome."

Then, being very careful not to look at her, he placed her bag next to the door and stepped back into the hall, one hand outstretched to her.

"I'll have the Vermont report," he clipped shortly. Jo's startled look made him add, more gently, "I want to study it tonight. Come to my office first thing tomorrow morning. We'll go over it together." Silently he urged: Come to my bed tonight and we'll forget it together.

The longing that swept through him shook Brett to the core. Hurry, damn you, he commanded silently, watching Jo fumble with the clasps on her attaché case. Hurry, because if you don't I'm going to step back inside, throw you down, and take you right there on that expensive hand-loomed rug my prowling brother paid for. The last thought brought with it a shaft of pain that blanketed Brett's mind with shocked disbelief.

Pain!

Automatically, Brett's fingers closed on the folder Jo extended to him.

Pain?

Automatically, Brett responded to Jo's baffled-sounding words of farewell. And automatically, Brett retraced his tracks to the elevator.

Why pain?

Examining the puzzling emotion, Brett absently slipped a twenty-dollar bill into the doorman's hand before slipping behind the wheel of the Porsche. The key to the puzzle eluded him as he fought his way through the late-afternoon traffic to Wolf's apartment, which *was* located in a posh section of the city.

Inside the elegantly decorated, bi-level suite, Brett abandoned his case inside the door and drew a straight line to Wolf's well-stocked bar.

"There should be no pain involved here. Except of the physical discomfort type."

Measuring two fingers of amber liquid into a short, squat glass, Brett wasn't even aware of speaking the assertion aloud.

58

After swallowing the aged Scotch neat, he was fully aware of being vocal.

"Damn," he muttered as the whisky burned a path to his stomach. "The idea was to quench the desire, Renninger. Not burn a hole in your guts." He added ice cubes and water to the second drink.

Sipping at the diluted whisky, Brett retreived his suitcase and climbed the free-standing staircase to the apartment's second level and the largest of the two guest bedrooms.

Standing dead center in the room decorated in muted tones of blue and pearl gray, Brett relaxed his fingers and let the case drop carelessly to the deeply piled carpet. He didn't even hear the muffled thud as the supple leather made contact with the wool fibers. His spine rigid, Brett fought against the urge tugging at him and lost.

Following the emotional dictate, Brett, cursing himself softly, spun around and strode from the room and along the short hallway to the master bedroom. Flinging the door open, he took one step inside then halted, his eyes riveted to the enormous bed—in which, Brett was sure, Wolf was undoubtably the master.

"Have you had her here, you bastard?"

The sound of his own voice was startling in its harshness. Still it persisted in erupting from his stiff lips.

"While that beautiful creature who bore your children went serenely, trustfully about the business of keeping your home for you in that classy pile of bricks beside the ocean, did you wantonly debase her, and yourself, on that damned island you call a bed, with *my* woman?"

The echo of his own words slamming back at his mind, Brett remained unmoving for a timeless moment, not seeing, not even breathing. Then, his eyes filling with something akin to horror, he slowly shook his head from side to side.

"No!" Brett's whispered denial came in cadence with his head motion. "No. I couldn't, I wouldn't do something as stupid as fall in love with her!"

Closing his eyes to blot out the offensive sight of Wolf's satin-sheeted playground, Brett's lips thinned in endurance of the shudder that rent the fabric of his soul. The body tremor caused a crackle in his breast pocket. In the silence of the room, the crackle had the muted ring of mocking laughter.

Raising his right hand, he slipped the long envelope from his pocket, then withdrew the legal document from it. A bitter smile twisting his lips, he opened his eyes and again focused on the huge bed.

"No, brother mine, soiling your own nest would definitely not be your style. You would ensconce her expensively, but apart."

The document Brett unfolded was the deed to the apartment he had so recently retreated from.

Retreat appeared to be Brett's order of the day, for now he backed away from his brother's sleeping quarters, quietly closing the door as he went.

If Brett had found it a struggle coming to grips with his unexpected, unwanted physical need for Wolf's partner in dalliance, that struggle was as nothing compared to facing the reality of a deeper emotional need.

Never a coward, Brett nevertheless decided that there were times when facing reality was better done with a few stiff belts. Striding out purposely, he went back downstairs to the bar and the comfort of twelve-year-old Scotch.

It was while sipping on his third glass of barely diluted whisky, his elongated frame perched tiredly on a leather-covered, thickly padded bar stool, that Brett finally conceded defeat to the indefinable emotion commonly called love.

God, he hated it.

No doubt about it, chum, he taunted himself wryly. This time your engine has completely jumped its tracks. One might be forgiven for falling hard for the wrong woman once. But twice? Brett shook his head sadly. You, sir, seemed to have developed a penchant for loose-limbed, loose-moraled, shockingly beautiful females. But at least the first one had not been staked out by another man—and that man the silver-eyed Wolf no less. Brett's soft, self-mocking laughter skipped the length of the short bar.

If she finds out, she will rip you apart.

So how do you go about keeping the very beautiful, very sexy, but, regrettably, also very intelligent Jo Lawrence from finding out?

Propping his elbow on the polished wood bar, Brett held his glass aloft and frowned at the amber contents, a self-derisive smile curving his lips.

You are not going to find an answer at the bottom of a bottle of Scotch, he advised himself judiciously. Finish your drink and go rustle up some food to soak up the booze.

The refrigerator, kept well stocked by Wolf's part-time housekeeper, yielded the makings of a Reuben sandwich, which Brett prepared with the same ease as he had breakfast earlier that morning.

Deciding coffee would be the prudent drink to have with his meal, Brett brewed a full pot and polished off the sandwich in between deep bracing swallows, all the while resisting the surge of memories of his first disastrous foray into the baffling emotion called love.

As a rule Brett was successful at keeping all recollection of his time with Sondra at bay, but this evening, taut with anger, actually aching with physical frustration, and saturated with whisky, the self-imposed mental barrier refused to stay in place.

Sighing in defeat, his beautiful male lips curling in a sneer of self-mockery, Brett refilled his cup, stretched his long legs out under the table, and let the memories rip.

Sondra Mallone had taken Brett's breath away from the first moment he saw her, greeting passengers as they entered the 745 bound from Chicago to Atlanta. His first thought had been that she was overall gorgeous. Of average height, Sondra had a neat, trim body with delectable curves, a fantastic mane of fiery red hair, and a face that could, and often did, stop men in their tracks. Of course, there was no outward indication betraying the fact that she also possessed the morals of a back-alley feline. Completely bowled over by her, it was a long time later that Brett learned, the hard way, that Sondra would sleep with anything that wore pants—if the pockets in those pants were heavily lined with gold.

Sipping at the strong black brew, Brett allowed his mind freedom to wander down the pathway to yesterday, allowed his senses to experience the trauma of the time he'd spent with Sondra.

Now, from a five-year distance, Brett realized he'd been a prime target for any Sondra who happened along. He'd been more than tired. After six weeks of flying from Atlanta to Dallas to Honolulu to San Diego to Chicago, on orders from Madam President to "pull the outer reaches of the company together," he'd been bone weary. As he'd also been without female companionship the entire length of those six weeks, he'd been horny as hell.

Enter the gorgeous redhead!

With a snort of disdain, Brett jackknifed to his feet and began clearing the table. When the kitchen was again restored to its usual neatness, he walked slowly to his temporary bedroom, extinguishing lights as he went. After a quick visit to the connecting bathroom for a brief ablution, the plying of a toothbrush, and the natural draining off of some of the liquid he'd consumed, Brett stripped to the buff and crawled between blue-and-gray striped percale sheets, only then allowing his memory free run once more. This time, their time together replayed in his mind in detail.

Anger tightened his frame, simmered in his eyes as Brett strode along the boarding ramp to the plane.

Damned incompetents! If I performed my duties with the

laxity of some of these airline baggage handlers, I'd be tossed out on my ear, Madam President's son or not.

The recipients of Brett's ire were the faceless airline employees who had somehow managed to mislay his bags between San Diego and Chicago. The mishandling in itself was bad enough but, on his second day in the windy city, he had been informed that his bags had been sent on to Atlanta and were awaiting him there. Thus Brett had been forced into an unscheduled shopping expedition. Brett detested shopping in general and clothes shopping in particular; he had remained furious over the incident throughout his entire five-day stay in the city. Nothing, not the fact that his exhausting back-to-back twelve-hour day meetings had gone so smoothly or the congratulatory phone call from his mother, had soothed his abraded temper. That is, not until he'd caught a flash of flaming red hair as he approached the entrance to the plane.

God, she's fantastic!

Anger forgotten, Brett increased his gait, plunging ahead for a closer inspection of the passenger-greeting stewardess.

"Good afternoon, sir." Sondra flashed perfect white teeth. "Your seat is lo—"

"Do you have a layover in Atlanta?" Brett interrupted softly, insinuatingly, his thumb and forefinger dipping into his breast pocket.

"Yes, sir, but . . ."

"If you feel the need of companionship." He again cut her off, pressing his embossed business card into her hand. "Give me a call." Giving her no time to respond or attempt to hand his card back, Brett strode into the plane.

Later, while delivering a Rob Roy to him, Sondra slid his card into the small handkerchief pocket on his suit coat with a whispered, "If you care to wait, I'll meet you in the departure lounge after we land."

If he cared to? Brett was grateful for the attaché case resting on his thighs, concealing the evidence of how very much he cared to wait. For the previous two weeks his body had been sending him signals of its need for release of sexual tension. Suddenly his need was centered on the tantalizing redhead.

Upon landing in Atlanta, Brett positioned himself at the long window in the departure lounge, his impatience camouflaged with cool composure, prepared to endure hours of waiting if necessary. The necessity did not arise as within a relatively short amount of time Sondra joined him at his sentry post.

"You're free to leave already?" Brett made no attempt to hide his pleasure at the sight of her.

"Free for three full days." Sondra smiled back at him.

"Three days!" Brett repeated, unabashedly delighted at the prospect. "Is that the norm for a layover?"

"No," Sondra admitted blithely.

"Then how did you manage it?" Brett grinned in anticipation.

"Wheedling, coaxing, and practically promising my firstborn to the girl who was due this layover."

Securing her elbow with his long-fingered hand, Brett steered her from the lounge. "Then let's get out of here before she changes her mind."

Smiling conspiratorially at each other, they hurried out of the terminal and into a cab.

Before the end of their first twenty-four hours together, Brett was thoroughly besotted with Sondra. She was not only gorgeous; she was bright, vivacious, and witty.

By the end of their second twenty-four hours, Brett decided Sondra was everything he'd ever wanted in a woman. He was so besotted he was beyond realizing that Sondra made a career out of being everything *every* man ever wanted in a woman.

Sondra's vacation never did end. The flight from Chicago to Atlanta was her last. After one particularly satisfying bedroom romp during their third twenty-four hours, Brett, positive he'd at last found a soulmate, proposed to her. They were married one week later at his mother's horse farm in Florida.

Brett, though not a confirmed workaholic, ran a close second in the energy and diligence he afforded the company. Sondra was a lotus eater to the marrow of her bones. The moment his diamond-encrusted wedding ring firmly encircled her finger, she prevailed upon him to come and play with her.

In truth, Brett needed very little coaxing to abandon duty for the intoxicating delights to be explored on the playground of her luscious body. For almost two years he was little more than a figurehead in his Atlanta office. It was only later that Brett would give thanks for whatever guidance had prompted him to hire Richard Colby as his assistant. For Richard not only held down the fort competently, he covered Brett's tracks completely.

The good life began to pall as their second anniversary crept over the horizon. Unnaturally tired, jaded, bored with it all, Brett announced his intention of going back to work one hungover midmorning.

At first, Sondra pouted prettily and coaxed beguilingly. When those tactics had no effect on Brett's determination, she turned on the waterworks. It was when the tears failed to dissuade him that she revealed the first glimpse of her true colors.

"God damn you," Sondra screamed at him. "What the hell do you expect me to do while you play at being the big corporate executive? Join a club of silly damned women who talk of nothing but their brats and redecorating the houses their husbands keep them chained to?"

Startled speechless, Brett had stared at her, unwilling to believe what he was hearing. Shock followed amazement as the tirade Sondra flung at him came straight from the gutter.

Though wealthy from birth, Brett had not led a sheltered existence. He had been all over the world. It would have been polite to say some of the places he'd been in were a mite unsavory. Yet he'd never encountered a female with Sondra's command of filthy language.

His head pounding from the effects of months of too much Scotch, too many late nights, and total abandonment to the physical senses, Brett, calmly walking away from her in mid-spate, strode into the bathroom and threw up.

From that point the marriage that never really was deteriorated rapidly. The twelve months that followed were sheer hell for Brett. Sondra, no longer concerned about his opinion of her, flaunted her true personality. She was still bright, if bitingly so. She was still vivacious, if frantically so. She was still witty, if sarcastically so. She continually turned Brett's stomach.

As one month dragged into another, Brett spent longer and yet longer hours in the office, more and more days on the road. He was fully cognizant of the audacious, unfettered life style Sondra was pursuing. At the dawn of their third anniversary he no longer cared; at least he thought he didn't.

His own personal breaking point came less then a week before their third anniversary. Brett had been in Philadelphia the previous week supervising the final details of a twin hotel-condominium complex the company was planning to build there. Although he was tired, he felt good, for he had successfully ironed out all the knots and twists that accompany a project the size and cost of the one in Philadelphia.

His mood soured slightly on entering the lavish condo Sondra had insisted on being installed in. Brett loathed everything about the place.

Ignoring his surroundings with singleminded concentration, Brett cut a direct path to the bedroom, his one desire being a hot shower and clean, cool, lightweight clothing. At the doorway to the bedroom he came to a jarring halt.

It was the middle of the afternoon and Sondra was in bed. She was not alone. The fact that she was in the act of defiling both him and his bed with another man was bad enough. That the other man had been a friend of Brett's since their university days was like receiving a kick in the teeth.

The other man was a very elite member of the old guard, old-money aristocracy, a prominent banker, and loaded—in more ways than one.

At sight of the writhing, moaning couple, Brett's feeling of well-being drowned in the anger that erupted at his core and surged hotly through him.

At sight of the nearly empty champagne bottle and forgotten glasses on the nightstand by the bed, his anger reached the boiling point.

But it was the sight of the small sugar bowl half full of cocaine that ignited the furious explosion that propelled him into the room.

Though his blood was running hot, Brett's mind remained icy cold. Fully aware of his actions, Brett strode across the deeply piled white carpet. Grasping his former friend by arm and thigh, Brett lifted the smaller man and tossed him to the floor.

"What the . . . !" The squeak slurred from the other man's throat an instant before he found himself flying through space.

"Brett! Stop this at—" Sondra's shrill command died on her bruised lips at the face of cold hauteur Brett turned to her.

"Pig." The condemnation that iced Brett's scathing tone twisted Sondra's features into a mask of fear. "Pig's the only name that suits you. You're worse than a whore. Well, though it may sound trite"—now he sneered—"you made your bed. Now you can wallow in it." Not bothering to glance at the man just regaining consciousness, Brett whipped around and strode to the door.

"It'll cost you a bundle to get rid of me," Sondra shrieked after him.

Pausing in the doorway, Brett slowly turned to face her, his expression amused, his smile relieved.

"And worth every dollar of it."

It had required six months, *and* every dollar of that bundle, but Brett had reclaimed his self-respect and his freedom.

Now, eighteen freedom months later, Brett derided himself for once again finding himself a slave to his own emotions. Though he would not have thought it possible, he felt a crushing need for another, if totally different, type of woman.

They are really sisters under the skin, Brett warned himself wryly.

I really should strangle the bitch and have done with it.

But what I'm going to do is get the hell out of her vicinity for a while and cool off. Vermont, here I come.

His lips curving in self-derision, Brett flung his arms over his head and went to sleep.

CHAPTER FOUR

For Jo, besieged by a barrage of questions and memories, escape into unconsciousness was not difficult to achieve; it was impossible.

Wandering restlessly, purposelessly through the large, roomy apartment, her distracted gaze skimmed sightlessly over the material rewards of her work effort.

The apartment itself was a reflection of Jo's success in her chosen career. The fact that she did not actually own it yet, or that the monthly payments were staggering, was immaterial. Jo was confident of her ability to meet those monthly payments. At least she had been before Wolf's horrible accident and the subsequent arrival of the disapproving Brett.

The furnishings, a reflection of Jo's personality, had been selected carefully, at her leisure, with little regard for cost. As yet the furnishings and bits and pieces of enhancing decor were sparse. It was less than six months since she'd taken possession of the apartment. Besides, Jo felt no driving compulsion to have the decorating chore finished. She had savored the purchase of each and every piece.

As Jo's chosen style of decor leaned from classic to ultra

modern, her task was made doubly difficult simply because the selection was abundant and varied.

Except for the kitchen and the apartment's two bathrooms, all the walls were painted a stark white. The living room was given life by the occasional splashes of brilliant color: the scarlet velvet that draped the large window with its stunning view of the city's towers; the blazing orange-red in the large print depicting a breathtaking sunset over the Pacific Ocean; the glaring lipstick red of the toss pillows littering the long white corduroy sofa and matching club chairs, and, underfoot, the rectangular scatter rugs in unrelenting black and white.

No, not at all the more common homey warmth. Yet it worked, and beautifully; the room invited conversation and relaxation. On this night Jo found little relaxation. Drifting in an aimless circle, her fingers touching a large glass ashtray here, the smooth surface of ebony tables there, she felt nothing, and saw less. Though the cause of her confusion had departed some fifteen minutes ago, Jo was still trying to grasp what had transpired while he stood at her door.

Was she, she wondered, so very infatuated with Brett she was beginning to imagine things? The night before she had felt certain he was on the point of kissing her before he'd turned away abruptly. Just moments ago she had received the impression that he was fighting a similar urge. Yet in both instances he had left her flat, and not very pleasantly at that! Was she reading something into Brett's behavior that simply was not there?

Hazel eyes cloudy with introspection, Jo walked slowly to her bedroom, switching off lights automatically as she passed them. With a featherlike touch to the dimmer switch mounted on the white wall of her bedroom, different but equally resplendent colors sprang into view. Here the draperies were of antique satin in a shimmering teal blue. The wall-to-wall carpet picked up the illusive hint of green in the drapes. A riot of blues and greens slashed diagonally across the satin bedspread. An impressionistic painting done in bold shades of blue was the only relief on one white wall.

Kicking off her shoes, Jo padded to the closet and began to undress, unaware of the carpet's soft fibers massaging her soles. Drat the man, she thought irritably, what was he thinking, feeling? Her distraction was evidenced by the fact that, although she was standing before the opened closet door, she dropped her clothes carelessly onto the floor. Seconds later Jo stood frowning under a hot shower. Usually the jet spray had a soothing effect. Tonight it simply was not working; in fact, nothing seemed to work for her anymore! Sighing tiredly, Jo stepped out of the tub, dripping unconcernedly onto the fluffy peach bathmat. Patting herself dry, she ignored her own reflection—no mean trick as the walls were tiled entirely in mirrors. There was not a hint of stark white in this room. Except for the mirror walls everything in the room was in the same soft peach shade as the mat she now dripped upon, including the roll of tissue set into the wall. The combination of mirrors and soft peach imbued the room with an innocent eroticism. The effect was not at all accidental; Jo had very carefully planned every room in the apartment.

Hanging her sodden towel neatly on the glass bar mounted on the wall, Jo glanced up and found her gaze caught by the unhappy expression in the hazel eyes gazing back at her. Had Brett been on the point of making a move on her? Devoid of enlightenment, hazel eyes stared at her. If he had wanted to kiss her, why hadn't he acted on the urge? He knew she was free. She knew he was divorced. And what did a kiss mean, anyway?

Long lashes fluttered in a quick blink. You may attempt to fool any other person in the world, Jo Lawrence, she chided herself, but never, never try to con yourself. From any other man a kiss would not only have no meaning, it would be forcefully rejected; from Brett Renninger, it might very well mean the end of existence as you know it and the beginning of a whole new, incredibly exciting world.

Wearing nothing but a dreamy expression on her lovely face,

71

Jo drifted into the bedroom and slid between wickedly expensive satin sheets. The feel of satin against her naked skin ignited a fire deep inside the very core of her being. Closing her eyes, Jo moved sensuously, her body growing vibrantly alive from the caressing touch of the cool, smooth material, her mind imagining that touch belonging to Brett's long, slim hands. Heat radiated from her now fiery core to lick hungrily through her veins, and Jo's trembling thighs parted in silent invitation. The low whimper that whispered through her dry lips alerted Jo to the folly she was indulging in. Moaning in frustration, she rolled onto her stomach and forced herself to lay perfectly still.

"Oh, God, why Brett?" Jo's cry was muffled by the silky pillowcase. "Of all the men in the world, why inflict me with the one who feels nothing but disdain for me?"

Jo grew still at the sound of her own voice, the context of her outcry. Why did Brett hold her in contempt? There were few people who knew her personal history. Still, could it be possible Brett had heard her rather pathetic story from one of them? Had he heard of her miserable attempt at playing mistress and dismissed her as a failure as a woman? Because she had failed. Gary Devlin had made sure she'd been aware of exactly had badly she'd fared in the male-female stakes.

The heat was gone, replaced by the chill of memory. Jo definitely did not want to think about Gary. Jo never wanted to think about Gary again for as long as she lived. But, given a choice between burning in the hell of desire's fire and reliving the hell she'd endured with Gary, she thought it prudent to think about him. Thoughts of him should not only keep her cool, they would very likely freeze her soul.

Gary. Had she really considered the possibility of spending the rest of her life with him? Yes, Jo admitted. At the beginning she had actually wanted marriage. Thank heaven Gary had hedged, opting for a trial, live-together period. That trial period had lasted a very short time. Jo shivered with the memory. She had not been able to hold Gary's interest for one full year! And, if he was to be believed, she had practically emasculated him as well!

Did all women who had reached a measure of success in their careers have this trouble in their relationships with men? Were all men intimidated by even the most mildly successful women? Jo didn't know the answers, and she was too private a person to ask the opinion of other professional women she knew.

Cool now, in body and mind, Jo rolled onto her back and stared into the darkness of her room. If their time together had emasculated Gary, she couldn't define what it had done to her. But she knew she was now afraid of any deep involvement with a man, and the very thought of making a commitment gave her the shakes. It's unbelievable, she mused sadly, how much damage two people can inflict on each other in such a short span of time. And it had begun so sweetly too.

She had met Gary while shopping one bright, warm morning in April in, of all places, a stalled elevator. Everyone on the car had become nervous immediately, including Jo. Gary had not. His tall, muscular frame propped lazily against the car's wall, he had coolly advised them to relax.

"This is at least the third time this has happened to me in this very car." Gary, a dry smile curving his lips, had offered the information in an attempt to calm a rather hysterical matron. "We'll be moving again shortly."

Within seconds of his promise the mechanism clanked into motion, then glided to a smooth stop at the next floor. Inside those seconds, his laughing eyes had captured Jo's and he'd winked conspiratorially. Acting completely out of character, Jo had winked back. As she stepped from the car he caught her arm in a gentle grasp.

"Now that our crisis is over," he'd whispered dramatically, "how about joining me in a celebratory cup of coffee?"

Jo couldn't help herself, she'd laughed aloud. "What, exactly, would we be celebrating?"

"Why, our very survival, what else?" He blinked owlishly at her, making her aware of the summer-sky blue of his eyes.

Completely charmed by his boyish smile, his dark, clean-cut attractiveness, and his engaging manner, Jo, flinging caution to the winds, went with him for coffee. Six months later she gave in to his plea to allow him to move in with her.

Less than a week after Gary had lugged his belongings up the three flights of stairs to her cramped, one-bedroom flat, Jo knew the arrangement had been a mistake. He was carelessly sloppy with his clothes, she soon discovered, leaving them laying in rumpled heaps all over the place. To someone as neat as Jo, the mere sight of the piles of soiled clothing induced a shudder. But even that irritating habit might have been bearable if it had not been combined with Gary's absolute refusal to help with the everyday household chores, claiming he wouldn't be caught dead doing "women's" work. But, by far, Jo's biggest disillusionment came on their very first night together.

Jo had been to bed with Gary before he'd moved in with her, of course, but always at his apartment, which he shared with a young accountant. Their sexual activity had therefore been less than satisfactory due, Gary had assured her, to the fact that his flatmate might walk in on them at any given moment. Yet, for some reason Jo could not explain even to herself, she had held firm in her refusal to having him spend time in her bed. When her capitulation came Jo had been every bit as surprised as Gary was.

In the darkness of a much more luxurious bedroom, Jo groaned in sympathy for the inhibited woman she'd been a few years ago.

Growing up in a home where her parents never displayed affection for each other, in fact rarely even spoke to each other except when absolutely necessary, Jo, harboring a wariness for the male-female relationship, had singlemindedly pursued first her studies, then her career. An only child, she had received an abundance of love from her parents, but always in separate doses. Jo was not yet ten years old when she realized her parents silently hated each other. Why they hated each other remained a mystery to Jo to this day. They never told her, she never asked.

Being a witness to this silent hatred through her formative years had inflicted fears as well as scars on her psyche. For as long as Jo could remember, everyone told her she was her mother all over again. In one respect this pleased her, for her mother was very beautiful. But in another way it frightened her, for her mother very obviously could not relate to any man. As she grew older Jo realized intellectually that looking like her mother did not necessarily mean she was *like* her mother. Still, no matter how she tried to convince herself otherwise, the fear of her own inability to express love for a man, either verbally or physically, would not be banished.

During her college and hotel-management training years Jo had dated infrequently, and always disastrously. Positive she would make a shambles of the evening, she always did. In fact, she said no so often that by her third year in college she had acquired the nickname No No Jo. It was only after she'd been working for some months that she began a slow emergence from her shell of fear. In the hotel business Jo naturally came in contact with different and varied types of people. Quiet and observant by nature, she studied the hotel guests and her fellow employees closely, most particularly the inner action between men and women. Slowly, as she conducted her secret servey, she came to the conclusion that she was not all that different from anybody else.

When, to Jo's own delighted surprise, she was promoted to assistant to the assistant to the head of the East Coast region of the Renninger Corporation and had to move to New York City, she discovered a whole new world to contemplate. Dedicated to her subject, and also to fill the hours when she was not at work, Jo devoured all the magazines devoted to the modern woman and every article she came across that dealt with the current mores on sexuality.

Gradually the tight bud of her self blossomed into mature young womanhood. Feeling free for the first time in her life, Jo felt ready for an adult relationship with a man. Then she met Gary Devlin. By the time their affair was over Gary had just about annihiliated all of Jo's hard-won confidence.

In personality they were complete opposites. Gary was outgoing, gregarious, and made friends easily, with just about anybody. Jo was as susceptible to his charm as most other women were. He was also the walking prototype of the clichéd "tall, dark, and handsome." It wasn't until after he moved in with her that Jo realized he was also vain, shallow, and extremely immature. That Gary was unspectacular in bed as well did not immediately become apparent to her. Having had only one painful, and abortive, sexual experience while in college, Jo really had no previous knowledge upon which she could base a comparison. Gary accused her of being, if not frigid, coldly unresponsive. Jo believed him, at least for a time.

The telling blow came when Jo was chosen for the coveted position of Wolfgang Renninger's assistant. Euphoric, soaring on a natural achievement high, Jo rushed home after work, burst into the apartment, and, flinging her arms around Gary, cried joyfully, "Guess what?"

As Jo had been rather withdrawn for several weeks, Gary eyed her warily, his expression suspicious.

"What?" he responded after a brief hesitation.

"I've been picked to replace James Mattern!" Jo bubbled, forgetting that, as Gary never had shown the slightest interest in her job, he hadn't the vaguest idea who James Mattern was.

"And that's good?"

"Good!" Jo exclaimed, laughing as he'd never seen her laugh before. "That's fantastic! At this moment, you see before you Mr. Wolfgang Renninger's new personal assistant!"

Gary was obviously unimpressed. His expression said "big deal" though he didn't voice the opinion. To her dismay Jo had learned over the eight months they had been together that, unless it was in some way connected with the world of sports, Gary's interest in business was nonexistent. But he was interested in money.

"Will it mean a raise in salary?"

"Of course, silly," Jo said teasingly. She named a figure, then waited expectantly for his whoop of delight. A chill washed all the joy out of her when he stepped back, his face stiff with outrage.

"But that's twice what I earn a year!" he exclaimed harshly. "Exactly what do you have to do for this Renninger?" Before she could shake herself out of her shock to answer, he added nastily, "Boy, is that poor jerk in for a surprise!"

Jo didn't need to ask what he meant. After weeks of his verbal digs about her ineptitude as a bed partner, she knew. Still she was hurt. She was also suddenly blazingly angry.

"Mr. Renninger's a married man!" she defended her employer.

"He's a man, isn't he?" Gary sneered. "And for the kind of money you just mentioned, he's going to expect one hell of a lot of assistance, and not only in the office either."

Jo wanted very badly to believe Gary was merely jealous of her boss, but she now knew better. Although it was painful and demeaning, she finally faced the truth. Gary did not love her. Gary loved Gary. Gary also loved the image he had of himself. That image could not bear the idea of a woman who was capable of earning twice his salary a year. Jo was not surprised when he spat a command at her.

"Tell him to jam his damn job."

"No," Jo said quietly but firmly.

Amazement gave his face a comical cast for an instant. Not in all the short time they'd been together had Jo so adamantly refused to do as he dictated. Then his expression turned ugly.

"Either you refuse this job or I move out of here." Gary flung the ultimatum at her in the tone of voice a child might use when threatening a parent with: If you won't let me have another piece of candy, I'll run away from home forever.

Jo answered in much the same way a weary parent might. "Shall I help you pack?" The difference between Jo's query and that of a parent was, Jo meant it. She had met his ultimatum with one of her own. And like the child he so obviously was, Gary resorted to verbal abuse.

"God! Am I glad I didn't let you talk me into marriage."

That was the mildest of the insults he snarled at her during the three day's required for him to find another gullible woman to move in with. When, finally, he was gone for good, Jo went through a brief but stormy period of weeping. Anger had kept her tight-lipped and dry-eyed throughout Gary's invective while removing himself from her flat. Unfortunately his final barb came via the telephone while she was at work, in Mr. Renninger's office.

"Is your boss there?" he'd asked innocently.

"Yes." Although she'd felt a warning prickle, she walked right into his nasty-little-kid trap. "Why?"

"You can tell the old boy I hope he gets his money's worth from you, but that I really doubt that he will. Even middle-aged men expect a little heat and cooperation from their bed partners once in a while." His derisive laugh burned Jo's ears as he hung up his receiver.

When the call had come through for her Wolf had pushed his chair back from the desk and walked to the window overlooking the busy avenue twenty-six floors below, thoughtfully allowing her a measure of privacy. Replacing the receiver with trembling fingers, Jo raised her eyes to the tall man at the window. Even though her chest felt tight from the pain caused by Gary's parting insult, she had to smile. Old boy? Middle-aged? Wolf Renninger? Her sight blurred by welling tears, she perused the height of him, the breadth of him, the muscularly athletic build that put Gary's to shame. A low, choking sound, part sob, part laugh, drew Wolf's attention. At the shattered look on her face his brows arched questioningly before coming together in a frown.

"What's wrong, Jo?"

It was not the question but the concern in his voice that released the flood of tears. Gulpingly, at times incoherently, Jo blurted out the whole miserable story to him, omitting only Gary's assertion that she was a cold, unresponsive woman. Sobbing out her unhappiness, she was hardly aware of Wolf crossing the room to take her into his arms, but she was grateful for the strong comfort of his embrace and the soothing strokes of his hand on her hair. There was nothing at all personal in his touch, and Jo was grateful for that as well. After the storm had passed he continued to hold her protectively for several minutes.

The sudden realization of her cheek resting on his tear-dampened shirt brought Jo to her senses. Embarrassed by her outburst and the position she found herself in, she stirred restlessly against his chest. Wolf immediately released her and stepped back.

"I-I'm sorry, sir, I . . ." Jo, feeling her cheeks grow hot, bit her lip in consternation.

Wolf's incredible silver eyes were soft with sympathy. "You don't need to apologize, Jo," he said quietly. Glancing down at his damp shirt, he smiled gently. "It'll dry." Then his smile twisted into a grimace. "He's not worth one of your tears, you know."

"Yes, I do know but . . . Oh, Mr. Renninger, I feel like such a fool!"

"First off, you can drop the Mr. Renninger bit." When she made to protest, he raised his hand to place one long finger over her lips. "I was going to request you call me Wolf anyway." A teasing gleam entered his eyes. "Besides, after what we've just been through together, Ms. Lawrence and Mr. Renninger would seem a mite formal. Don't you think?"

Jo smiled back at him, if hesitatingly. "I suppose so," she acceded, sounding unconvinced.

"Don't 'suppose so,' know so," he chided. "I've always insist-

79

ed on a first-name basis with my assistants. We work too closely together to have it otherwise." It was then that Jo learned that Wolf was not only kind but forthright. "I like you, Jo. I have since the first interview I gave you. You are bright and alert and ambitious, and I like that. But, like my wife, you have retained your femininity, and I like that too. Friends?"

Soon after Jo had begun working in the New York office she had heard, via the office grapevine, of how Wolf's wife, Micki, adored him. At that moment she understood why.

Wolf's brother Brett was something else entirely.

Brett.

Rolling onto her side, Jo groaned aloud in protest against the intrusive image of the object of her unwilling affections. After that shaming debacle with Gary, she had felt positive it would be a very, very long time before she'd find anything attractive in another man. Yet, here she was, a little more than a year later, sleepless, achy, and longing for the sight and touch of a man who very obviously did not like her.

But there had been those moments when she'd sensed desire in him, desire for her. Or was she seeing emotions in him that simply were not there? Why did he dislike her so?

"Oh, hell!"

With the exclamation Jo turned onto her side, pounding the pillow in an attempt to vent her frustration. She was weary of the questions that buzzed incessantly inside her head, tired of searching for answers that were not there. Clutching the pillow close to her body, she shut her eyes tightly, certain she was in for another sleepless night. Within seconds Jo was oblivious to the world. She slept long, and deeply, her rest unmarred by remembered dreams.

Feeling and looking better than she had in well over two weeks, Jo sailed into Brett's office the following morning mere moments after he'd issued a rough-voiced command for her to do so. His appearance betrayed his own restless night. Though he was dressed immaculately, as usual, his eyes had a flat, dull look, faint white lines of strain edged his compressed lips, and a pallor underlay the toast tan on his cheeks.

"I'm leaving for Vermont after lunch," he said bluntly the minute she'd closed the door behind her. "I have no idea how long I'll be gone. It may be days, it may be weeks. Can you handle things here in my absence?"

"I have before." Jo was sorry for the arrogant-sounding assertion the minute it was out of her mouth. Would he think her statement too confident? The way his lids narrowed convinced her that he did. But, damn it, Brett knew her capabilities by now, didn't he? Brett gave further proof of his tiredness by shrugging instead of snapping at her.

"I'm relieved," he muttered irritably, tossing the folder that contained Wolf's project across the desk to her. "Okay, let's get at this. There's a lot to cover and I'm pressed for time."

Several times during the following hour and half Jo had to fight back the urge to scream at him. Brett fired questions at her with the rapidity of a machine gun, merely grunting when she knew an answer, grating "why not?" when she didn't. Finally, after about his tenth "why not?" Jo's tenuous hold on her temper snapped.

"I don't know because your brother chose to keep this project to himself!" Feeling as though her back was to the wall, Jo lashed out at him. "You know I believed this project had been scrapped. You *know,* and yet you persist in badgering me with questions I can't possibly be expected to know the answers to. Don't play games with me, *Mr. Renninger!"*

For an instant the flatness fled from his eyes and they glittered like sunlight on gun metal, then the light was gone and Brett lowered his eyes to the slim gold watch on his wrist. "I have a luncheon appointment," he droned without inflection. "Take the folder back to your office and familiarize yourself with the contents. I'll stop by and pick it up before I leave for Vermont."

Raising his head he stared at her, his expression remote, his eyes again dull gray with disinterest. "You may go now."

Dismissed! She had been dismissed like a bothersome child! Jo had to bite her lip to keep from crying out in protest. Both chilled and subdued by his manner, Jo withdrew into herself before rising to her feet, her composure her only shield against Brett's attitude. "Yes, sir." Jo was amazed at the degree of coolness her tone conveyed, for inside she was anything but cool. Actually, she wanted to run back to her office and weep with frustration. Moving with calculated slowness, she walked out of his office, closed the door carefully, then, her composure slipping, ran along the hall to her own office.

You must have masochistic tendencies. Jo made the silent observation while sitting slumped in her high-backed desk chair. It was over an hour since she'd beat a hasty retreat from Brett's office. In that time she had done nothing but stare at the walnut paneling that covered the wall facing her desk. She had not found a single solution to her emotional condition on the beautifully grained wood. Why was she putting herself through all this? Hadn't she had enough pain with Gary? Why couldn't she simply dismiss Brett from her mind as ruthlessly as he'd dismissed her from his sight? The questions repeated themselves with boring insistency. The answer was always the same: I love him.

Love. What the emotion did to a woman should be against the law of both God and man! What unadulterated fools it makes of us, Jo decided sadly. Who needs it, anyway? she railed at herself. You do, her self mocked smugly. I'm losing my mind! Am I actually arguing . . . with myself? Tearing her gaze from the wall, Jo jumped to her feet and stalked to the oversized window behind her desk. Yes, I am actually arguing with myself. It seems that love does that to us too. It makes us irrational! Who but an irrational being would invite pain into her heart?

Staring at the minuscule pedestrian and vehicular traffic on the avenue far below, Jo sighed in exasperation. How many, she wondered, out of the millions that jammed this greatest of all cities, how many people have indulged in a like self-analysis? And how many have reached any concrete conclusions? Probably none. A wry smile twisted Jo's soft lips. Don't feel like the Lone Ranger, girl, the odds are that you have plenty of company. So why don't I feel reassured? The smile growing into a grimace, Jo turned and walked slowly back to her desk. Forget it. Forget *him*, she advised herself. Sliding onto her chair, Jo picked up the now-hated folder. As she opened the cover Brett strode into her office.

"Hard at it, I see," he observed complacently.

Jo didn't know whether to laugh or cry. She did neither. Instead, she held his strangely intent gaze steadily, silently challenging him to do or say anything clever or smart. Fortunately, perhaps for both of them, he read her mood correctly. His expression wary, he arched an attractive eyebrow at her.

"Any questions?"

At least a hundred, Jo thought. "None," she answered.

"Good." Turning abruptly, he walked to the door, then paused, his hand on the knob, in much the same way he had weeks before. "Oh, yes, he said softly, "I've made up a list of things to do while I'm gone." Sliding his left hand into his jacket pocket, he withdrew a sheet of paper. Even from across the room Jo could see the list was lengthy. Holding the paper between thumb and forefinger, Brett waved it languidly in the air. "You'll take care of everything"—the brow inched higher—"won't you?"

"Yes, of course," she replied quietly, fully expecting him to backtrack and hand the paper to her. Brett didn't move.

"Of course," he repeated in a near whisper, his tone dry.

He's going to make me go to him! The realization struck as a taunting smile feathered Brett's lips. Standing stock still, Brett's eyes transmitted an order for her to get up. Resentment burning like acid in her throat, Jo pushed her chair back and stood up. Suddenly she knew what this little charade was all about. With cool deliberation Brett was making it clear exactly who was the boss and who was the lackey. Would you like me to shine your shoes, sir? Jo had to compress her lips to keep from voicing the question. The mood he was in, he'd very likely say yes, she decided sourly as she crossed the carpet to him. Her restraint nearly snapped when he smiled in self-satisfaction.

"I've written down the phone number where I'll be staying," he murmured silkily. "If you have any problems, call me. Don't, I repeat, do not even consider calling Wolf. He is in no condition to be bothered with you." Slowly, as he was speaking, his tone went rock hard.

Thoroughly confused, Jo frowned. Why in the world would he think she'd call Wolf? Had he no confidence in her ability at all? Did he believe she'd run to his brother at the first little snag she encountered? More hurt than insulted, Jo snatched the paper out of his hand, her gaze skimming the list swiftly.

"I think I can handle it," she assured him. And anything else you can dream up, she tacked on silently.

"Do you think so?" His tone sent a chill rippling down her spine. Could the man read her mind? Releasing his grasp on the doorknob, Brett took the single step necessary to close the distance between them. "Do you really think so?" Slowly, his eyes holding hers, he lowered his head.

Jo did not have to fight to keep from stepping back; quite the contrary, she had to fight a sudden need to step into him. Holding herself tautly still, she watched his descending face, positive he'd turn away at the final moment. She was wrong. When his lips brushed hers her eyes widened in astonishment, then her long lashes fluttered and lowered. That whisper touch brushed her lips a second, then a third time. A ripple of pure delicious sensation shivered through her. Why, why was he teasing her with these almost kisses? And why didn't he touch her, embrace her, crush her to him?

Fully conscious of what she was doing, Jo parted her lips in silent invitation. Although he still made no move to bring his body into contact with hers, Brett accepted her invitation at once. Open hard male lips fused with Jo's, moving slowly to engulf and encompass. A soft half sigh, half moan rose in Jo's throat, only to be muffled by the intrusion of Brett's stiffened, searching tongue. Electrified, Jo stood, trembling violently, longing to feel her softness molded to his hard length, aching for the feel of his hands on her overheated skin. Still he did not touch her.

Jo felt rather than heard the groan that passed from Brett's throat to hers an instant before he deepened the kiss. Revealing raw hunger, his lips consumed while his tongue made a masculine demand for active participation from hers. Jo responded to his demand without hesitation, parrying each thrust, riposting in turn, savoring the sweet male taste of him. Now the murmur that issued from his throat had more the sound of growl than moan, a feral sound that spoke to something wild deep within Jo.

And wildly sweet was the sensation of her blood rushing through her veins, converging in her head, making her legs weak and her need strong, pounding out one cry in her mind: Touch me, touch me, touch me. Still Brett did not touch her.

Brett's plunging, scouring tongue was everywhere, learning everything about the moist interior of her mouth. Her mind spinning, her senses going crazy, desperately afraid she'd collapse at his feet any second, Jo's lips clung to his. Growing deeper, more possessive, more demanding by each instant, his kiss went on and on, reducing Jo to a receiver of the erotic messages Brett was transmitting through the medium of his mouth. Then, suddenly, he ended it. Drawing away with obvious reluctance, he lifted his head.

There was no power on earth, certainly not her shattered will, that could have prevented Jo from swaying when his anchoring lips were removed. Bereft, disoriented, she waited long seconds for the floor to stop shifting under her shaky three-inch heels before raising leaden eyelids. The gaze that met hers came very close to undoing her completely. Smokey gray with passion, Brett's eyes bored into hers, underlining the messages his lips had sent to her. He wanted her, very badly, but for some unfathomable reason of his own, he had exerted every ounce of control he possessed to keep from laying even one finger on her body. As if his eyes were an open book, it was all there for her to read. The only pages missing were the ones explaining why. Refusing her the opportunity to ask questions, Brett straightened to his full height and stepped back, his hand grasping the doorknob.

"You look very beautiful today," he said softly, throwing Jo into deeper confusion with the first compliment he'd ever given her. "That color is very becoming on you. You should wear it more often."

Then he was gone and Jo stood staring at the door he'd closed so very gently. Pulling herself together, if loosely, Jo backed up until the back of her thighs bumped her desk. Sinking onto the solid wood support, she released a long, heartfelt sigh. Well, if nothing else, one question had been erased from her mind. Gary had repeatedly accused her of being unable to physically respond to a male advance. Moments ago she had responded with every quivering particle of her being. Unashamedly she admitted to herself that, had Brett asked it of her, she'd have sunk to the floor for him without hesitation. In amazement, Jo realized that for the first time in her life she wanted, really wanted to experience a man's physical lovemaking. A tiny, sad smile feathered her lips fleetingly. How grand! Here she was, at age twenty-eight, prepared to offer everything of herself for the first time in her life and the donee of her largess flaunts his iron control in her face.

The thought was chilling, but had to be examined. Brett's involvement in their mouth embrace had been as total as her own, Jo was as sure of that as she was of leaves falling in autumn. But he had not touched her, had not taken advantage of the opportunity to assuage the hunger he'd revealed through his kiss. Why hadn't he? The answer was obvious, at least to Jo. She had spent most of the last three weeks with him. She had seen the expression of disdain and often contempt on his face when in her company; Brett hadn't made the slightest attempt to hide his feelings. For reasons known only to himself, Brett simply did not like her. So then, did a man . . . a man like Brett Renninger . . . make a lover of a woman he could not like personally? Jo asked herself. Not very likely, she concluded unhappily. And where does that leave me? She wondered. Absolutely nowhere.

But he does think I'm beautiful! Grasping at the thought for all she was worth, Jo glanced down at the dress she'd hastily chosen that morning. She had not known until she'd walked out of her apartment that the garment had been the perfect choice for a crisp fall day. The wool-blend material was in a vibrant burnt orange that rivaled nature's brilliant autumnal display. The dress was cut in simple, classic lines that did full justice to Jo's slim yet curvaceous figure. Jo's lips twitched wryly as she remembered the enormous price that had been discreetly printed on the little frock's tiny price tag. At the time of purchase Jo had gasped at the cost. Now she was glad she had given in to temptation and whipped out her credit card before she'd had time to change her mind!

The buzzer on the intercom on Jo's desk peeled the information that her secretary, Reni, was back from lunch and back to work. And, apparently, Jo decided as the number-one button on her phone began to blink, so am I.

Leaning to the end of her desk, Jo lifted the tan receiver and asked with a briskness she was light-years away from feeling, "Yes, Reni?"

"Mr. Renninger's on line one, Jo," Reni reported calmly.

For one second Jo was certain she could not manage a normal tone. Fourteen questions jumbled together into a solid mass in her head. One stood out in glaring clarity: Is he going to ask me to go with him?

"Yes, Mr. Renninger?" How in sweet heaven had she contrived that coolly professional note?

"Ms. Lawrence, I hope you can help me. I need some information and Brett's secretary tells me he's out of the office."

Eric Renninger! Why hadn't Reni told her the caller was Eric

Renninger? Closing her eyes against a sudden, ridiculous sting, Jo drew in a deep breath before answering softly, "Yes, your brother left less than an hour ago, Mr. Renninger. I'll be happy to help you, if I can. Exactly what do you need?"

While she was being her most businesslike self, a vision rose to play havoc with Jo's concentration. The vision had slate-gray contemptuous eyes, a harshly unyielding countenance, and a mouth designed to make thinking women weep.

Her eyes foraging over the desk in an effort to escape the taunting image, Jo's glance settled on the cream-colored folder. Perhaps he hadn't found it all that easy to control himself. The austere Brett Renninger had forgotten what he'd originally come into her office for!

CHAPTER FIVE

Purring like a sleek, well-fed cat, the Porsche hugged the highway that unwound like a ribbon into the magnificent mountains of New England. Though now past the peak of brilliance, the world-famous foliage blazed in the waning afternoon sunlight, a spectacular free show for anyone with the eyes to see. Brett's awareness of fall's breathtaking display of colors was at a shallow surface level. His glance noted the panorama, his mind didn't register the glory of it at all. The tiny, picturesque villages tucked into the folds of Vermont's sun-kissed mountains went virtually unnoticed by gray eyes bleak with introspection. Grappling with his own conflicting emotions, he was immune to summer's fiery exit.

Why, Brett berated himself scathingly, in the name of peace of body if not mind, why didn't you take her right there in her office? She was willing. Hell, she was more than willing, she was eager! And you were damned near incinerated! The memory of the blast furnace created by the simple method of placing his lips to Jo's ignited a fresh burst of fire inside Brett's already overheated body. Lord! How many females had he kissed since he'd discovered how exciting the fusing of two mouths could be somewhere around his fifteenth birthday? A lot more then he cared to remember. Yet never before had he experienced the instantaneous, electrified arousal Jo's sweet lips had sent crashing through him. Even now, hours later, every living cell in his body cried more, more, more.

You are very definitely losing your grip, chum!

Slicing a glance to the rearview mirror, Brett grimaced at the unnaturally pale visage momentarily reflected in the small rectangular of silvered glass. Without even trying, you win the "big stupe" award! There's a blotch on your psychological makeup. Only a true glutton for punishment would go panting after the wrong type of woman twice!

Yet, against all the rationale he could muster, Brett wanted to possess Jo Lawrence with an intensity that shook his so recently well-ordered existence. The emotional hold she was beginning to have on him had been the very element that had induced his exertion on his control. The knowledge of how perilously close he'd come to losing restraint still had his hands trembling as they gripped the steering wheel. With sardonic humor directed at himself, Brett relived his hasty departure from Jo's office.

His arms aching with the need to hold her against his hardened body, his *body* screaming with the need to invade hers, Brett had literally run after he'd closed the office door between them. Never before in his life had he been so sorely tempted to throw all caution, propriety, and plain common sense to the wind! The battle that had raged inside his most sexual of organs, the one he formally called his rational mind, had been of mammoth proportions. The fact that reason had won imbued an intellectual satisfaction that in no way appeased the physical hunger. Against all the arguments he could manufacture, he wanted her, all of her, last night, this afternoon, tonight, and, the most sobering, frightening thought of all, for every one of the forever days and nights to come.

Brett's fingers worked spasmodically on the wheel. Frowning at his reflexive response to the mere thought of touching Jo, he advised himself to stop the lustful window wishing and concentrate on the job of work that was growing closer with each passing mile. He had things to do, and people to see, and he needed a clear mind and steady hand to accomplish the task he'd set for himself. Now, more than ever, he was determined to at least get the ball rolling on this project Wolf wanted.

One of the people he had to see was a Casey Delheny, the architect Wolf had chosen for the multi-unit. That Brett had never heard of Delheny before was not at all unusual. He was kept doubly busy looking after his own bailiwick. He rarely ever poked his nose into either of his brother's domains. Besides, were he inclined in that direction, Wolf would probably tell him to butt out. Brett smiled at the realization that their mother would very likely back Wolf. Violet Renninger had worked diligently at raising strong, independent sons!

That morning Brett had had his secretary call the architect to arrange a conference meeting. She had reported back to him that Delheny had a full schedule for the next day but would be happy to join Brett for dinner at the restaurant in the motel where he'd reserved a room.

If the man was that busy he was probably an excellent architect, Brett decided as he neared his destination less than fifty miles from the New Hampshire state line. Not at all disgruntled at having to wait on Delheny's convenience, Brett planned on spending the day checking out the building site and surrounding terrain. Wolf had delineated the proposed project with his usual painstaking care. Though Brett fully expected to find everything exactly as Wolf had described, still, he had to see for himself.

The motel was one of a large chain, fairly new, and decorated to blend in with the locale in an elegant early American motif. Thinking the early Americans never had it so good, Brett found his own way to the large, comfortable room assigned to him. He was tired but, having eaten nothing since lunch, he was also hungry. After depositing his case on the luggage rack, he washed his hands, splashed cold water on his face, then strode out of the room again in search of sustenance, preferably in the form of a two-inch thick steak with a side order of Scotch and Scotch.

On entering the motel lobby, Brett had noticed a sign advertising a restaurant lounge. Back in the lobby, he followed the direction marker on the sign to a dimly lit room. As he neared the lounge entrance the melodic sound of an expertly played piano assailed his ears, along with the slightly offkey blending of several voices. Over half the tables in the large room were occupied with quietly conversing patrons. Every one of the high stools around the piano held a would-be soloist. The combined strains of a Billy Joel hit of a few years back was not at all unpleasant.

Settling his elongated frame into a well-padded chair at a table in a far corner of the room, Brett smiled when a discordant note rose above the harmonizing voices. His smile broadened as, undaunted, the man who had hit the sour note continued, still slightly out of tune, till the end. And he joined in with his fellow patrons when they offered a round of applause for the impromptu rendition.

The atmosphere in the lounge encouraged relaxation and conviviality, and Brett felt the tensions of the day ease out of his taut body. With conscious determination he relegated the disturbing thoughts that had traveled north with him to the farthest corner of his mind. The ambiance of the lounge imbued a feeling of well-being. Brett convinced himself good food would fill the emptiness inside.

The menu presented to him by a soft-spoken waiter was limited but included an open steak sandwich that Brett promptly ordered, medium rare, with French fries and a small salad. He also ordered Scotch but, remembering his foolishness of the night before, requested both ice and water in it. He had consumed the steak and salad and was putting the finishing touches to his fries when a young woman entered the lounge, glanced around, then, straightening her shoulders, walked directly to his table.

"Mr. Renninger?" she asked with just the tiniest bit of hesitation.

"Yes." Brett eyed her interestedly but discreetly. Small, well rounded without being at all heavy, the woman was not actually pretty. Her looks were too strong to be defined as anything but striking. Her features were almost sharp. Her eyes were almost slanted. Her mouth was almost too full. Yet the combination was appealing. Hair as fair as Brett's own was styled into a shining cap that framed her face to advantage. His perusal completed in seconds, Brett smiled in welcome of the diversion she presented. "What can I do for you?"

"May I sit down?" Interpreting his smile correctly, the hesitation disappeared from her voice.

Was she trying to pick him up? The idea intrigued Brett. Besides, he was curious as to how she'd known his name. "Please do," he invited softly, rising to pull a chair away from the table for her. Brett didn't get the chance to question her identity for she launched into an explanation as he reseated himself.

"My name is Marsha Wenger," she said quietly. "Casey Delheny told me you were booked into this motel." When this statement drew one pale brow into an arch, she clarified. "I asked for you at the desk. The clerk told me you were in here."

"I see." Of course, he didn't, but, what the hell. He shrugged mentally. He wasn't going anywhere, and she *was* attractive. "May I order you a drink?"

"Yes, please." She paused, eyeing his empty glass. "That is, if you're having another."

Brett's smile was unknowingly sardonic. "Oh, I was planning to have several others."

"All right then, I'll have white wine." Although her smooth tone had not altered, it was obvious his smile had confused her for a tiny frown appeared momentarily between her perfectly arched blond eyebrows.

Satisfied with having thrown her slightly off balance, Brett's smile grew into a grin as he motioned to the waiter for a refill.

He remained quiet, scrutinizing her with what he knew was unnerving intentness until their drinks had been placed before them and the waiter had departed. Then, lifting his glass in a silent salute, he sipped appreciatively, lowered his glass, and queried softly, "I can't help but wonder why Delheny would tell you where I'd registered." His smile turned suggestive. "Unless Casey decided I'd appreciate a little entertainment and diversion."

Although Marsha seemed startled at Brett's use of the architect's last name, her surprise was forgotten with his final conclusion.

"Casey decided no such thing!" she declared heatedly. "I am *not* a pros— call girl, Mr. Renninger!" Drawing a calming breath, she went on more quietly. "Casey mentioned your name quite casually and I—"

"Casually, Ms. Wenger?" Brett interrupted silkily, then added thoughtfully, "I beg your pardon. Is it *Ms.* Wenger?"

"Yes, it is." Marsha sipped distractedly at her wine. "And I said casually because . . . oh Lord, I'm screwing this up, and I wanted so badly to make a good impression!"

Now that he had her thoroughly rattled, Brett relaxed completely. You are a chauvinist bastard, he accused himself unrepentently. Somewhere on the very fringes of his conscousness Brett knew he was, in a very convoluted way, trying to get at Jo through this stranger. Yet, unwilling to face the power his vulnerability placed in Jo's hands, he refused to give a second thought to his own lack of logic. At this moment he simply enjoyed that fact that he had unnerved *any* woman.

"Don't despair, Ms. . . . may I call you Marsha?" he inquired respectfully—much too respectfully.

"Yes, please do. I-I—" Marsha had obviously not missed the nuance of a drawl in his overly polite request. Her expression revealing that she was indeed despairing, she grasped her glass and drank thirstily.

Suddenly Brett tired of the roasting game. Relenting, a little, he prompted, "You were saying my name was mentioned causally?"

"Yes, well, not really casually." Marsha took a final gulp from her wine, then dove head first into an explanation. "We had lunch together yesterday, Casey and I. When I mentioned"—she winced over the word—"that I'd just mailed a résumé off to you, Casey told me you were due to arrive in Vermont sometime today." She wet her lips before continuing. "The name of this motel was not offered. I asked Casey point blank where you would be staying."

"Résumé?" Brett pounced on the one word.

Marsha winced again but answered at once. "Yes. Through a friend in New York I learned about the managerial position open in your offices. As I'd been considering relocating to New York City for some time now, I decided to apply for the job."

"Go on," Brett prodded.

"That's all!" She smiled apologetically. "At least it was until yesterday. When Casey said you were coming here I decided to seek a personal interview with you."

"Here? Now?" Brett's expression and tone wiped away the image his casual slacks and sport shirt projected, revealing the hard businessman that was never very far from the surface. "A bit unorthodox, wouldn't you say?"

Marsha had the grace to blush with embarrassment. But she espoused her cause just the same. "I know," she admitted boldly. "But I have always believed that the only way to get something is to go for it fearlessly. Up until now my method has always worked."

Brett laughed. He had to. The woman's honesty genuinely amused him. Settling more comfortably in his chair, he fixed her to hers with eyes sharp with interest. "Okay, Marsha Wenger, fire at will. Give me a verbal account of what is contained in your résumé."

Leaning forward tensely, Marsha began speaking in a tone devoid of inflection. Her recitation went on nonstop for a full twenty minutes. When she was finished she sat back and matched Brett stare for stare, her expression composed with the knowledge that her credentials were impressive.

In actual fact, Brett *was* impressed. He was also relieved. The open managerial position Marsha had referred to was the New England area manager's job, which had not been filled since he'd figuratively kicked Bob Harley upstairs, the day he'd gone to the New York offices at his sister-in-law's request. Brett had lost count of the exact number of people he had interviewed for the job during the last three weeks. Most of the applicants had been unqualified, some had been overqualified. Now, incongruous as it seemed, in a motel in Vermont, at a very late hour, Brett had found his new manager!

"You got it."

"I-I beg your pardon?" Marsha blinked in surprise. After his long silence, it was clear his sudden pronouncement had startled her.

"The job." Brett smiled. "It's yours. When can you start?"

Marsha straightened abruptly, as if she'd been pinched in a very delicate spot. "At once!" she squeaked, then hedged. "Or, that is, as soon as I can relocate to the city."

"All right." Brett nodded his acceptance. "If you'll drop all the pertinent information off here at the desk tomorrow, I'll call it in to the office and have personnel fill out the necessary forms."

Marsha opened her mouth to agree but before she could speak Brett added, "Are you employed now?"

"Yes."

"You'll want to work out notice." It was not a question. Brett's tone indicated she had better want to work out a decent notice.

"I gave my firm a month's notice three weeks ago." Marsha was not quite successful in hiding her annoyance.

It would seem quite a bit happened three weeks ago, Brett thought wryly. The thought reminded him of Wolf and his own temporary tenancy as head man in the New York office. The

96

thought also reminded him of Jo, and that coated his voice with irritation.

"You do realize, I assume, that I'm only filling in for my brother, and the status quo might change when he's back in command?" At the harsh sound of his voice Brett modified his question-statement. "Understand, he will take my recommendations under consideration, but the final decision is his."

"Yes, Casey outlined the current situation." Marsha smiled. "I was also led to understand that *if* you hired me, your brother would very likely retain me." Her smile widened, revealing small, straight white teeth. "Casey seems to know your brother quite well."

"Indeed?" Brett murmured coolly, wondering at both her smile and her opinion. How buddy-buddy had Wolf and this Delheny become? he mused. He did not voice the question to Marsha, preferring to judge the extent of the men's friendship for himself.

Marsha appeared to take Brett's coolness and preoccupation as a hint for her to leave for, after swallowing the last of her wine, she picked up her purse and pushed her chair away from the table. Her actions drew an alert, questioning glance from him.

"I've taken up enough of your time," she explained. "I'll leave you to enjoy the rest of the evening."

"Alone?" Brett's smile held sheer enticement. "Stay and join me for another drink," he invited softly. "We'll discuss your problem of relocation."

Brett found Marsha as easy to charm as most of the other women he'd come in contact with . . . excluding Jo Lawrence, that was. Again the flashing memory of Jo sent a spasm of annoyance through him. Damned woman! He'd wipe all consideration of her out of his mind, or kill himself in the effort! Giving Marsha his warmest smile, he underlined his desire to keep her company. "You will stay, won't you?"

"Well, yes." She laughed, a soft, melodic sound that was easy on Brett's ears. "If you like."

"I do," he assured her firmly, consigning all thoughts of a tall, willowy body, a breathtakingly beautiful face, and a pair of maddeningly arousing lips to the farthest reaches of hell. Brett was content to smile at Marsha encouragingly until their fresh drinks were served, *then* he encouraged her to talk. "Tell me exactly what has to be done to accomplish this move to the big city."

"First"—she held up a long, slim forefinger—"I must finish out my month's notice which, in actual days, amounts to seven. Then I'll have to face the distasteful task of going through my things to decide what I want to take with me and what I will store temporarily. My friend has offered me the use of her sofa until I can find a place of my own, so I can't take too much of my own stuff along." She paused to gaze contemplatively into her wine. When she again raised her eyes to him, they were cloudy with consternation. "I understand finding a decent apartment in the city is the next thing to impossible."

"But not completely impossible," Brett assured her bracingly. While she'd been speaking a germ of an idea had stirred to life in his mind. Now, playing for time to allow the germ quiet in which to sprout, he took a long moment to taste his drink, savoring its bite on his tongue. In his foolishness over one kiss, Brett felt sure he'd revealed far too much of his feelings to Jo. Here, sitting next to him, was a way to disabuse her of any notions she might have conceived about his emotional state. The consideration that he'd be using Marsha didn't bother him in the least. He would be helping her as well and he'd be careful she was in no way involved afterward. The decision made to proceed, Brett put his hastily formed plan into action.

"As a matter of fact, when I call the vitals into personnel tomorrow, I'll have my assistant scout out a place for you." His smile could only be described as intriguingly wicked. "Ms. Lawrence is highly competent. I'm sure she'll have no trouble at all in finding the perfect place for you."

"Oh, but I can't infringe on your assistant's time like that!" Marsha protested, if not too convincingly.

Now Brett's smiled came very close to nasty. "She'll love it," he promised. "Apartments are her 'thing.'"

Though she looked suddenly skeptical, Marsha grasped at the offer. "Well, if you're positive she won't mind?"

She won't be given a choice, Brett thought with relish. Aloud, he merely reassured her. "She'll adore the search," he murmured facetiously. Controlling a prod from the devil to laugh out loud, Brett spun out another strand to his deception web. "I will be in Vermont for at least two weeks. If you can clear up everything here by then, you can drive back to New York with me." His smile was now sugar coated. "You could add the saved air fare to the rent money." His grimace was sincere. "The cost of renting decent living quarters is astronomical."

"So I've heard, and so I'd be a fool to argue over your offer." She grinned. "Thank you."

With a twinge of guilt he didn't wish to recognize, Brett waved her thanks aside. They talked of other things then, the beauty of Vermont, the many and varied attractions it had to offer, not the least being the skiing, and Brett's purpose in being in the state in the first place.

"Casey did tell me about the project some time ago," Marsha said when Brett finished his very brief account. "But I guess I assumed the project would be dropped, at least until your brother was fully recovered from his injuries."

Sipping his drink, Brett reached the conclusion that this Casey Delheny talked too damn much for the Renningers' own good. Where in hell had Wolf found this blabbermouth? Carefully concealing his thoughts from Marsha, he watched her polish off her wine.

"Would you like another?"

"No, thank you." One well-manicured hand, complete with raspberry-colored lacquer, covered his when he went to signal for the waiter. "I must be going. My alarm clock rings at the

99

same early hour every working day, no matter what time I stumble into bed."

"I'll be in touch with you as to exactly when I'll be leaving for New York," Brett promised.

"Oh, you'll probably be running into me all over the place while you're here." She grinned. "In a town this size, people have to work at not tripping over each other every other day or so." With a final grin and a wave of her hand, she strode lightly from the room.

Having risen when Marsha stood up to leave, Brett watched her retreating back in appreciation of her shaply form. Even in the soft light from the small lamp that burned scented oil that had flickered away steadily during their conversation, Brett had reevaluated his initial judgment of her age. When she'd entered the lounge, he had guessed her age at mid to late twenties. Now he felt sure she was within striking distance of his own thirty-five years. Twenty-five or thirty-five, he mused, Marsha Wenger is one very attractive woman; smart too.

Brett moved to sit down again, then, changing his mind, decided to call it a night. He paid the check the waiter promptly presented to him, added a tip that from the man's grin insured Brett would be remembered the next time he entered the lounge, and, fighting a yawn, sauntered from the room. Traversing the motel corridors from lounge to elevator, then from elevator to his room, he gave up fighting the tiredness pulling at him and yawned widely. It had been a long, tension-filled day. The hours Brett had escaped consciousness the night before had not counted more than three. He was beat to a fare-thee-well. And fare-thee-well was the case as Brett slipped into sleep mere minutes after slipping, buck naked, between the cool sheets.

Ten hours of uninterrupted sleep did wonders for Brett's mental condition. Waking with the bright October sun on his face around mid-morning, Brett stretched hugely before springing off the bed. He felt good, raring to go, but he also felt empty. By the time room service delivered the large breakfast he ordered, Brett was shaved, showered, and dressed to go roaming the project's site in jeans, a soft cotton shirt, a finely knit cashmere pullover, and tan suede desert boots.

In no particular hurry whatever, Brett savored every sip of the tart, chilled grapefruit juice, every forkful of creamy scrambled eggs, every crunching bite of golden-toasted English muffin, and every satisfying swallow of rich, dark coffee. Replete with good food and ready to face the day, Brett pushed the tray aside and reached for the telephone. The digits he heard register numbered eleven. The voice that answered at the other end of the line had already been familiar to him at age ten. The voice belonged to his mother's housekeeper at the horse farm in Florida. Even now it seemed to Brett that Elania Calaveri had been in residence at the farm forever. When he responded to her hello, Brett's tone was warm with affection.

"Good morning, Elania. How are you today?"

"Still kicking." The reply was a stock one, reserved for the offspring of her employer. Brett's retort was also stock.

"Anyone I know?"

Elania's chuckle was as hearty at seventy-odd as it had been at forty-five. "Your brother if he don't start behaving himself. I swear, that man is the worst patient I've ever cared for."

Brett was fully aware of the fact that Elania Calaveri was the main reason Wolf had been transferred to the farm instead of his own home to recuperate. Having grown up in the streets of Sicily, Elania was one tough cookie. Nobody, not Wolf or even the hard-nosed businesswoman they all called Mother, gave Elania an argument. If Elania decided Wolf was going to recover completely, Wolf had damn well better do it, and without complaint! Smiling at the thought of the fire Wolf was under, Brett politely inquired if his brother was up to speaking on the phone.

"I wouldn't know why not." Elania gave a long-suffering sigh. "He's been up to driving me to distraction since before six this morning. Hold on till I prop the prowler up."

Brett's appreciative smile still lingered on his voice when he responded to Wolf's growled, "What's up, Brett?"

"Mind your own sex life," Brett shot back, laughing at Wolf's groaning response to his feeble attempt at humor.

"You have a sex-oriented mind, baby brother," Wolf accused grittily.

"Merely following in your size fourteen shoes, big brother," Brett chided laughingly. "May I inquire how you are today?"

"In comparison to what? The wreck of the *Andrea Doria*?" Wolf drawled dryly before, relenting, he allowed affection to color his tone. "How's it going, Brett?"

"Hey, big prowler! You're the one in the sight of Elania's formidable gun, not me!" Brett laughed. "Compared to the heavy weather you've got to ride out, my job's a piece of cake!" Brett's opaque terminology in reference to Wolf's injuries had been deliberate, simply because he knew an openly solicitous query would not be welcomed warmly.

"Yeah, I know, but don't tell the boss." Wolf's dry tone didn't quite succeed in masking his weariness. "If she finds out how easy I usually have it up there, she'll probably create a new region just to keep me out of trouble."

The tired huskiness in Wolf's voice shot instant concern through Brett yet, knowing his brother would not welcome a display of that concern, he decided to claim an appointment and end the conversation. "Look, lazybones, I'm going to have to hang up in a minute. I have to see a man about a house," he paraphrased an old saw. "But first, tell me how Micki and the kids are making out in Florida."

"Basking in the sunshine." Wolf's voice held a smile. "I'd let you talk to Mick but she's having her riding lesson at the moment." His soft chuckle hummed through the wire to draw a smile from Brett. "She's doing pretty good at it," Wolf added. "She's only tumbled twice."

Brett's smile disappeared. "Was she hurt?" he asked sharply.

"Micki! Hell no!" Wolf actually chortled. "That hoyden's got more bounce than half a dozen tennis balls. At the rate she's going, she'll put all the rest of us in the shade in no time."

Mingled with the relief Brett was feeling was a growing urgency to cease and desist for Wolf's voice was now definitely reedy. Before he could ease into saying good-bye, Wolf asked a question that jolted him upright in his chair.

"How is my best girl working out as your assistant?"

"JoAnne Lawrence?" Brett asked tightly, stupidly.

"Well, of course, Jo," Wolf chided. "Isn't she something?"

Oh, she's something, all right, Brett mentally sneered. "Yes, she's very efficient."

"Jo is more than merely efficient!" Wolf defended strongly, much *too* strongly, to Brett's way of thinking. "I'd say she could give your Richard Colby a run for his money any day of the week!"

Richard Colby's not wealthy enough to even gain Jo's notice, Brett retorted silently. "Perhaps so," he hedged. Then, simmering with renewed anger, and hating it, Brett rushed on, "Look, old son, I really do have to get cracking. If I don't get the chance to call you again, I'll see all of you sometime over the holidays. Give my love to Micki and the kids."

After he'd cradled the receiver, Brett reached for the large manila envelope that had been delivered to him with his breakfast tray. Gone was the feeling of well-being he'd wakened with. He felt tense, and angry, and all because Wolf had asked about an employee. Had the query been about any other employee, Brett would have considered it the natural interest of an excellent employer, which Wolf was. But the question had not been about any other employee, it had been about Jo, and that annoyed Brett unreasonably.

A quick perusal of the envelope's contents was all that Brett required to assure himself of Marsha Wenger's qualifications. Everything she'd claimed the night before was true. She seemed perfect for the vacant manager's position.

Holding the pertinent papers in one hand, Brett lifted the

receiver and made another long-distance call, this time to the New York offices. He spoke first to the personnel manager, setting the gears of Marsha's employment in motion. Then he asked to have the call switched to Jo's office. While waiting for the interoffice connection to be made, a slightly cruel smile of satisfaction curled his lips. Brett's anger intensified with the frisson of warmth the sound of Jo's voice sent rippling through him.

"Jo Lawrence," she answered, as she always did.

"I have a job for you," Brett said without preamble.

"Yes, sir?" she clipped alertly.

Against his will Brett thought about the previous day and how the soft lips that had just moved in answer felt molded to his own. He could see her, he could taste her, and it hurt like hell. Groaning silently, he pushed the memory aside. When he spoke the roughness of his voice reflected the effort he was exerting to maintain his anger.

"I have found someone to fill the New England manager's job. It's a woman. Her name is Marsha Wenger. She'll be needing an apartment. I want you to find her one." Ignoring her muffled gasp, Brett went on ruthlessly, "You have two weeks. I'll be bringing her back to the city when I return." He paused long seconds, then added silkily, "Are there any questions?"

Even long distance Brett could hear the slow, deep breath Jo quietly drew into her lungs. After releasing it just as slowly she said calmly, "Yes, one. What if I'm unable to find an apartment by then?"

Brett knew Jo was holding on to her temper with every fiber of her being. The knowledge pleased him greatly. Keep a lid on it, beautiful, he advised silently. You can't afford to blow your stack now. Your lover's in no condition to protect you. And if you explode at me, I'll teach you how to behave! The method of how he'd accomplish this teaching process tantalized Brett's senses a moment. Then he *came* to his senses.

"In the event you're unable to find a *suitable* place for Marsha," he said smoothly, "I suppose she'll have to bunk with you until one *is* found."

This time Jo didn't gasp. This time she choked. "Stay with me!"

"You heard it. So you'd better get to work." Very gently, Brett replaced the receiver. Now let's see how efficient the assistant-mistress really is, he thought savagely.

Contrarily, as he strode from the room, Brett found himself hoping Jo would prove her capabilities to him. Shaken by his vacillation, he brought himself up short. You fool, he raged, you're so hot for her you don't know what the hell you do want! Scratch that, he jeered, storming out of the motel. You know exactly what you want . . . her! Her mouth, her body, everything that *is* her!

Brett worked the worst of his agitation off striding to, around, and from the huge land area Wolf had purchased for the multi-unit condo complex. The site was close to the base of the overlapping mountains and near existing ski trails. Off to the left, appearing to hang on the side of the tallest mountain, an attractive lodge sat in regal solitude. From studying Wolf's report, Brett knew exactly how many people the lodge could cater to. The motels located farther down in the valley accommodated some of the overflow but, when the skiing season was at its peak, quite a few hopeful schussers had to be turned down when seeking rooms. Wolf had estimated that with the growing popularity in the winter sport, the number of disappointed skiers would double, if not triple. Wolf's plan was for a Renninger complex to take up the slack, and make a great deal of money in the bargain.

Being a true Renninger, Brett fully approved of his brother's plan. As he walked back to the motel, his mind raced with ideas. Gone was the constraining anger of the morning. He had work to do. A great deal of work. And the first thing on his agenda was an in-depth discussion with the architect, Casey Delheny.

It wasn't until he'd finished a late lunch and had returned to his room to get Wolf's report from his briefcase that Brett discovered he'd come away without it. As a general rule, forgetting things was not at all his style . . . no matter what the provocation! And Jo's sweet mouth had been some provocation! Disgusted with his unusual lack of thoroughness, Brett snatched up the receiver and made yet another long-distance call. Jo's voice hadn't changed in the four hours since he'd heard it; it still had the power to fire his blood.

"Jo Lawrence."

"Fancy that!" Brett exclaimed in his most drawling drawl.

"Yes, sir?" The patience of a saint weighted her tone.

"I forgot the report," he said flatly. *I forgot to make love to you,* he thought longingly. "I want you to shoot it up—"

"I shot it up to you yesterday afternoon," Jo interrupted very gently, very sweetly. "You should be receiving it soon." There was a telling pause, then she asked nicely, "Is there anything else, *sir?*"

Fresh-mouthed woman! The thought had no sooner entered his mind when Brett had to concede the truth of it. Jo's mouth had been delightfully fresh. Suddenly needing to jar her with a zinger, Brett purred, "Have you found Marsha an apartment yet?"

"Well, I'm considering one," she zinged back. "But there are a few details I want to check out before committing 'Marsha' to it."

So help me, the minute I'm back in New York, I will strangle that witch! Brett found it heavy going not to laugh. She was an amusingly beguiling witch, after all! "I'm glad to hear it," he growled in an effort to conceal the smile in his voice. "Maybe you just might be worth the enormous salary Wolf is paying you."

"Oh, Mr. Renninger, sir," Jo simpered. "Please believe me, I am worth every penny of it." Apparently she considered it her turn to hang up on him, for she did so, quite as gently as he had that morning.

Jo's parting assertion ate at Brett for the remainder of the afternoon. At one point, pacing the room in frustration, he

106

caught himself thinking: She's nothing but a damned high-priced . . . At that moment, shocked at the direction his thoughts were taking, Brett forced his attention back to the folder that had been delivered to his room less than half an hour after she'd hung up on him. Brett played at being the dedicated businessman for several hours before giving up the farce.

A brisk shower and clean clothes did little for his disposition. Deciding what he needed was a stiff drink, Brett went to the motel's elegant dinning room some twenty minutes early for his appointment. After lining the maitre d's palm with a respectable inducement, he was ushered to a table with a flourish. He was three quarters into his second whisky when he glanced up to observe the maitre d' escorting a breathtakingly lovely redhead across the room. Wondering who the knockout was, Brett ran his eyes over her tall, well-proportioned body appreciatively. When the smirking maitre d' came to a stop at his table, Brett rose to his feet, one brow arched in query.

"How do you do, Mr. Renninger?" the knockout said, extending a long, slim hand. "I'm Casey Delheny."

Not another one! The protest jumped unbidden into Brett's suddenly alert mind. Wolf *has* been busy since I visited him last!

Within fifteen minutes of accepting Brett's hand during their cordial greeting, Casey simply and neatly disabused him of his initial opinion. Oh, Brett was quick to realize that Casey was indeed in love! But not with Wolf Renninger. The man she talked about in glowing terms of admiration and respect was a Sean Delheny, her husband of eleven months.

Gradually, as they savored their expertly prepared Chateaubriand and steamed fresh vegetables, Brett learned that Casey not only truly liked Wolf but that he would forever hold a place of affection in her heart. Wolf had introduced Casey to Sean. Over dessert, still smiling faintly at the idea of Wolf in the role of matchmaker, he acquired the additional information that Sean was the contractor Wolf had chosen to build the multicomplex and that he would be joining them for drinks after dinner.

"But why didn't he join us for dinner as well?" Brett wondered aloud.

"Because the appointment had been made with me," Casey explained. "Sean didn't want to, in his words"—she smiled—"horn in."

"He felt left out?" Brett asked sharply, responding to the hint of censure in her tone. Casey's shrug was eloquent. "Believe me, had I known of Wolf's intention to contract Mr. Delheny, I would have included him in on our meeting, whether he was your husband or not. I didn't know."

"But I don't understand," Her slight head movement caused a rippling in her hair that made Brett think of undulating waves on fire. "Didn't Wolf mention Sean at all?"

Before Brett could answer, a tall, brawny man with hair the exact same shade of red as Casey's came to a stop at their table. Brett immediately knew who the man was by the way her eyes lit up. After the introductions were made and fresh drinks ordered, Brett gave Sean a thumbnail account of the conversation prior to his arrival, then he answered Casey's last question.

"I didn't speak to Wolf about my decision to go ahead with this project." This time Brett's shrug was eloquent. "Wolf very obviously wanted this complex. I intend to give it to him. But, as his condition precludes any involvement with business matters, I am proceeding with the report he'd drawn up." He glanced at Sean and shrugged again. "Your name is not in the report."

"But surely Ms. Lawrence knew of Wolf's intention to give the contract to Sean!" Casey exclaimed. "She's closer to Wolf than his own shadow."

Even as Brett assured Casey that Ms. Lawrence knew no more about the project than he did himself, his mind seethed with renewed anger. Exactly what, he fumed, had Casey inadvertently let slip with that last remark? Was she aware of the liaison between Wolf and Jo? For that matter, had everybody been aware of the affair but him?

The questions teased Brett's mind throughout the rest of the evening, hovering on the edge of his consciousness while he officially hired Sean as project contractor, discussed the pros and cons of the job ahead, and made plans to meet with the couple again the following day in Casey's office. After bidding the Delhenys' good night, Brett went to his room to spend most of the night tormenting himself with even more questions, questions that conjured visions, visions that drove his anger into fury. And, at regular intervals, he repeated one phrase as if in hopes of convincing himself of its truth.

Damn it to hell, I do not love her!

Surprisingly, after that one tension-filled night, Brett found little difficulty in sleeping. Perhaps it was due to the hours he spent pouring over architectural drawings with Casey. Perhaps it was due to the hours he spent tramping over the building site with Sean. Then again, perhaps it was due to the evening hours spent in getting to know Marsha Wenger.

Brett called Marsha to invite her out to dinner the very next day. Squashing a ridiculous feeling of being in some strange way unfaithful, he shoved all thoughts and considerations of Jo from his mind. Marsha proved to be a delightful companion, easy to talk to and easy to laugh with. When she invited him in for a nightcap after he'd escorted her to the door of her apartment, Brett accepted, knowing full well he was going to at least attempt to make love to her. The scene that ensued would have been ludicrous, had it not been so sad.

Marsha made it clear that she was willing, so willing that the nightcaps were forgotten the moment they closed the apartment door. She came into his arms before the sound of the door closing faded in the room. Her softly welcoming lips moved with hungry abandon in time with his, sapping his strength as they sipped his taste. Their move from just inside the door to the bedroom was made smoothly, effortlessly, as were their movements as they undressed each other. It was after they embraced on the bed that they grew awkward. It simply did not work, and the harder they tried, each convinced the failure was their own, the less it worked. Brett finally ended the farce.

"I'm sorry," he muttered, appalled at his lack of a potency he had always reveled in. Rolling onto his back, he stared at the ceiling fighting a clawing fear that didn't bear thinking about.

"It's not your fault," Marsha whispered wretchedly. "I thought, after all this time . . ."

The misery in her tone caught his sympathy, the context of her words caught his attention. "All this time? I don't understand."

"I very foolishly divorced my husband last year when I found out he had been with another woman." Turning her head, she faced him unashamedly with tears trickling down her face. "I say foolishly because I've since learned it was the first and only time he had ever strayed." She smiled sadly. "He did have reason to seek solace elsewhere. At the time I was so wrapped up in getting my career off the ground, I neglected to remember we had a partnership."

Brett frowned, not in the least enlightened or reassured. "But I still don't—"

"You are the first man I've been able to relax with since I left my husband over a year ago." Marsha sighed. "I thought that . . . maybe this time I could"—she actually blushed—"you know? I couldn't stop thinking of him, all the time you were . . . I love him." She blinked against a fresh onslaught of tears. "I really am sorry, Brett."

"Yes, so am I." Reaching out his hand, Brett brushed the tears from her cheeks. "Not only for you, but for myself as well." His smile was as sad as hers. "It was not entirely your fault." Brett had never confided his most personal thoughts to anybody, not even Sondra. Drawing a deep breath, he decided that now, perhaps more than ever, he needed a confidant. "You weren't the only one unable to stop thinking of another. She has never belonged to me. Maybe she never will." A long sigh whispered through his lips. "But I love her. I shouldn't. I don't want to. But I do."

They spent the night together. Brett asked no questions, Marsha didn't either. They did not make love. Giving and receiving comfort simply by holding each other close, they finally slept, secure in a friendship forged during the sharing of despair.

Two weeks later, after spending nearly all his evenings with Marsha, Brett left Vermont for New York. Marsha went with him.

CHAPTER SIX

The cab jarred to a splashing halt at the curb. Irritated, frustrated, and soaking wet into the bargain, Jo thrust a bill at the driver. Not bothering to ask for a receipt this time, she pushed open the door and stepped out of the cab, being careful of the miniriver rushing along the gutter. The cabbie pulled away from the curb as Jo was trying to hang onto her handbag and open her umbrella at the same time. The resultant spray of cold water against the back of her legs elicted a muttered, very unladylike curse from her anger-tautened lips. The umbrella slipped from her chilled fingers, exposing her bare head to the cold late October downpour. Straightening her arm with a jerk, Jo dashed for the entrance doors of the tall office building.

Inside the warmth of the building, she paused to catch her breath. I must be totally out of my mind, Jo thought waspishly. No marginally intelligent person would run around like some kind of a nut looking at apartments in this weather! I wish Brett Renninger would go to . . . Atlanta! Sighing with the realization that she really wished no such thing, Jo sloshed her way to the bank of elevators that would whisk her to the twenty-sixth floor and the comfort of her office, a place she'd seen very little of during the previous two weeks, most of which had been cold and rainy.

"Good grief, Jo, you look like you've just been pulled from the river!" Reni greeted her with wide-eyed exclamation. "You also look half frozen!"

Slumping back against the door for a moment's respite, Jo attempted a reassuring smile. "I think it's safe to conclude that Indian summer is truly over," she offered dryly. "That rain feels like it could turn into sleet without halfway trying." A shiver shook her slender body. "Why didn't I simply go home and call it a day?" she wondered aloud.

"Because you're dedicated?" Reni asked teasingly.

"Or not too bright," Jo retorted, pushing away from the supporting panel. "Well, since I'm here, I may as well stay. I might even surprise everyone and actually get some work accomplished." Stiff fingers fumbling with the large buttons on her wine-color raincoat, Jo planted wet footprints on the beige carpeting as she walked to her own office. "But"—she paused to level an arched glance at Reni—"all has not been in vain."

"You've found a place for her!" Reni piped hopefully.

"Yes, I've found a place for 'her.'" Jo smiled in satisfaction. "I've paid the first month's rent, the last month's rent, and a security deposit." Her deepening smile softened the forbidding line of her lips. "Someone, either 'her' or our exalted leader, owes me a lot of money." *God! I hope it's her and not him!* Ever since Brett had literally ordered Jo to find an apartment for Marsha Wenger, she had been torturing herself with the possibility of a relationship between him and the woman he'd so quickly hired for the vacant manager's position. The very idea of Brett sleeping with the unknown woman during the last two weeks didn't bear thinking about. Yet Jo had thought of little else but that! She had read the data on the woman that Brett had mailed to personnel; the woman was indeed qualified! Jo prayed that Marsha Wenger's qualifications extended only to the position of area manager and not to the much higher position of Brett's current bed partner.

"Are you all right?"

Reni's worry-ridden voice brought Jo out of her disheartening speculation. Shivering again, Jo shook her head. "No, as a matter of fact, I'm not," she answered candidly. "I'm cold, and wet, and, as I missed lunch, starving." Shrugging out of the limp raincoat, Jo opened the door to her office. "Call the executive dining room and tell that ego-inflated chef I'd like an omelet and a gallon of hot tea."

Reni's giggle drew a grin from Jo. At one time or another, every person in the building had felt the lash of the sarcastic tongue of Hans Vogel, self-proclaimed chef extraordinary. Everyone that is except Wolf and Brett, the brothers Renninger. They'd have either fired him or decked him—possibly both!

Jo walked into her office, then walked out again moments later, a char-gray suit and a pale-blue blouse that had just been delivered at the office from the dry cleaners draped over one arm. As she sailed by Reni she smiled devilishly. "Don't tell anybody but, while I'm waiting for my lunch, I'm going to make use of the mahout's private bathroom. Maybe a hot shower will chase the shivers."

Jo returned to her office warm of body and dry of clothes, to find her tea and food covered and waiting for her. Ah! She sighed silently, sipping the hot brew. Being the assistant to the big man *did* have its compensations at times. But not always, she quickly reminded herself. There were other attendant duties that were downright onerous! Like running around in inclement weather finding the impossible find! This gal had better be good, she thought grimly, then cringed in contemplation of exactly what Marsha Wenger might be exceptionally good at.

Glancing unnecessarily at her desk calendar, Jo chewed a bite of the egg mixture thoughtfully. It was sixteen days since Brett had whirled into her office and then out again, leaving her shattered from one touchless kiss! During those two weeks she had

114

swung from longing for the sight of him, to the gleeful consideration of taking a contract out on him with a hit man. Of course, Jo hadn't the vaguest idea of how to go about hiring a hit man, but that in no way impaired her enjoyment of the idea! Where in the . . . whole of New England was the kiss-and-run devil? she asked her nearly empty plate reproachfully.

After the lunch tray had been removed Jo got to work—or, at least, she tried to work in between glances at her digital desk clock. Where was the dratted so and so, anyway? He'd said two weeks, it had been sixteen days. When was he coming back? The questions skipped in and out of Jo's mind at regular intervals as the clock pulsed its way toward five, the last one always being: Why should I care? After the way he'd treated her before he left, then spoken to her on the phone, she really should not care if she never laid eyes on him again! But she did care, so deeply it scared her senseless. How very Cinderellaish; falling in love with the boss! Jo scowled at the contract she was holding in one hand. And Brett was certainly no Prince Charming! Focusing on the legal jargon, she reread the words that had little more meaning this time than they had the previous three times she'd read them.

"How impressively industrious she is!" The loved, hated, dreaded, longed-for drawl crept to her from the office doorway. "Perhaps I should reward her with a raise." He paused, deliberately Jo felt sure. "Or could I devise a more ingenious form of compensation?"

Good saints preserve us! Was this man trying to drive her mad? At the sound of Brett's husky drawl, Jo's entire system had hummed with joy. Quickly glancing up, the hum had switched to a screech of fury. Brett was not even looking in her direction, but was instead gazing down at a small blonde who could be no other than the new manager, Marsha Wenger. Jo had to fight an urge to fling the contract at his damnably handsome face. Controlling herself with difficulty, Jo smiled prettily through her gritted teeth.

"Welcome back, sir," she said overly politely. Rising graceful-

115

ly, Jo nodded her head with queenly condescension at the petite blonde. "And this must be Marsha?" She arched one dark brow elegantly at Brett, receiving a frown that might have been fear-inspiring if she'd been in a frame of mind to be intimidated. As Jo wasn't in such a frame of mind, she countered his frown with a brightly inquiring expression.

"Yes." The way Brett bit off the word was a clear warning to Jo that she was skating on very thin ice. "Marsha Wenger, my brother's . . . ah . . . assistant, JoAnne Lawrence." Brett's smile drew a chilling line down Jo's spine. "Have you found an apart-ment for Marsha, Ms. Lawrence?"

Jo felt the double insult as sharply as if he'd slapped her face! Not only had he hesitated derogatorily over the title of assistant, but he'd refused her the courtesy of introducing Marsha to her in turn! Quelling a sudden, degrading need to cry, Jo lifted her head proudly.

"As a matter of fact, *sir,* I have," she answered in an extreme-ly soft voice. "I think Ms. Wenger will find it eminently *suit-able.*" Jo figuratively flung the last word at him.

"I knew you could do it." Brett's smile was positively feral. "I told Marsha you have a . . . thing . . . for apartments."

Jo was thoroughly confused, and not only by Brett's odd tone and equally odd phrasing. Marsha's expression of bemused com-passion as she glanced from Jo to Brett and then back to Jo again had Jo wondering what the devil the woman could possibly be thinking. Had she missed something along Brett's hurtful con-versation route? Or, Jo cringed inwardly, had she been the target of Brett's barbed tongue prior to their arrival at the office? The very thought coated Jo's response with acid.

"Well, my 'thing' worked." Picking up a long white envelope from the desk, Jo held it out to Brett, forcing him to cross the room to her. "You will find all the information in there." Care-fully avoiding his touch, she placed it in his hand. "As you will see, there's a detailed account of money owed to me."

"Just give me a total and I'll write out a check for you," Brett snapped, thereby practically admitting his intention of "keeping" Marsha.

The pain that stabbed through Jo was unbelievable in its intensity. Though Marsha opened her crimson-tinted lips, Jo beat her into speech.

"There is no hurry, sir. I'm in no danger of either starvation or eviction." Fleetingly, Jo wondered at the strange look of fury her assurance sent flashing over Brett's face, but she was too upset to probe for reasons. "Now, if there's nothing else pressing"—she glanced at the clock's digits as they moved to five fourteen—"I've got a blasting headache, and I'd like to go home." It was not a lie or an excuse. Within the last few minutes Jo's temples had begun to beat like a demented drummer! Along with the pain in her head was the sickening feeling that the omelet she had consumed earlier was not going to stay down!

Her discomfort must have been visible, for Brett's cold expression changed to instant concern. "Of course!" he agreed to her leaving at once. Then, confusing her even more, his tone softened into what sounded very like tenderness—although Jo felt sure she was mistaken, probably due to her headache. "Look," he urged, "sit down for a moment while I call for a car." When she would have protested, he added adamantly, "I won't have you running for a bus in this weather."

Jo had to choke back a peel of hysterical laughter. After running for days in rotten weather, Sir Fairhaired Knight belatedly blunders to the rescue! Her stomach lurched and Jo sat down with a plop. Oh, fantastic! she thought sickly. He finally comes home, and I feel decidedly ill! At that moment the room began rocking.

"Brett!" Jo heard Marsha's warning cry through a fog of dizziness. "I think Ms. Lawrence is really ill!"

When Jo woke, she was in her own nightgown, in her own bed, with only a cloudy recollection of how she had gotten into either one of them. Lying still, she probed her memory for enlightenment.

As the clouds dissipated, bits and pieces of the puzzle began falling into place. With sudden clarity, Jo remembered the expression of alarm on Brett's face when he'd turned from the phone at Marsha's cry of concern. Never could she recall seeing anyone move quite so quickly as he did when he whipped around the desk to where she was slumped in her chair.

"God! She looks terrible!" he'd exclaimed in an oddly hoarse tone. Then, even more oddly, he'd gently pressed his palm to her forehead. "Good Lord! Jo, you're burning up!" He'd turned aside then to Marsha, saying harshly, "I've got to get her home."

Jo squirmed uncomfortably at the memory of what had happened next. Brett, his face set in lines of determination, gently slid one arm beneath her legs and the other arm around her back, to lift her gently. Still, with all his care of her, the already spinning room tilted and Jo's roiling stomach revolted, making her ignominiously sick, all over the expensive carpet and Brett's handmade Italian loafers.

Writhing in remembrance, Jo heard her own reedy gasps of apology, could hear again Brett's murmured, "Don't, Jo. Don't worry about it! The dammed shoes are unimportant!" Clutching her tightly to his chest, he had issued clipped orders to Jo's secretary. "Tuck her coat around her, then get on the horn and have a cleaning crew sent up here. I'm taking her home." After the coat was wrapped securely in place, he strode to the door, tossing over his shoulder, "And get a doctor . . . the best." He rattled off Jo's home address as he crossed the outer office.

Now Jo had total recall of the dizzying ride down on the elevator and of Brett's arms tightening reassuringly as he strode out of the lift and across the lobby. She could feel again the sting of sleet mingled with cold rain on her flushed cheeks, could clearly hear Brett's muttered curse as he dashed for the protection of the limo. Now Jo's face burned with embarrassment instead of fever as her awakened memory replayed the scene enacted in this very room after their rather over-the-speed-limit run from the office building to her apartment. Although she had been barely conscious by the time Brett carried her into the bedroom, Jo had struggled with him when he'd started to undress her. Concentrating fiercely, she attempted to reconstruct his exact wording of admonition.

"Damn it, Jo. Stop fighting me! You're ill, and you must rest, and you can't very well do it fully clothed." At this point her recall was not quite as total for he'd gritted his teeth, or something. At any rate, only snatches of what he'd muttered remained clear. "Obstinate woman . . . you'd think I was Jack the Ripper or . . . will you be still . . . Jo, please, I'm not so desperate for you I'd—"

Whoa! Hold it! Jo brought her thoughts to a jarring stop. Had Brett said "I'm not so desperate for you" or "I'm not so desperate for a woman"? Jo wanted to believe it was the former, though she was certain it was the latter. In any case, he had finally managed to remove all her clothes and slip a nightgown over her head, all the while displaying a patience Jo would not have believed him capable of.

Then came the doctor, very distinguished looking and extremely irritated at having been called out in such weather. Brett toppled him off his high horse with one scathingly unrepeatable pronouncement. Now, hours removed from the incident, Jo could smile at it all, but at the time she'd been appalled at hi arrogant crudeness.

Thoroughly cowed, the good doctor had examined Jo expert ly, then, in an affronted tone, told Brett that she had contacte a virus.

"She's to have nothing by mouth for twenty-four hours afte the cessation of vomiting," he'd intoned self-importantly. "Ther a very light diet for a day or two after that." Gazing down at her he'd frowned. "Her pulse is a little rapid. Has she been under strain?"

To give the devil his due, Jo now admitted to herself that Bret had had the conscience to flush, if lightly.

"Perhaps," he'd answered tersely. "I'd have no way of know-

119

ing for certain, as I've just returned from a two-week business trip."

Both men jerked to attention when Jo choked. A business trip indeed! Funny business! Monkey business! Physical business! Jo's spasm of choking subsided as she ran out of old accusations. Her reaction to Brett's pious excuse gained her a calming hypodermic needle in the posterior. Jo had fallen asleep within minutes of receiving the injection.

How long had she slept? Twisting her head around to the small alarm clock on her nightstand, Jo discovered two things: the first that she had slept approximately four hours as it was now nearing eleven P.M., the second that her headache and queasiness were gone. She felt extremely tired but no longer sick. Sighing in relief, she snuggled down again then groaned when she rubbed a tender spot on her derriere. Within seconds the door to her room was quietly pushed open and Brett's tall frame was outlined in the doorway by a light in the hall behind him. When he saw she was awake, and alert, he smiled.

"You groaned, madame?" His smile widening, he sauntered into the room. "You must be feeling somewhat better," he opined, studying her closely. "You've lost all that gorgeous green color." Bending down, he touched her forehead lightly. "The fever's gone too. What you need now is rest." His fingers lingered, then slowly trailed down her temple and over her cheek.

Her breathing suddenly shallow, Jo had to grit her teeth against the urge to turn her head to seek his palm with her lips. She felt lightheaded again, only this time she knew her loss of equilibrium was not caused by a virus. Still his fingers lingered, stroking her cheek, her jawline. When one long forefinger sought the delicate line of her lips, Jo knew she had to say something to break the tension twisting through her. Raking her mind, she blurted the first thought that entered.

"How . . . how did you know I was awake?" she babbled breathlessly, then nearly fell apart altogether with the gentle smile that curved his lips. But her purpose was achieved for he straightened slightly and lifted his hand to indicate a small, dimly lit box on the dresser.

"The intercom," Brett replied blandly. "I have the volume turned up as high as it will go. I could hear the slightest rustle every time you moved."

"But where did it come from?" Jo frowned. "I've never seen it before."

"I had Doug pick it up when I sent him to my apartment for some clothes." Straightening fully, he reached out to switch on the small lamp on the nighttable. Doug Jensen was Brett's driver, the same one who had helped her into the car that afternoon. Jo moved restlessly with the memory of how very sick she'd been in the car, this time all over the expensive upholstery.

"I'm sorry," she whispered contritely.

"Sorry?" Brett repeated blankly. "Sorry for what?"

"The carpet, your shoes, the car. I'll pay to have them cleaned."

"Forget it." His hand sliced the air dismissively. "They have been cleaned. The only thing I want you to concentrate on is getting well." Now his hand moved to his head, fingers raking through the blond strands distractedly. "Though you obviously did have at least a touch of a virus, the doctor seemed inclined to think your problem was more exhaustion than anything else." Gray eyes captured hers. "What have you been up to these last two weeks?"

What had *she* been up to? What had she been up to! He dared ask that? When *he* was the one who had assigned her the duty of finding *suitable* living quarters for Marsha Wenger? Jo was still feeling very tired, and very weak. Now she was beginning to feel very, very edgy.

"What have I been up to?" she grated. "Why, I've been sitting in my office with my feet propped up on my desk, manicuring my nails, talking on the phone to all my friends, and generally goofing off. Isn't that what one is supposed to do when the boss is away?" Jo paused to draw breath, then demanded heatedly,

"What the hell do you think I've been up to? I've been up to the end of my patience with running around in all kinds of weather, trying to scare up a decent apartment for your latest . . . manager."

"Jo!" Brett cautioned softly, "calm down. The doctor said you are not to—"

"Calm down! Ha!" Really agitated now, Jo jerked to a sitting position, unmindful of the skimpiness of her nightgown. "I'll calm down when you and your stupid questions get out of here! I'm tired and, now that I think about it, I haven't felt quite right for days. Still, with your demands in mind, I've chased all over this blasted city examining some very unsuitable flats." She grimaced. "I'm so weary of the very word *apartment*, I could scream. And I do wish you'd get out of mine." The angry spate had consumed all of her breath and most of her energy. Feeling shaky, Jo eased back against the pillow with a soft sigh, her heavy eyelids dropping.

It was quiet for long minutes, much too quiet. Jo knew that Brett had not moved from beside the bed. She couldn't hear him breathing, but she knew he was there. Lifting her eyelids to mere slits, she stared at him balefully.

"Are you still here?"

"Do you always ask the obvious?" he retorted. "I'm here and I'm going to stay here . . . through the night."

Brett's flat statement sent a spurt of renewed energy zinging through Jo and, still unaware of her nearly naked state, she shot upright. "You are not!" she denied wildly. "I don't want you here. I'll be perfectly fine. All I need is a good night's rest and I'll—"

"You will stay in that bed for at least three days," Brett's adamant voice cut through her protest sharply. "Maybe longer if you don't behave."

"You . . . you can't . . ." she began sputteringly, only to be cut off again.

"I not only can, I will," Brett promised. "So be a good girl and stop arguing." A tiny smile quirking the corner of his lips, he ran an encompassing glance over her from hair to waist. "You know what?" he mused rhetorically. "Even in a state of . . . ah . . . dishevelment, you look very delectable." The quirk spread to a devilish grin. "If you're feeling so feisty, how about a quick wrestling match?"

Jo knew Brett expected her to clutch the covers to her chin with a maidenly blush. She was furious, yet she could not control the bubble of laughter that vibrated her vocal chords. "How many falls?" she gasped. "Two or three?" Placing her balled hands on her waist, she deliberately expanded her chest by drawing in a deep breath. "The mood I'm in at this minute, I'll probably pin you in seconds!"

Brett's grin disappeared and his eyes narrowed. "The mood I'm suddenly in, I'd let you pin me," he said seriously. "In fact, I'd enjoy it immensely." He took one step closer to the bed, then halted, as if catching himself. "I think you had better go back to sleep now," he warned softly. "You need R and R, not A S A." Turning abruptly, he started for the door.

A S A? Blinking, Jo racked her mind, finally giving up as he reached for the door knob. "What *is* A S A?"

"Abundant sexual activity, of course." The devilish grin flashed again as he stepped through the doorway and quietly closed the door.

Jo slowly slid into a prone position. That son of a something! Would he always have the last word in a confrontation with her? She knew he'd merely been amusing himself with her, yet . . . yet, Jo sighed. Stop dreaming, she chided herself. So he kissed you once, so what? So he's been very kind through this sickness thing, so darn what? You mean nothing to him. You are an employee. And, of course, now there's Marsha the manager! Oh, damn!

When she woke the second time, the angle of the sunrays in her room told her it was midmorning. While stretching herself into full wakefulness, Jo discovered two things. First, she realized that she was very hungry. Second, she found that she ached all over. What you need, my girl, is a long, hot shower, she told herself firmly. Her firmness wavered a bit when she slid out of bed and stood up. Jo wavered too. Brett entered the room as she was inching her way to the bathroom.

"What in hell do you think you're doing!" he roared. "Get back in bed!"

Afraid she'd fall on her face if she so much as paused, Jo continued groping along the wall to the bathroom. "I feel grubby," she panted. "I'm going to have a shower."

"Forget it."

As shaky as she was feeling, Jo probably would have docilely, happily gone back to bed had he said anything else. "Forget it" definitely did not make it as a convincer, except to convince her to keep going—if it killed her! Jo kept moving with dogged determination. "I said I'm going to take a shower, and I meant it. Go away, Mr. Renninger."

"Be sensible, Jo. You can't even stand up straight. Go back to bed." Jo hadn't heard him move away from the doorway, but now he was right behind her. His hands on her shoulders were warm, and reassuring, and, thankfully, supporting. "Let me help you."

"Do what? Take a shower or get back into bed?" Jo could have bitten her tongue for the smart, too-fast retort. She felt his fingers flex spasmodically into her shoulders, then she felt his warm breath feather her cheek.

"Both," he whispered. "If you like. In fact, I'll even join you—in both—if you like."

The idea was appealing, too appealing. Jo shrugged to dislodge his hands and found herself sitting on the floor. She didn't know whether to laugh hysterically or cry hysterically. She did neither, she simply sat there, listening to Brett swear as he bent to help her up.

"You have got to be the most obstinate woman I have ever met!" Though his voice was harsh, his hands were extremely gentle. "How the devil you ever got around Wolf—" He broke off to stare at the tears welling up in her eyes. "What's the matter?" he demanded, his face a study in concern. "Did you hurt yourself?"

"No." Jo shook her head, then sniffed. "Only my pride. What a dumb thing to do."

"Surprise, surprise!" Brett grinned. "We finally agree on something."

"But I really must have a shower," Jo murmured in a very conciliatory tone. "I feel so yucky. Please, Brett." The art of practicing cajolery was new to Jo. Not knowing quite how to go about it, she unconsciously did the right thing. Lowering her incredibly long lashes slowly, she repeated, "Please."

Brett was not at all a novice to the art, nor was he immune. A slow smile gathering along his lips, he knelt beside her. "Yucky, humm?" he murmured close to her ear. "Sounds uncomfortable." Raising his hand, he combed his fingers through her long, tangled mass of dark hair. "Okay, Delila." His quiet voice held a hint of teasing laughter. "You've chained me to the pillar. You may have, not a shower, but a bath. On one condition."

Victory within her grasp, Jo decided to push her luck. "Why not a shower? It's so much faster," she coaxed. "And on what condition?" she added quickly, hoping to put him off stride. Jo suspected her ploy wouldn't work. She was right; it didn't. Brett merely laughed aloud at her.

"First things first, my greenhorn temptress." A thread of tenderness wove through his chiding tone. "Consider your present position." Brett's gaze swept her crumpled form. "You could not remain erect with a wall to lean on. How were you planning to manage a curtained shower stall?" One silky blond brow arched exaggeratedly. "Have I made my point?"

"Point taken," Jo mumbled ungraciously. "But—"

"You simply do not quit." Brett shook his head in mock despair. "On to point two. My condition is, while pleasant, at

125

least for me"—here his tone hardened—"absolutely necessary. I will supervise your bath."

The silence that descended on Jo, and the room, was eardrum-cracking. To maintain that one could hear a pin drop would be to understate the case; one could possibly have heard a feather flutter to the floor. Unfortunately, for Brett, the silence was short-lived and shattered by a female screech.

"You will what!"

"There is certainly no lack of strength in the lungs here," Brett observed to the room in general. "You heard me, sweetie. No supervision, no bath . . . and no arguments. Got that?"

Jo did not require an interpreter of facial expressions to tell her Brett was not talking to hear the melodious sound of his own voice. He was dead serious and equally determined. As wishing he'd drop dead, period, was no solution to her immediate problem, Jo declined from voicing the observation. She was quiet a long time—a very long time—wrestling with the pros and cons of her boxed-in situation. Brett simply remained still, metaphorically playing out enough rope. She either bathed with an audience of one, or she crawled back into bed without even as much as cleaning her teeth. Yuck! Of course, being a product of an age with a fetish for cleanliness, Jo hanged herself.

"Oh, all right!" But she couldn't quite let it go at that. "If you're so dammed desperate to play voyeur while a woman bathes, let's get it over with."

Brett did not become angry at her nasty barb. He cracked up with laughter. Flinging himself onto the carpet, he roared at the ceiling. "Oh, goody," he gasped between barks of laughter. "I've been waiting thirty years to leer at a woman in her bath. Now, that erratic, erotic pleasure is to be mine." As Jo glared at him, Brett whooped with delight. "And not only is this woman beautifully pale of skin from a recent illness"—he paused to compose himself then went on—"she is also a trifle sick in the head."

Her back ramrod straight, Jo stared down at Brett in solemn consideration. Set into lines of superior austerity, Brett's face

126

was breathtaking in its classical perfection. His visage softened by warmth and genuine amusement, he stole Jo's heart along with her breath. Suddenly, for reasons Jo didn't want to examine too closely, she was eager to undress for this perfect example of the magnificent male in his prime. Still, wary of his motives concerning much more than a silly bath, Jo was determined not to reveal her eagerness.

"You do have a rather strange sense of humor, Mr. Renninger." Jo offered her opinion with a solemnity that mirrored her expression. "Still, I would guess the undraped female form holds no mystery for you . . . humm?"

Brett literally fell apart again. The seizure of mirth lasted for several minutes, during which Jo fought valiantly against the onslaught of reciprocal laughter. When, at last, Brett brought himself under control, he sat up facing her and grasped her face in his hands.

"You know what?" he asked seriously. "*You* have a rather strange talent for tapping a deep emotional response from me, be it anger, or amusement, or . . . whatever." Jo would have liked to question the whatever part, but he added, frowning in thought, "I don't think I've laughed that spontaneously in at least twenty years." The corners of his mouth twitched with that funny quirk Jo was beginning to realize was all his own. "You may be a little weird"—he allowed the quirk to grow into a smile—"but you're a kinda nice weird." With that, he lowered his smiling lips to hers.

Turning her head, Jo robbed him of his target. "Brett, no!" She fought the insistent tug of his hands. "I haven't brushed my teeth!"

Brett's hands sprang away from her face as another paroxysm of laughter shuddered through him. "Okay, I give up!" Springing to his feet, he stared down at her, his chest actually rumbling with the effects of his amusement. "I'll run your bath for you. I'll even prop you up while you do your thing with a toothbrush. Then I'll wait right here, outside the door, while you perform your ablution ritual." He started for the bathroom, then paused to slice a sharp-eyed glance at her. "You know, I think you may damn well be worth every penny Wolf is paying you."

There was an underlying note in his voice that caused a chill in Jo's bones. Up until Brett's last statement, sexual tension had been drawing her nerves to a vibrating tautness. And riding the back of that tension was the faint spark of hope that Brett had revised his original opinion of her. With his sudden withdrawal the tension snapped and the tiny spark of hope was doused. What was it about her that turned him off? Jo asked herself as she sat, miserable and uncaring of her disheveled appearance. Listening to the rush of water into the bathtub, she stared into nothingness and scoured her mind for answers.

The physical attraction was not one-sided, Jo knew that. Brett felt the tug of sexual awareness every bit as strongly as she did. That single kiss they'd shared had revealed the depths of the physical desire Brett felt for her. Would he, she wondered tormentedly, have given in to his need a moment ago if she had not stopped him? As usual, when Jo began searching for answers to questions about the element of constraint between Brett and her, all she found were more questions. Circles, circles, circles. Whenever she contemplated Brett Renninger, her mind took on the characteristics of a carrousel.

"Have you passed out with your eyes open?" Brett's drawling query fragmented Jo's bemusement.

Oh, why couldn't she hate him? Or, at the very least, dislike him as he so obviously disliked her? Shaking her head more at herself than in a silent reply to him, Jo was unaware of the appealing picture she made with her mass of hair a riot around her head and shoulders and her slim, long-limbed body covered with the sheerest of nightgowns. All she was aware of was the suddenness of Brett's impatience with her.

"Well?" he snapped. "Are you going to sit there for the rest of the morning? Your water's getting cool."

As if she were a child, or a total incompetent, Brett assisted

Jo into the bathroom. His hands impersonal of touch, but firm of grip, clasped her about the waist while she brushed her teeth and cleansed her face. Then he left her, his dubious expression a silent question of her ability to get into, then out of the tub without doing injury to herself. Quelling the urge to scream in frustration, Jo stepped into the warm water, a soft "oh" of delight whispering through her lips.

Brett had not only filled the tub to less than an inch from the rim, he had sprinkled her scented bath crystals into the water. Sighing with pleasure, Jo slid down into the fragrant silkiness. The soothing warmth lapping her chin, she closed her eyes in contentment and promptly dozed off.

"What am I going to do with you?" Jo's eyes flew wide at the sound of exasperation in Brett's voice. He was standing beside the tub, hands on his hips, actually scowling at her. "The idea was to become clean, not dead." Snatching a fluffy peach bath sheet from a glass towel bar, he held it out in invitation. "Let's go, water baby, bath time's over."

"You promised to wait outside!" Jo exclaimed accusingly.

"I waited outside," he grated. "Twenty minutes, to be exact. That water has got to be cold by now." He shook the towel lightly, impatiently. "Out." It was not a request but a definite order.

It was at that moment that Jo realized she was covered by nothing more than clear liquid. The fact that Brett had seen everything there was to see of her the afternoon before had little impact on her now. Feeling herself flush, and hating it, Jo launched a verbal attack.

"*You* get out!" she snapped. "I am perfectly capable of getting out of the tub all by myself." With deliberate insolence she swept his lean length with hazel eyes sparkling with anger. "If you don't move quickly," she threatened softly, "I swear I'll splash water all over your elegant suit." And elegant it was too, all three pieces of expertly tailored wool blend in a rich dark brown that

129

contrasted beautifully with his pale-gold hair. Brett's response to her threat not only startled Jo, it shocked her.

"Screw the suit! I have dozens of suits. I have only one of you." His eyes narrowed in warning. "If you do not stand up and step out of that damned tub in five seconds," he enunciated clearly through gritted teeth, "I swear *I* will haul you out of there bodily. And I won't concern myself about what I touch, or how roughly I touch it."

Her head lifted in defiance, her eyes challanging him, daring him, Jo rose from the water slowly and stepped delicately onto the peach carpet. Then, her head back, her bearing regal, she stood before him in nature's covering of blushing ivory-toned skin.

Except for his eyes, Brett didn't move. For several seconds he didn't even breathe. Starting with Jo's now-sodden, tangled hair, his glinting gray gaze inched the length of her body to the tips of her water-wrinkled toes. When his eyes slowly returned to hers, he stared into their depths as if he were trying to search out the deepest secrets of her soul. The intensity of his gaze stopped the breath in Jo's throat and liquefied all the strength in her body.

"God! You are beautiful!" Brett's hushed, reverent tone drained all defiance, all resistance from her. "Your hair is beautiful." Slowly, holding the towel aloft, he moved to her. "Your skin is beautiful." Flipping the huge terry sheet behind her, he wrapped her in its voluminous folds. "Your eyes are beautiful." Sliding his arms around her, he drew her to him. "And your mouth." His arms tightened to crush her to him. His voice lowered to a murmured groan. "God, your mouth!"

The mouth that Brett groaned over trembled in reaction to a sudden, searing need racing wildly through Jo's body. She was afraid, afraid of her own ineptitude, her own inadequacy, but she was also powerless against the force that urged her to arch her neck and raise her lips to him in silent offering. Brett pounced on her offering with the vengeance of an angry deity. With a

130

guttural growl her lips were taken inside his mouth to be devoured, nibbled on, and then gently laved by his searching tongue.

Giving in completely to the rioting sensations storming her body, Jo worked her arms free of the confining towel and coiled them around his neck, driving her fingers into the silken strands of his hair. The heat rising inside her found a measure of release as she obeyed his silent command to part her lips, wider and yet wider. All rational thought suspended, Jo's mouth consumed while being consumed. When Brett's stiffened tongue pierced into the moist warmth, Jo drew a moan from him by curling her own tongue around his. This time Brett placed no restraint upon his hands. His impatient mutter filled her mouth, and then the towel was torn from her body and tossed aside.

His hands moving restlessly over her back, Brett slid his lips from hers. Biting little kisses sensitized her skin from the corner of her mouth to the delicately curved edge of her ear. With a maddeningly slow, erotic rhythm the tip of his tongue dipped in and out of her ear. When his evocative play forced a groan from Jo's dry throat, Brett's hands moved down to cup her rounded bottom to pull her up and into the burgeoning hardness of his body.

"Will you part your thighs for me as quickly as you parted your lips, water baby?" he coaxed softly into her ear. Lost to everything but the need to have him fill every particle of her being, Jo complied to his coaxing with a whimper of surrender. The whimper turned to a gasp as Brett thrust his body against hers. Even fully clothed, Brett's arousal imprinted itself on her forcefully. Releasing his grasp on her, he brought his hands up to cradle her face. His eyes glinting like new steel in bright sunlight, he stared down at her.

"I must have you," he said clearly, fiercely. "Against all reason . . . and my better judgment, I *will* have you. In all probability we will both regret it afterward but, while the fire rages, I will feed my appetite for you on it."

A cold finger of unease poked warningly through the fog of passion clouding Jo's mind. There was something wrong here, something in the harsh tone of Brett's voice, and the rigid set of his features, something that looked frighteningly like disgust, both for her and himself. Not understanding this new element of fear he'd injected into their intimacy, Jo attempted a protest.

"Brett, no . . ."

"No?" he snarled, obviously misinterpreting her protest as a refusal. Grasping her by the shoulders, Brett spun her around, roughly pulling her back to his chest, imprisoning her easily by clamping his hands over her breasts. "Look at yourself," he ordered tersely. In a room of mirrors, there was no possible way to avoid looking at herself. Jo recognized the incongruity of the picture reflected back at her, she stark naked, Brett fully clothed. But that incongruity was not the point Brett was trying to make, as he very quickly proved.

"How dare you tell *me* no?" he demanded. "Just look at yourself. Your lips are wet and parted in anticipation, your eyes are dark with desire, and your entire body is quivering with sexual hunger." Watching her examine herself, Brett spread his fingers with cool deliberation. Immediately her hardened nipples thrust through the opening. Moving his hands slowly, he stroked the tips of Jo's breasts with his index fingers. When Jo could not deny the aching moan that whispered through her lips, Brett lowered his head to place his lips to her ear. "Now tell me no." As if to reinforce his point, he rotated his hips enticingly against her derriere. "If you still dare."

Jo's rational thinking process dissolved as Brett continued to stroke and manipulate her tingling nipples. Following the dictates of a passion flaring out of control, she arched her spine to press her aching breasts into his hands and twisted her head around, seeking his mouth with her avid lips. Grunting in satisfaction, Brett released his hold on her breasts to sweep her up into his arms. His mouth clinging to hers, he carried her into the bedroom. As he came to a stop beside her bed, Brett lifted his

132

head, then froze when his glance brushed the nighttable. Cursing softly, vehemently, he set her reluctantly on her feet. Thoroughly confused, Jo stared at him in disbelief.

"Brett, what . . ."

"Gertrude will be here in approximately fifteen minutes," he cut her off harshly, still staring at the table and the small alarm on it.

"Gertrude?" Jo repeated blankly, then, because she only knew one Gertrude: "Gertrude Jorgeson? Wolf's housekeeper?"

"Yes. *Wolf's* housekeeper."

The sudden, inexplicable anger in his tone and stiffened body as he turned away from her created an empty, bereft feeling inside Jo. What had she done to anger him? Surely her response had been evidence enough of how badly she wanted him? Fighting a creeping sense of failure, Jo bit down hard on her lower lip as she watched him stride to the double dresser against one wall, pull open a drawer, then, without bothering about being selective, plunge a hand in. Grasping the first garment he touched, Brett withdrew it and flung it at her with a tersely snapped "Cover yourself."

Jo could not have been more shocked had Brett slapped her, hard, across the face. Blinking furiously against the sudden sting of tears, she pulled the filmy mid-thigh-length nightie over her head. By the time she'd tugged the short gown into place, Jo's hurt had given way to anger.

"What is Gertrude Jorgeson coming here for?" The cold, grating sound of her voice surprised Jo, and spun Brett around to face her.

"She's going to look after you for a few days." Brett's voice was as cold and grating as hers had been. What, Jo cried inside, had happened to all the passion of moments ago?

"I don't need anyone to look after me!" she exclaimed hotly. "I'm perfectly all right."

Cool eyes swept her from head to toe. "You are *not* all right. People who are all right do not throw up and then faint. Nor do they fall to the floor the way you did a little while ago." Now Brett's eyes hardened in determination. "You will not return to the office until Monday."

"But this is only Tuesday, Brett!"

"Not before Monday," he repeated firmly. "And that is a direct order."

"But—"

"I said that's an order," he roared. "Now, get into that damn bed and stay there. Gertrude will be here shortly." Shooting his wrist from his cuff, he glanced at his watch. "It's just as well I remembered Gertrude's imminent arrival before undressing," he drawled—insultingly, Jo thought. "It's almost noon and I have an appointment at one." Shrugging his shoulders as if their abortive lovemaking was of little importance, Brett turned and walked from the room.

Still standing beside the bed, her eyes wide from the impact of his parting observation, Jo crossed her arms around her middle and hugged herself tightly in an effort to contain the pain clawing at her insides.

CHAPTER SEVEN

Monday morning Brett sat in his office, his gaze riveted to the digital clock on his desk. When the numbers read nine oh five, he thought, I'll give it five more minutes, then I'll call and order her to come to me. The small rectangle that contained the digits blurred as the phrase "come to me" echoed in his mind. Brett had not seen Jo since he'd walked out of her bedroom the previous Tuesday noontime. Now what he wanted, what he really wanted more than anything else in the world, was for Jo to come to him without the order to do so ever being issued. Brett knew, deep down in his bones, that what he wanted and what he'd get were two entirely different things. After the way he'd left her, he knew there was no way Jo would come anywhere near him without being summarily ordered.

His gaze still fixed on the dark wood-encased clock, Brett absently slid his hand across the desk to a pack of cigarettes lying to one side. Shaking a cigarette from the pack, he placed it between his lips and lighted it with a bright red disposable lighter. His fingers toying with the lighter, flicking it on and off repeatedly, Brett drew the acrid smoke deeply into his lungs, sighing with pleasure as he exhaled.

In the quiet room the clicking sound of the on-off play of his thumb drew his attention and his gaze shifted to his hand. His eyes bleak, Brett drew on the cigarette again, savoring the bite of tobacco on his tongue. Wisps of whitish-gray smoke swirling from his nostrils, Brett smiled in wry self-derision as he again brought the filter tip to his lips.

Brett had quit smoking, cold turkey, four months after his divorce from Sondra had become final. He had quit because the realization had struck suddenly one grim, hung-over morning that he had slowly increased his habit to three packs a day. The realization had been sobering in more ways than one. Since that morning fourteen months ago, Brett's consumption of alcohol had been curtailed drastically and he had not had as much as one drag of a cigarette. Had not, that is, until last Tuesday afternoon when, the tension that rode him demanding some form of release, he'd walked into a cigar store near his building and purchased a carton of the filter-tip 100s and the inexpensive plastic lighter. His first cigarette had induced lightheadedness. His second had instilled a quasi-calming effect. By the time he'd finished his third, Brett was hooked again. He had purchased his second carton that morning before entering the building.

Slicing a glance at the clock, Brett punched out the butt in the ashtray his secretary had unearthed for him, then immediately lighted another. His smile containing equal measures of self-disgust and self-amusement, Brett reached for his telephone. This morning Jo did not answer as usual.

"Yes, sir?" Her voice came crisply to him over the wire.

I'm *sir* again. Brett's twisted lips smoothed into a genuine smile. How long would it be, he wondered, before he was again Brett to her? Inside his head he could hear the exciting sound of her passion-thickened voice whispering his name.

"Mr. Renninger?" Jo's crispness had fled before confusion at his silence.

"You have to be told?" Brett drawled slowly.

"You want me in your office?"

In my office. In my apartment. In my bed. Anywhere and everywhere, Brett tormented himself with the tantalizing thought an instant before replying to her leading question.

"If you can find the time, Ms. Lawrence."

"Now?"

"If you will." Brett sighed loudly, exaggeratedly, then gently replaced the receiver.

The moment Jo walked into his office Brett felt the presence of the invisible wall she'd erected between them. The presence was as cold and forbidding as her expression. If he was any judge of women, and Brett had cultivated a discernment since Sondra, he was in for a very chilly period. His nerves tightening with tension, Brett waved her to a chair, then wondered what in hell he'd say to her. Perhaps, he mused, clearing the air would melt the ice. But first he needed a weed. Lighting a fresh cigarette from the end of his last one, Brett watched Jo's eyes flicker from him to the half-empty pack and then back to him again, a frown drawing a faint line on her brow.

"I—I didn't know that you smoked!" she blurted starkly.

"I don't . . . or, at least, I didn't." Now Brett frowned. "I used to," he explained. "I quit some time ago."

"But obviously . . . " she began.

"I started again," he said sharply.

"Why?" Jo retorted just as sharply, displaying little evidence of employee constraint.

Why? Why? The word echoed mockingly inside his head. Why, because I've got the hots for my brother's woman, Brett wanted to snarl, and it's driving me insane, that's why. The weeds are a substitute satisfaction, you beautiful bit— Brett clamped the lid on his thoughts. Longing to fondle something much softer, Brett fondled the plastic lighter.

"Maybe the pressure of business is finally getting to me," he answered dryly. "How are you feeling?" His sudden change in topic startled her and, for some perverse reason, that pleased him. Watch it, Renninger, he warned himself. If you derive

137

pleasure from drawing the mildest reaction from her, you're in bigger trouble than you imagined.

"*I'm* feeling fine." She eyed him uncertainly, then shrugged, as if thinking *why not?* Are you all right?" she asked warily.

Brett started to laugh, choked on the smoke he'd just drawn into his lungs, then coughed violently. "You're priceless," he gasped, gulping air into his tortured lungs. "The look on your face!" As the coughing fit subsided, he shook his head. "Were you wondering if you should call for help?"

"Will I need it?" Jo arched a dark brown questioningly.

There's a distinct possibility you will. Brett shrugged off the urge to voice the observation. Now was not the time. There was something he had to say first.

"Jo, about last week . . . "

"I don't want to talk about it!" she interrupted sharply. "Do you have work for me to do?"

"We're going to talk about it whether you want to or—"

"No!" Jumping out of the chair, she stood trembling and poised for flight. "If you have nothing for me to do—"

"SIT DOWN!" Brett barked the command. "I'll tell you when you may leave this office."

Her eyes shooting sparks at him, her delicate nostrils flaring with rebellious agitation, Jo defied his authority. "You can't make me . . . "

"Who the hell's going to stop me?" Partly amused, partly angry, Brett flung the question at her arrogantly. Jo did the one and only thing that could stop him cold. Calmly lifting the telephone receiver, she stared at him coolly as she punched the button for his secretary.

"Mrs. Jenkins, get me Wolf Renninger in Florida, please," she instructed the woman quietly. "I'll wait till you've made the connection."

"Damn you, Jo! Hang that phone up." Brett was so furious he had to push the order through his gritted teeth. You should have known better, you fool, he lashed himself scathingly. You really should have known better. Why did you assume, even for one wild moment, that she'd let you order her around? She's got the ear of the big prowler, his ear and every other vital part of him. You, big mouth, are only his baby brother! Berating himself, Brett watched as she spoke into the receiver.

"Cancel that Florida call, Mrs. Jenkins. We've resolved the problem." Cradling the receiver gently, Jo looked at him impassively. "We have resolved the problem. Haven't we?"

Leaning back in his chair, Brett studied her through narrowed lids. "You really would have called him, wouldn't you?"

"Yes," Jo replied simply. "I really would have called him."

"Because I raised my voice to you, you'd have taken the risk of disturbing him," Brett persisted coldly. "Regardless of his condition, or what a whining call from you might do to him, you would have called him?"

Even though Jo's features tightened, she answered coldly, "That's right, I would have." She pause to draw a deep breath, then coldly reinforced her position. "Let's have one thing clear here and now, *Mr.* Renninger, sir. I am your *brother's* assistant, not yours. At least, fortunately, not on a permanent basis. I am not a lackey. I am not a go-for. I am not the resident whipping boy. And I will not be spoken to like any of the above. If you are in a foul mood, find someone else to snap at." A derisive smile curled her lips. "You can always call Richard Colby," she suggested sweetly. "And chew him out." Her smile hardened. "May I leave now?"

Taut with anger, Brett curled his fingers around the chair arms to keep himself from springing from the seat and sprinting around the desk to her. He wanted to slap her smirking face. He wanted to shake the living hell out of her. But, more than anything else, he wanted to kiss her insolent mouth. You are in big trouble, boy, Brett advised himself, running a calculating glance over her. This one's got you tied in knots that would make a sailor blanch. Play it cool, chum, play it cool.

"Sit down, please," he said in a carefully controlled monotone.

"Why?" Jo didn't move.

Somehow Brett contained the curse that danced on the tip of his tongue. Forcing himself to relax, he sat up straight and folded his hands on his desk. One could hardly throttle a woman if one's hands were folded! "This is a business office, and . . . "

"Oh! You noticed, finally," Jo taunted coolly.

Of course, one could always *un*fold one's hands. Brett didn't. Instead, he drew a deep, cautioning breath. "You're right," he admitted, swallowing the taste of gall. "I stepped out of line . . . " He paused, then added firmly, "Here." He paused again, but her only reaction was a tightening of her lips. "It won't happen again." Once more he paused briefly. "Here."

"Why do I feel less than reassured?" Jo murmured tersely.

Brett could feel his facial muscles tightening with the insult. "I said I'll keep all our discussions on an impersonal basis here in the office. If I give you my word on it, will you sit down?"

Jo stared directly into Brett's eyes for several seconds, then slowly, stiffly sank to the very edge of the chair. Brett knew the elation he felt at her compliance was out of proportion to the situation, yet he savored the acknowledgment of her acceptance of his word. Staring into the hazel depths of her eyes, he nodded his head slightly. "Thank you." His husky tone caused a ripple in her mask of withdrawal, and that sent his elation up a notch. God! he mused, visually crawling into a hazel ensnarement. With very little effort, this gal could slip a ring through my nose and keep me grinning throughout the entire process! Time to pull your head together, Renninger, before you find yourself down for the count. Think of something, anything, but get your concentration back on the business of buildings.

"The Vermont project is underway." The suddenness of his stark statement shattered the tension Brett could feel sneaking along his nerve ends. It shattered a great deal of Jo's assumed composure as well. Two hazel traps blinked in momentary confusion, releasing their captive. "It would have been less awkward for me up there if you had seen fit to inform me of Wolf's decision to contract Sean Delheny for the job."

"But I didn't know he had!" Jo protested. "How many times do we have to go over this argument?" she added impatiently. "Brett, I will tell you once more that I had thought Wolf had scrapped the whole idea."

"Well, at least I'm Brett again." Brett was barely aware of murmuring the thought aloud. Jo hastened to assure him the status quo could revert at an instant's notice.

"For as long as you behave by maintaining a professional attitude."

The "behave" got to him. "I'm not a little boy, Jo," he purred with deliberate silkiness. "Be very careful of how you speak to me. You cannot remain in the building forever." He smiled gently, very gently. "Are you receiving my message?"

The expression that flashed across Jo's face activated a curl of excitement in Brett's lower region. She had obviously received his message loud and clear, and, although she now had her expression in rigid control, for a fleeting instant he had read blatant eagerness on her face. Oh, yes, my sweet, the time for A S A draws closer and closer for both of us, he promised silently.

"Brett, I did not know about Wolf contracting Sean Delheny." Jo's quiet but forceful disclaimer snapped the erotic thread Brett was weaving. Consigning his designing plans for their future of sensuality to the edge of his mind, he brought his concentration back to the cold world of business.

"Okay, but I felt like a fool. First of all, I didn't even know Casey was a woman! Then I find out Sean had his nose out of joint because he hadn't been included in our first meeting." Brett shook his head in memory. "As I said, I felt pretty foolish when Casey introduced me to Sean."

"I'm sorry. I could have saved you that embarrassment. I just never thought to tell you the architect was a woman. Of course, I knew that Casey and Sean were married, and that Sean was a

141

building contractor, but . . . " She let her voice trail off as she shrugged lightly.

Brett's shrug reflected hers. "It's over and done with. Sean is now officially under contract. I suggested a few minor changes in design, which Casey is working on now, but, for all intents and purposes, the project is underway." Without consciously thinking about it, Brett lighted another cigarette, drawing in deeply before continuing. "Before I left Vermont I tossed the ball into your court. I instructed both the Delhenys to send their reports to you." Pushing his chair back abruptly, he stood up and strolled to the wide window behind his desk to stare up at the overcast sky. When Jo didn't respond for several seconds, Brett turned back to her. "Can you handle it?"

"Yes."

A tiny smile quirked the corners of Brett's lips as he silently applauded the simplicity of her affirmation. In effect, what Jo was telling him with her quiet assertion was "I'm good at my job, and I know it." In that respect Brett could empathize with her; he felt exactly the same way about himself. Brett went momentarily still with the realization of sharing yet another character trait with Jo. In his mind, he slowly ticked off the things they had in common. They were both good at their chosen work and knew it. They both had a somewhat offbeat sense of humor. They both enjoyed good food, especially of the breakfast variety. During the hours Brett had spent in Jo's apartment while she'd been sleeping, he had made a tour of the rooms. On completion of his inspection he'd decided her taste was excellent—very likely because it reflected his own. And, last but definitely not least, they shared a mutual physical hunger. The parallels were enlightening . . . and a little scary. Brett was positive he did not want to feel this affinity with *any* woman, let alone another man's woman!

"You don't believe me?" Jo's strained tone fragmented Brett's conjecturing.

"What?" Brett shook his head to clear his mind. "Oh, yes, of course I believe you. I . . . ah . . . was thinking of something else." Something I wish I'd never considered, he added mutely. "Understand, if there are any snags, or major problems, we'll work them out together but, well, I'd like the freedom to get on with an idea of my own."

Jo's immediate interest was evidenced by her alert expression and the eagerness of her blurted, "What idea?"

"I'm considering a complex, a very large complex, in the Pocono Mountains in Pennsylvania." His gaze steady on her taut form, Brett waited to see if she'd react at all. He didn't have long to wait. Jo was still for a moment, then, an appreciative smile baring her white teeth, she nodded her head once.

"Can you get the property?" She shot the question at him hopefully.

"There's a realtor negotiating the deal now, but I want to be there." He lifted his shoulders. "The man is completely qualified yet"—he smiled deprecatingly—"I want to be there."

"Of course you do." Jo's return smile said tomes more than her simple words.

A gentle quiet settled between them. An understanding quiet Brett had never before experienced with a woman. It was good. They both felt it and reacted to it. Neither one of them moved, nor did they break that fragile quiet with speech. But they spoke to each other with mirroring smiles and glances that touched and locked. Jo, a wondering look widening her eyes, finally snapped the both of them back to the here and now.

"When are you leaving?"

There was an odd, almost frightened edge to her carefully controlled voice that Brett was in complete communion with. He felt it himself, the accord, or *simpatico*, or whatever it was that shimmered between them—it kind of frightened him too. He also was careful of betraying no nuances in his tone.

"I can clear my desk by Wednesday," Brett said hopefully.

"Then go," she chided softly. "I'll mind the store."

Brett grinned, unknowingly revealing his relief at her willingness to assume command in his absence. When he'd gone to Vermont three weeks previously he'd had everything under control. Now things were beginning to hum a bit—the way things usually did when the youngest of the Renningers got into gear—and it was a definite relief to know he had a second in command in New York who was the equal to Richard Colby in Atlanta. Still grinning, he walked back to his desk. Propping a hip on the edge of the cluttered surface, Brett picked up a thick manila envelope and handed it to Jo.

"The Vermont project thus far. Skim over it. If you have any questions, jot them down. We'll confer tomorrow afternoon." Brett arched a pale eyebrow at her. "Okay?"

"Yes."

Again that simple matter-of-factness. Damned if she isn't something else, Brett mused, watching her rise and move to the door. As Jo reached for the knob, another consideration struck him.

"By the way—" He halted her action. "I've fully briefed Marsha on the project. As the New England manager, she will be at your disposal."

Five minutes later, Brett still stared at the door Jo had closed so very carefully behind her. What the hell had happened to all that understanding that had been flowing back and forth between them? Suddenly Jo had turned into the queen of ice! Surely it could not have been because he'd suggested she utilize the talents of another employee? But then, what the hell had chased all the warmth from her eyes and voice? All he'd done was mention the New England area manager and Jo had turned on the frost. Women! Shaking his head, Brett circled his desk and sat down. Just when a man thought he was beginning to understand a female, she spins and throws one at him from left field!

As arranged, Brett met with Jo on Tuesday afternoon. The minute she entered his office Brett sighed with the realization that she had apparently applied her makeup with Jack Frost's paintbrush; he was still getting the ice treatment. Their meeting

144

was terse, brief, and to the point. She claimed to have no questions whatever. Brett took her word for it. The minute she left his office, Brett called Marsha front and center.

"Has Jo been in touch with you about the Vermont deal?" Brett shot the question at Marsha before she'd even seated herself.

"No." Marsha made no attempt to conceal her surprise, or her curiosity.

"Why?"

"No special reason," Brett hedged. "I was merely wondering."

"She's the one, isn't she?" Marsha murmured sympathetically.

"What one?" Brett's tone leveled a definite warning.

"Oh, Brett." Marsha chose to ignore the danger. "You know 'what one'. The one whose memory kept you from performing at"—she paused at the sudden stiffness about him, but went on fearlessly—"full capacity, shall we say?"

Brett's reaction was immediate and startling. "Damn it, Marsha!" he snarled, jumping to his feet to stalk to the window, then back again. "Do I taunt you by reminding you of your failure that night?"

"I'm not taunting you, Brett."

"Then what the hell—"

"Brett," she cut in gently. "You're laying a smoke screen, and you know it. Jo is the one, isn't she?"

"Yes," he grated harshly. "Christ! Am I that transparent?"

"Of course not." Marsha smiled. "And you know it. But I was with you when you came back last week, remember. I could actually feel the tension between the two of you. And I saw your face when it became obvious that she was ill. Poor Brett, you've got it pretty bad, haven't you?"

"Sometimes bad." Brett smiled whimsically. "And sometimes good. But at all times frustrating."

"As to that, I have a million questions." She held up her hand at the frown that drew his brows together. "None of which I'd dare ask. But isn't there any way you can resolve the situation?"

"Oh, my dear Marsha, I fully intend to resolve the situation," Brett assured her softly. "In my own time, and in my own way."

"There are times"—Marsha grinned—"my dear Brett, when you actually give me the shivers."

"Oh, sure," Brett said dismissively. Moving restlessly, he strolled to the window. "By the way, are you all settled in?" he asked idly.

"To what? The job or the apartment?"

"Both," he grinned. "But primarily the job."

"Fairly well." She grinned back. "Why do I have this sensation you have a particular reason for asking?"

"Maybe because I have a particular reason for asking," he retorted dryly. "I'm going to hit the road again on Wednesday," he explained seriously. "I was wondering if you had any questions before I leave."

"Where are you off to this time?" Not for a minute did Marsha think the query impertinent, which said much for the closeness that had developed between them in the brief time they'd known each other.

"The Pocono Mountains in Pennsylvania. I'm considering a condo complex there," Brett explained sketchily.

"For the skiers?"

Brett smiled. Marsha was sharp, but she was not quite as sharp as Jo. Jo had immediately picked up on his motivation. Oddly, knowing Jo was half a step ahead of most pleased him immensely.

"Partly." He nodded. "But I suspect that, before too long, that area will be booming the way the Jersey coast is now."

"Legalized gambling?" Marsha's eyes widened.

"The possibility is there." Brett shrugged. "What the hell, Columbus took a chance."

"And he's dead," Marsha drawled, straightfaced.

"Yes, well, nobody gets out of this life alive," Brett out-drawled her. "Well, do you have any questions?"

"None that I can think of offhand," she assured him.

"In that case, I have an assignment for you." Choosing his words carefully, Brett continued, "While I'm away I'd like you to use your connection with Casey Delheny to keep abreast of what's going on up there." Restless again, he measured the carpet in strides. "Jo has been put in complete charge but—"

"You don't trust her?" Marsha asked softly.

"I trust her implicitly!" His tone suddenly harsh, Brett stopped pacing to glare at her. "*But*, should she require assistance, I want you armed with the necessary data."

"Oh, boy," Marsha breathed softly. "You *do* have it bad." Before he could bite her head off, which he appeared ready to do, she asked, just as softly, "Are we friends, Brett?"

"You know we are," Brett snapped. "But that does not give you the right to—"

"Brett." Marsha silenced him with a wave of her hand. "Let me give you a bit of"—she shook her head at his scowling look—"not advice, but information. You know, the grapevine in this building is very alive and very active. I've picked up a few interesting bits and pieces since I've been here."

Positive she was going to say Wolf's name, and equally positive he did not want to hear it, Brett tried to shut her up. "I'm not interested in company gossip, Marsha."

"Then you should be," Marsha insisted, determined to have her say. "I'm told she's frigid."

"What!" With the memory of Jo's eager mouth, the way she melted against him, and her eyes, smokey with desire, teasing his mind, Brett was hard put not to laugh.

"Or afraid of men, or something. At any rate, she appears to have little or nothing to do with them. And they have tried, boy, have they tried! Apparently every eligible, and not so eligible, man in this building has approached her at one time or another.

147

The rebuff is made gently, and very politely, but it is definitely a rebuff." Marsha shrugged. "I just thought you should know."

"And now I do," Brett replied roughly. "And now the subject is closed." No sane person argued when Brett used that roughly threatening tone of voice. Marsha knew better than to set a precedent.

Brett was away from the office for ten days. Ten days during which he was very busy, and strangely lonely, and tormented by thoughts of Jo. Only once did he give thought to his last conversation with Marsha, and then only fleetingly. Incredible as it seemed, apparently no one at the office had an inkling of the affair between Wolf and his assistant. That fact confirmed Brett's opinion of the two of them: Wolf and Jo were intelligent individuals.

One consideration did occur at regular intervals during those ten days, and that was his stated trust in Jo. Did he trust her? Brett asked himself repeatedly. Always, he answered his question with a question: How could he trust a woman who was involved with a married man? Yet, after days of self-questioning, Brett finally answered his conscience with the truth: He would trust her with his life.

It didn't make much sense, at least not Brett's kind of sense, but there it was, like it or not. He trusted her. He loved her.

On the flight back to New York, Brett told himself he was as dead as Columbus!

It was raining when Brett landed at Newark. It was raining when he dashed from the taxi to the doors of the Renninger Building. The cabbie had told Brett the radio newscaster had said there was a possibility of the rain turning to snow. The front desk receptionist informed him the TV newscaster had said there was a chance of snow. Not one of them told him what he wanted to know. After ten days of longing for her, missing her, the only subject of interest to Brett was Jo Lawrence.

On entering his office, Brett's first act was to ask his secretary to call Jo and request she join him. "And phrase it to her exactly that way," he instructed the shocked, middle-aged secretarial wizard.

To pass the time while waiting for Jo's arrival, Brett lighted a cigarette, then drummed on his desk with the tips of his fingers. Beginning to feel a trifle foolish staring fixedly at the wood-grained door, he swung his gaze to the window, then wished he hadn't. The direction of the wind was driving the rain against the pane and, intermingling with the drops striking the glass, Brett could discern the occasional splat of a snowflake.

"Whoever heard of snow a week and a half before Thanksgiving?" he muttered in disgust.

"I beg your pardon?"

"There's snow mixed with that rain!" Brett growled, swinging around to confront the tormenter of his nights. Then Jo smiled at his disgruntlement, making him feel more a fool than before. God! She's all I think about for over a week and, when I finally get back, I complain about snow! You had better nail this woman down pretty soon, old son, Brett advised himself. For if you don't, they're going to come and cart you away!

"Well, don't blame me." Jo actually laughed at him. "I didn't order it."

Lost in his own thoughts, Brett stared at her in confusion a moment. Then the dawn broke in his mind. The snow! "Oh, well, I'm not used to the stuff. The South doesn't get a great deal of it."

"Do tell!" Jo gave a fair imitation of a Southern drawl.

Brett was immediately suspicious. Why was she so downright chipper this afternoon? One word sprang into his mind. A name. A name he didn't even want to think, let alone say aloud. Nonetheless, there it was. Wolf! Had she been in contact with her lover? Damn it, if she had he'd beat her!

"You appear to be in fine spirits today," he probed carefully.

"And why not?" Jo grinned. "I received the report you sent me three days ago." Her grin widened into a full, breathtaking

149

smile. "You closed the deal on the property you wanted. I think that's plenty of reason for high spirits. Don't you?"

Brett nodded, grinned, and just sat staring at her. She is so damn beautiful, he thought achingly. Her smile alone brightens the dismal day. In concession to the weather, Jo was dressed in a full, dove-gray wool skirt and a pullover sweater in hot pink that clung to her figure to the point of making Brett's hands itch. Her long, slim legs were encased to the knee in black stack-heeled boots of soft, pliant leather. Considering the overall picture she presented, Brett decided she looked terrific. He also decided he'd love to undress her, very, very slowly. The beginnings of a frown marring her face drew him, reluctantly, out of the promise of a delightfully erotic daydream.

"Now the work begins on it," he said abruptly.

"Have you decided on an architect?"

"I was considering Casey Delheny," Brett said thoughtfully. "I was really impressed with her designs for Vermont. What do you think?" Brett's question was not rhetorical. He really wanted her opinion, and he let it show in his tone.

"I think Casey's an excellent choice. Wolf thought so too. He'd inspected several of the buildings she'd designed and was very impressed. He also approved of the work of her interior designers."

Although Brett was not pleased with her use of Wolf as a reference, he let it slide. "Yes, I've seen some of her buildings myself, and I like the work of her interior designers as well. Okay, we'll go with Casey and let her use her own people."

"Do you always make decisions this quickly?" Jo laughed in a tone slightly tinged with awe.

"Usually." Brett shrugged nonchalantly.

"But don't you have to consult with headquarters?"

"Are you kidding?" Brett grinned. "I consulted with headquarters until I was afraid the phone lines would melt between Pennsylvania and Florida." His grin widened. "And do you want to know what the final word from the head honcho was?"

Of course Jo nodded. "Mama told me, and these are her exact words, 'You picked up the ball, now run with it.'" Brett laughed out loud.

"Incredible!"

"I suppose." Brett shrugged. "But then, Renninger's is not run like most companies. In the first place it is entirely family owned and managed. Madam President *gives* orders, she does not take them." A gentle smile curved his lips. "In the second place, Mother gave each one of her sons the opportunity to do one complete job on his own. It was my turn. The Pocono project will be my baby."

"But what if you fail?" Jo blurted.

"No problem," Brett drawled. "She'll kill me."

Jo stared at him aghast for an instant, then joined him in laughter. "I think I'd like your mother," she said, when she could finally speak.

"I know Mother would like you," he assured her. "In fact, she wants to meet you."

"Me?" Jo blinked in astonishment. "Why would she want to meet me?" She eyed him warily. "And how would you know?"

"She told me." Brett met her wary glance with a smile. "While we were burning up Bell Tel's East Coast lines, she asked me how I was muddling along without the redoubtable Richard Colby. I told her I was indeed not muddling, but skimming, as I had Richard's double in drag in the New York office." Jo's gasp produced a slashing grin from Brett. "Again I quote my revered mother: 'I have got to meet the woman *you* admit is as competent as Richard!' she said quite seriously."

"Yes, well, the next time your mother is in New York, perhaps she'll peek into my office." Everything about Jo's attitude told Brett she didn't believe a word he said. "Now, back to the business at hand. Are you going to have the preliminary specs for the building drawn up by our people, or are you going with a general contractor?"

"What I said to my mother was incorrect." Brett groaned.

151

"You are not like Richard. You are much, much more of a slave driver." Jo frowned. Brett got back to the business at hand. "I've decided to use Sean Delheny as general contractor. As with Casey, I've seen some of his work. I've also discussed it with the people he's worked for. The decision was unanimous: Sean is one damned good ramrod. He's done some fast-tracking."

Jo was well aware that the term fast-tracking applied to bonuses earned for a construction job completed ahead of schedule. Jo was also well aware of Sean's track record. He was very careful. He was very good. He got a job done right, usually ahead of time. Brett knew she made it her business to be aware of such things.

"Does Sean know he's been appointed for yet another Renninger project?" Jo asked dryly.

"Of course." Brett acted shocked, as if she should have known better than to even ask. "He's in the mountains now, checking out the local talent for subcontracting. I plan to confer with him again after Thanksgiving."

"Which reminds me," Jo sat up straighter in her chair. "I'm going to be out of the office most of Thanksgiving week. I'm going home for the holiday. I still have some vacation time due me."

"No problem." Brett shrugged. "Clear it with personnel."

Long after Jo had gone back to her own office, Brett sat, again contemplating the grain in the wood door. All his hopes of the previous ten days metaphorically laughing at him as they floated out the window. There were four days left to this week, four days in which he had one hell of a lot of work to catch up on. Next week she'd be gone. Come to that, so would he, as he had to fly to Atlanta to brief and be briefed by Richard. Then he was off again to Florida for Thanksgiving. A schedule, Brett decided glumly, that allowed little time for seduction.

Pushing his chair back, Brett shoved his suddenly tired body erect and stalked to the window to glare out at the rain that was rapidly changing to snow. At first he had envisioned taking Jo to his own bed. Then, growing desperate, he'd decided *her* bed would do just as well. Now, in a state of constant frustration, he'd happily make use of any damned bed or reasonably flat surface!

I think I was happier, he thought irritably, when all I wanted to do was strangle her.

During the remainder of that week, Brett saw more of Marsha than he did of Jo. A minor crisis had cropped up at a Renninger motel nearing completion in Massachusetts, and Marsha had come to Brett, mad as hell, because the ramrod of the project flatly refused to deal with a woman. When reason and diplomacy failed to budge the jerk, Brett had resolved the problem by telling the man to "Eat what you're served, or get the hell away from the table." If the injection of instant education didn't exactly cure the man's ailment, it did treat the existing symptoms; the ape decided he could work with Marsha.

In Atlanta, to Brett's immense relief, he found that Richard had everything under control, as usual.

"Are you attempting to ingratiate yourself into my office?" Their conference concluded, Brett and Richard were relaxing over a drink in one of Brett's favorite bars.

"Of course." Richard nodded. "The way I figure it, at the pace you've been working at since you and Sondra separated, you'll begin to burn out any day now." His grin was pure Machiavellian. "I intend to be prepared when Madam Pres finds herself in need of a new head man in Atlanta."

Free of tension for the first time in over a month, Brett leaned back in his chair and raised his glass in salute. "Good luck," he drawled, a grin lightening the new lines of strain on his handsome face.

Brett could afford the salute and the encouragement, very simply because he knew his assistant had no designs on his position. Richard Colby, small, dapper, urbane to his fingertips, was quite satisfied in his position as first assistant, and Brett knew it. Of course, Richard knew Brett knew it. Richard's mild

153

threat was as close as he'd come to asking Brett to slow down. Brett, though appreciating Richard's concern, had no intention of paying heed to it.

Brett was in Florida barely long enough to sit down at the overloaded dinner table with the Renninger clan. Within the eighteen hours he was at the farm Brett learned that: Wolf was mending, if slowly; Micki was well, and pleased with the way Wolf was mending; their offspring were full of sun and the devil; Eric and his family were happily increasing, as Eric's wife was pregnant with their third child; his sister Di was smugly displaying her son's ability to perform back flips, and his mother was, as always, the indestructible head of Renninger Corporation—and all the assorted younger Renningers.

Then Brett was off again, this time to Pennsylvania and his prearranged meeting with Sean Delheny. Not once during Brett's quick visit to the farm had JoAnne Lawrence's name been mentioned. Not once had the image of JoAnne Lawrence been far from Brett's mind. In fact, by the time Brett returned to the New York office in early December, his thoughts of Jo had become so obsessive he was afraid that if he didn't see her soon he'd begin snarling at everyone around him like a dog with distemper.

Brett began snarling upon arrival at his office the following morning. He had wakened early feeling good with anticipation and had even caught himself whistling while standing under the shower. Walking to the office briskly in the cold December air, he had counted the blocks and then the pavement squares to his building. Entering the outer office, Brett had politely asked Ms. Jenkins to buzz Jo and request her to join him. Ms. Jenkins reply stopped him cold two paces from his office door.

"Ms. Lawrence isn't in, sir. She flew to Vermont yesterday."

Later, through Marsha and his second assistant, a young eager beaver named Bob Kempten, Brett learned that Casey Delheny had called about some technical problem and Jo had decided to investigate personally. By the time Jo returned, two days later, most of Brett's staff were circling him from a distance, as if he were a rabid dog. Determined he'd see her the minute she was back in her office, Brett left a terse note for her on her desk. The message consisted of three words: Get in here.

"You wanted to see me?" Jo asked as she gently closed the door to Brett's office.

Brett was standing at the window, trying to stare holes through the low-hanging, dirty-gray clouds. At the sound of his door being opened every muscle and nerve in his body tensed, but when he turned to face her he presented a picture of total relaxation. At the sight of her, her cheeks pink from the cold, her dark hair tousled from the brisk wind, and her lips slick with freshly applied gloss, Brett had to clamp his back teeth together to control the urge to go to her and pull her into his arms.

"What was Casey's problem?" Brett tossed the question at Jo as he strolled to his desk. As if, at this moment, I care, he thought, reaching for the pack of cigarettes on his desk to give his hands something to do instead of reaching for her.

"Nothing really earth shattering, and nothing I couldn't handle."

Every one of Brett's senses screamed an alert. There was something wrong here, something in Jo's tone. Eyelids narrowing, Brett studied her more closely, his sharpened glance probing past the glow imbued by being out of doors. Her eyes were opaque, refusing an observer access to her thoughts. Her features were carefully controlled, devoid of expression. Her attitude was of polite, cool detachment. All the questions he'd planned to ask her about Vermont fled before the confusion that fogged Brett's mind.

Before he'd left New York for Atlanta they had been on friendly, almost warm terms. Now Jo looked at him as if he were a stranger, and a not too appealing one at that. What could have possibly happened to change her? Brett wondered. And in such a short amount of time?

"Are you . . . all right?" Brett inquired gently, carefully feeling his way.

"Actually, no." Jo's lips tightened.

Brett's chest tightened too. "Is it something to do with that trouble in Vermont?" Even as Brett asked the question Jo was shaking her head in the negative. "What then?" he demanded, if softly.

Jo drew a deep breath, which nearly drew a groan past his compressed lips; Jo did fill a sweater to advantage.

"I'm not feeling right." She hesitated, then rushed on, too quickly. "I don't feel exactly ill, but I don't feel exactly well either. I'm . . . I'm tired all the time. Perhaps it's a holdover from the virus I contracted a few weeks ago."

Garbage. Brett knew Jo was lying, he *knew* it . . . yet, why? "Have you consulted a doctor about your symptoms?" Brett knew the answer to that too. He was right.

"No." Not a muscle in her face moved, only her lips. "I-I think all I need is some rest." Now she hesitated again, as if girding herself for battle. "I've used up all my vacation but, with your permission"—she grimaced, as if the last word was distasteful to her—"I'd like to take a leave of absence the last two weeks of this month."

"Jo—" Brett began, only to be cut off at once.

"That's not all . . . sir."

Sir again! Brett very nearly winced. Controlling the need to go to her and shake some life, some emotion, into her and evoke some *response* from her, Brett muttered, "Go on. What else do you want?"

"Permission to stay at the motel in Ocean City." Jo stared at him coolly.

"You want to go to the beach in December!" Brett exclaimed in an amazed shout.

"I want to rest!" Jo shouted back, revealing tension for the first time since entering his office. "It will be quiet there. And I love

156

the sea. May I stay in one of the rooms there?" she insisted, her tone again without inflection.

"Aren't you going home for Christmas?"

"No!" The denial shot out of her.

Brett now had part of the answer, but only part of it. He was sure something had happened while she'd been home at Thanksgiving, and apparently that something had been unpleasant. Brett was equally sure that was not the complete answer. Her attitude toward *him* had changed drastically, so it was also something to do with him that had caused this cold front she was presenting. But what had he done? Brett raked his mind and came up blank. If she'd only talk to him, or scream at him . . . but, from her attitude, it was obvious she was not going to budge from behind her icy mask. Damn it, he raged inwardly, what can I do but let her have what she wants? Nothing.

"If you're going to stay there the entire two weeks, one room won't do," he said flatly. "You'll get cabin fever before the first week is out. Stay in the apartment."

"But . . . "

"Don't argue!" Brett was skating very close to the edge of his patience, and it showed. Jo subsided at once. "I'll call Wolf's housekeeper, Mrs. Jorgeson, and ask her to have the utilities turned on and to clean the place for you." Standing abruptly, he slid his hand into his pocket and withdrew a gold keyring. After working two of the keys off the ring, he leaned across the desk and handed them to her. "I'll also let security know you're coming." A sardonic smile twitched at his lips. "I don't think you'd enjoy spending Christmas in the slammer for breaking and entering."

Jo's expression didn't change, in as much as she still showed no expression at all. "Thank you." Her voice had a cool, withdrawn quality that sent a shiver through Brett.

Brett mentally gnawed at the problem of Jo's attitude long after she'd left his office. In fact, he was still racking his brain for an answer after her leave of absence had officially begun. He

157

saw little of her during the two-week interval, and what he did see of her alarmed him. She was pale, she looked liked she was not getting enough sleep, and she was much too subdued. The Jo Lawrence he had come to love had been anything but subdued.

As Christmas grew nearer, and the office employees grew merrier, Brett's worry and frustration jelled into determination. Four days before Christmas he reached the end of his patience. Whether Jo liked it or not, she was going to get company. Damn it! He owned the place, didn't he?

Late that afternoon Brett signed the release for the employees' Christmas bonuses, locked his desk, and pushed his chair back. As he was shrugging into his coat the phone rang. Snatching up the receiver impatiently, Brett growled, "Ms. Jenkins, I told you I was leaving. I'm taking no calls."

"I'm sorry, Mr. Renninger, but I was sure you'd want to speak to this party."

Brett immediately thought of Jo. "Who is it?"

"The boss."

Brett smiled at the wizard's dry tone. Hell, he didn't know she was capable of dry humor! "You're right, Ms. Jenkins. I'll take the call." The moment Brett heard the switch click in, he drawled with his usual insolence, "Yes, sir?"

"I should have beaten you as a child," his mother said decisively, then added maternally, "You are coming to the farm for Christmas, aren't you?"

"Yes, of course," Brett assured her. "I should get there late in the afternoon on Christmas Eve."

"Good, we'll see you then," Violet said briskly. "By the way, if your Ms. Lawrence has no other plans, bring her with you," she tacked on as an afterthought.

Brett mulled over his mother's invitation all the way to Ocean City. Even though she had expressed a desire to meet Jo, it seemed odd to Brett that his mother had chosen this particular time to do it. Christmas was always a family time at the Renning-

158

er manse, wherever that happened to be when the holiday rolled around. There was, of course, one unavoidable consideration, and that was that Wolf had made a special request of Violet to include Jo. Merely speculating on that possibility torched a blaze of anger inside Brett.

By the time he drove onto the motel parking lot, Brett had mulled himself into a fury. Deep inside his conscience, Brett knew he had no right to demand anything from Jo. At the same time, consciously Brett knew he was about to demand everything from her.

The small car, parked near the entrance doors, looked slightly forlorn on the large lot. As he pulled the Porsche up beside it, the term run-about slithered into Brett's mind. Had Wolf signed his name to a check for the toy? Brett tormented himself with the query as he strode to the wide glass doors. After making sure the doors were securely locked again behind him, Brett took the stairs two at a time, then loped along the hallway to the apartment. Key at the ready, he hesitated a moment, then unlocked the door and stepped inside.

Jo was standing with her back to the oversized window, having obviously spun around at the sound of his entrance. She did not look frightened, or even surprised. In fact, Brett had the strange sensation that she'd been expecting him. His anger changing to an even more basic emotion, Brett stood still for a moment, eating her with his eyes. Even though it was still early evening, Jo was dressed for bed in a lilac-and-orchid striped silk robe over a paler orchid nightgown. Her face was free of makeup and her hair was slightly mussed. Brett decided to muss it even more.

Without as much as a word, watching her eyes, Brett walked to her, shedding his suede jacket and dropping it to the floor as he went. With cool deliberation he walked right into her, a primitive thrill leaping in his loins at the shock of their colliding bodies. Then the aching emptiness of his arms was filled with the softness of her and his restlessly moving hands delighted in the silk material covering her back. Still staring into her eyes, Brett read surrender in the soft hazel depths.

The clean scent of her filling his senses, the feel of her soft breasts crushed to his chest, and his own now-raging desire snapped the thread of communication between Brett and his conscience. Damn Wolf! Damn the whole damned world! He must have this woman.

Giving Jo time to protest, or turn her head aside if she wanted to, Brett lowered his head slowly. The fact that Jo did neither, but parted her lips instead, set Brett's heart racing. Gently, gently, he cautioned himself as he touched his lips to hers. But then, at Jo's instant response, all thoughts of caution dissolved in the blood that went rushing through his veins. Suddenly filled with the need to conquer, Brett pressed his mouth against hers, unmindful of the low growl that swelled his vocal chords. Jo reacted by clasping his head to pull him deeper into her mouth.

Sliding his hands down her back, Brett grasped her rounded bottom and lifted her up to meet the urgent thrust of his body. At the same time he inserted his tongue into the sweet moistness of her mouth. Jo rewarded Brett's efforts with a low groan. Sweeping her into his arms, Brett strode to the bedroom, his lips locked on hers. Coming to a stop beside the bed, he allowed himself the pleasure of sliding her body down his as he settled her on her feet.

Every one of Brett's senses urged him to rip the robe and nightgown from Jo's body then tear his own clothes off. Clamping hard on his back teeth, Brett brought every ounce of control he possessed into play. He had waited too long for her to rush the moment. No, there'd be no ripping or tearing here. No hurried, frantic coupling. Brett fully intended to enjoy every minute of the love play. He fully intended Jo to enjoy it as well.

Slowly, tenderly, Brett removed the robe and nightgown, then stepped back to feast his eyes on her. Beautiful, God, she's beautiful, he thought, inching his gaze over Jo's nakedness. Her breasts were not large, but firm and high. Her waist curved in

160

neatly before flaring out again to rounded hips. Her legs were long, shapely as a dancer's, tapering to slim ankles and feet. And her thighs! Brett's gaze lingered on Jo's smooth thighs a moment, then slowly rose to meet her eyes.

"Brett . . ." It was the first word spoken, and her only word. The plea drew his eyes to her face.

"It will be good, Jo. I promise," Brett said in a hoarse voice he hardly recognized as his own. "Do you believe me?"

Jo swallowed, then wet her lips, making Brett long for the feel of her pink tongue in his mouth. "I—I want to believe you, but you don't understand. . . ."

"I don't need to understand," Brett cut her off urgently, positive she was going to attempt to tell him about Wolf. "It *will* be good. I swear to you."

Tugging the spread, blanket, and top sheet free, Brett tossed them to the bottom of the bed, then, lifting Jo again, he lay her in the middle of the mattress. Straightening, Brett swiftly shed his clothes, his gaze locked on hers. When, finally, he stood before her as God had made him, he searched her face for signs of approval—or disapproval. Brett was not unaware of his attractiveness to women. Many of the women he'd dated, and slept with, had been articulate in their praise of his masculine good looks. Now, stripped of all the expensive trappings, Brett trembled as he watched Jo's eyes examine him. His trembling increased with excitement when he saw her eyes widen on sight of his arousal. Brett's excitement building, he watched her gaze shy away from, then return to his manhood before climbing up his body to his face.

"I—I'm not sure I can . . ."

That's as far as Jo got before, sliding on to the bed beside her, Brett closed her mouth with his own. Yet Jo's attempt at protest had shaken him. The prospect of rejection goading him, Brett set out to seduce her.

His lips teased hers. His teeth nibbled on the tender flesh inside. His tongue made gentle forays into the recess of her

161

mouth, then thrust deeply over and over until she moaned and clung to him, silently begging for more. At the tiny sound Brett deserted Jo's lips to plant stinging kisses down her neck to the hollow at the base of her throat. The flutter of Jo's pulse against the tip of Brett's tongue set fire to his blood. Enjoying the sensation of liquid flames racing through his body, Brett ventured farther south. His lips adored the satiny smoothness of her breasts, his tongue worshipped the hardening nipples. Driven now by a passion running rampant, Brett closed his lips over one rigid nipple and drew gently, shivering with the resultant tightening in his loins.

His hands stroking Jo's softness, learning all the places that caused a movement or murmur of response from her, Brett imprinted his lips onto the skin of her body. His own ardor rising, he dipped his tongue into her navel, then slid his moistened tongue the length of her abdomen and around the perimeter of her dark triangle. Loving his work, Brett tongue-kissed Jo's legs to her insteps, then backtracked up the inside of her thigh. When his lips reached their desired destination, Jo stiffened.

"Brett, no! I . . . "

It was too late. Determined not to be denied, Brett tasted the honied sweetness of her. His hands clasped to her hips, he kissed and caressed her silky warmth. Jo remained stiff for a moment, then a smile touched Brett's lips as he felt her begin to move slowly, then with increasing frenzy, her breath rasping through her moaning throat.

"Brett, Brett, please . . . oh, please . . . "

In all of his fantasies about Jo, never had he hoped to hear her plead for him to love her. Sliding his body up between her thighs, Brett placed his lips lightly to hers.

"Did I promise you it would be good?" he whispered into her mouth.

"Yes!" she gasped, sending a shudder through his body.

"And have I pleased you so far?" he murmured, nipping at her lower lip.

"Yes," she moaned, sending a shaft of near pain into the lower part of his body.

"Shall I continue?" he teased, sliding his tongue along her teeth.

"Oh, yes," she sobbed, sending his control into retreat.

Brett talked to himself to keep from rushing and ruining it all: Take your time. There's no hurry now. You've waited and waited what seems like forever for this. Wrest every ounce of sweetness from it.

All the while he was advising himself, Brett was moving over Jo. Gently he settled himself between her enticingly soft thighs, pausing a moment to stroke her heated core with one hand while caressing a breast with the other. The movement of Jo's hips encouraged entrance and, sliding his hands beneath her, Brett lifted her to meet him. Then, slowly, savoring every incremental movement, Brett penetrated into the satiny sheath that felt like it was fashioned for him alone. Deep within her warmth, Brett felt himself savoring every sensation as he and Jo moved in slow rhythm as one.

The slow savoring could not last. For the first time in his adult life Brett's control shattered completely. Never had he experienced the fullness of the love act—a joining of mind and soul as well as flesh—and only now with this most magnificent of women. Increasing the tempo, Brett moved faster, and still faster, thrusting his body against and into hers, thrilling to the feel of her legs embracing him tightly, exulting to the strength with which she thrust her body against his.

Brett's body was bathed in sweat and his hands felt the slippery wetness of Jo's, and still he prolonged the final moment, waiting for her. When that moment happened for her, he stilled, holding her close, absorbing the shudders into his own body. When her shock waves had subsided, Brett began moving again, stroking deeper, and yet deeper, desperate to possess, equally desperate to be possessed. The explosion came within seconds of her own, and now Jo clutched him to her to cushion the reverberations.

When total sanity returned, Brett carefully moved from Jo's body to the bed. Without a word he drew her into his arms, close to his side. Then, his lips at her forehead, he murmured, "Thank you, water baby. Now, go to sleep."

Long after Jo's even breathing indicated to Brett that she was sleeping deeply, he lay awake, holding her soft body tightly to his own. Staring into the darkness, Brett attempted to sort out the tangle of conflicting emotions vying for supremacy in his mind. First and foremost was the indisputable fact that what he'd just been through had been *the* most shattering sexual experience he'd ever had. Even thinking it seemed strange, yet Jo had somehow enveloped him totally, not merely physically but spiritually as well! Stranger still was the stark realization that, not only did he not mind the . . . ensnarement, for want of a better word . . . he was actually rejoicing in it. He loved it! Hell, now, to himself, holding Jo close in a pitch-dark room, Brett felt free to revel in the truth that he loved her!

Pushing all other considerations aside, Brett whispered the words aloud.

"I love you, JoAnne Lawrence, completely, unconditionally, and, very likely, forever."

The vow at last spoken, even to one who could not hear, Brett sighed contentedly and went to sleep.

CHAPTER EIGHT

The sound of the wind, moaning like a soul in torment, woke Jo. Lying still, she listened to the shiver-inducing noise as gusts beat against the wide bedroom window in ineffectual fury. It was no longer dark beyond the pane, yet still not fully light, the time of morning when the lowest temperature reading is usually registered. In her mind, Jo pictured the ocean and breakers whipped to whitecapped frenzy by the gale. All that potentially destructive elemental force, she mused sleepily. So very near.

A smile of contentment curved her kiss-swollen lips. She was warm and safe. The warmth came, Jo acknowledged, not so much from the covers tucked around her shoulders but from the heat radiating from the body beside hers. The feeling of safety came not from being inside a roof and four walls but from being enclosed within two strong, masculine arms. Dismissing the weather as not worth consideration, Jo snuggled closer to Brett's body, luxuriating in the delicious sensation of his nakedness against her own.

God, he was wonderful! A grin tugged at Jo's lips. *She* was wonderful too! She was a woman! Not merely a female, but a living, breathing, sexually responsive woman! Brett had proved it to her. Proved it in the most primitive way possible. He had made her his, figuratively as well as literally. Brett did not know it, and Jo prayed he never would, but with his possession of her he had earned himself a slave. Jo had been in love with him last night. This morning, what she felt for him came so close to adoration, it scared the wits out of her. Still, perhaps enslavement was worth the price for enlightment. All her fears and insecurities concerning her ability to respond physically to a man had been swept from her mind by the pulsating rush of sexual fulfillment.

Go to hell, Gary Devlin!

Jo gulped back a gurgle of laughter and snuggled still closer to Brett. She felt terrific! She felt fantastic! She felt . . . Jo compressed her lips to contain a fresh surge of laughter. She *felt* Brett's hand stroking slowly up the inside of her thigh!

"Are you trying to tell me something with all your wiggling around?" Brett's breath whispered over Jo's temple an instant before his tongue outlined the edge of her ear.

"I—I was just thinking how cold the wind sounds, and how warm it is in here," Jo explained, her breath catching as his hand found the apex of her thighs. The entrapped breath vibrated in her throat producing a tiny gasp when his long fingers began combing through the dark thicket.

"I have a feeling it's going to go from warm to red hot very quickly if you continue wiggling your fanny like that." Brett punctuated his assertion by stabbing the tip of his tongue into her ear.

Jo's tiny gasp matured into a deep-throated moan as Brett's fingers slid lower to explore the moist heat of her core. And it was heated! The realization was both a shock and a delight to her. She, JoAnne Lawrence, the woman who had believed herself incapable of responding physically to any man, had become meltingly hot by the simple process of snuggling closer to Brett's warm, naked body. She was ready for him! She was actually ready for him! To a sexually experienced woman that sudden arousal would not have come as a surprise. To Jo it seemed a miracle.

Go with the flow. The buzz phrase drifted through Jo's mind and, reacting to it, she moved her hips sensuously. Brett reacted to her movement by exploring the region in depth. Soft, inarticulate sounds she was barely aware of making tickling the back of her throat, Jo arched her body, instinctively inviting deeper penetration.

"You like that, do you?" Brett murmured into her ear.

"Yes!" Jo admitted between shallow gasps. "Oh, yes!"

"Then you might return the favor," he chided softly.

Return the favor? For an instant Jo's passion-clouded mind grappled with his request. What . . . Oh! Did Brett mean for her to . . . ? But, of course, what else could he mean? she thought fuzzily. Were men also turned on by having their bodies stroked and caressed? Brett answered the question for her in a low groan.

"Touch me, Jo! Please. You can't imagine how long I've ached for you to touch me."

Shyly, hesitantly, Jo lifted her hand and placed her palm against his chest. Then, slowly, she stroked, a growing sense of wonder widening her eyes at the smoothness of his skin. When her fingers brushed lightly over the flat male nipples she paused, a question rising to tantalize her mind. All too vividly Jo remembered the piercing pleasure she had experienced from the touch of Brett's lips to her breasts. Would Brett experience a similar reaction? Intrigued by the idea, Jo shifted her body around until she was positioned almost on top of him. With a soft sign, Brett obligingly made a half turn onto his back. Lowering her head, Jo dropped a string of delicate kisses across his chest. When her lips reached the tight nipple she hesitated and a shiver rippled through Brett's body.

"Jo, please, don't stop now!"

His hoarse, excitement-tinged groan encouraging her on, Jo closed her lips around the taut bud and laved it gently with her tongue. Amazingly, Brett gasped and actually writhed beneath her. His response had the strangest effect on Jo. She was suddenly filled with a heady sense of power. *She* could make him writhe in pleasure! How marvelous! At the same time, Jo recognized that her own sexual tension was increasing. She'd had no idea of how exciting making love to a man could be!

All timidity forgotten, Jo continued to explore Brett's body with her lips. By the time she dipped her tongue into his navel, Brett's breathing had a raspy, uneven sound and his hands moved restlessly over her upper arms and shoulders. All the while her lips dropped tiny kisses, her palms were absorbing the feel of his skin. At his navel she again hesitated briefly, then bravely skimmed her lips down the concave of his abdomen to a hair-rough thigh. Now Brett's hands were in her hair, stroking, tugging gently in a silent plea for her to bestow the ultimate caress.

Understanding immediately, Jo stilled for an instant. During that instant a minibattle raged. Could she? Did she want to? No! Yes! Damn it! Was she not a woman after all? Brett's hips thrust provocatively. The feeling of power washed over her again. Swiftly, before she could change her mind, Jo bent her head, sank her fingertips into his hard buttocks, and granted his mute request. Brett's low groan of intense pleasure urging her on, Jo caressed him gently, finding to her amazement that the more pleasure she gave him, the more she received herself.

Brett withstood Jo's ministrations for several moments, then he grasped her shoulders and growled softly, "Come up here and kiss my mouth, water baby, I want to feel your body covering mine."

Slowly, tormentingly, pausing at strategic spots to kiss teasingly, Jo sinuously slid up his body, unashamedly reveling in Brett's raspingly uttered words of praise.

"You're fantastic, do you know that? You've made me want you so badly I'm trembling all over." Then, when her mouth lightly touched his: "God! The scent of you! The feel of you! The taste of you!"

168

Digging his fingers into her hair, he pulled her head to his, his mouth taking hers hungrily, his tongue a hot spear branding her mouth as his own. Brett's lips locked onto hers, he grasped her by the hips and lifted her up, then settled her onto his body, branding her again with another spear.

Gasping aloud at the depth of his penetration, Jo let her head drop back and began to move her body in a slow, undulating motion.

"Yes, Yes," Brett crooned unevenly. "Perfect. God! You're perfect."

The lazy tempo was maintained for several minutes during which Jo felt the tension twisting into a wildness inside. She moaned as Brett's hands stroked lovingly over her tautly arched neck to her shoulders and then to her aching breasts before settling firmly on her hips. Slowly, directing her with his hands, Brett increased the tempo, his own body arching to meet hers. His action fed the wildness growing in her, and, grasping his wrists with her hands, Jo accelerated the tempo to a frenzied crescendo. Brett exploded under her. There was no holding back for him this time. Jo sensed his loss of control and gloried in the realization of having been the instrument of his loss. Reality receding, Jo had the uncanny sensation of soaring through space, and then simultaneously they went crashing through the time barrier. For sweet, pulsating seconds time stood still while their entire beings experienced the highest of the highs. Then, slowly, gently, they drifted back to earth together.

Jo opened her eyes to the awareness of her head resting on Brett's shoulder, her face pressed to the curve of his neck. In gratitude and unspoken love she placed a kiss on his moist skin. Brett's arms tightened around her momentarily, then relaxed.

"Are you uncomfortable, darling?"

Wanting to lock the sound of it in her mind and heart, Jo closed her eyes at the endearment. Uncomfortable? How could she possibly tell him that, at this moment, she desired nothing more than to remain coupled to him forever? Dreamily, she murmured something unintelligible and allowed him to disengage her body from his.

"Are you going to sleep again?" Brett teased, lightly caressing her thighs with one hand.

"I hope so," Jo murmured drowsily, lifting a lazy hand to cover a yawn.

"Self-indulgent wench," Brett chided. "I was hoping you'd come with me."

"With you?" Jo forced her heavy eyelids up. "Where are you going?"

"I thought I'd run on the beach." That quirky smile twitched his lips. "That is, after I've rested a bit. You do take the starch out of a man."

"Run on the beach!" Jo exclaimed, choosing to ignore the double meaning attached to his assertion. "Are you mad? It's cold out there! And windy! Don't you hear it screaming around the building?"

"I'd have to be stone deaf not to." He laughed. "I'm not afraid of the wind."

"I'm not either," Jo assured him around another yawn. "But that doesn't mean I want to run in it. Good night, Brett."

Brett's laughter grew stronger. "But it's morning, honey. See? It's broad daylight."

Casting a narrowed glance at the window, Jo obligingly observed the broad daylight, then she pulled the covers up to her chin and closed her eyes. "So it is," she agreed. "Good night, Brett." Inside her mind, Jo was savoring the taste of his "honey."

"It *is* cold out there." The statement was made through lips that moved against Jo's ear. "And you *are* so nice and warm." His hand wove an erotic pattern up her thigh to cup the tightly curled thicket. "Wonderfully warm." With his other hand Brett drew her head back into the curve of his neck. "Maybe I'll sleep awhile with you. *Then* I'll run on the beach."

The second time Jo woke that morning she noticed three things at once. The wind had died down; the sun was shining brightly; and she was alone in the bed. Apparently Brett had decided to run on the beach. In Jo's opinion, anybody who would even consider running on the beach, or anywhere else, on a cold December morning was slightly animal crackers, but, she thought shrugging, each to his own brand of self-torture. For Jo, the torture would come in the form of the first meal of the day. Jo was a lousy cook. She could knit like a dream, needles clicking away at a dizzying rate of speed while whipping up anything from a simple scarf to a full-length coat, but turn her loose in the kitchen and within minutes it was a disaster area.

After a warm, revitalizing shower, Jo tugged skin-tight jeans over her slender hips and pulled a thigh-length, baggy sweatshirt over her head, then winced as she stroked a brush through her mass of tangled hair. When the dark mop had been beaten into submission, Jo tossed the brush aside and padded barefoot out of the bedroom. She was standing at the kitchen sink, filling the electric percolator with cold water, when Brett swung into the apartment, out of breath, sweaty, and looking sexy as hell in a navy-and-white jogging suit.

"Hi!" he panted, flashing her an ice-melting grin. "If you give me ten minutes to jump in and out of the shower, I'll prepare brunch." Not waiting for a response, he loped across the living room and disappeared down the short hall to the bedroom.

Brunch yet! Jo smiled as she scooped coffee into the small basket. All the while she'd been showering, one worry had nagged at her mind: What would Brett's attitude toward her be now? The morning after! His spontaneous greeting and easy grin had laid that particular worry to rest. Oh, there were other worries and considerations Jo realized she'd eventually have to deal with, but they could wait until after she had fortified herself with food.

As if he'd timed it, Brett strode into the kitchen as the coffee-pot gurgled its last perk. Running a swift, encompassing glance over his lean frame, Jo decided he looked even sexier in tight, brushed denim jeans and a white velour pullover than he had in

171

the jogging outfit. Without hesitation, Brett drew her into his arms.

"Now I can wish you a proper good morning," he said, lowering his head to hers.

Brett's lips touched hers gently, almost tentatively, until he felt her part her lips in response, then his kiss deepened, although not in demand, but more like a learning process. Wanting to learn more herself, Jo put every ounce of herself into the meeting of mouths. When Brett drew back to gaze down at her, his eyes shimmering like silver, Jo promptly decided she'd adore being wished a proper good morning in that fashion every morning for the rest of her life. Smothering a sigh of regret for the impossibility of foolish dreams, she smiled tremulously back at him.

"How are you feeling?" The smile changed into a frown as Brett examined Jo's upturned face minutely. "When you left the office last week, you looked about ready to unravel. Are you feeling any better . . . now?"

Jo did not miss Brett's deliberate hesitation before the word now, and she knew he meant right now, since the night they'd spent together. Should she take a chance and tell him how deeply his lovemaking had affected her? Could she bare her soul to this man? Don't be a complete fool, the voice of cool logic warned scathingly. Remember what happened the last time you spoke of your feelings to a man. Staring up at Brett, Jo could actually hear the echo of Gary's taunting gibes. Gary's ridicule had been hard enough to take; somehow Jo knew she would not be able to bear it from Brett. No, Jo cautioned herself, play it cagy, play it down, but for God's sake, play it safe!

"I'm feeling much better." Jo avoided the word now. "I simply needed some rest . . . as I told you last week."

Brett's sigh revealed to Jo how disappointing her reply had been. Like all men, she thought in sudden irritation, he wanted his ego stroked! Well, damn it, women had egos too! And she sure hadn't heard any soul baring from him!

"If you're feeling so much better," Brett chided gently, "why are you scowling at me in exactly the same way you were last week?"

"I'm hungry." Jo blurted the first excuse that came to mind. "I thought you said you were going to make brunch?"

From his expression, it was obvious that Brett didn't buy her disclaimer. But, fortunately, it immediately became obvious he was not going to push the issue. His grin back in place, if a trifle strained, he released her and stepped back.

"Okay, we'll leave it for now." A definite warning underlined his light tone. "Have you got anything interesting in the fridge?" Without waiting for a reply, he strode to the almond-toned appliance.

"I have the usual breakfast foods, eggs, bacon, juice," Jo enumerated, following him.

"Then I guess that will have to do." Brett sighed dramatically. "How about a bacon omelet? You wouldn't happen to have a green pepper and an onion, would you?"

Jo did, and the resultant meal was delicious. As she polished off the last bite of toast, Jo pondered on the hows and whys of Brett's culinary skill. He had whipped the meal together with the panache of a professional chef—making as many dishes dirty in the bargain. How had he learned to cook like that? And, more important, why? Brett had grown up in the proverbial lap of luxury. Why would anyone born to a family of wealth learn to cook? Especially a male? And this particular male didn't merely cook, he created!

All of a sudden Jo felt very uncomfortable. Musing on the circumstances of Brett's culinary expertise brought home the realization of how very little she knew about him. Brett was still virtually a stranger to her, and she had shared his bed! What must he think of her? Had she been merely a convenient, easy lay? A cold shudder rippled along Jo's spine. Unable to look at him, she lifted her cup and stared into her coffee. Oh, God! Jo thought bleakly. What had she let herself in for here? Loving

Brett as she now did, Jo felt sick at the idea of him using her simply to assuage a physical need.

"Were you planning to do anything today?" Brett's quiet voice shattered Jo's introspection.

"No." Jo forced herself to look at him. "There really isn't much to do in a resort town in December." Now she forced herself to smile. "I didn't come here to *do* anything. Remember? I came here to rest."

Jo's smile disintegrated at the memory of why she had needed to get away from everything. First there had been that disheartening visit home for Thanksgiving. Then, already feeling depressed, she had gone to Vermont, only to have Casey confirm what she had suspected about Brett and Marsha. And still, knowing they had been lovers before they came back to New York, she had not only not repulsed him, she had welcomed him into her bed, and herself! In the cold light of a winter morning, Jo told herself that loving Brett was no excuse for her self-indulgence. If she suffered later she had only herself to blame. But she could not think of it now, not with him sitting opposite her, frowning at her lengthy silence. Shaking herself out of her blue funk, Jo rose and began clearing the table, deciding she'd have to think it all through later.

"What's wrong?" Brett's fingers closed around Jo's wrist as she reached for his plate. "Why are you so quiet?"

"I'm always quiet." Jo made a feeble attempt at a smile. "Didn't you know? I have always been quiet. It comes from being an only child and being alone so much." She was babbling, she *knew* she was babbling, but Jo hoped that by expanding on his second question, she could avoid answering the first one.

"You're not alone now." Brett's tone implied a lot more than his flat statement. Jo sensed that he was telling her something that, in her emotionally confused mind, she simply wasn't hearing. Brett didn't give her time to ponder on his meaning. "You do realize I'm going to stay here with you, don't you? That is, at least through the twenty-third." The twenty-third was two days away. Two very short days, Jo thought, sighing and lowering her eyes to the long fingers lightly clasping her wrist. Two days in which to soak up the sight of him, the feel of him, and then he'd be gone until the next time he decided to add spice to his sexual life by changing bed partners. The thought hurt so badly Jo closed her eyes, blocking out the vision of implied imprisonment. An instant later Jo's eyes flew wide at Brett's soft pronouncement. "When I leave I'm taking you with me."

"Taking me with you?" Jo blurted, rather stupidly, she was sure. "Where?"

"To the farm." Brett's lips tightened, as if in anger. "In Florida."

"But I can't go . . . " Jo began in protest.

"Yes, you can. And you will." Brett's tone indicated there'd be no arguing over the matter. "I was instructed to, and this is an exact quote, 'Bring her with you.' "

"By whom?" Although she was positive the answer would be Wolf, Jo asked anyway. Wolf was the only person who knew her family situation. Thus Brett's answer came as a complete surprise.

"By Madam President, herself."

"Your mother!"

"The one and only," Brett concurred softly.

"But why?" Oh, God, had Wolf discussed her with his mother? And, in turn, had his mother taken pity on her? Jo felt sick. And more than a little angry. Damn it, she didn't want or need pity!

"Who knows what motivates the great minds?" Brett replied in a careless tone that was belied by the glitter of speculation in his eyes. It was patently obvious to Jo that something about his mother's invitation had angered Brett too. The realization reinforced her decision not to go, and, shaking her head sharply, she told him so.

"I won't go with you."

Jo was totally unprepared for the swiftness of Brett's reaction to her refusal to accompany him south. Rising abruptly to his feet, he gave a sharp tug on her wrist that impelled her against his hard chest. Releasing her wrist, he imprisoned her within his arms, crushing her soft breasts to the rock hardness of him.

"You will go with me," Brett contradicted with soft menace. "When I leave here on the twenty-third, and when I fly south on the twenty-fourth." Releasing her as abruptly as he'd caught her to him, he said briskly, "Now, let's get this mess cleaned up." His lips curved into a wickedly alluring smile. "I want to go back to bed."

"You can go straight to hell!" Really angry now, Jo planted her balled fists onto her slim hips. Who the hell did he think he was talking to . . . the upstairs maid? Was there an upstairs maid? Jo shrugged the irrelevant thought aside. Damn him! One night in the sack and he acted as if he owned her! Well, Madam President's fair-haired boy was about to learn that Jo Lawrence would not be owned . . . by anyone! She might love him but she'd be damned if she'd pander to him! She had learned the folly of pandering to a man the hard way. Never, never again, she vowed. "If you're feeling the need to work off the enormous breakfast you consumed," Jo said scathingly, "go beat your feet on the beach again." Her nastily voiced advice was followed by a loud gasp as she was immediately hauled into his arms.

"Oh, but I'd much prefer working off my 'enormous' meal by beating my body against yours," Brett purred with deliberate crudity. "Are you going to fight me?" One pale eyebrow arched elegantly. "Make me subdue you?" His lips twitched into a devilish smile. "How very intriguing."

"Let me go, Brett," Jo gritted warningly. "You'll get nothing from me by force." Jo groaned silently. If he didn't release her at once she'd be a goner! Already the melting process had begun, and she could feel the effects in the lower part of her body. Oh, God! Maybe the transition from female to woman had not been so wonderful after all. She was vulnerable to him now, much too vulnerable.

"Force!" Brett exclaimed on a soft burst of laughter. "Oh, honey, there'll be no need for me to use force." His liquid silver gaze seared her face. "Whether you realize it or not, your eyes are soft with desire. Your lips are parted, ready for mine. And" —his hands slid down her back to cup her derriere—"your hips are moving against mine very invitingly." Slowly, inexorably, he drew her against the hardness of his thighs and aroused manhood. "I accept your invitation," he murmured lowering his head. "Just as you are going to accept my mother's."

Jo wanted to scream a denial, and she would have if Brett's mouth had not taken hers so sweetly. Damn him, she sighed, mingling her breath with his. Damn him for being the only man able to ignite her physical fire! Fully cognizant of what she was doing, hating and loving it at one and the same time, Jo coiled her arms around Brett's strong neck and gave herself up to the moment.

The moment stretched into most of the afternoon! By the time Brett allowed Jo to drift into sleep, she was completely fulfilled and thoroughly exhausted. This man, she thought groggily, swiftly losing her hold on consciousness, has more than enough stamina to accommodate two women! Jo should have been upset by the observation, and she would have been if she had not drifted so far along the path to slumber.

The third time Jo woke it was to an oddly familiar stillness that was in no way connected to the fact that she was alone in the bed. Frowning as her mind groped for an explanation, Jo stared at the darkened bedroom window. A faint splat against the pane brought instant recognition. It was snowing!

Snow. Jo's pulses leaped with a ray of hope. If it were to snow long enough, and hard enough, maybe she and Brett would be stranded through Christmas! Savoring the possibility for more reasons than she cared to examine too closely, Jo snuggled deeper under the covers. She really should get up, she supposed vaguely. But then, she yawned, why should she? She was here to rest, wasn't she? And she certainly hadn't had a great amount of rest since Brett's arrival. The man was a sexual dynamo!

Groaning aloud, Jo rolled onto her side. Oh, damn! Jo was reminded of the last observation she'd made about him before falling asleep. Damn! Damn! Damn! Why had she gone to Vermont? Why had she gone home for Thanksgiving? Why had she ever been born? She didn't want to think about Vermont. She didn't want to think about Thanksgiving. She didn't want to think, period. The room was too quiet. Quiet was inductive to contemplation. Sighing in defeat, Jo flopped back onto her back and let memory have its way.

On arriving in Brookhaven, the small southeastern Pennsylvania town Jo had grown up in, she had been greeted warmly, if separately, by her parents. The evening before Thanksgiving had gone rather smoothly, Jo thought. But then, of course, there were church services to attend and a united false front to maintain for the benefit of her parents' fellow church members. Thanksgiving morning had not been too bad either, as her father had gone hunting, which put her mother into a good mood. That is, except for the note Jo's father had left on the kitchen table for her.

Her eyes beginning to sting, Jo lowered her lids and bit on her lip. If she lived forever she would never forget that note! How very like her father it had been, and all over an early phone call from Marybeth, a friend of Jo's from their high school days. He'd written:

My dear successful and independent daughter,
Marybeth will call you about nine thirty. She called earlier (would you believe seven thirty?) but I told her that, like most normal people on a holiday, you were still in bed. As you were still asleep, you could not answer the phone. Inasmuch as you could not answer the phone, Marybeth could

178

not talk to you. I told her to call again somewhere in the neighborhood of nine thirty, because I doubted you'd be up much before then. If you were to sleep till ten, and Marybeth calls at nine thirty, she still would not be able to speak to you. Anyway, if the phone rings at nine thirty, and you are awake to hear it, it will probably be Marybeth. Happy Thanksgiving, darling,

Daddy

At first Jo had laughed at the note, another in a long line of similar, whimsical missives. And then she had cried, because he was so dear and trying so hard to appear lighthearted in the face of his unhappiness. As fate would have it, her mother had entered the kitchen as Jo was wiping the tears from her cheeks. In response to her mother's concern over her tears, Jo had silently handed her the note. After skimming the lines, her mother had smiled bitterly.

"All men can be charming when it suits their purposes," Ellen Lawrence said dryly.

"Oh, Mother." Jo sighed, beginning to feel the familiar tightness in her stomach that usually appeared on her visits home. "Why do you always use that tone of voice when talking about Daddy?"

"Because he's a man," Ellen retorted. "I would have thought your experience with Gary Devlin would have taught you that they're all the same. They want one thing from a woman, then, once they get what they want, they no longer want her."

Jo remained perfectly still in hopes that her mother would expound on her subject. To date, this outburst was the closest Ellen had come to explaining the problem between herself and her husband, Mark.

"You'd do better to concentrate on your career," Ellen went on. "And forget the myth about finding happiness with a man. That kind of happiness exists only in fairy tales."

179

Jo knew from her mother's flat tone that the subject was now closed, and she had learned nothing of why she had always felt that she was hovering in the demarcation zone between opposing forces.

As usual, when Jo returned to New York the day after Thanksgiving, she felt depressed and vaguely responsible for the failure of her parents' marriage. Intellectually Jo knew she was in no way at fault, just as she knew, intellectually, she was not a cold, unresponsive woman like her mother. Lord, hadn't she lain awake night after night aching for the touch of one particular man? Somehow knowing something intellectually did not erase the scars carried over from childhood.

Jo sniffed in the silence of the bedroom. Then, as if her visit home hadn't been depressing enough, she had received that call from Casey Delheny! Why the hell hadn't she followed her first impulse and sent *her* assistant up to Vermont? Because she'd been hoping for a mental diversion, Jo derided herself. What she had found had had more the effect of a blow to the solar plexus. Oh, the technical problem regarding the application of one of Casey's designer's ideas to the existing plumbing plans had been relatively easy to unwrinkle. Relating to what Casey had confided to her over one too many drinks the night before Jo was due to return to New York was infinitely more difficult to handle.

"Are Brett and Marsha still together?" Casey had asked Jo morosely, swallowing almost half of her third martini.

"Together?" Jo had prompted softly, telling herself Casey, unhappy because of her lengthy separation from Sean, who was still in the Poconos, was talking through a gin-and-vermouth haze.

"Yes, you know, like in bed. That kind of together." Raising her glass, Casey gulped down the remainder of her drink. "The kind of together Sean and I have been doing damn little of lately." Waving her glass in the air, Casey indicated to their waiter that she wanted another drink. Tilting her head, she ran an assessing glance over Jo. "You know, I do believe Brett's even

180

more of a live wire than Wolf is." She laughed insinuatingly. "Businesswise *and* otherwise. I swear, he and Marsha spent every night together locked inside his room. Yet he was hard at work bright and early every morning."

Jo had returned to New York more depressed than before, even though she had suspected an affair between Brett and Marsha since he'd called her and as much as ordered her to find an apartment for Marsha. Walking into her office the morning she returned to find that insultingly terse note ordering her to "get in here" had been the absolute last straw for Jo. Suddenly bone weary, she had gone to Brett's office in a cold rage, prepared to resign if he refused her request for a leave of absence. She had to get away, to think and to rest.

Circles, circles, circles. Would this mental merry-go-round never end? Jo sighed. Lord, she was tired of her own thoughts! How many times must she plow over the same row before she found ground fertile enough to sprout some answers? Were there any answers? Jo moved restlessly between the tangled sheets, enjoying the sensuous feel of the fine percale against her naked skin. A smile of physical contentment softened the taut line of her mouth. Brett had given her the answer to one question, perhaps the most important one. Her initial response to him had been an outright revelation! Always before, with Gary, she had gone positively rigid the moment he began to enter. But then the moment of penetration had always come mere minutes after he had drawn her to him. Now, after experiencing Brett's lovemaking and the infinite care he took to arouse her body to the point of readiness that equaled his own, Jo realizied that Gary had only been interested in self-gratification, not mutual satisfaction. In the expertise stakes, one might say that Brett crossed the wire before Gary ever left the gate.

The rather silly analogy amused Jo. Pushing back the covers with one hand, Jo lifted her other hand to smother a giggle. Jumping off the bed, she shook her head in amazement; she never giggled! Giggling was strictly for teenage girls, usually in connec-

181

tion with teenage boys! Telling herself her gray matter was beginning to flake, Jo grabbed up her robe and strolled to the bathroom.

Standing under the stinging-hot shower spray, Jo came to terms with what she had already decided subconsciously. She would accept whatever Brett offered her of himself for as long as he offered it.

Turning around, she dropped her head to allow the hot spray to massage the tension out of the muscles in the back of her neck. Her decision was probably not a very intelligent one, Jo mused, sighing blissfully as the jet fingers reduced her muscles to rubber. I want him, she argued in her own defense, even if I have to share him. An image of Marsha Wenger rose to torment Jo's mind, and she gritted her teeth in determination. Bump Marsha Wenger! Brett's here now, with me, and I'll hang on to him for all I'm worth, even if it means going to Florida with him. And while I'm there, I just might strangle that blabbermouth Wolfgang Renninger!

Applying the same sharp intellect that had earned her the position of assistant to Wolf, Jo ruthlessly refused to use the old feminine cop-out of not being able to live without Brett. She could survive very well, if not too comfortably, without him and she knew it. Then again, why should she? At this moment in her life she was deeply in love, and she was Brett's, mind, body, and soul. When her time with him was over, she would accept the hand dealt to her without a wince. What the hell! Jo shrugged, oddly cold within the cascading hot water. She didn't want commitment either. Did she? Of course not, she assured herself bracingly. Jo was so consumed with her own rationalizing, she didn't hear the door being opened or feel a draft when the shower curtain was inched aside.

"Have you taken to sleeping in the shower now too, water baby?"

With a gasp that grew into a gurgle, due to water in the mouth,

Jo flung her head back to glare at Brett. "Are you trying to drown me?" she sputtered indignantly.

"I don't have to," Brett drawled dryly, unmindful of his shirt as he reached in to turn the water off. "You're doing a pretty good job of it yourself." Curling a now soaking wet arm around Jo's waist, he lifted her off her feet. "Out, water baby, before you wash yourself down the drain."

"Brett!" Jo protested his handling of her, although she didn't struggle. Only a complete idiot would take the chance of slipping out of one arm to land in a painful heap on the hard floor of a bathtub! "I was not falling asleep! I was letting the hot water work the ache out of my muscles!" Jo was so annoyed she was unaware of exactly what she was admitting to. As Brett set her carefully onto the fluffy bath mat, Jo shrugged off his arm. "And I wish you'd stop calling me that ridiculous name!"

"But I like that ridiculous name." Brett grinned. "I also like to look at you when you're all wet and slippery." The grin grew up to be a leer. "You are one sexy baby when you're wet." Bending to her, he licked a drop of water from the tip of her breast. "Hmmm . . . nectar," he murmured throatily, curling his tongue around the swiftly hardening bud before, very gently, closing his teeth on it. "And ambrosia." He passed judgment on the taste of her.

"You're positively mad!" Jo gasped, unconsciously arching her back to give him better access to his point of interest. "Oh, Brett . . . what are you doing?" Jo knew full well what he was doing; she could feel the results of his suckling lips through the nerve endings in her loins.

"You don't know?" Brett teased, skimming his tongue across her body from one breast tip to the other. "Maybe I'm not doing it right." Before her startled eyes, he dropped to his knees. "I guess I need a lot more practice. But first, I think I'll get rid of this sopping shirt." Straightening, he whipped the garment up his body and over his head, tossing it aside carelessly. It landed in the bathtub with a soft plop that neither he nor Jo heard.

Then, his hands clasping her lightly around her rib cage, his eyes watching hers, Brett enclosed one nipple inside his mouth.

It was the most incredibly erotic action Jo could imagine, Brett watching her, while she watched him make lover to her body! Lightheaded, feeling her knees begin to buckle, Jo grasped Brett's shoulders to keep from falling, a purring moan tickling the back of her throat.

"Ah . . . perhaps I am doing it right." He laughed softly. Slowly, tantalizingly, he lavished attention on her midsection, stringing moist kisses down to her navel. When he dipped the tip of his tongue into the indentation, Jo shuddered and gasped his name aloud. "You're trembling," he breathed against the damp skin stretched tautly over her abdomen. "From the cold outside, I wonder, or the heat inside?"

Quickly losing touch with reality, Jo sagged against him and, at the feel of his tongue dancing around the edge of her delta triangle, she lost all control of her legs and sank to the floor before him. It was a short, fast trip from her knees to her back. The soft fibers of the bath mat caressed Jo's spine while the prickly hair on Brett's chest caressed her breasts.

With her feet flat on the floor, and her knees bent and angled out, Jo should have been uncomfortable. She wasn't. Even the chafing sensation of Brett's jean-clan thighs against the inside of her own was more exciting than abrading. The realization of his arousal as he arched his body into hers was more exciting still. Brett's hands captured Jo's breasts as his mouth captured her lips. The assault on her senses was total. Spearing her tongue into his mouth, Jo dug her nails into his shoulders, glorying in the grunt of pleasure that exploded from his throat as he thrust his hips in reaction.

"I've got to get out of these damn jeans." He groaned, heaving himself up and away from her with obvious reluctance. "Stay warm for me, babe," he pleaded hoarsely, his hands fumbling with the belt buckle.

In fact, he didn't get completely out of the jeans. As Brett was about to lever himself to his feet, Jo called his name softly, beguilingly. The jeans, along with the silky very-brief briefs he wore underneath them, were forgotten the moment they pooled around his knees. Whispering her name in a voice made rough with urgency, Brett filled Jo's body with his own.

The tension building inside Jo coiled tightly, and still more tightly, until, Brett's name filling her mind in an endless scream and reverberating in the tiled room like an arching whimper, it snapped, springing her into near oblivion where she was conscious only of the ecstasy shuddering through her and the sound of her own hoarsely cried name beating against her eardrums.

Jo surfaced from the mind-blanketing fog of sensuality to the awareness of the crushing weight of Brett's collapsed body on hers and the soothing sensation of his hand stroking her hip. She was still wet, only now the moisture that sheened her body was the natural result of strenuous physical activity. Raising a lazily limp hand, she smoothed her palm down his equally slick back, her sensitized skin monitoring the responsive shiver that followed the path from shoulder to waist.

"God! You are one exciting woman," Brett rasped through uneven breaths, the tip of his tongue testing the saltiness of her skin. "I feel as though I've been pulled through the wringer and hung out to dry."

"Is that good?" Jo murmured, gliding her hand up his back to tangle her fingers in his sweat-dampened hair.

"Extremely good. In fact, it's what all the noise has been about all these many centuries." Brett laughed softly. "What do the French call it? The little death, or some such?"

"Some such." Jo sighed contentedly. "It must be true for I feel a little dead right now."

Brett's bark of delighted laughter pried her heavy eyelids up, and Jo stared, bemused, into his laughing face. Oh, happy saints, he was handsome when he laughed like that, but then, he was handsome when he didn't laugh like that too. At that moment,

Jo knew she could refuse him nothing. Apparently, possibly because of the dreamy expression on her face, Brett knew it too.

"You'll stay here with me through the twenty-third?" Brett was all seriousness now.

"Yes." Jo smiled as she felt his chest expand, then depress on a sigh of relief.

"And you'll go with me when I fly south on the twenty-fourth?" His chest expanded again, then became still as he held his breath.

"Yes." Jo's smile deepened as his sharply released breath feathered her cheek. Why ruin the effect by telling him she had decided to go with him before his exhausting inducement?

"Hmmm . . . have I told you you're beautiful?" Brett nibbled gently along Jo's jawline.

"Not nearly enough." Jo laughed as he nipped on her chin in tender punishment.

"And did I thank you for wringing me out so deliciously?" He teased her lips apart with his tongue.

"I think your wringing was more than enough thanks." Jo admitted to her own intense pleasure in his body.

"Do you suppose we could manage to drag our two wrung-out bodies into the shower?" Brett's eyes were silver bright in appreciation of her candid reply.

"I suppose we better had," Jo mimicked his heavily laid on drawl. "Because if I don't get up very soon, the fibers of this bath mat are going to be imbedded in my back, and your chest hair will be imbedded in my front."

Jo felt the expulsion of air into her mouth a millisecond before she heard his shout of laughter. Displaying what she considered a disgusting amount of energy, Brett eased his body carefully from hers, then sprang agilely to his feet. His shoulders still quaking with laughter, he kicked his legs free of jeans and briefs before bending to help her up. When Jo winced at the twinge of pain the sudden exertion caused in her thighs, Brett grinned wickedly.

"All that standing under a hot shower to ease overworked muscles for nothing," he commiserated falsely, making her aware now of what she had unconsciously admitted to him earlier. "But don't fret, darling. If the hot water doesn't work this time, just keep in mind what the physical fitness enthusiasts claim." Afraid to ask, Jo arched a delicately winged brow at him. "Why, that regular workouts will keep the muscles from tightening up." His grin telegraphed the punchline. "And I intend to work those muscles very regularly."

For two days Jo basked in the light of Brett's lovemaking and approval. And for two days she ate better than she had since leaving home at age nineteen. Brett did all the cooking. Jo did all the cleaning up. Personally, she thought she was getting the better of the bargain. In bed, Brett was demanding but gently so and, with his expert guidance, Jo emerged from behind her psychological wall of inhibitions. Never had she felt so free, so light, so at ease in the company of a man. Unselfconsciously, she teased him, sometimes dryly, other times wickedly. Brett, laughing often, responded in kind, leaving no doubt that he was enjoying himself every bit as much as she was.

Nervous apprehension began eating at Jo as the purring Porsche entered New York City. What would she find on arrival at the farm in Florida, besides a houseful of Renningers? Why had Brett's mother invited her there on a traditionally family-oriented holiday? Had Wolf related to his mother Jo's less-than-happy family situation? And if Wolf had turned blabbermouth, why? He's probably getting bored from inactivity, Jo answered her own question. Intermingled with the whys revolving in her mind was one recurring assertion. She did not want to go to Florida.

She was going to Florida. Jo examined the thought as the plane soared into the bright winter sunlight the following afternoon. She had coaxed and wheedled and pleaded to no avail the night before. Brett had remained adamant. Oh, he had loved being coaxed, and wheedled, and pleaded with, and he laughingly admitted it, but he had remained adamant none the less.

Strangely, Brett had grown tense during the drive to the airport and had barely spoken to her since he'd buckled her into her seat belt. Now, sitting stiffly in her seat, Jo studied his rigid profile wondering what emotional tick had burrowed into his craw. He looked, she finally decided, like a man set in his determination to do a particularly unpleasant duty.

Trying to relax, Jo closed her eyes to the sight of Brett's harshly set features and her mind to futile speculation. But one thought persisted. Was Brett tired of her already? It was not a thought conducive to in-flight relaxation.

Relaxation in the form of sleep snuck up on Jo while she wasn't looking. She woke to the mild jolt of the wheels touching down and the realization that her seat belt had been fastened for her. Brett was busy stuffing papers into a large attache case and ignoring the fact that she sat beside him. The moment the plane came to a stop he stood up, only then deigning to notice her.

"I think you'll be warm enough if you drape this over your shoulders." Brett held up the golden-beige cashmere thigh-length coat Jo had worn onto the plane. "The pilot said the temperature is in the low fifties."

How wonderful, Jo thought wryly, turning her head to glance out the small window. He doesn't say one word from New York to Florida, then he gives me a weather report! As she could discern nothing in the darkness except the blue-tinged lights delineating the runway of the small, private landing field, Jo turned back to face him again. Brett's features still gave the impression of having been carved in granite. As she rose to her feet, hands smoothing the matching cashmere skirt she was wearing, Jo sighed tiredly. What the devil was bugging Brett, anyway? If he was bored with her company, why had he insisted she accompany him? For one mad second Jo was tempted to confront him with the question, then, mercifully, the madness subsided. In all honesty, Jo admitted to herself that she was afraid of what his answer would be. For all her self-assurances of a few days earlier that she would accept whatever Brett offered of himself for however long he offered it, she was beginning to live in fear of him walking away from her.

Standing mutely before Brett in the narrow aisle, Jo closed her eyes at the brief touch of his hands on her shoulders as he draped her coat over the emerald-green silk blouse she was wearing. How had it happened so quickly? How could it be that within a period of four days she knew that losing Brett would be as painful to her as losing a vital part of herself? Her throat closing in panic at the mere thought of his rejection of her, Jo preceded Brett to the door on legs suddenly unsteady.

The mild early-evening air felt balmy after the biting cold of New York, yet Jo wished herself back along the coast of Ocean City. The snow she had hoped would continue for days had lasted less than an hour but the wind had been blowing steadily, nipping at exposed cheeks and noses right up until they had boarded the small, sleek private jet.

On the ground, Jo could see little more than she'd viewed from the plane's window. Other than the lights positioned on the roof of the low building she assumed was a hangar, the surrounding area was as black as the inside of a leather glove. As Brett, his hand at her elbow, escorted her over the uneven ground, Jo began to discern the outline of a long vehicle as their destination. As they approached the car Jo saw a man standing beside it. When they were within three feet of him, he swung the back door open.

"Evenin', Mr. Brett," the man greeted laconically.

"Hello, Josh," Brett replied in the most civil tone Jo had heard from him in hours. "The mild weather feels good after the cold up north." Brett grinned, handing Jo inside the roomy backseat of what she could now see was a black Cadillac limousine.

"Gunna rain," Josh replied with the implied wisdom of a native.

"Perhaps you're right." Brett shrugged. "But it feels good just the same," he tacked on, settling his long frame beside Jo on the plush seat as their bags were loaded into the trunk.

"Wouldn't know, never been up north," Josh grunted before closing the door smartly.

As the car rolled smoothly onto a blacktop secondary road, Brett sliced a glance at Jo. A glance Jo felt all the way down to her toes.

"Are you comfortable?"

What would he say if I said no? Jo wondered. Brett's behavior in combination with her nervousness was making her irritable.

"Yes." How could one not be comfortable enscounced in the back of a luxurious car? she thought waspishly. "Is it very far to the farm?"

"No. Not far," Brett replied slowly, then, in an oddly intense tone: "Are you getting anxious?"

"Anxious?" Jo frowned. Why did he sound so uptight? *He* didn't have to walk into a houseful of strangers. Thank heavens Wolf would be there! "A little," she admitted. "It will be wonderful to see Wolf again."

"Thanks."

Astounded at the bitter note in Brett's tone, Jo stared at his averted head for several minutes. What in the world? Why had he said "thanks"? And in that tone? Surely he hadn't taken her eagerness to see Wolf again as an insult to him in his capacity as replacement employer? Brett had simply never struck her as the type of man who'd need employee adoration—loyalty, yes, adoration, no. Brett was too confident of himself to feel petty jealousy over his brother's popularity. So then, why the bitter thanks? Shaking her head in utter confusion, Jo turned away to glance out the window. All she saw was total blackness created by a combination of night and smokey-gray windowpanes. Actually feeling Brett withdraw into himself, Jo stared at the blackness, biting her lip to keep from demanding he tell the driver to turn around and take her back to the airfield.

By the time the car glided to a stop in front of the house, Jo's nervousness had drowned in the flood of her rising anger. How dare Brett insist she come south with him only to ignore her? Damn him! She'd enjoy this unexpected, unwanted holiday if it killed her!

Stepping out of the car, Jo stifled a groan. The horse farm, Brett had called it. So, naturally, she'd been expecting a farmhouse! Or perhaps a ranch house, maybe. What Jo was looking at was an elegant structure that would have looked right at home dead center on any antebellum plantation! The house was illuminated by spotlights on the outside and a blaze of indoor lights from every window on the ground floor.

As they mounted the three wide steps to the front door, it was flung open by a small, wiry woman who looked to be in her late sixties. Hands on her hips, the woman waited until Jo and Brett had stepped over the threshold, then she lambasted Brett in the tone of a field marshal.

"Well, young man, it's about time you got here." Dark, still-young eyes snapped a quick encompassing glance over Brett. "Much later and you would have missed Christmas Eve altogether." Now the dark eyes did their snapping dance over Jo. "And you must be Ms. Lawrence?"

"Yes, this is Ms. Lawrence," Brett answered for Jo, who was busy staring at his smiling face in consternation. How could he leap the distance between bitterness and lightheartedness so effortlessly? Jo wondered. The sound of her name shattered her bemusement. "Jo, this is Elania Calaveri, housekeeper to my mother and friend to us all."

"How do you do?" Jo murmured, offering her hand.

"So so," Elania replied surprisingly. "My arthritis is acting up. It's going to rain."

Jo had to hold her breath to keep from laughing. Brett made no attempt at self-containment. Laughing aloud, he wrapped the small woman in his arms and hugged her tight. "Josh said the same thing, so I guess it must be true."

"Of course it's true," Elania scolded. "Josh is no fool." Disentangling herself from Brett's embrace, she held out her hand. "I'll take care of your coats and bags. The gang's in the living room." She frowned at Brett. "Your mother expected you before dark. Now get in there. Supper will be in an hour."

Throughout Elania's tirade, Jo had been glancing around the enormous hall, admiring the wide, curving staircase, aware of the murmur of voices issuing from behind two oversized doors to her left. Feeling somewhat as if she'd stepped back into history, Jo was barely aware of Brett slipping the coat from her shoulders to hand it to Elania.

"Do you like the house?" he asked softly, his gaze following hers as it touched a beautifully made parson's bench along one wall.

"Like it?" Jo breathed in awe. "It's absolutely beautiful." Dragging her enthralled gaze from the rich patina of the parquet floor, she looked at him in amazement. "You grew up in this house?"

"Off and on," Brett drawled. "When I wasn't in the house in Miami, or the original family homestead in Lancaster, Pennsylvania."

"Your family's from Pennsylvania?" Jo exclaimed.

"Yes," Brett frowned. "I assumed you knew that."

"But . . . how would I have . . . "

"Brett Renninger!" Elania interrupted impatiently. "Your mother is waiting. You can show Ms. Lawrence over the house after dinner."

"Yes, of course." As if he suddenly remembered he wasn't speaking to her, Brett's face closed up again. "Come along, Jo. Mother's waiting." An odd grimace fleetingly twisted his lips. "They are all waiting."

Shepherding Jo across the wide hall, Brett slid the two intricately carved doors apart and motioned for Jo to precede him into the living room. As she stepped through the portal Jo did not actually see the generously proportioned room, or the many exquisite pieces of furniture that adorned it, or even the people

192

who reposed on the delicately crafted, probably priceless, chairs and settees, although she was aware of all of them. From the moment of entrance, Jo's gaze homed in on the man sitting in a wheelchair, his left leg encased in a hip-to-toe cast that stuck out straight as a board in front of him, his left arm nestled close to his chest inside a sling, and his right arm outstretched, palm up, to her. As Jo had noted months ago, there was very little facial resemblance between the man beckoning to her and the man standing behind her. As if drawn by a magnet, Jo unhesitatingly crossed the room to Wolf Renninger.

"Ah . . . " Wolf's masculinely attractive voice revealed satisfaction. "There's my girl." When Jo placed her hand in his, Wolf's fingers tightened in reassurance. "How are you, Jo?"

"I'm . . . I'm fine, Wolf," Jo finally managed to whisper around the thickness in her throat. Blinking her eyes against a surge of hot moisture, she smiled tremulously at the man she loved almost as much as her father and easily as much as she would have an older brother. Wolf's year-round golden tan had faded somewhat from confinement to the house, and he had lost weight but, in essence, he was the same ruggedly attractive man upon whose broad shoulder Jo had cried—not once but several times. This tough-tender man was the only living person Jo had ever confided in about her mixed-up emotional state. And now, the realization flashed through Jo's mind, that state had progressed from unsettled to near chaos. Pushing all thoughts of herself aside, Jo studied him intently. "How are *you*?"

"As you see"—Wolf laughed, indicating his immobilized left side— "out of commission." A grin lit his face, revealing even white teeth. "But only temporarily. We'll talk later, Jo, but now—" His right hand covered a slim one resting on the arm of the chair. "You remember my wife, Micki?"

"Yes, of course." Jo's glance shifted to the woman sitting on Wolf's right. Jo had met Micki on several occasions and each time her original opinion that Micki was the perfect mate for Wolf had been reinforced. After two months in the Florida sunshine, Micki was tan, and healthy looking, and more lovely than ever. Jo's smile was soft and genuine. "You're looking very well, Mrs. Renninger," Jo complimented quietly. "The climate? Or your husband's improvement?"

"A little of both, I'm sure." Micki smiled serenely. "But more the latter than the former," she hastened to add when Wolf's dark brows drew together in a mock frown. "You're looking as beautiful as ever yourself," Micki returned Jo's compliment. Before Jo could respond, Wolf made a motion with his hand for Jo to turn around.

"And now, my dear." Wolf grinned. "Gird yourself to meet . . . " He paused for dramatic effect. "The Boss." Wolf's eyes telegraphed the message that he was fully aware of her nervousness. His smiled confided that he was also fully aware that Jo would never betray her nervousness. Her composure intact, Jo turned to face the president of Renninger Corporation, actually amused with the realization of how very well Wolf knew her. "Mother," Wolf said gently as Jo crossed the room to the fair, still-beautiful woman, "my assistant, JoAnne Lawrence."

"How do you do, Mrs. Renninger?" Jo murmured in a tone of complete self-containment. "Thank you for inviting me."

"The pleasure is ours, JoAnne," Violet Renninger assured Jo, then on a delightfully light laugh, she exclaimed, "We must use first names here! Do you realize there are three Mrs. Renningers in this room?" Waving her left hand, she said, "We'll take the introductions as we sit." Turning to her left, she said, "This is my second son, Eric."

Jo pivoted to face the man patiently standing next to his mother and felt the breath catch in her throat. Eric Renninger was the most incredibly handsome man Jo had ever seen. Dark-haired like Wolf, Eric had sapphire-blue eyes that sparkled with good humor and a singularly endearing smile.

"I feel I know you, JoAnne," he said warmly. "I've heard so much about you." Before Jo could ask the stock question, Eric answered it. "All of it good. So good, in fact, that, if ever either one of my brothers gives you as much as an uncomfortable moment, you call me. I'll have an office ready for you within twenty-four hours."

Feeling the tension being drawn out of her by these warm welcoming people, Jo laughed easily. "Thank you, Eric. I'll definitely keep your offer in mind."

Releasing the hand Jo had offered to him, Eric made a half turn to his left. "And this very pregant lady is my wife, Doris. Darling, the much raved-about JoAnne Lawrence."

Doris Renninger was Jo's second shock within minutes. Compared to Eric's heart-stopping good looks, Doris was actually plain—except for the most arrestingly lustrous eyes Jo had ever gazed into. Dark brown with gold highlights, Doris's eyes glowed with an inner beauty.

"How do you do, JoAnne?" Doris smiled. "I'm sure this must be an ordeal for you, so I'll simply keep the ball rolling. The woman sitting next to me is the baby of this clan. Diane, called Di by all."

Di, as fair as her mother and brother Brett, had the same attractive smile that Jo was beginning to think of as pure Renninger. "Hello, JoAnne," Di chirped. "Besides yourself, I am the only woman in this room who is not a Renninger. And all because of this good-looking dude standing by me. JoAnne, I'd like you to meet my husband, Hank Carlton."

"The pleasure is mine, JoAnne," Hank assured in a rich baritone, taking Jo's hand in a warm, solid grip.

"And mine. Thank you, Hank," Jo replied, beginning to feel a trifle groggy. At that moment, Violet revealed how astute she was.

"You must be parched by now," she said crisply. "Will you have a cocktail? Or a glass of wine?"

"White wine would be lovely." Jo turned to smile at her hostess. "Thank you." Relieved as she was, Jo knew there was more to come. "But where are the children?"

"Having their supper in the kitchen, fortunately." Violet's

softened eyes belied her last word. "They'll be descending on us soon enough. Hank, would you get JoAnne a glass of wine? And you, child, take that chair beside Wolf. Maybe *you* can keep him in line."

"Fat chance." Wolf chuckled, echoing Jo's exact thoughts.

"Now," Violet went on in an aggrieved mother tone, "where *is* Brett?"

"Right here, sir." Brett's tone was deliberately insolent and drew every eye in the room to where he lounged lazily yet elegantly against the closed double doors. "I didn't want to intrude on Jo's . . . ah . . . moment of excitement." As he spoke, he pushed his slender frame away from the doors and strolled into the room, a cynical smile playing on his chiseled lips.

Watching him, Jo felt a thrill, both of apprehension and appreciation. Why the sarcasm and cynicism? she wondered in confusion. While, at the same time, she accepted the fact that, although Brett wasn't quite as rugged looking as Wolf or as handsome as Eric, he was the only male she really cared to gaze upon. Sighing for her own seemingly hopeless love, Jo observed Brett's greetings to his family from beneath lowered lashes. As Brett made his way, hugging the women, shaking hands with the men, around the room, Jo registered the increased rate of her heartbeats. When Brett came to a stop in front of Micki, Jo felt a stab of pain in her chest at the softness of his eyes and the tenderness in his smile.

"And how are you, darling?" he murmured, bending to kiss Micki's tan cheek.

"I'm fine . . . now, Brett," Micki murmured back. "Welcome home."

"Thank you, love." He held her hand a moment longer, then he cocked his head at Wolf, his eyes sharply assessing. "Well, big prowler, you look like you might just make it," he drawled in the same insolent tone he'd used earlier.

"You can bet your Porsche I'll make it, baby brother," Wolf

retorted, every bit as insolently. "If only for the pleasure it will give me to boot your ass out of my office."

Everyone in the room, including Brett, laughed, except for Jo, as Violet gently chided her eldest. "Behave yourself, Wolfgang!"

Jo's initial foray into the Renninger stronghold presaged the entire visit. The children were children. Delightful in their excitement of the day to come. Christmas day dawned, not cold and bright as Jo was accustomed to but mild and rainy, as Elania and Josh had predicted. The day, as all happy days are wont to do, seemed to flash by in a continuous din of laughter and family camaraderie. Though Jo had been fearful of receiving gifts proffered by people she had just met, the Renningers displayed both breeding and tact by offering none.

By the time the small jet with Jo and Brett enscounced inside soared again into the blue sky, its nose pointed north, Jo's mind was a seething mass of emotions and impressions, some good, some bad. The good impressions derived from eight days spent in the company of a truly "together" family whom, in the security of their affections for one another, had unhesitatingly included Jo within their circle of bantering communion. Savoring the memories of each day, most of which were rainy or gray outside, all of which were sun-bright inside, Jo tucked them away in a safe corner of her mind, to be taken out and enjoyed whenever she felt down.

Every one of Jo's bad impressions had been instilled by Brett. Though he had appeared to be relaxed and every bit as holiday-spirited as the rest of his family, Jo had seen through his light-hearted facade, possibly because she had come to know him so intimately. Throughout their entire visit, Brett had treated Jo with unfailing politeness. In fact, so very polite had he been, Jo had been repeatedly tempted to smack his face!

Now, sitting beside him as stiffly as she had on the flight south, Jo tried, as she had continuously over the past eight days, to equate this silent, hostile man with the ardent, laughing lover she'd come to know in the apartment in Ocean City.

197

Failing miserably in her attempt to understand Brett, Jo spent every quiet mile of the flight preparing herself for his leave-taking. A mask of cool composure blanking her face, Jo writhed with pain inside, knowing the pain was only a tiny measure of the agony that would strike her with Brett's final good-bye.

CHAPTER NINE

His facial muscles beginning to ache from being kept under rigid control, Brett curled his long fingers inward and grasped the arms of the seat to keep himself from reaching out to pull Jo into a hard embrace. Smothering a sigh, Brett faced the ills tormenting him. His arms ached to hold Jo's softness close. His lips burned with the need to crush her mouth. His body screamed to lose itself in the velvety warmth of hers.

Damn. And damn. And double damn! Brett had been mentally swearing, sometimes mildly, other times violently, for the better part of nine days. There was a knot in his stomach that felt like a rock. His neck was stiff from tension. And, after eight days of celibacy, he felt mean with frustration. Exerting every ounce of control he possessed, Brett sat statue still, staring straight ahead, positive that if he moved he'd explode, his bitterness and incrimination destroying the woman he both loved and hated.

You need help, buster!

Right.

A muscle twitched at the corner of Brett's jaw. God helps those . . . Great! Terrific! Now I'm not only talking to myself,

I'm answering myself! They're going to find a quiet room for you, Brett cautioned himself scathingly, if you don't do something, and soon, about this crazy situation. But what the hell *can* a man do when he finds himself involved with a woman who belongs to another man? Another man who just happens to be his own brother. Resting his head against the seat back, Brett closed his eyes.

There has to be some way, some answer.

Sure, there's an answer to everything. All you have to do is find it! The problem teased and tormented Brett as the jet streaked through the winter sky. One by one he rejected each solution that his mind presented for inspection.

The most obvious solution was, of course, to simply walk away from her. To do what? Brett wondered. Merely asking himself the question was enlightening. Always before, through any kind of personal upheaval, including the last months he'd been with Sondra, Brett had invariably found surcease in his work. The business of speculating on real estate had excited him from the first time he'd ventured into his mother's office at the advanced age of ten. Now the very thought of the work waiting for him in his office merely added to the weariness Brett was experiencing.

Weariness, and frustration, and anger. Three very debilitating emotions. Brett's nervous system had become ragged from those emotions, and others, during the last nine days. You had better get your head together, chum, Brett advised himself wryly. If you're not careful, your blood pressure is going to go up and your natural resistance is going to go down. God! What an unholy mess!

Wolf.

Brett exhaled a long, drawn-out sigh, no longer caring if the woman sitting beside him heard or not. Never, never would he forget the joyful expression that had momentarily set Jo's face aglow at her first sight of Wolf. Brett was positive none of the others in the room had seen that fleeting, betraying look of love on Jo's face—with the possible exception of Wolf himself. But then, Wolf's rugged features had worn a like expression.

Moving restlessly in his seat, Brett could see again Wolf's outstretched arm, could hear the emotion in his brother's voice as Wolf growled, "There's my girl." Brett's teeth clamped together in much the same way they had on Christmas Eve, but then it had been to keep himself from snarling "Wrong, Wolf, Jo is *my* girl now." And that had only been the beginning of a week full of instances when Brett had not only wanted to snarl but to lash out both verbally and physically.

They had all fallen in love with her, every one of them. His mother; Eric, Doris, Di, Hank, all the kids, Elania, and even, before Jo had been there two full days, Micki. Brett sighed again. If nothing else, he could congratulate himself on a job well done in convincing Micki of Wolf's fidelity!

Jo was depressed now. Brett felt he could actually feel the vibrations of sadness that enveloped her. Yet, up until the moment he had handed her into the car to leave for the airfield, she had been lighthearted and carefree, seemingly content simply to be within the radius of Wolf, Micki or no Micki.

How many times during their visit had he conquered the urge to grab hold of her to shake some sense into her? Brett smiled in derision. About as many times as he'd conquered the need to go to her room during the night to restake his and her claim.

What the hell had they talked about? The question stabbed at Brett's mind at regular intervals. On the three separate occasions Wolf and Jo had been closeted together in Wolf's bedroom, of all places, what had they discussed? It sure as hell had not been one Brett Renninger, for Jo had emerged from those meetings flushed and laughing! She wasn't laughing now. In fact, Brett had the distinct impression Jo was within a hairsbreadth of breaking into sobs.

Brett realized with a jolt that he had never seen Jo cry. Not even when she'd become so suddenly and violently sick in the office had she given way to tears. She had been appalled at soiling his shoes and the carpet and the car, but she had not wept. And another time, her eyes had welled up—but she hadn't given in. If she cries now, he thought savagely, I'll beat her; then she'll really have something to cry about!

Brett shifted position, as if unable to find comfort in the confining seat. The discomfort was in his head, not his butt, and Brett knew it. He also knew that were she to lose a single tear, he would haul her into his arms, promising anything, anything in an effort to stem the flow.

Lord! What a mess!

You have a problem, my son?

Yes, Lord. You see, I love my brother but I love his woman too.

That is not very bright of you, my son.

But, Lord! How many women does one man need? Besides, I thought the wolf mated for life.

You're definitely losing it, Renninger, Brett chided himself in wry self-amusement. You keep playing these funny little games in your mind and you are going to find yourself weaving baskets instead of building condos for the rich and near rich. You have *got* to resolve this situation one way or another, and soon!

All wry self-amusement fled before a rising flood of despair. What could he do? Exactly what in hell could he do? Perhaps if they talked about it. But what would he say? Could I stand to hear Jo say she loves Wolf and could never give him up, even if it meant ending her relationship with me? Brett asked himself. No, I could not stand it, he replied honestly. Could not. As far as Brett could see he had two choices. He could accept the status quo, or he could take a walk.

Jo was too close. How could he think clearly with her sitting less than two feet away? It had been over a week since he'd held her in his arms. And, damn it, it had been the same length of time since she'd held him.

Brett was a proud man and he knew it. Now, although the taste was vile, he swallowed that pride. He *wanted* the feel of Jo's

202

arms holding him close to her softness. He *yearned* for the touch of her fingers stroking through his hair. He *longed* for the sound of her voice whispering love words against his lips. Walking away would not erase the wanting, the yearning, the longing, and Brett knew it. He would just have to learn to live with the status quo.

"Brett."

Brett came slowly, reluctantly out of a half sleep in which he was reliving the days spent along the shore with Jo. Turning his head, he opened his eyes to stare into hazel depths darkened by disillusionment. God! He'd give his soul to be able to set those amber flecks glimmering like gold in happiness.

"It's time to fasten your seat belt for landing."

Brett nodded in answer and, straightening his cramped body, turned away. Even her voice has a dead, toneless sound, Brett thought tiredly, automatically engaging his belt. Taking Jo to the farm had been a mistake, just as he'd known it would be. What arrogance had led him to hope that three days and four nights with him would be enough to wipe the memory of Wolf out of her mind? For, in truth, that was what he had hoped for. But they had been such wonderfully contented days, and such satisfyingly ecstatic nights. Brett had convinced himself Jo had become as lost in him as he was in her. At any rate, he qualified mentally, he had tried to convince himself. Yet, even before they'd boarded the plane the tightness had begun in his insides, and it had continued unabated until now he had the sensation of carrying a rock around in his gut.

"Will there be a car waiting?"

"Yes, of course." Brett was immediately sorry for the impatience edging his tone. For God's sake, man, he berated himself, she asked a simple, quiet question! Was it really necessary to snap at her? It's either snap or beg, and I sure as hell cannot and will not do that!

Jo asked no further questions, nor did she make any remark whatever from the time they left the plane till the limousine drew up in front of her apartment. Brett broke the silence once, to inquire if Jo's car had been returned to New York from Ocean City.

"Yes, sir," Doug replied promptly. "I drove it in myself. It's parked in the garage at Ms. Lawrence's apartment."

Telling Doug to wait for him, Brett followed Jo out of the car and into the building. Traversing the hall beside her, Brett felt his lips twist in a grimace when Jo dug the large oddly shaped key from her purse. At the door to her apartment, he frowned at her trembling fingers as she stabbed at the slot in the lock.

"You're tired." Brett was careful to keep his tone free of inflection as he set her case inside the door. "We'll talk later. After you've had some rest." Jo's reaction startled him in its swiftness.

"No!" Jo spun to face him. "We will *not* talk later." Her eyes were no longer sad. They actually seemed to shoot sparks at him. Her voice was no longer quiet. Her tone was razor sharp with anger. "I don't know what sort of game you think you are playing, Brett, but you can deal me out of it. I thought I could . . ." Jo paused, as if to steady herself. "But I can't . . ." Her breath caught, then she repeated, on a sigh, "I just can't." Very slowly, very quietly, Jo closed the door in his face.

His body rigid, Brett stood frozen for one full minute, then, swinging around, he strode back to the elevator. What prompted him to do it, Brett had no idea yet, as he approached the security guard's desk he paused, then stopped.

"Do you remember who I am?" Brett ask the guard arrogantly.

"Yes, sir, Mr. Renninger." The man snapped to attention smartly. "Ms. Lawrence gave you clearance to enter at will two days before Christmas."

"That's correct." Brett's lips smiled at the man. "I wanted that point quite clear. I may be back some time later this evening, and I did not want any hassle over admittance. I will not have

Ms. Lawrence unnecessarily disturbed. Are we in accord?" Brett deliberately arched one brow imperiously.

"Yes, sir."

What a bastard you are, Brett accused himself wryly as he pushed through the entrance doors. But then, if you never take a step, you never get anywhere, in *any* direction, he exonerated his rather overbearing behavior.

In the car, Brett gnawed on the wisdom of returning to see Jo later that evening. He *knew* his attitude had been less than charming throughout their stay at the farm. On reflection, he admitted he'd acted out the part of the name he'd moments ago called himself to the letter. Why couldn't he just go to Jo and confess that he was so miserable, because he was so miserable?

On entering Wolf's apartment, Brett set his suitcase aside, tossed his jacket onto a chair, poured himself a double shot of Scotch then, telling himself he had to be hungry since he'd eaten nothing since early that morning, ambled into the kitchen. Opting for eggs, as he was certainly not in the mood to wax creative, he popped two slices of bread into the toaster while melting butter in a small frying pan. Breaking two eggs neatly in one hand, he dropped them, yolks intact, into the sizzling butter. A moment later he turned away from the stove to butter the toast, then, turning back, he grasped the handle of the pan to shift it gently back and forth a few times before, with a slight snap of his wrist, the eggs slid up and over, perfectly flipped. Brett waited another moment, then lifted the pan from the burner to slide the over light eggs onto a plate. He had taken three steps to the table when, spinning around, he walked to the sink to dump the combined eggs and toast into the disposal. Brett tossed back the last of his whisky as the mechanism ate his supper.

My mother would have a fit!

Smiling not unlike a devilish young boy, Brett returned to the living room for a second helping of his liquid meal. His second double shot tempered with ice and water, Brett climbed the stairs to his bedroom. Between long sips at his drink he undressed slowly. Glass in hand, he strolled into the bathroom where, again between sips, he brushed his teeth, shaved his face, and showered his body—this action minus the glass. By the time Brett had pulled on suede slacks, a soft sweater, and ankle boots, his glass was empty. Retracing his steps, he went back to the bar. After carefully measuring three-fourths whisky, one-fourth water, and adding two ice cubes, he lifted the glass.

"No!"

The glass landed on the smooth surface of the bar with a crash, its spilled contents unnoticed by the man who was scooping his jacket from the chair on his way toward the door.

His bootheels hitting the sidewalk with a muffled thud, Brett strode purposefully in the direction of Jo's apartment. Damned if he'd lie awake one more night, aching with the memory of how good their lovemaking had been! Damned if he'd give up on a relationship he *knew* would be satisfying to the both of them—if she'd give it a chance to get off the ground! And damned if he'd let her get away with closing the door in his face!

Plunging a hand into his coat pocket, Brett withdrew a cigarette and brought it to his chilled lips. Raising the plastic lighter, he cupped his hand over the end to shield the flame from the cold wind. The lighter clicked on, then off again. His movements uneven from the anger coursing through his body, Brett grasped the unlit cigarette from his lips and flung it to the street.

"No!" He growled softly, harshly. "No more substitutes to pacify frustration!"

At his destination, Brett nodded curtly to the doorman, and a moment later he dipped his head again to the security guard. Neither man attempted to impede his progress.

At Jo's door, Brett stabbed the button to her doorbell with quick impatient motions of his forefinger. Nothing. Grumbling an expletive that would very likely have shocked the neighbors, had they heard it, Brett slipped his hand into his slacks pocket and withdrew his gold keyring. Detaching the large key from the others, he unlocked the door and stepped inside.

"Jo?"

Nothing.

"Jo?" Brett crossed the living room to the bedroom. "Where are you?" Brett's question was answered not by a voice but by the sound of the shower in the bathroom. As he entered the room, the sound came to an abrupt stop. Standing in the middle of the room, facing the bathroom door, Brett waited. Two minutes. Five minutes. Nuts! He was pulling the sweater up over his shoulders when Jo came out of the bathroom tying the sash on the striped robe she'd worn in the apartment in Ocean City.

"Brett!" His name exploded from her lips with a gasp. "How did you get in here?"

"I'm a second-story man in my off hours," Brett muttered through the soft wool.

"And what do you think you're doing?" Jo demanded, charging across the room to stand before him, hands on hips.

"I'm getting undressed for bed." Staring her in the eyes, Brett tossed the sweater aside and began working on his belt buckle.

"Like hell you are!" Jo choked in fury.

"Like hell I'm not," Brett corrected softly. "It seems bed is the one place you and I can communicate. And, the way I feel right now, I just might communicate through most of the night." As he lowered the zipper on the slacks, Brett watched Jo stiffen with outrage. Well, he shrugged mentally, at least when she's furious she talks to me.

"You know," she finally managed through gritted teeth, "for an educated man, you certainly have a flair for crudity."

"Nothing crude about it," Brett contradicted smoothly. "And you know it." Slowly, deliberately, he let his eyes caress her body, feeling a quickness in his loins at the realization that she was wearing nothing but satiny skin underneath the classy, sexy robe. "I said we'll talk later," he went on softly, unselfconsciously stepping out of both slacks and briefs. "And we will talk . . . later." By now Jo's eyes were wide, her gorgeous lashes

207

fluttering, her breath coming in short, angry puffs. God! Brett marveled. She is one beautiful woman.

Reaching out, Brett caught the tie belt of her robe and began loosening the knot.

"Brett!" Her throat worked spasmodically as she swallowed. "Brett, you can't do this! I won't let you."

Brett slid the loop free.

"Brett! Stop this!" Jo demanded in an unconvincing whisper.

The knot untied, Brett gently slid the silky material off Jo's trembling shoulders. Dropping his arms, he stood still, drinking in the longed-for sight of her. It had been nine nights since he'd held the slim loveliness of her close to his own hardness. It seemed more like nineteen years. Stifling a groan, Brett reached out again, this time to lightly grasp her shoulders. The feel of her under his hands set off a chain reaction Brett could not have controlled had his life depended on it. Sliding his hands urgently down her back, Brett drew the warmth and softness of Jo against him, a sigh of real pain escaping his tightly constricted throat.

"Jo . . . my Jo."

Brett, unaware he was saying it all, felt he needed to say so much, much more, yet all that came out was her name. The tips of her breasts touched his chest with the effect of electric probes, creating shock waves that spiraled wildly through his body. Brett's arms tightened convulsively, crushing her to him. His hands, hungry to touch her everywhere at once, moved with restless abandon from her shoulders to the base of her spine and back again.

"Oh, Brett! Oh, Brett."

There was a universe of mixed-up meanings contained in the husky, defeated sound that whispered into Brett's mind as well as his ears. His mind, totally absorbed with the overriding need to make her finally, irrevocably his, caught only the nuance of passion in her tone. Elation singing through him, Brett took her mouth with commanding force. Jo's capitulation was immediate and frenzied. Her hands skimmed the length of his body to grasp his buttocks, fingers clenching, urging the ultimate intimacy.

Brett literally went wild. Shuddering with the desire rocketing through his body, he began moving, backing her to the bed. Then he was on the bed, on Jo, in Jo, taking, taking, wanting more, and yet more, greedily demanding she give everything of herself, his body quivering in exultation of the primitive possession, his mind chanting: mine, mine, mine.

It was over very quickly. His head thrown back, Brett could feel the tug of strain on the taut tendons in his neck. Striving, driving, propelling himself to the very limit of endurance, Brett gasped harshly at the intensity of near pain at his moment of culmination, reveling in the echoing gasp that was torn from Jo's throat.

In a state of complete collapse, Brett lay with his head against Jo's breast, dragging great gulps of air. Brett lay still while his body went through the process of regeneration. His mind, emerging from the fog of sensuality, began clicking away like a well-made timepiece.

Never, never, not even that first time with Jo in Ocean City had Brett so completely lost contact with reality during the act of lovemaking. And never had he wished to remain so completely lost. Even in his exhausted condition a burst of adrenaline shot through his system at the memory of what he'd just experienced. Brett had always doubted the existence of the absolute sexual pinnacle. He doubted no longer.

Monitoring Jo's still-rapid heartbeat, a thrill snaked through Brett's insides. Jo had not surrendered! The thrill changed direction to skitter up his spine. Jo had *not* surrendered! If he had been impatient, rough, demanding, and he had, Jo had been equally so. He had witnessed the same tautness cording her slim white neck that had tightened his with tension. He had felt the sting of her oval nails in his buttocks as her fingers flexed and gripped in a frantic effort to draw him deeper and yet deeper into her body as if in craving to absorb him totally within her being. His lips now tasted the salty flavor of her sweat-sheened skin. Joyous delight followed the path of the thrill. In no way had she surrendered!

I love her! I love her. With my mind, with my body, with my soul! God! Why can't she love me too?

Brett felt an unfamiliar hot sting in his eyes and his brain went numb for an instant. He could not! He could not! He hadn't wept since his father's death during that stupid yacht race! Holy Mother of God! What *was* he going to do? The mere possibility of losing Jo now froze his heartbeats. I can't let her go, Brett's mind roared back to life. I cannot let her go.

The slight stirring of Jo's body beneath him alerted Brett to the realization that he was very likely crushing her slim frame with his weight. Easing himself from her, he stretched out beside her on the now-rumpled spread. Brett knew he should move, if only to get under the spread. Jo was so quiet. Was she sleeping? Shifting onto his side, Brett gazed down on her, a tender smile curving his lips at the sight of the dark swath of hair partially covering her face. Raising his hand to her face, he gently smoothed the swath away from her temple before trailing his fingers to her cheek. Several obstinate silky strands clung to Jo's eyelashes. Being careful not to startle her, Brett brushed her lashes with his fingertips, then became absolutely still.

Jo's lashes were wet! Her face was *wet!* Why was she crying? Had he hurt her! But she had not cried out, had not withdrawn in any way! Quite the opposite, she had attacked, consumed, devoured! As if, as if . . . A chill pervaded Brett's body. Jo had responded to him with all the fervor of a woman with the man she . . . No! Brett closed his eyes in an attempt to block out a face. He could not close his mind to the taunting whisper of a name.

Wolf.

Brett shook his head sharply once.

No. No. Please, no. He didn't want to hear it. Still, he had to know.

"Why are you crying?" His voice was soft, but tight with strain. "Did I hurt you?"

"No!" Jo's lids flew up and her head moved briefly on the pillow.

"Then why are you crying?" he insisted.

"It . . . it's nothing, really." The nothing started a fresh flow trickling down her cheeks. "I'm . . . being silly."

"Is it him?" To keep from shouting, Brett whispered. "Were you thinking of him?" Suddenly incensed, he leaned over her, his face close to hers. Teeth clenched, he rasped, "Was *he* in your mind . . . while *I* was in your body?"

"Brett!" Wide-eyed, Jo stared at him. "I don't . . . "

"Was he?" Brett's shout cut across her voice.

"NO!" Jo shouted back at him. "It's over, Brett. I swear it's over. It's been . . . "

"All right!" Brett again cut her off harshly. "I don't want a blow by blow of the ending." He leaned even closer to her. "As long as it is completely over. I want your word on that, Jo. I won't allow you to use my body to appease a hunger for another man."

"Use *you*?" Jo exclaimed on a shriek. "How—"

"Your word, Jo," Brett inserted quietly, ominously.

"You have it!" Jo actually snarled at him. "And don't you ever, ever again accuse *me* of using *you*. Do you understand?"

"Perfectly." Brett's teeth snapped together. Now what? Brett wondered, returning her glare fiercely. Well, when in doubt . . . kiss the bitch! Closing the inches that separated them, Brett covered her mouth with his own.

At first Jo's lips remained stiff and tightly closed. Then they softened. Then they parted. Then they grew warm. The warmth quickly turned to heat. Heat burst into flames. Instant replay; another conflagration. Tongues pierced, hands searched, bodies melded, one into the other. Who owned whom?

Normal breathing restored, Brett drew Jo's sleep-heavy body close to his own. Already half asleep himself, the thought wafted

211

through his mind again. Who owned whom? Beginning to drift, Brett lifted a hand to smother a yawn.

Who owned whom? Who cares?

The automatic alarm that jangled inside Brett's head every working morning at seven fifteen pried his eyes open the next morning. His eyes wide open, he frowned. When, he asked himself, had he and Jo made the move from on top of the spread to beneath the covers? Memory stirred and Brett vaguely recalled waking in the night feeling chilled. Rousing Jo, he had coaxed her up enough to allow him to pull the spread and covers down. She was back to sleep before he'd finished tucking the blankets around the two of them.

Throwing his arms over his head, Brett stretched his body awake. Lord, he was hungry. He needed some food. He needed a shower. But, first, he needed a kiss. Turning onto his side, he propped his head up on one hand. His expression soft, Brett studied the woman he loved. In sleep, Jo was even more beautiful, but in a different way. She looked younger than her twenty-eight years, defenseless, more vulnerable. Staring at Jo's sleep-flushed cheeks, her tender mouth, and her wildly disordered hair, Brett felt his throat constrict with emotion.

How could it be possible, Brett mused, to want to protect to the death and inflict pain on a woman at one and the same time? For Brett did suddenly feel fiercely, savagely protective of her. Yet there had been times, and probably would be again, when he wanted to hurt her. Strange. Frowning in concentration, Brett raked his mind for a single memory, a single instance when he'd ever felt so very strongly about another woman. His mind came up blank. Oh, he'd experienced the usual instinctive protectiveness for Sondra. Sondra had been his wife and as his wife she deserved his protection. Brett smiled. What he'd felt for Sondra paled to transparent in comparison to what he was feeling now for Jo. Brett's smile broadened in self-derision. Of course, he had faced the fact long ago that what he'd felt for Sondra had more to do with self-indulgence and infatuation than love. The woman

212

he gazed upon now Brett loved with every fiber of his being. Brett's smile vanished.

On consideration, the whole concept was pretty damned scary!

Brett lowered his head, then caught himself up short less than an inch from her lips. Don't wake her, let her sleep, his conscience advised. She gave you infinite pleasure during the night, not once but several times. Let her sleep, she has earned it. His smile back in place, Brett eased his body away from Jo's and off the bed.

Twenty-odd minutes later Brett was tugging his crumpled sweater over his head when a slight movement on the bed caught his attention. Pulling the garment into place, he glanced up to find Jo watching him guardedly.

"Good morning." Brett offered the greeting in a neutral tone.

Jo continued to watch him unblinkingly, her expression wary. "Good morning," she responded in a sleep-husky murmur. "Have you eaten?"

"Not yet." Brett stood still, his hands at his sides, regarding her closely. What was she thinking? The alert, somewhat fearful expression in her eyes puzzled him. It was almost as if she was waiting for an inevitable blow to fall. Why? Unable to come up with an answer, Brett shrugged. "I thought I'd stop for something to eat on my way back to the apartment."

"I see," Jo replied tonelessly.

What does she see? Brett felt a stirring of anger. What the hell was going on in that beautiful head of hers? Jo ended his fruitless search for answers.

"You were going to leave without waking me?"

The mild reproach in her voice put a spur to his anger. "Of course not!" Brett was barely aware of his fingers curling into his palms. Cool it, chum, he cautioned himself. Make haste slowly here. What had he expected from her this morning? The query was rhetorical, and Brett knew it. He'd expected Jo to be as she'd been on the mornings they'd wakened together in Ocean City . . . warm, responsive, smiling. The disappointment that lanced

213

through Brett robbed him of a portion of the energy he'd felt on awakening. Choosing his words carefully, Brett went on, "I had every intention of waking you. I put the coffee on to brew. It should be ready in a few minutes." A small smile Brett didn't particularly like shadowed Jo's lips.

"The holidays are over," she said flatly.

"Jo, what . . . ?"

"You'd better go," she interrupted impatiently. "You'll be late. And so will I."

Now what in hell . . . ? Brett frowned. Was she throwing him out? After last night? Oh, no! No way! Brett's balled hands tightened into hard fists. "I was going to suggest you take an extra day off."

"Why?" Jo shot the word at him.

Why? Brett was hard put not to laugh. God! He'd have thought it was obvious. He had loved her to a standstill; she'd been exhausted when he'd finally allowed her to rest. Come to that, so had he . . . and he felt, or at least he *had* felt, like he could fight his weight in wildcats. An unknowing, sardonic smile played on his lips. Hell! He was having trouble fighting his weight in JoAnne Lawrences! Exasperation serrated the edge of Brett's tone.

"Why not?"

"I don't want to stay home!"

"Then don't!" Brett snapped. Immediately regretting his loss of patience, Brett drew a deep calming breath. Jo was still lying flat on the bed, the covers up to her chin. Very probably, Brett decided, because she was naked. He didn't like the connotations to that consideration. During their time together by the ocean, Jo had been completely unselfconscious with him. An uncomfortable sensation of defeat crawled along the floor of his stomach. Hanging on to his temper, Brett explained calmly, "You had requested a leave to rest. What with one thing and another" —he shrugged—"you've had very little of it. I thought you could take the day to just . . . catch up."

"I'm fine," she assured him quietly.

"Okay, then I'll see you in the office?" Brett lifted one eyebrow slightly.

"Yes."

Brett didn't move. Staring into her eyes, he waited to see if Jo would say anything else. She didn't. She stared back at him, her expression also one of waiting. Say it. Now. The command flashed from Brett's brain to his lips.

"I'll transfer my things tonight." Barely breathing, Brett watched Jo's eyes flicker and widen, observed the sudden rigidity of her body.

"W-what . . . " Jo stopped to clear her throat before continuing in a husky whisper, "What are you saying?"

"I'm moving in with you." Brett heard the steel underlining his soft statement. From her expression of shock, it was obvious Jo heard it too.

"Brett, is . . ." Jo paused to moisten her lips with the tip of her tongue. "Is that wise?" Grasping the covers in one hand, she sat up to stare at him in consternation. "I mean, word of it will zing through the office grapevine within a week!"

Brett had to put a clamp on the elation that was dancing wildly through his system. He had won! Hot damn! He had won! Jo had not denied him the right to share her world or her body! She was simply concerned about propriety! He swallowed a whoop of laughter.

"Need I tell you what the office gossips can do to, and with, themselves?" he drawled. The amusement swelled at Jo's expression of censure. How in hell, after being Wolf's mistress, had she retained her naivete? The query killed Brett's amusement. Why had he had to think of Wolf, and the role he'd played in Jo's life, now? A fresh spurt of anger threatened to swamp his elation. *Had* played, Brett repeated in an effort to contain his emotions. The operative word here is *had*. While calming himself, Brett let his eyes feast on Jo's invitingly disheveled appearance. Taking one step toward her, Brett caught himself up short. You've got

215

to go to work, Renninger, he cautioned in an attempt to quell the sudden need to hold Jo in his arms. Get started on the day, he advised himself. The night will come more swiftly if you keep busy in the interim.

"Why are you staring at me like that?" The wariness was back in Jo's expression and her voice cracked with uncertainty.

"I'm thinking about having you for breakfast," Brett answered softly, his elation soaring again as her wariness and uncertainty were washed away by a look of surprised delight.

"I think you'd probably work a lot better on bacon and eggs," Jo replied, straightfaced.

This time Brett made no effort to contain his laughter. "I'd say you are probably right," he agreed, grinning. "Even though it won't be near as much fun." Brett held his breath. Was the tension gone for good? Was the easiness between them back to stay?

"Perhaps not," Jo murmured. Then, to Brett's delight, she fluttered her long lashes at him coyly. "You could always plan on having me for dessert. Anticipation sharpens the appetite, you know."

Brett took another step toward her. "If my appetite gets any sharper," he growled, "I'll slash myself on it and bleed to death." Brett had no qualms whatever about admitting to Jo how very much he desired her. Hadn't he admitted as much silently, with his body, throughout the long night?

"Poor darling," Jo cooed. The "darling" electrified Brett; still, he could appreciate her teasing. "So neglected. So deprived. How long has it been, dear, since a woman took pity on you?"

Sheer enjoyment of her tempered Brett's arousal. Laughing softly, he strode to the bed. "I don't want 'a woman.' I want one woman." Bending to her, he brushed her mouth with his lips, afraid to allow himself a deeper taste of her. He had to get to work! "And that one woman had better rustle her rump because, if she's late to work, I'll dock her pay."

216

Leaning back, Jo surveyed him with a superior expression. "In case you've forgotten, I am a sal-ar-ied employee." She smirked.

"Yes, I know." Brett smiled sweetly. "But then I could always demote you *and* put you on an hourly wage. I'm sure Bob Kempten would jump at the chance to have your job." Brett regretted the teasing barb the minute he uttered it. Jo was Wolf's assistant. How many times had she reminded him of that fact? Too many. Well, if she had plans of beating him to death using Wolf's name as a stick, he had certainly given her the perfect opportunity to get off the first whack.

"Oh, I'm quite sure you're right." Jo's purring voice sent a chill down Brett's spine. Here it comes, he thought tiredly. "But would he also jump at the chance to sit on your lap?"

The breath Brett was fully aware of holding sighed silently through his grinning lips. "Are you going to sit on my lap?" he asked with exaggerated eagerness.

Jo's expression turned woeful. "I'm a loyal employee." She sighed loudly. "If I must, I must."

Brett's laughter bounced off the walls. You had better get your can out of here, ol' buddy, he urged himself. Or there is no way you'll see the inside of your office this day. Still laughing softly, Brett spun away from the bed to stride across the room. Scooping his jacket off the chair he'd tossed it onto the night before, he slanted a devilish glance at Jo.

"Move it, water baby," he ordered gently. "I want to see you in my office at nine thirty." Still grinning, he sauntered out of the bedroom.

That evening, as promised, Brett transferred his clothing and few personal belongings to Jo's place, ignoring the taunting thought that he was moving out of Wolf's apartment into Wolf's apartment. As he stowed his shaving gear onto the medicine cabinet shelf Jo had cleared for him, Brett decided to contact a real estate agent about finding another place for them.

Surprisingly, they made the adjustment of living together very quickly and, within two weeks Brett wondered how he'd ever thought he was content living alone. They learned and accepted each others faults—in Jo's case, her habit of kicking her shoes off the moment she entered the apartment and forgetting to pick them up again; Brett did it for her. In Brett's case, his failure to replace the cap on the toothpaste tube; Jo did that for him. They worked together well. They played together joyously. They laughed together often.

Near the end of January Brett asked Jo if she'd like to go skiing. Jo's response was less than enthusiastic.

"I don't know how to ski, Brett. And, to be honest, I'm not all that eager to learn how."

"You could give it a try, honey," Brett coaxed, itching to get on the slopes again. "If you don't like it, you could always relax by the fire with a hot toddy while I attempt to break a leg."

Jo hesitated but Brett gave her such a woebegone expression she laughingly relented and agreed to go with him, exactly as he'd hoped she would.

"Terrific!" Brett exclaimed as eagerly as a kid might have. Jumping out of his chair, he walked restlessly around the living room, unaware of the gentle smile curving Jo's lips as she watched him. "Let's see now." He began making plans aloud. "Accommodations are no problem. I've retained the room at that motel up in Vermont for office space in case I needed it." Brett was equally unaware of the slight tightening of Jo's lips. "I have that meeting in Atlanta next week." Jo had absolutely refused to go to Atlanta with him. Brett was still not completely reconciled to her stand on Atlanta but, with this new victory, he decided to stop badgering her about it. "Suppose we say the week after next?" One brow lifted quizzically, he swung to face her. "Okay?"

"You love skiing that much?" Jo laughed.

"Yes," Brett answered simply. "And I haven't stepped into boots once this winter."

This time Brett was fully aware of Jo's gentle smile. "Okay," she agreed softly. "The week after next."

Brett thanked Jo, twice, after they'd turned out the light in the bedroom that night.

Atlanta was a drag for Brett, even though the meeting he'd set up with a local realtor proved satisfying to both of them. Brett missed Jo as much as he would have the loss of his right arm. His impatience to get all existing details cleared up did not go unnoticed by Richard Colby.

"Is she beautiful?" Richard asked out of the blue while they were discussing swamp drainage, of all things, the day before Brett's departure.

"Very," Brett responded immediately. Then, his tone dangerous, Brett retorted, "Why?"

"No reason." Richard, unperturbed by Brett's tone, smiled easily. "It's obvious you can't wait to get back to her. Why wait till tomorrow? We can clean this drainage thing up by dinnertime. I can handle all the nitpicking details myself. There's no reason you could not fly back to New York tonight." His smile broadened. "Unless, that is, you're enthralled with my company."

Brett's smile was as broad as Richard's. "Thanks, buddy. Remind me to give you a raise."

"Why do you think I made the suggestion?" Richard drawled dryly.

It was late by the time Brett let himself into the dark, silent apartment. Moving cautiously but unerringly, he made his way through the living room to the bedroom. Inside the bedroom he placed his case carefully out of the way, then stood still to allow his eyes to adjust to the unrelenting darkness. When he had his bearings, Brett walked softly to the side of the room's one large window to tug gently on the cord that worked the draperies. The heavy, lined drapes slid silently apart giving access to a pale shaft of moonlight. A low moaning sound froze Brett in his tracks as he turned from the window. Every sense alerted, he focused his gaze on the moonlight-washed figure lying on the bed.

Jo moaned again and, frowning with concern, Brett crossed to the bed in three long strides. The sight that met his eyes stole Brett's breath.

Jo was lying on her back in the center of the bed, her arms flung wide, her fingers grasping at the sheet, nails scratching the smooth surface. Her naked body was only partially covered, and even as Brett stared her legs thrashed about, dislodging the blankets completely. Gazing transfixed at her white skin gleaming in the moonlight, Brett felt a kick of desire in his loins. A sighing sound drew his eyes to her face. Her head moved restlessly as another sigh whispered through her slightly parted lips.

She's dreaming, Brett concluded in bemusement. Watching her legs, Brett's heartbeat accelerated. She's dreaming she's making love! Brett closed his eyes as another low moan sent a shiver of excitement careening through his body. Barely conscious of what he was doing, Brett opened his eyes, then, fastening his gaze on her writhing body, he began to undress. When the last piece of his constricting clothing had been discarded, Brett stepped up to the bed. Sliding onto the cool sheet beside Jo, he ran one palm lightly from her ankle to her hip. Immediately Jo's leg moved to press against his hand and a low groan of need murmured from deep in her throat. Brett was sliding his hand over her rib cage when a chilling thought stopped him cold.

Who is she dreaming she's making love with?

Watching her, wanting to know, not wanting to know, Brett closed his mind to the visage and name of one man. She's mine, he raged silently. Awake or asleep, Jo is mine! Blocking out the idea that what he was doing could very well be wrong, Brett deliberately took possession of her silky-skinned breast.

"Brett."

Not even a whisper, hardly more than a sigh, yet his name swelled to a joyous crescendo in Brett's mind. Jo was dreaming *he* was making love to her! Unhesitatingly, Brett carefully slid his body between her soft thighs, determined to make her dream a reality. Covering her gently, yet not joining their bodies, Brett touched Jo's parted lips with his own. Before entering her, Brett wanted her fully conscious of who was doing what to whom. The touch of his lips and hands feather light, Brett adored her body.

"Brett?" Jo's voice was fuzzy. She was not yet fully awake.

"Yes, love?" Brett murmured, kissing the corner of her mouth.

"Oh, Brett. Is it really you?" Jo was coming out of sleep, but falling into passion. Her hands forsaking the sheet, she grasped Brett instead.

"Yes, love," Brett assured softly. "It's really me." He gave her the feel of his tongue along her bottom lip for proof.

"I missed you so." Jo's arms tightened; her thighs relaxed. "Don't make me wait. Please." She arched her body to his with the plea and sighed when Brett granted it.

Moving slowly at first, savoring the velvety softness of her, Brett twined his fingers in Jo's hair and kissed her tenderly on her cheeks, her eyes, her chin. When his lips brushed hers she groaned.

"Kiss me. Love me. Oh, Brett, I need you." The moan deepened into a sob. "I need you." That's when the brainstorm hit him. Teasing her with his body's slow strokes, Brett brushed Jo's quivering lips again.

"Marry me, Jo." Brett's voice was low but firm with conviction.

"What!" Jo's heavy lashes fluttered, then lifted. She stared at him with passion-clouded eyes. "What did you say?"

"Marry me." Brett increased his stroke, restraining a smile at the immediate response she made with her body.

"But . . ."

"We're good together, love," He brushed her lips harder. "You know we're good together. Not just like this." Brett thrust against her, then slowed again. "We're good together in everything."

"Brett, we can't!" Jo's breathing was shallow now and getting more shallow with each passing instant. "We don't . . . "

Brett closed her mouth with his own, certain he didn't want

to hear whatever she was going to say. He let his tongue match the motion of his body. When Jo was clinging to him, whimpering in need, Brett denied her his mouth.

"Will you marry me, Jo?" Brett stopped moving entirely.

Jo seemed unable to open her eyes. "Brett . . . please," she wailed.

"Will you marry me, Jo?" Brett kissed her very hard, and very fast.

"Yes."

The whisper trembled through Jo's lips. Relief trembled through Brett's body. Strength, power, followed on the heels of relief and, positive he could fly at that moment if he so wished, Brett gave in to the fire raging in his body.

Sated physically, satisfied emotionally, content in his mind, Brett lay cradling Jo's relaxed body close to his own. "Are you asleep?" Moving his head slowly, he brushed a few damp tendrils away from her temple with his lips.

"Yes." Jo's warm breath tingled the skin on his chest.

Lifting one hand to her chin, Brett turned her face up to his. "You won't back out. Will you, Jo?" he asked quietly, staring directly into her love-softened eyes.

"No, Brett, I won't back out."

Brett fought the urge to close his eyes in relief. Although he wasn't overjoyed at the underlying note of calm acceptance in Jo's tone, he consoled himself with the realization that her tone had also contained firm conviction. For now, Brett decided he could live with the knowledge that Jo would not attempt to repudiate her agreement to legalize their union on the grounds of duress. They could make it work, he *would* make it work, Brett vowed. He had to because he really had no other choice; Brett knew he could not let Jo go now. Brett knew also that he belonged to Jo every bit as much as he felt she belonged to him. It was somewhat scary but, Brett shrugged mentally, there it was. Bending to her, he kissed her tenderly.

"We can be married in Vermont next week." The suggestion

made, Brett held his breath, waiting for her reaction. He didn't have to hold his breath long.

Jo's eyes, suddenly clear, alert, widened in shock. "Next week?" Her voice cracked and she cleared her throat. "Vermont? Brett, I can't be ready to get married in less than a week!"

Positive he detected a note of panic creeping into her tone, Brett tightened his grasp on Jo's chin. "You can be ready." To punctuate his assertion he kissed her deeply. "You *will* be ready." His mouth crushed hers again. "We will be married"—another brief kiss—"next week . . . in Vermont. I'm sure Casey and Sean will be delighted to stand witness." Brett's punishing kisses were beginning to backlash. Feeling his body harden with renewed passion, Brett conveyed his need to Jo with his mouth, and his tongue, and his groaning words.

"Say yes again, Jo, please."

"To which question?" Jo gasped as he trailed his fingers from her chin to her breast. "The one you're asking with your words? Or the one you're asking with your body?"

Laughing softly, Brett sucked gently on her lower lip. "Say yes to both."

"Yes to both," Jo parroted at once, then qualified, "On one condition."

As by now the fire racing through Brett had consumed his brain, he would have consented to almost anything. "Name it," he murmured into her mouth.

"This time"—Jo hesitated, then rushed on—"I want to make love to you."

This was a condition? Laughter shook Brett's body. Flinging his arms wide, Brett threw himself back away from her to lay stretched out on the bed. "Take me," he cried, grinning wickedly. "I'm yours."

Brett was to remember his words several times over the days that followed. And, everytime he did, he felt again the thrill he'd experienced in being taken by Jo. Lord! When that exceptional woman decided she was going to make love to a man, she put her heart and soul into the effort. Days later Brett's body still tingled from the effective way she'd tormented him with her soft, caressing hands and her sweet, hungry mouth. Marriage to Jo, Brett decided, still lost in bemusement, should prove to be one interesting experiment.

Surprisingly, as the days until their departure for Vermont shortened, Brett found himself growing more and more nervous. Why the tension? Why the jumpiness? Why the crawly sensation in his stomach? Brett quizzed himself repeatedly. It was not as if he were being coerced into matrimony. Quite the contrary. If a charge of coercion were to be leveled, *he'd* be the guilty party. Strange, he thought, he had no recollection of any nervousness at all before he and Sondra were married. There were moments, many in number, when Brett wished he hadn't quit smoking . . . again. Brett's thinking process danced around the edges of the answer to his uptight feeling right up till he and Jo arrived in Vermont.

As Brett had predicted, Casey and Sean were both delighted and flattered to be asked to witness the nuptials. Casey, bubbling over with the news that she was pregnant, threw herself into the wedding spirit and, by the time the legalities were taken care of, had made all the arrangements for the ceremony.

Brett and Jo were married in a picturesque New England church on a Thursday morning in early February. Immediately following the brief service, Casey and Sean whisked them off to an equally picturesque but decidedly elegant restaurant for a champagne wedding breakfast that lasted through four bottles of the expensive wine and most of the afternoon. From the restaurant, the Delhenys poured Brett and Jo into a cab with the advice to do everything they might do.

"Which should take you until sometime tomorrow afternoon," Casey confided laughingly.

It was then that Brett, not drunk by a long shot, but feeling little pain, faced the reason for his nervousness during the previous week. In a word, Brett identified his malady. That word was fear. The cause and symptoms had vanished when Jo signed her name to the marriage certificate.

The first thing Brett did after he'd locked the motel room door was kiss his new bride, satisfyingly and thoroughly. The second thing he did was lift the telephone receiver and dial his mother's private office number in Florida. When his mother answered in her endearingly brisk tone, Brett, wasting no time on formalities, went directly to the reason for his call.

"Jo and I were married this morning, Mother." Not being able to resist, Brett added insolently, "We'll accept a large check for a wedding present." From behind him, Brett heard Jo's shocked gasp and grinned. His grin widened at his mother's retort.

"You'll accept what I choose to give you, smart ass." There was a telling pause, then Violet said solemnly, "Congratulations, Brett. JoAnne is a lovely young woman." Violet's tone changed to reveal confusion and a tinge of hurt feelings. "But why didn't you let us know? You could have been married at the farm."

"I've done that. Remember?" Brett's grin was gone, replaced by a grimace. Brett had coolly and deliberately chosen not to inform his family about his plans simply because he knew his mother would suggest the farm as a perfect site for the wedding. Brett's reason for not wanting to be married at the farm had absolutely nothing to do with memories of Sondra and everything to do with Wolf being in residence there. At his mother's sharply indrawn breath and murmured "Oh, Brett, how foolish of me. I'm sorry," Brett made an effort to soften his rough tone. "It's all right, sir, forget it. Besides, I wanted to go skiing on my honeymoon."

Following his mother's request, Brett handed the phone to Jo, then stood patiently while she responded to her new mother-in-law's well wishes. When the connection to Florida had been broken, Brett again handed the receiver to Jo.

"Your turn to face the firing squad," he teased. "But make it quick, love, your bridegroom is getting itchy."

Wondering at the odd expression on Jo's face, Brett studied

225

her as she placed the call. There was something wrong with Jo's family situation, Brett knew. Something that had hurt her. And, although Brett knew Jo had informed her parents that she was getting married, it was obvious she was not happy about making this call. Brett listened intently to Jo's short, terse conversation, anger stirring when she winced at something that was said to her. The moment she'd replaced the receiver, Brett enfolded Jo in his arms.

"It's all right, water baby," Brett soothed as she began to weep. "Don't cry, love."

"You don't understand," Jo sniffed, burrowing into his chest. "Talking to my mother always makes me cry. You see, my mother and father hate each other. And it's so sad . . . They're both so very unhappy."

What could he say to comfort her? Coming from a happy family, Brett hadn't the vaguest idea. So, instead of words, he comforted her with caresses. Jo didn't cry very long.

CHAPTER TEN

Jo woke to the delicious sensation of her husband's lips exploring her face.

Her husband! A shiver of pleasure rippled through Jo's mind and body. Brett's arm, bent at the elbow, made a V on her chest; his fingers combed through the tangled mass of her hair. Circling his wrist with her hand, Jo lifted it to peer at the face of the slim gold watch he'd forgotten to remove in the heat of the moment the night before. The digits pulsed to eleven fifteen. She had been Mrs. Brett Renninger for over twenty-four hours!

Eleven fifteen! Good heavens! Jo stared at the watch in disbelief. She never slept past nine in the morning, not even on her days off or on holidays! Of course, that was before one very handsome man breezed into her life, and her bed, keeping her awake until the darkness of night gave sway to the pearl gray of predawn. A memory thrill tiptoed down Jo's spine. Had any bride ever had a more ardent bridegroom? Had any bride ever experienced such consummate ecstasy? Jo very seriously doubted it. But, even so, it was time to get up! Even if she infinitely preferred to lay luxuriating in her marriage bed.

"Brett?"

"Hmmm?" Brett's warm breath caressed her ear.

"Do you know what time it is?" Gulping back a gasp, Jo managed a steady tone.

"Time to make love to you again?" Brett responded immediately, hopefully, gently nipping at her earlobe.

Jo tried, and failed, to suppress the laughter that bubbled into her throat. "What are you?" she demanded in a falsely stern voice. "Some kind of sex maniac?"

"No," Brett denied calmly, poking the tip of his tongue into her ear. "I'm every kind of sex maniac." Raising his head, Brett gazed at her with eyes so soft with tenderness, Jo's throat closed with emotion. "But," he qualified seriously, "I only suffer this libido madness when in the company of one particular woman. The rest of the female population is absolutely safe from me."

Even Marsha Wenger? Jo, cautioning herself against being stupid, ordered the question to remain silent. As far as she knew, Brett had not seen Marsha outside the office since he'd followed her to Ocean City. Marsha's loss is my gain, Jo decided with a feeling of ruthlessness she had never before experienced. Brett is *mine!*

"Have you been eating raw oysters and swallowing vitamin E capsules while I wasn't looking?" she teased, banishing all consideration of Marsha.

"Not necessary," Brett murmured, the quirk at the corners of his mouth telegraphing the coming grin. "Merely touching you here—" His wrist slipped out of her hand and his fingers blazed a fiery trail from her throat to the tip of one breast. "And here—" His fingers drew a straight, tantalizing line down her body. "And especially *here*—" His fingers slid into the moist warmth of her. "Is all the aphrodisiac I need." Brett moved his fingers enticingly and Jo, her breathing already erratic, arched her hips into his hand. All traces of Brett's grin disappeared as his eyes swept down over her body.

Jo felt the heat rising in her in reaction to his close scrutiny of her responsiveness. Watching her intently, Brett stroked a

228

particularly sensitive spot, his eyes flaring silver with passion when her body writhed in pleasurable agony. Embarrassed by having him witness her abandoned response, Jo tensed her muscles in an attempt to withdraw from his maddening fingers.

"Brett . . . what are . . . you doing?" Jo pushed the protest out between short, rasping breaths.

"There are many ways of giving and receiving pleasure, love," Brett said softly, continuing his mind-divorcing slow stroke. "Together you and I are going to explore most of them. Relax, darling," he husked, luring the tension out of Jo's muscles. "Enjoy. I am."

Jo was beyond protest. Closing her eyes, she surrendered to the moment and the clamoring demand of her body for release. Jo knew Brett was watching her every frantic move, hearing her every labored breath but, suddenly, inexplicably, she no longer cared. Instinct or unformed intelligent reason routed all shame. Brett was her husband, the man she loved more than her own life. How could she feel shame in loving his lovemaking? She couldn't. Sighing in relief, Jo reveled in the enjoyment Brett offered her, thinking, vaguely, his turn would come.

Jo's vague thoughts proved correct some fifteen or twenty minutes later. When the last of his shudders had subsided, and his weight was a sweet heaviness on her seemingly boneless body, Brett lifted his head to kiss her softly. "I love—" He paused— because he was still out of breath? Jo wondered, afraid to think or even hope—then, disappointingly, he went on, "being with you, being around you, being in you." As if, no matter how much he had, he couldn't get enough of her, Brett kissed her again. "You love it too, don't you?"

"Yes," Jo admitted, swallowing the tightness in her throat that presaged tears in her eyes. "I love it too." The sense of defeat, of disappointment, was crushing. She had known Brett was not in love with her, still Jo had dared to hope. Hope gone, Jo consoled herself with the thought that, although Brett was not in love with her, he was not in love with any other woman either.

The very idea of Brett loving another woman made Jo tremble in fear of losing him.

"Are you cold, love?" Brett asked at once, then answered for her. "Of course you are." Carefully lifting his weight from her, Brett rolled to the edge of the bed and sat up. "Come along, darling. A hot shower will warm you up." Tilting his perfectly sculpted head, Brett slanted a teasing look at her. "Then, after you're all nice and warm, I'll take you skiing, and you can get cold all over again."

Pushing all thoughts of being unloved, and all consideration of other women from her mind, Jo arched one brow and taunted dryly, "Why are you so good to me?" The instant the gibe was out of her mouth Jo realized she'd let herself wide open for a zinger. Brett's slow grin told her she was right.

"Because you're such a hot number in the sack," he shot back every bit as dryly. "And because I had the proper up-dragging," he added, deadpan.

Jo refused to acknowledge the twinge of pain Brett's taunt had inflicted. He was obviously teasing, besides, with him, she *was* a hot number in the sack. Instead of feeling hurt, Jo chided herself, you should feel complimented. Not two years ago another man had damned near convinced you you were a walking, talking iceberg! You should be thankful for what you do have, not cry for what you don't have. And, right now, you have a husband who dearly loves to tease. Get with it, girl!

"Dragging is the perfect term," Jo rejoined, getting with it for all she was worth. "Insofar as your mind being dragged through the dirt, that is."

Leaning to her, Brett scowled threateningly. "Are you implying I have a dirty mind?"

"Oh, no." Jo smiled sweetly. "I'm *declaring* you have a dirty mind." Jo was up and running to the bathroom before she'd finished speaking, flicking the lock on the door a hairsbreadth before Brett reached it.

"Let me in, love," he coaxed, rattling the knob. "I promise I won't beat you . . . much."

Standing inside the door, Jo rested her forehead against the wood panel. She hated being separated from him, even by a hollow door. Dear God! Jo thought wonderingly, How is it possible to love so deeply? If he ever leaves me I'll . . . I'll . . .

"Jo." Brett's forlorn tone brought a smile to Jo's lips. "Please let me in."

"Will you buy me diamonds?"

"Yes."

"Will you buy me furs?"

"Yes, yes."

By now, tears running unheeded down her cheeks, Jo was shaking with laughter.

"How about a Maserati?"

"Are you crazy?" he bellowed. "Do you have any idea what they cost?"

Brushing impatiently at her wet cheeks, Jo unlocked the door.

Although Brett extended their stay in Vermont, the days disappeared like spring snow in warm sunshine. They spent most of their afternoons skiing, Brett on the high runs, Jo with the beginners. Their nights and mornings they spent alone, usually in bed. They were sitting in bed on their last morning, sipping coffee, when Brett asked casually . . . far too casually:

"What if you're pregnant?"

"I'm not," Jo answered calmly, ignoring the sudden wish that she was.

"How do you know?" Brett persisted. "We've certainly tried hard enough."

"I'm on the pill, Brett." Drawing a deep breath, Jo looked him straight in the eyes. What was he probing for? Jo speculated, searching his eyes for an answer. Was he hoping she was pregnant? Was he praying she wasn't? His eyes darkened with confusion and something else Jo could not identify.

"Since when?" Brett's quiet voice made Jo uneasy.

"Since the day you moved into my apartment," Jo replied in her self-enforced calm. "I already had the prescription. All I had to do was have it refilled." Jo grew chilled at Brett's sudden shuttered, withdrawn expression.

"Of course." He smiled wryly, increasing Jo's chill. "How stupid of me." Moving with a swiftness that startled Jo, he slid off the bed and stood up. "I guess we'd better pack. We have a long drive ahead of us."

Brett remained terse and withdrawn throughout the entire drive back to New York. Both confused and hurt by his quick change in attitude, Jo gave up her frustrating, fruitless attempts to draw him into conversation forty-five minutes into the trip.

Watching his expensively gloved hands control the powerful sports car with effortless ease, Jo sighed silently. This was not the first time Brett had coldly shut himself away from her without explanation. Was he opposed to her taking birth control pills? If so, why hadn't he simply told her he was? She'd like nothing better than to flush the things down the toilet. God! Jo shivered in the warmth of the car's heater. A good screaming match would be preferable to this freeze-out.

Sliding down into the supple leather of the bucket seat, Jo rested her head on the high seat back and closed her eyes. Would she ever understand this complex man she'd married? She knew his body intimately and his mind not at all. What motivates him? she mused. He works like a Trojan, yet doesn't need the money he accumulates. He laughs and teases like a carefree boy, then broods like an overburdened man. He amuses me. He confuses me. He scares me to death. Unaware of the sharp-eyed glances the object of her thoughts slanted at her periodically, Jo sighed in longing for the carefree boy who amuses.

Jo opened her eyes briefly when she heard a clicking sound, then closed them again as Brett finished sliding a tape into the machine attached to the underside of the dashboard. The music that filled the small interior of the car surprised her. If she'd been

232

asked to guess what kind of music Brett enjoyed, her last guess would have been Paul Williams, yet that's who she was now listening to! Losing herself in the singer's odd yet enchanting voice, Jo let her thoughts drift.

There was a danger in allowing one's thoughts to drift, Jo found to her chagrin. Unfettered, thoughts tended to drift in the wrong direction. Unwelcomed by Jo, the memory of her two phone calls to her mother sidled into her mind. Sighing again, she gave the memories free rein, hoping she'd then be able to put them out of her mind. Jo had made the first call to her mother the day after Brett's wildly unorthodox proposal of marriage. Quite like Brett had done when he'd phoned his mother after the fact, Jo had not beat around the bush.

"I'm getting married next week," Jo had said starkly, wincing at her mother's gasp of dismay.

"You're out of your mind!" Ellen had exclaimed angrily. Not "do you love him?" Or even "to whom?" Just "You're out of your mind."

Jo had dug her nails into her palm in reaction to the scorn in her mother's voice. Controlling her tone with sheer will, Jo had replied, "Perhaps so but, nevertheless, I'm getting married." Then, though unasked, she offered the name of the groom. "I'm going to marry Brett Renninger."

"Your boss?" Ellen asked with sudden interest.

"Yes." Jo had been totally unprepared for her mother's next words.

"Well, when the bubble bursts, at least you'll have money to fall back on."

"I'd never accept money from Brett like that, Mother," Jo had said with quiet determination.

"Now I'm convinced you're crazy," Ellen had retorted disgustedly. "Well, I won't waste my time wishing you happiness. The rich ones are even worse than the men without money. They can always buy their way out, and they know it. What I do wish

233

is that you'll change your mind before it's too late. Live with him, if you must. But think twice before you commit yourself."

Jo stirred restlessly, wondering when Brett had changed the tape. Now the sexy voice of Neil Diamond swirled around her head from the car's four speakers.

"Are you hungry?" Brett's voice was soft but the unexpected sound of it startled Jo into opening her eyes.

"No." Thinking the denial too uncompromising, Jo added quietly, "Are you?"

"No."

Anger flared inside Jo's mind. Arrogant beast! Apparently being uncompromising doesn't bother him! I should have listened to my mother! Jo regretted the thought immediately. No! She was not sorry she'd married Brett. Even if she did long to punch his lights out at this moment! Closing her eyes, Jo deliberately dredged up the memory of her second phone call to her mother. Knowing Brett was listening to her side of the conversation, Jo had chosen her words very carefully.

"It's Jo, Mother," she'd said with all the lightness she could muster. "I'm calling from Vermont to tell you Brett and I were married this morning."

"You have my deepest sympathy." Ellen sighed before adding, "Is he there with you now?"

"Yes, Mother." Jo had fought to keep her tone even.

"Tell him I said he's to take good care of you, even though I know he probably won't." There'd been a pause, then her mother had gone on in a muffled tone, "I love you, honey. I wish . . . I wish . . . well, it doesn't matter what I wish. I *do* hope you'll be happy, but . . . " Her voice trailed away.

Feeling the hot sting of tears behind her lashes, Jo opened her eyes and sat up abruptly, shaking her head sharply to dislodge the sound of her mother's sad voice.

"What the hell?" Brett sliced a frown at her. "What's the matter?"

"Nothing. It's nothing. I got a cramp in my neck from my

awkward position," Jo improvised, lifting her hand to rub the side of her neck. "It's fine now."

Brett returned his attention to the highway but his frown remained in place. "Even so, I think it's time we stopped to stretch and, while we're doing it, we might as well eat something."

The restaurant Brett found was unpretentious but clean and the food was superior. Jo ate less than half her dinner. Brett drank his. When he motioned the waiter to indicate he'd like a third Rob Roy, Jo reached out impulsively to grasp his hand.

"Brett! You've got quite a distance to drive. If you expect me to get into the car with you, don't have another drink."

Brett Renninger was not at all used to being told what to do, and Jo knew it. She also knew there was no way she'd ride in a car with a driver who was not only in a foul mood, but three sheets to the wind as well. Her resolve rock hard, Jo stared defiantly into Brett's icy, narrow-lidded eyes. Amazingly, Brett relented first, albeit angrily.

"A wife of little more than a week," he sneered, waving the waiter away. "And already you're issuing ultimatums." Brett extracted several bills from his wallet and tossed them on top of the check the waiter slid discreetly onto the table. Glancing back at Jo, he pinned her to her seat with eyes the color of cold steel. "This is the second time I've backed down to an ultimatum from you." Brett's voice was as steely as his eyes. Jo, her spine tingling with apprehension, had a memory flash of their confrontation in his office the day she'd lifted the phone to call Wolf in Florida. Raising her chin, Jo managed, just, to meet his stare unflinchingly. "Three strikes and you're out, sweetie," Brett said grittily. "Don't push your luck . . . or me too damn far."

Jo's gasp burst into the tension hovering in the air between them. Was Brett threatening her? Well, of course he was! Jo swallowed the taste of panic. What, exactly, was he threatening her with? The promise of physical retaliation? Jo rejected the idea at once. Without knowing how she knew, Jo was positive

Brett would never raise his hand to her in violence. Then what form would his retaliation take? The answer that stole into Jo's mind was accompanied by a choking nausea in her throat. He'd said "three strikes and you're out." Out as in: out of a job? Out of his life? Out of his sight? Out of a husband? Jo was very much afraid Brett meant every one of the outs that marched through her rattled brain.

The nausea lasted only a moment, then fled before the onslaught of fury. If Brett Renninger thought he could frighten her into quivering submission, he was in for a very rude awakening! Gritting her teeth, Jo leaned across the table to enable him to hear the rage in her soft voice.

"Don't you ever threaten me again. *You* are the one who followed me to Ocean City. *You* are the one who moved into *my* apartment. *You* are the one who insisted on marriage." Jo paused to gulp air into her constricted lungs, then, forcing her teeth apart, made a threat of her own . . . or at least attempted to.

"If you ever threaten me again, I'll . . . I'll. . ."

"You'll what?" Brett inserted in a quiet tone that in no way concealed his own fury. "Call the big prowler?"

"I don't need Wolf to protect me from you," Jo retorted. "Now, if you are tired of me, or bored with this situation you forced the both of us into, take a hike!" Pushing her chair back, Jo jumped to her feet, grabbed her coat, and, still glaring at Brett, underlined her position. "I don't need you, Brett," she lied convincingly. "I don't need any of the Renningers." Sliding the coat around her shoulders, Jo strode out of the restaurant.

For the remainder of the drive to New York the sports car took on the qualities of an abandoned tomb. There were moments when Jo was certain the silence would shatter her eardrums.

It was early evening when they arrived at the apartment. Jo's fury had long since burned itself out. By the time she walked into her bedroom, Jo was combating an overwhelming feeling of loss. Disregarding Brett's warning, she had issued one final ultimatum. She had figuratively pointed out the direction of the door. Now Jo was terrified Brett would literally walk out of it. Throwing her coat at the chair she had spent weeks shopping for, Jo stood in the middle of the room, stiff as a board and scared witless.

"Jo?" As soft as it was, Brett's voice jerked Jo around to face him.

"What?" Jo was amazed at the steadiness she'd managed to convey. In actuality, she was afraid to hear whatever he was about to say.

"I'm not at all tired of you." Brett walked to her slowly as he made the tension-relieving statement. As he drew near, Jo could see that all his anger was gone too.

"You're not?" Jo had to fight the urge to fling herself into his arms.

"No." Brett shook his head, a conciliatory smile tugging at his lips. "I'm also not bored with our situation."

"Then . . . why . . . ?" Jo gazed at him in confusion, her eyes begging for an explanation.

"It was the mention of a preexisting prescription for birth control pills." Brett shrugged, as if trying to rid himself of an unbearable weight. "No man likes to be reminded of his predecessor." Raising his hand, he touched her hair very gently. "I'm . . . sorry." Brett's hesitation was telling; he did not make apologies often. The relief that washed through Jo was shocking in its intensity.

"I'm sorry too," she whispered, blinking against a sudden rush of tears.

Jo gulped back a sob as she was hauled into Brett's arms. God! It was heaven, like being ushered into a warm room after standing naked in the freezing night. Burying her face in his chest, she slid her arms beneath his jacket and around his waist.

"Honey, are you crying?" The concern in Brett's voice was nearly Jo's undoing.

"No." Sniffing, Jo rubbed her face against his rough wool sweater.

Brett's long fingers caught her chin to lift her face to his scrutiny. "You are crying. And I'm a bastard for making you cry. Honey, don't." He brought his other hand up to brush at the tears. Bending low, close to her ear, Brett whispered in a teasing drawl, "If you stop crying, I'll buy you the Maserati."

A bubble of happiness burst inside Jo, creating shock waves of laughter that could not be contained. "And the diamonds?" She sniffed through a peel of laughter.

"And the diamonds." Brett sighed exaggeratedly.

"And the furs?" Jo fluttered her lashes at him.

"I'm afraid the furs will cost you," Brett said seriously.

Jo's laughter died in her throat, killed by the abrupt change in his voice. "Cost me?" she repeated blankly. "What will it cost me?"

"You'll probably consider the price too steep, but . . . " Brett paused, his tone solemn, then, he went on quietly, "I'd prefer it if you didn't take the pill anymore."

"Not take it!" Caught off guard, Jo stared at him in consternation. If things were different between them, if he loved her instead of loving to be with her, around her—Jo shivered in memory—in her, she'd glory in conceiving, carrying, and bearing his child. But Brett did not love her. He did not yearn to have proof of that love expressed in the form of a child. Brett's sole reason for asking her to discontinue the pill had more to do with pride than any other emotion. In his own words, Brett did not like being reminded of his predecessor—Gary Devlin. Still, after basking in the warmth of his arms and recent concern, Jo shuddered with the fear of having him revert back to the cold stranger he'd been all day. Could she refuse his request? Dare she refuse him?

"Tough decision, huh?" Brett's soft voice held a betraying thread of tension, tension that Jo now knew could quickly change to icy withdrawal.

Jo's sigh was the harbinger of her approaching capitulation. She didn't like it. In fact, she resented his use of coercion, especially this type of coercion, yet she knew she would yield in the end. She really hadn't much of a choice. It was either give way or face the cold stranger. Damn! Her mother was right, Jo thought distractedly. Being in love hurt in more ways than Jo had ever thought there *were* ways! If Jo had once believed Gary was a manipulator, she now knew he was a piker in comparison to Brett Renninger; Brett was a master of the art!

"Jo?" Brett was losing patience. He was attempting concealment with his low tone and the tender way he brushed her forehead with his lips, but Jo could hear the warning knell of impatience loud and clear.

Jo's face sought comfort in his sweater again. "All right, Brett." Tightening her arms around his waist, Jo clung to his lean frame in silent, possessive desperation, facing the unpalatable truth that she would very likely do anything to keep him satisfied—and with her. "I'll stop taking them . . . if that's what you want."

"Yes. That *is* what I want."

Holding him tightly, Jo could feel the tension easing out of his body. Could feel that tension being replaced by an unmistakable quickening. Brett's long thigh muscles tightened to press against hers in an urgent, demanding way. Moving his body suggestively, Brett made Jo excitingly aware of his arousal.

"You won't be sorry, love." Brett's caressing words were every bit as enticing as his body language. "I promise, you won't be sorry."

Jo's capitulation was complete; she was his, mind, body, and soul. Of course she knew it and, if his triumphant laughter as he urged her toward the bed could be used as an indicator, Brett knew it too.

The month of February seemed even shorter than usual for Jo. Except for a few minor irritants, and one glaringly jarring incident, Jo sailed through the cold, snowy month wrapped in a warm cocoon of marital bliss.

As the one glaring incident occurred when Brett tenderly draped a breathtakingly beautiful, full-length sable coat over her shoulders the day after he'd witnessed her disposal of the controversial pill, Jo was also wrapped in the cocooning warmth of shockingly expensive fur, even though she had resisted the gift on general principle. There was too much the feeling of payment about the coat. When Jo tried to explain her feelings to Brett, *he* took offense.

"Payment?" he barked, pulling her face close to his by tugging on the wide collar. "What do you mean? Not, I hope, like in 'for services rendered'?"

As that was exactly what she had meant, Jo winced and bit her lip, thereby giving herself away. Jo did not want a sable coat. She had never wanted any kind of fur coat. Warily studying Brett's frowning face, Jo ran her palms over the luxurious fur while advising herself to be prudent. From the look of him, she would have to be completely mad to refuse his gift on any grounds.

"It . . . it is a beautiful coat," she offered lamely, sighing when his frown deepened.

"I know *that!*" Now Brett narrowed his eyes. "*I* chose it. I did not call the shop and order it. I went to the store and picked it out for you." All the time he was speaking his voice grew softer, causing Jo's skin to tingle in warning. "But whether or not the damn thing is beautiful is beside the point. You didn't answer my question."

"Brett . . . "

"No!" Brett cut her off roughly. "I think I don't want to hear your answer. Please just say thank you, Jo."

Jo said thank you. As a matter of fact, Jo said thank you in more than words. Less than an hour after he'd sprung the coat on her, he was smiling again. Jo fully realized that to keep him smiling at her she'd wear the coat, and, to keep him so deliciously ardent, she'd even wear it to bed if he asked her to! Marriage was a compromise—wasn't it? Besides, she felt singularly honored by Brett's assurance that he had personally selected the garment. She knew the schedule Brett maintained better than any other person, including his secretary. Brett's days began early and ended late, and every hour between was packed with meetings, conferences, reports to go over, phone calls to receive or make, and various other details he insisted on seeing to himself. That Brett had thought enough of her to take the time to shop, when she knew full well his loathing for shopping, was a compliment to her. Jo accepted his compliment gratefully and told her sense of moral insult to cool it. Her principles had not been compromised! Since when did a husband have to pay for favors?

The irritants that marred Jo's otherwise euphoric month of wedded bliss were simply that, irritants, all concerned with the office. The major irritant was the mere sight of Marsha Wenger. Fortunately Jo saw the New England area manager seldom, but every time she did see Marsha, Jo smiled coolly and cursed silently. That what she was experiencing was rampant jealousy, Jo readily admitted—to herself. It was a new emotion, one Jo was positive she could very well have done without. She hated it and the mean way it made her feel, but there it was, all blatant and green eyed. Strangely, Jo had never felt the slightest twinge of jealousy over Gary, and the females had fluttered all over him wherever they had gone. Reluctantly, Jo faced the fact that what she had felt for Gary had been infatuation . . . and a rather shallow infatuation at that. She hadn't been in love with Gary at all, merely in love with the idea of being in love! It was a home truth Jo accepted, then put from her mind. Perhaps everyone had to experience the trauma of near love to appreciate the real thing when it finally did come along.

Early in March, Brett was away for the longest five days Jo had ever lived through. Both Brett and Sean were in the Poconos, ironing out some labor union wrinkles, and while he was away Jo began to understand Casey's attitude of the previous December. At the time, Casey had been frustrated and bitchy, and all because Sean had been away. During the five days, and what seemed like twice as many nights, that Brett was away, Jo was tormented by a like frustration and bitchiness. Thinking about Casey had given Jo some purpose though. In an effort to fill the lonely evening hours, Jo's knitting needles clicked away at a furious pace. A tiny, delicately fashioned pair of booties in a soft shade of yellow appeared the first night she was alone. Jo's industry of the second night produced a small matching cap. By the time Jo put her work aside on the third night, her eyes stinging from strain, her yarn was over half gone and an infant's sweater was easily discernable as it grew beneath her needles. The fourth night of Brett's absence the knitting lay forgotten as Jo worked on a report she'd brought home from the office. But, on the fifth and, Jo fervently hoped, the last night, she was busy knit, purl, knit, purling, when she heard the sound of a key turning the lock on the front door. The furious clicking stopped as, joy leaping through her entire body, Jo glanced up to see Brett stride into the room.

Brett looked tired, and windblown, and cold, and absolutely beautiful. He was outfitted in dark corduroy jeans, low boots, and a thigh-length, pile-lined suede jacket, and he looked like he'd just left the project site. Jo, both surprised and delighted by his early return, opened her mouth, but before the words of welcome and question could be formed, Brett explained in three terse words.

"I missed you."

Jo stopped breathing at the expression in Brett's eyes as he crossed the room to where she was sitting. His eyes, shot with silver, raked her face avidly before slowly drifting down over her body. When his glance touched the knitting, still clutched in her hands, his glance held, a frown drawing his brows together.

"Why do I get this uncanny image of a nineteen forties Hollywood scenario?" Brett's eyes remained fastened on the knitting as he muttered the question.

Bemused by the query, probably because she was still tingling all over in reaction to his admittance of having missed her, Jo shook her head in confusion. Nineteen forties? Hollywood? It was Jo's turn to frown. What the devil was Brett talking about?

"I'm afraid I don't understand, Brett. What scenario?"

Jo's baffled tone drew his intent gaze to her face. "Oh, you know." Brett's reply was oddly terse. "You must have seen it on the late-late movie at least once. It's the scene in which the young wife uses this type"—a quick movement of his hand indicated the knitting Jo was still clutching—"of contrivance to tell the young husband the 'big' news."

Jo's frown deepened. Feeling extremely dense, she glanced down at her work. Oh, gosh! Surely Brett didn't think . . . ? But of course he did. What else could he mean? Lifting her head, Jo studied Brett's face in an effort to discern his emotional reaction to his own hasty judgment. Her visual probe went unrewarded; Brett's expression was devoid of reaction. Whatever he was feeling, Brett was keeping it completely to himself.

"Brett, I think you might be jumping to the wrong conclusion here." Jo lay the knitting aside before continuing. "I'm knitting the sweater set for Casey's baby."

"Then you're not pregnant?" Brett's voice was flat, a trifle gritty, and maddeningly unrevealing.

Was he relieved? Was he disappointed? Jo didn't know, and not knowing was both frustrating and irritating. There had been moments during the last month when Jo had felt a closeness between them, a kind of coming together mentally that was every bit as exciting as their satisfying physical union. Jo longed for that closeness to mature. Having Brett lock his feelings away from her about something as important as the possibility of a child imbued in her the fear that their relationship had not progressed at all!

"No, Brett, I'm not pregnant." Jo sighed in sudden weariness.

"And damned glad of it." Brett's smile was cynical. "Right?"

Then and there Jo decided she hated his cynicism. Damn it, she *did* want his child! Jo also wanted to spend the rest of her life as his wife. But she was afraid. She was scared silly of this commitment they had rushed headlong into. Hell! Jo still wasn't even sure Brett liked her as a person, even though he no longer looked at her with open disdain. What were her chances of ever hearing him promise a lifetime commitment to her? As clearly as if Brett were speaking the words aloud at that minute, Jo heard his voice of months before: "While the fire rages, I intend to have you." It was the fear of the fire being consumed by its own intensity that made Jo answer:

"Yes, Brett, I am glad I'm not pregnant." Forcing herself to look into his eyes, Jo challenged him to declare himself on the issue. "Aren't you?"

Brett didn't quite pull off a shrug that was intended to be careless. "To tell you the truth, I really don't know. The possibility of you becoming pregnant has been on the fringes of my consciousness ever since I asked you to stop taking the pill." Removing his jacket, Brett walked slowly to the closet to hang it up. As he turned back to her he frowned. "I like kids. I've always enjoyed being around my nieces and nephew. I've never given much thought to having a child of my own." Brett's brief smile held traces of bitterness. "Sondra didn't want children either."

Jo shot to her feet. How dare he equate her with his former wife? If only half of what she'd heard about Sondra via the office grapevine was true, Sondra was nothing more than a playgirl, interested in no one except Sondra. Her feelings smarting from Brett's bitter dart, Jo planted her fists on her hips and glared at him.

"Back it up, Mr. Renninger!" Jo's voice trembled with hurt anger. "This seems to be your night for jumping to conclusions . . . all of them wrong! I did not say I don't want children. What I said was, I'm glad I'm not pregnant. I meant, at this time." Jo paused to draw breath and to try and get a grip on her turbulent emotions. Sondra indeed! She had no idea of the picture she presented to Brett in her silk robe with her hair a tumbled mass around her quivering shoulders and her hazel eyes flashing amber sparks at him. All Jo realized was she had to set Brett straight on this score once and for all.

"I also like kids! And, though you might find it extremely hard to believe, I have the required amount of maternal instincts!"

"Jo . . . "

"Let me finish!" Off and running, Jo trampled Brett's attempt to speak. "Good grief, man! We've only been married a month! We've hardly had a chance to become accustomed to each other, let alone a new individual! I just don't think now is . . . "

"JO!" Brett shouted her down. "Will you please shut up?"

Brett's bellow had the desired effect; Jo's mouth closed, her eyes opened wide in shock. Jo had seen Brett in a cold rage. She had seen him locked inside icy withdrawal. Once he had even raised his voice to her. But she had never actually heard him yell, at anyone. There was no way Jo could mask her surprise. She blinked once, then stared at him, the inside of her bottom lip caught between her teeth.

Brett, his nostrils flaring with his rate of inhalation, took the two steps necessary to bring him to within inches of Jo. Lifting his hand, Brett raked long fingers through his hair, ruffling the thick ash-blond waves. "I get the message, Jo." Brett sighed, then smiled apologetically. "And, of course, you're right. We haven't become accustomed to each other yet." His hand moved from his hair to hers, not raking now but stroking, smoothing. "We're going to have to work on the mutual learning process." Brett's tone was soft now, gentling. "Okay?"

Staring into his eyes, as soft as the feathers on a gray dove, Jo felt all the tension and irritation drain out of her. It was always the same. All Brett had to do was lower his voice and look at her tenderly, and she was completely his. It's not fair! A small spark of defiance tried to make itself heard above the flutter of

Jo's pulse. It is simply not fair for him to have this much control over me, when I have no effect whatever on him. Well, that wasn't quite true and Jo admitted it. She did have some effect. Jo could see the effect on Brett's body and in the tiny flame beginning to leap in his eyes. Jo knew she had the power to arouse Brett's body. There had been moments when she'd connected with his mind. Why couldn't she touch his heart?

"Okay, Brett." Jo acceded to his request in a whisper that betrayed the unhappiness her thoughts had churned up. Not even hearing the sound of her own voice, and unaware of the cloudy sadness dulling her eyes, Jo could only guess at the strange expression that moved spasmodically over Brett's face. Had it been anyone else, Jo would have concluded the expression was one of quickly suppressed pain. But not Brett; Brett had no reason to feel pain and every reason to feel triumphant. Brett had won . . . again. "How do you suggest we go about this learning process?" Jo recognized the stupidity of her question even as she voiced it. Damn this man for owning the ability to rattle her so effortlessly!

Brett's lips twitched in the quirky smile that had become so very endearing to Jo. "I know how I'd like to go about it," he said teasingly. "I've slept alone for four nights." The quirk progressed at its usual rate into a grin. "Let me rephrase that statement. I tried to sleep alone for four nights. I did not succeed very well. I missed you like hell, Jo." By the time Brett had finished speaking the grin was gone.

Jo was long past deciphering Brett's intricately simplistic admission. Merely knowing he had missed her was enough, for now. "I—I missed you too, Brett, that's why I picked up the knitting in the first place. I didn't know what to do without you here." The murmured confession escaped through Jo's unguarded mental barriers while she was otherwise occupied by becoming lost inside the gray prison of Brett's eyes. Vaguely, Jo wondered why the flame in those gray depths suddenly leaped wildly. As it was where Jo had wanted to be since he'd walked into the room, she never entertained the thought of resistance when Brett drew her into his arms. Home. Jo sighed with relief. The scent of him, his aftershave, the hint of whisky on his breath, even the faint, woolly odor of his sweater, all were now the scents of home to Jo.

"I was going to suggest we go the usual route in our learning process." Brett's lips skimmed her forehead. "You know, open a bottle of wine, get comfortable on the sofa, and talk until we run out of words." As if drawn by a lure too enticing to resist, his lips made a direct path down her small nose to her mouth. "But, on consideration, four days without you is three and a half days too long. We'll still have a bottle of wine, but I think we'll drink it in bed." Brett's lips teased Jo's for mind-bending seconds. "After we've communicated in a more basic language," he whispered into her mouth.

Brett proceeded to converse very fluently without speaking a syllable. He began the dialogue with his lips, and his tongue, and his hands. Then, with his body, Brett presented a brilliant dissertation on communication. Distracted by sensations seemingly tripping over each other as they raced crazily through her body, Jo was ignorant of the fact that her own silent thesis was being presented with equal eloquence.

Brett eventually did get around to opening a bottle of wine, but only after they had both had a short, reviving nap and a long, revitalizing shower. Brett went to the kitchen while Jo remade the thoroughly disordered bed. Clad in the striped silk robe, she was reclining against the headboard when Brett strolled into the bedroom, a bottle of white wine and two glasses in one hand and a tray of sandwiches in the other.

"It's a good thing this is Friday night," he observed dryly. "As I'm planning to lay siege to your mind, and your body, through most of it."

"Actually, I was thinking of going into the office tomorrow," Jo lied unconvincingly. In truth, she had glumly looked forward

247

to pacing the apartment till he came home. "There's a report I should finish to have ready for mailing on Monday."

Placing the tray of sandwiches on her legs, Brett slid onto the bed beside Jo and poured wine for the both of them before bothering to reply. "I could give you my opinion on your report," he drawled, arching one brow as he lifted his glass to her in a silent salute. "But I seem to recall shocking you the last time I gave a similar opinion concerning one of my suits." His devilish eyes made a liar of his innocent expression. "I believe you were in the bathtub at the time."

"Conjured up a rather strange picture too," Jo speculated thoughtfully. "Sounds exceedingly dull to me. I mean, really, a suit and a report?" She yawned delicately.

Brett fell apart and, in the process, splashed wine on his chest and the mid-thigh-length navy blue toweling robe he was wearing. When his roar of laughter subsided to a low chuckle, he shook his head in bemused amazement. "You are the only woman I have ever known who could do this to me," Brett confessed around a grin. "Come to think of it, I don't know anyone else who can make me laugh like you can." Sobering, he leaned to her to kiss her gently. "It feels good to laugh with you." When Brett lifted his head he was smiling. "Come to that, practically everything we do together makes me feel good. How about you?" he probed blatantly.

Jo's smile was a reflection of Brett's. "Makes me feel good too," she offered softly. "For the most part, I've enjoyed our being together."

"For the most part," Brett repeated quietly. "Well, that's a start." Picking up a piece of sandwich, he examined the ham-and-cheese filling as if he'd never seen it before. "Time for the learning process to begin, I think." Taking a tentative bite, he chewed it thoroughly and washed it down with a healthy swallow of wine. "I already know you are terrific at your job, knit like a wizard, and can't cook worth a damn," Brett finally continued. "What other talents, or lack thereof, are contained within the beautiful package you call yourself?"

"I'm great in bed." It was not a declaration but a question, if a teasing one. Although Brett obviously understood, he chose to treat Jo's query as a statement of fact.

"Granted." Brett's concurrence was made in all seriousness. "What else? And please feel free to elaborate."

Jo hesitated briefly, then, thinking—what have I got to lose?—opened her mind, if not her heart, to him. "I am, by nature, quiet. But I think I told you that before?" Jo arched a brow at him in question; Brett nodded. "I like almost all kinds of music, from classical to country western. I love movies, especially science fiction. I have a passion for clothes that by far exceed my budget."

"No longer," Brett inserted at this point of her litany. "I'll take care of your clothing bills."

Jo stiffened noticably. It was the sable-fur dilemma all over again. The last thing Jo wanted to do was stir Brett's anger. On the other hand, she didn't want him paying her bills either. Why having Brett assume financial responsibility for her should make her feel like a kept woman, Jo didn't know, unless it had something to do with Brett not loving her. Jo had conscious knowledge of being his wife; the emotional impact was missing. She would much prefer to pay her own bills. Now, for Jo, the problem was how to convey her feelings to him. Brett was way ahead of her.

"Don't say it, Jo," he warned softly. "We've got the beginnings of a good picnic going here." Jo was well aware Brett was not referring to the impromptu supper he'd put together. "Don't rain on it."

"Brett . . . I—" Jo faltered. Was her independence really worth the price of this tenuous reaching out they had embarked on? She *was* Brett's wife, all legal and binding—or at least as binding as any marriage could be in this enlightened age. Leave it, her common sense advised. Meet him halfway, see what develops.

You have nothing to lose and the world to gain. "I play a fair hand of poker."

Brett stared at her blankly for an instant, then a grin of mixed delight and relief instilled animation; he grinned like a summer-time-happy boy. As if he were suddenly starving, Brett wolfed down another sandwich. Waving his hand at the depleted plate, he ordered her to follow suit. "Dig in, honey." Brett's grin removed the sting from the barb that trailed his invitation. "*I* do know how to put a sandwich together."

They ate and drank in silence until the plate and bottle were empty, then Brett made himself comfortable by stretching his long length out full and throwing his arms over his head.

"I'm going to toss another responsibility at you next week," he told her lazily.

Busy brushing bits of breadcrumbs off the sheet, Jo didn't even look up. "Really?" she replied idly. "What sort of responsibility?"

"I'm going to put you to interviewing applicants." He yawned. "The job bores the hell out of me."

"Applicants?" Jo glanced up to frown at him. The only applicants Brett ever personally interviewed were for managerial positions, and, to Jo's knowledge, there were no positions of that type open. "Applicants for what?"

"New England area manager." Brett exhaled in exasperation. "We've got less than a month to replace Marsha, Jo."

Marsha! Jo froze. Marsha was leaving the firm? At first the news thrilled Jo. Then the thrill was chased by apprehension. Why was Marsha leaving? And why hadn't Jo known about it? Had Brett deliberately kept the information from her for reasons of his own? Jo could think of only one reason Brett would have for keeping silent, and that reason did not bear thinking about. Pushing a sudden, explicit image of Brett and Marsha together in much the same way Jo and he were now, Jo made a production out of finding the last, tiniest crumb.

"Why is Marsha quitting?" Jo directed her question at the smooth sheet.

Brett hesitated for seconds that were pure agony for Jo. "Well," he began slowly, "I know all she'd say was her reason was personal but—" Again he hesitated, drawing Jo's nerves to quivering tautness. "What the hell, you are not only my assistant but my wife. Marsha's going to follow her husband."

Jo could not have been more stunned if Brett had told her Marsha was going to have a sex-change operation! Added to Jo's bafflement at Brett's seeming assumption that she'd known of Marsha's intention to leave the company, Brett's revelation of a heretofore unheard of husband left Jo totally speechless. Had she been beating her emotions to death since December for nothing? Had there ever been anything personal between Brett and Marsha? And does being in love make jackasses of everybody? This last consideration jolted Jo out of contemplation and into speech.

"Brett, let's clarify a few details here." Jo's voice contained a harsh undertone. She was fed up. She never had liked playing games, and this love game was starting to get to her. As Jo had never particularly liked mysteries either, she wasn't about to tolerate Marsha's. "Detail one," she said flatly. "I knew nothing about Marsha's resignation. Detail two: I knew nothing about a husband."

"Former husband," Brett inserted.

"Former or otherwise," Jo bit angrily. "Which brings about detail three: I was under the impression that you and she had indulged in a flaming affair last October in Vermont." Sitting up straight, Jo stared Brett directly in the eyes, defying him to deny an alliance with Marsha. When Brett didn't respond immediately, Jo added, "And what the hell do you mean, former husband? If they are no longer married, why is she chucking an excellent job to follow him?"

"Are you finished?" Brett asked softly. "Or are there more details on your list?"

"I'm finished." And very likely in more ways than one, she

added silently. But, good grief, how long could she go on living with this silliness? Jo demanded of herself. Sex, in itself, was not a panacea, the be-all and end-all of any relationship . . . let alone marriage! There had to be more or, if there was not, then her mother was right!

"Detail one." Brett's quietly controlled voice intruded on Jo's introspection and riveted her attention. "I honestly believed you did know of Marsha's resignation. She tendered it this past Monday." He regarded her steadily. "I thought I'd mentioned it before I left for the mountains. I'm sorry, but I was rushed. Okay?"

Jo let a nod suffice for reply. If he was on a roll, she certainly wasn't going to call a halt now.

"Detail number two is a little more involved. Marsha has been unhappily divorced for over a year. The marriage fell apart because Marsha, admittedly, neglected it in favor of her career." Brett shrugged. "Apparently, like most men, Marsha's husband labored under the illusion that he should come first. When he discovered he didn't, he sought comfort elsewhere."

"How delightful!" Jo exclaimed. "He sounds like a real charmer. And Marsha is going to repress her ambition to chase *him*?" Incensed at the very idea of what Marsha was doing, Jo momentarily forgot how relieved she'd felt on hearing of the woman's intentions mere moments ago.

Brett's expression hardened at her outburst. "Why the hell must it always come to this?" he demanded angrily. "Why do all career women feel they must carry this equality banner to the outer limits?"

"Because that's where it belongs!" Jo retorted.

"But, damn it, Jo!" Brett shot back. "Is there no workable solution? Men are only going to back up so far! When they have reached the wall, then what happens? Something has got to give."

"You mean some*one* has got to give!" Jo protested. "And, of course, that someone had better be female!"

"Not necessarily," Brett denied Jo's allegation.

"Oh, but it is in the case of Marsha, isn't it?" Jo sneered. She was angry, really angry, and yet she was trembling with excitement. She was actually loving every minute of this argument! Geared for mental battle, Jo missed the significance of her enjoyment, and that was that the lines of communication were wide open!

"Jo!" Brett shouted in exasperation. "Marsha loves the man. She has been miserable for over a year! But she has decided to meet him halfway . . . no more. Can you honestly sit there and insist she's wrong?"

"Brett, how can you insist she is only meeting him halfway?" Jo argued heatedly. "She's giving up her job. She's going to him. What, exactly, is *he* doing? No! Don't tell me, I know. *He* is waiting for her to come to her senses! Right?"

"I don't believe this! I positively do not believe this." Brett glanced around the room as if seeking guidance. "We are actually fighting over another couple's marital problems!"

"Yes," Jo responded impulsively. "Isn't it fun?"

Brett grinned, then sobered almost at once. "It would be, if we didn't have a few problems of our own." Brett met Jo's glance and held it. "There was no affair in October." He hesitated, then went on determinedly, "But not for lack of trying on my part."

Jo sat perfectly still, staring at him, while her conscience went to work on her. She longed to dissect his last statement, but did she have the right? No, she did not, her conscience advised. In actual fact, she'd had no right to ask him about October in the first place. Obviously Brett had assumed she'd pounce on his admission.

"No questions?" he probed, a strange note of disappointment edging his voice. "Aren't you curious . . . at all?"

Jo sighed. "Yes, I'm curious. But it really is none of my business. Is it?" After the effervescence of their argument, Jo felt flat. "What you did, and who you did it with, before we married,

253

is, in fact, none of my business." Jo broke the hold his eyes attempted to maintain.

"And so, of course, I have no right to ask you about your previous affair." Brett's tone had a corresponding flatness, tinged with accusation.

So he did know about Gary! Jo raised her eyes to encounter a blank wall. Brett had withdrawn. The lines of communication had snapped. Following Brett's example, Jo mentally withdrew.

"Not in that manner." Jo was amazed at the distant sound of her own voice.

"It doesn't matter." Brett's shrug had the impact of a blow to Jo's heart.

He doesn't really want to know, because he really doesn't care! The thought froze Jo's mind. Moving carefully, as if afraid she'd shatter into a million shards of ice if she hurried, Jo slid off the bed and walked into the bathroom thinking. The learning process is now over.

CHAPTER ELEVEN

Brett sat behind his brother's desk, staring fixedly at an unopened pack of cigarettes lying within inches of his hand. He had placed the pack on the smooth surface as a reminder of his own avowal of no more pacifiers. But it had been a very long three weeks since he and Jo had reached dead end the night he'd returned from Pennsylvania.

Why hadn't they been able to break free of constraint since then? Brett was afraid he knew the answer and simply didn't want to face it. Damn it, if she loved me . . . The desk chair was shoved back roughly as Brett jerked to his feet.

Stalking to the window, Brett scowled down at the miniature people scurrying about their business twenty-six stories below. God! He wanted a cigarette! How many times had he fought down the desire to seek comfort in that unopened pack during the last three weeks? Brett smiled in self-derision. More times than he wanted to remember. The need for a cigarette was the least of the desires Brett fought against.

If she loved me.

Brett was relieved at the intrusive noise of the buzzer on the telephone. Swinging back to the desk, he scooped up the receiver.

Before he could speak the "Wizard" said, "Mrs. Renninger on line two, sir." Brett's distraction was evidenced by his subdued greeting to his mother. He forgot to call her sir.

"Yes, Mother?" he queried after pressing the proper button.

"Are you feeling all right?" Violet demanded in concern.

Brett frowned. "Yes, of course. Why?"

"If you have to ask, I must be working you too hard," Violet answered. Then, without warning, she sprang her news on him. "Wolf has been declared fit to go back to work. He has decided to remain at the farm until after Easter. That gives you a week and a half to clear up whatever you're on at the moment and regear your mind for Atlanta. You can bring him up to date when you and JoAnne come down for the holiday. You *were* planning to come down for Easter, weren't you?"

Brett was in no mood for pretense. "I really hadn't thought about it," he admitted starkly.

"And now you don't have to," she shot back at him. "It's family conclave time, Brett. I'm considering another branch on the Renninger's company tree. Wolf needs to be brought up to date. And you sound like you need a rest. When will you and JoAnne arrive?"

Brett couldn't deny the smile that curved his tight lips. "What rank did you carry in the marines?" As the question was moot, he went on through her laughter, "We'll fly down sometime during holy week. I cannot be more definitive at this point. Okay?"

"I guess it will have to be." Violet sighed. "Sometimes I think I trained my sons too well. Give my love to JoAnne, Brett."

Give my love to JoAnne. The phrase revolved in Brett's head long after he'd replaced the receiver.

I want to give my love to JoAnne.

Does JoAnne still love my brother?

Did JoAnne ever love my brother?

Does JoAnne know how to love?

Is Brett going completely mad?

256

Tune in tomorrow for the next thrilling installment of "Brett Renninger takes a header."

Brett came to his senses with the realization that he was in the process of opening the forbidden pacifier. Stupid ass, he berated himself, flinging the pack from him with such force it ricocheted off the wall to skim over the floor to where it came to rest under the desk. In disgust, Brett turned his back to glare out the window.

They had come so close that night, so very close to a breakthrough, to a meeting of the minds as well as of the flesh. Brett swallowed the bitter taste of defeat coated with self-destructive jealousy. Both emotions were unfamilar and unacceptable to him. Brett knew he would have to do something to rectify the situation, and soon. The question was what?

I hate this!

The silent cry came from the soul. There was nothing new or unique about the protest. Brett had been living with it now for what seemed like most of his life. Stalemate. To Brett, the marriage was in a position of stalemate. So what do you do? he taxed himself. Write it off? Brett refused to as much as consider calling it quits without a fight.

What had gone wrong? Brett's lips curved wryly. What had ever been right about it . . . other than the purely physical? Then again, there had been some moments, times when he and Jo had been in smooth accord. Those times had been a lure, a teaser, promising a rich relationship if they could bridge the gap.

That was what had been so exciting for a little while the night he'd come home from the Poconos. Brett could still feel the tremor of expectation that had shivered through him that night. For a brief, breathless moment, he had allowed himself to believe Jo was beginning to care for him. Jo had talked more openly than ever before, she had even revealed signs of resentment for Marsha. For an instant, Brett had actually convinced himself Jo's resentment was caused by jealousy. Euphoric, Brett had felt the time right to mention Jo's affair with Wolf. Jo's sudden, chilly silence had said more than any lengthy explanation. Jo had stopped talking and, during these interminable three weeks, had conversed on a surface level. It was only after they were in bed that Jo displayed animation.

Brett felt his body harden in reaction to a flashing image of Jo, her breathing shallow, her lips parted, writhing and moaning beneath him. Their physical union was as close as Brett had ever hoped to get to perfect. The strange thing was, his desire appeared to be feeding itself. The more Brett had of Jo, the more he wanted her! Satiation was transient. Hunger was self-renewing. Need. Need. Need.

Turning abruptly, Brett strode back to his desk. He didn't have time to indulge in wishful thinking. His movements purposeful, Brett drew a pile of reports to the center of the desk. After reading the first sheet of paper contained in the first report for the second time, he closed the folder and pushed the pile away again. Resting his head against the chair's high back, Brett stared sightless at the large photograph of the first Renninger-built condominium on the wall opposite his desk.

His concentration was a thing of the past. Perhaps his mother was right and he did need a rest. Brett's smile was both bitter and derisive. He certainly didn't expect to get much rest at the farm! Not if he had to play the role of watchdog around Jo and Wolf. At the thought, Brett went rigid in the well-padded chair.

Is this what being in love had brought him to? Brett shuddered at the idea of himself sniffing at the heels of his wife and brother.

God damn it! No! He'd see them both in hell first! She was not worth it. No woman alive was worth it! Damn Wolf! Damn Jo! And damn my own love for her! If, when Wolf is once again in residence behind this desk, they still want each other, I'll go back to Atlanta alone! I can live without her!

But, oh God, I love her!

A short distance down a wide, plushly carpeted hall, Jo sat in a similar, if smaller office, at a similar, if smaller desk, coming to a similar, if softer decision. Jo had not damned Wolf. Jo had not damned Brett. Jo had not even damned herself. Jo had reached the same conclusion as Brett. She would remain in New York when Brett went back to Atlanta.

The relationship they had so very suddenly dived into was crumbling with equal swiftness. How long could she go on living with a stranger? Jo had grown weary with the repetition of the question. How long could she bear coexistence with a man who was always polite, most times even pleasant, a searing flame in bed, but a stranger nonetheless?

Was it worth it? Jo lowered long lashes over eyes stinging with hot moisture. Another failure. Was she to go through life drifting in and out of affairs? Successful in her chosen career, ineffectual in any personal relationship? Or was her mother right after all? Was it all a hoax, a shimmering facade—this idea, or ideal, or a real, lasting love between a man and a woman?

Rebellion stirred deep inside Jo. If the whole concept of love was nothing more than a myth, then what was the purpose of life? Without the humanizing presence of love, romantic love, humans would be reduced to the lowest level, and life itself would become a barren waste. Every atom of intelligence Jo possessed rejected the cold precept. Her mother was wrong! She *had* to be wrong! Jo refused to view life as a grinding ordeal, or humans as automatons, untouched or unsoftened by the gentle kiss of love.

Why can't Brett love me?

Shivering, Jo opened her eyes to stare at the plain, narrow gold band on her left ring finger. Jo wanted to live to be a very old lady and still be wearing that gold band when she closed her eyes for the last time. But without Brett's love, the ring was valueless.

Reflective of her husband's actions, Jo pushed her chair away from the desk and walked to the window. If only Brett had not mentioned her affair with Gary in quite that accusing tone! Or was she too sensitive about that fiasco? Why couldn't they just sit down and talk like two intelligent, mature adults? Maybe she ought to look Brett straight in the eyes and say: I love you. Now what are you going to do about it? Jo sighed. She knew full well that it was the fear of Brett's answer that kept her from speaking to him about her feelings. Still, Jo knew that something would have to give, and soon. She simply could not continue to live in this void.

Jo stood at the window a long time, her thoughts revolving, always coming back to the same point. Something, or someone, would have to give. Jo had the very uncomfortable feeling that the someone would be JoAnne Lawrence Renninger.

Since their marriage, whenever Brett was in the office, he came for her when it was time to go home. It was after six before he strode into Jo's office that afternoon. As usual, the sight of him set Jo's pulses racing. Today Brett's grim expression increased the pulse rate to a gallop.

"Are you ready to leave?"

For all the work she'd accomplished, she might as well have stayed home in the first place! Jo refrained from offering the information. Come to that, there hadn't been all that much work to do! Had Brett been as idle as she these last weeks? Jo rejected the idea at once. From all reports, he had not allowed his first wife to interfere with his work, and he had been in love with her! Jo nodded in answer and began collecting her briefcase, handbag, gloves, and coat, suppressing the longing to have the power to interfere with his daily routine.

"Well, at least I'll soon be saying good-bye to this place." Brett made the thickly drawled observation as they entered the apartment.

Startled, and more than a little shocked, Jo's gaze trekked Brett's as he scanned the room. She would have sworn he liked the apartment! The full content of his statement hit her in a rush. Was Brett obliquely telling her he was leaving her? Jo's fear hid itself behind a calm tone.

"Are you going somewhere?" God! She sounded bored! And, from the sharp glance Brett sliced at her, he did not appreciate her enforced smoothness.

"*We* are going somewhere," Brett enunciated harshly. "I had a call from Mother today." Removing his coat, Brett held it in one hand and reached for Jo's with the other. "She is expecting us at the farm for Easter," he continued as he hung the garments in the closet. Jo felt pinned by his steely eyes when he turned to face her. "It's time to return to Atlanta." Brett walked to within a few inches of her before adding, "Wolf's ready to resume control of the New York office."

"But that's wonderful!" Jo momentarily forgot her own unhappiness on hearing about Wolf's recovery. Brett brought her back to earth with a crash.

"Are you going with me?" Brett's quiet tone conflicted with the muscle jumping in his jaw.

To where? Jo wondered in confusion. To Florida or Atlanta? And why was he suddenly so tense? And, damn it, why did he sound so relieved about leaving the apartment? Ask him, you fool! Jo opened her mouth, then closed it again, damning herself for the coward she'd become. Fortunately, Brett unwittingly gave her a reprieve.

"I told Mother we'd fly down the middle of next week," Brett went on when it became obvious she was not going to respond. "It seems there's a family conference awaiting us. Will Wednesday be convenient for you?"

"Yes, of course." Jo frowned. "What is the conference all about?"

"Who knows?" Brett shrugged. "But, knowing Mother, it will probably mean more work for all of us."

Brett breathed in deeply as the plane soared off the runway into the clear morning sky. After a week of figuratively holding his breath, it was a relief to breathe without constraint. At every minute of every hour of every day Brett had expected Jo to tell him she was not going with him. Now, with Jo strapped into the seat beside him, Brett allowed his taut body to relax. The ending would come soon enough. Until the final moment was upon him, Brett wanted her right where she was, by his side.

My beautiful, fragile-looking, tough-as-a-marine wife. Brett smiled sadly inside his mind. Since meeting Jo the previous October, Brett had revised every one of his opinions about her but one. At that time, he had concluded that Jo was a confection spun of pure steel. Now Brett knew his conclusion had been correct. Then again, perhaps Marsha's theory held merit. Maybe Jo simply did not like men! Not once in the two months they had been together had Jo looked at another man with even a hint of interest. As to that, Jo hadn't revealed a hell of a lot of interest in him, either, except in the bedroom!

Brett had to clench his teeth against the bitter laughter that rose in his throat. Now, there's a switch! Weren't men forever getting rapped for being unable to communicate outside of the bedroom?

Crap!

Brett had never consciously thought about it before but, at that moment, he decided that most of what he'd heard and read about the differences between the sexes was simply that . . . so much crap. Once the obvious hurdle was cleared, the fact was there was very little difference between the male and the female.

The fact denoted equality.

The thought sprang into Brett's mind and refused to be dislodged. In all honesty, he had to admit, at least to himself, that Jo was indeed his equal. How often had he heard the expression "she thinks like a man"? As far as Brett was concerned that expression was more of the same crap. He had witnessed Jo in action. Jo did not think like a man. Jo thought like a highly intelligent human being. Brett personally knew several men who were not half as bright as she.

They should make a brilliant combination, Brett mused. The ideal team. So, why didn't they?

Because she does not love you.

Square one. From a distance that seemed like light-years, but was in fact not yet two full years, Brett acknowledged that the love he'd thought he'd felt for Sondra was as water compared to wine in what he felt for Jo. What he felt for Jo was a totally different kind of loving. Other than in the physical sense, he'd really not needed Sondra. Brett knew he needed Jo, in every sense known to man. If he required proof, all Brett had to do was remember the desperation he'd felt while making love to Jo ever since he'd received the phone call from his mother. For Brett, the act had gone far beyond the physical coupling of a man and a woman. In effect, what he had been attempting to do was draw the essence of Jo into himself; in a sense, to store up on her for a rainy day. And yet Brett still felt empty.

Emptiness has to be filled with something: Brett filled his personal void with anger. His fury was unreasonable and he knew it. Yet there it was, eating through him like a hot tongue of fire. Anger at Wolf, the brother he idolized. Anger at Jo, the woman he adored. Anger at himself, for getting involved in the first place. Brett's anger fostered determination. He could not . . . would not give Jo up without a fight!

The same black Cadillac with the same taciturn driver was waiting for them at the small airstrip in Florida, only this time the sun was shining brightly and the temperature hovered in the mid-seventies. There was not a hint of rain, either in the air or on the horizon.

Jo, grateful for Brett's suggestion that she wear light clothing, looked around with interest as they walked to the car. The airstrip and the small office-hangar had the appearance of having been plunked down in the middle of nowhere, so isolated were they.

Josh's greeting was every bit as terse and laconic as it had been in December. Brett's reply was as tight-lipped. Dismissing both men from her mind, Jo sat close to the smoked-glass window, her gaze skimming over the lush green pastureland they were driving through.

"Those trees are beautiful!" Jo exclaimed, indicating the huge pines that dotted the pastures and the large, tree-shaped cones that decorated the grass beneath the widely spread branches.

"Yes."

Brett's short reply robbed Jo of her delight in seeing Florida basking in the sunlight. Her first glimpse of sleek Thoroughbreds ambling serenely behind white rail fences restored her enthusiasm. Jo had never seen a Thoroughbred horse before, yet even she could recognize the fine lines and elegant appearance of the animals. It was not exactly love at first sight. Oh, the horses were very beautiful, but they were also very large. Jo decided she'd prefer to admire from a distance.

The drive seemed much shorter, and the house much larger, than before. As the car glided to a smooth stop in the curving driveway in front of the house, Jo was again struck by its likeness to pictures she'd seen of antebellum plantation homes. The word tranquility sprang to Jo's mind. As she stepped from the car, Jo fervently hoped she'd find a measure of that tranquility while she was within its walls. As Jo and Brett mounted the steps, the door was flung wide open.

Elania Calaveri was exactly as she had been in December. Jo smothered a bubble of laughter as the woman again took Brett to task.

"Well, what a surprise!" Elania exclaimed in mock amazement. "Only half of holy week gone and you're here already! Are you sick or something?" As they entered the imposing hall, the housekeeper directed her comments to Jo in a confiding manner. "Never could keep this hellion in one place for very long. He was always eager to be gone, even as a boy. He'd be up and out of the house so early, I had to teach the scamp to cook his own breakfast to make sure he'd get a decent meal inside him, as he seldom came home before dark."

Jo shot a gleaming glance at her scowling husband. One bursting sentence from Elania had cleared up the mystery of how and why Brett had learned to cook. Eager to be gone. The words reverberated in Jo's mind. Did that explain Brett's strained behavior of the past several weeks and his obvious relief about leaving the apartment soon? Was the adult Brett still the same as the boy—eager to be gone? Caught up in speculation, Jo missed Brett's greeting to Elania, snapping to attention when she heard her name.

"I'm sorry, I was . . . admiring the house and didn't hear what you said," she lied unevenly when Brett repeated her name impatiently.

"I said," Brett reiterated, "Elania has just told me that none of the others know we've arrived as they are in the dining room having lunch. Would you like to freshen up before we join them?"

Annoyed by Brett's too-quiet tone, Jo answered sharply, "Yes. If you don't mind?"

"If I had minded," Brett bit back, "I wouldn't have asked in the first place." Ignoring the tiny gasp that burst through Elania's suddenly tight lips, Brett ushered Jo up the stairs.

On her first visit to the house, Jo had been delighted with the bedroom Elania had escorted her to. Now she followed Brett as he swung in the opposite direction at the top of the wide staircase. Apparently, Jo mused, this side of the house contained the family bedrooms. A twinge of pain twisted in her chest as she wondered how much longer she'd be a member of the Renninger family.

The room Jo trailed Brett into was large and square and definitely masculine in decor. Jo loved it immediately. The absence of unnecessary clutter appealed to the Spartan in Jo. Standing just inside the door, Jo inventoried the rich dark-brown carpet and matching drapes, the bold broad stripes of alternating brown and white in the bedspread, and the stark white of unadorned walls. An overstuffed, comfortable-looking chair in a blazing red-orange gave the room focus and color. Jo did not have to be told that Brett had selected the decor himself. In some strange way the room was Brett.

"I love it." Jo might as well have said "I love you."

Brett's face relaxed at her stamp of approval. "Somehow I knew you would." He stared at her intently for a second, then indicated a door on the wall to her right with a wave of his hand. "The bathroom. You don't need to fuss, it's only family." A smile flickered over Brett's tautly drawn lips. "You always look perfect anyway."

Jo stared at him, unable to move for an instant. Would she ever get past the point of melting inside at the slightest suggestion of a smile from this man? It's not fair, Jo protested silently. It's simply not . . .

"If you don't move," Brett's sensuously warm voice drew her out of her thoughts, "I might be tempted to demonstrate the resiliency of the mattress on my bed." His lips curved invitingly. "Are you as hungry as I am?"

Incredibly Jo was suddenly starving, in exactly the manner Brett's slumberous eyes told her he was! How was it possible? Had they not skipped breakfast in favor of . . . Jo shivered in memory of the feast she and Brett had indulged in that morning. Fleetingly, Jo concluded that if they could remain in bed forever, they would have no marital problems. She wanted him, again, very badly, but, there was more to a marriage than that. There had to be. "Brett, I . . . " Jo's breath caught in her throat as he took a step toward her. "They are all down there," she finished lamely.

"And we are all up here." Brett took another slow step. "All two of us." His smile promised everything. "The perfect number for a luncheon party." One more step, and Jo felt like she was coming apart at the seams.

"But we haven't even seen Wolf yet!" Jo grabbed at the excuse in desperation. What if Elania had mentioned their arrival? What would they all think? The change in Brett was as confusing as it was sudden. His body stiffening with tension, Brett pivoted away from her.

"Yes, of course, Wolf." His back to her, Brett stood as still as

266

if carved from rock, his voice as hard. "Will you go do whatever you have to do, so we can get out of this room?"

Jo wanted to scream. Jo wanted to throw things. She walked into the bathroom. How did one keep up with a man whose moods changed with mercurial swiftness? Jo stared at the pitifully wan face reflected in the mirror above the brown-and-white marbleized sink. With the eyes of a critic, she examined the makeup she'd applied so carefully that morning. Her pale cheeks were in need of a touch of the blusher brush. Her disordered hair needed taming. Jo pictured the needed articles inside the flight bag Brett had placed on the long double dresser as he'd entered the room. She could either go and get the bag, or ask Brett to hand it in to her. Jo's eyes avoided her face. Lifting her hands, she smoothed the mass of dark hair. She would not ask him for anything and, when she did walk out of the room, she would be ready to go downstairs. Brett was in a strange mood. He had been moody for weeks. The smell of showdown was in the air around them. Jo knew the slightest incident could trigger it. Raising her long lashes, Jo read the plea in her own dull hazel eyes; not now, not today, hold on to him as long as you can.

Jo's smoothing hands drifted down over the wheat-color suit jacket she wore over a crisp orange shirt, then down over hips covered in a pencil-slim skirt that partnered the jacket.

"Jo!"

Jo's hands stilled at Brett's impatient call. Dismissing the sad-eyed woman in the mirror, Jo opened the door and walked out of the room, her spine straight, her shoulders back, her head high, and her expectations gone. The sight of Brett had the usual, melting effect on Jo's senses. In casual slacks and sport coat, Brett didn't project quite the forbidding appearance as when he was decked out in battle array of conservative, three-piece business armor.

They descended the romantic staircase in an unromantic silence. As they neared the dining room the muted sound of genial conversation filtered through the closed double doors. Drawing a deep breath, Jo forced a smile to her stiff lips, prepared to follow Brett's lead in whatever image he created concerning their marriage.

Determined to play out the role of the happy bridegroom if it killed him, Brett pasted a parody of a smile on his face. His facial muscles ached in protest of the switch from down to up. Over the last weeks those muscles had grown used to the down position. As Brett followed Jo into the dining room, the ache was relieved by the scene that met his eyes. Brett frowned. Where were Eric and his family, and Di and her brood? The question spun out of his mind at the sound of his brother's voice.

"Will you look at the delicious creature!" Wolf's liquid-silver eyes swept Jo's willowy body. "What a delightful treat for dessert!"

Everyone laughed. Everyone but Brett. Cursing silently, Brett ordered a faint smile to his lips thinking, with shocking savagery, You touch her, big brother, and you're dead. Every muscle in Brett's body tightened. He hated it, yet there it was. Brett knew without doubt that should Wolf presume to lay one hand on Jo, he would find himself on the floor, on his back, and hurting like hell. Without conscious command his fingers curled into his palms, readying for action that didn't come.

"Wolf! Will you never learn to behave?" Violet chastised, bestowing a welcoming smile on Jo. "Come sit by me, JoAnne. It's long past time you were welcomed into the family." She shot an arched look at Brett.

"It's been a busy winter, Mother." Brett offered the lame excuse for not bringing Jo to visit sooner, then strode to where Wolf had risen in place at the end of the table. "You're looking good, big brother." The truth of his compliment brought an equal mixture of joy and pain to Brett. He had prayed for Wolf's recovery, while at the same time dreading it. Brett knew Wolf's return to vigor might well mean his own loss. The emotions in conflict inside him were tearing him apart.

Wolf's silver eyes darkened with concern. "I'm sorry I can't say the same about you. You look very tired, Brett." Wolf's glance sliced to Jo. "Are there problems?"

"No! I . . ."

"No more than usual," Brett cut across Jo's too-hurried denial. "I'll be glad to get back to running one region." Terminating the subject, Brett turned to kiss Micki's cheek in greeting, then frowningly directed his gaze back to his mother. "Eric and Di not here yet?"

"No. And they won't be coming." Violet waited till Brett seated himself opposite Jo before explaining. "Dirk is covered with chicken pox." She smiled in sympathy for Di's youngest child. "And, as Doris has been having mild cramps for several days, her doctor has forbidden her to travel."

"But it's not Doris's time yet. Is it?" Brett truthfully couldn't remember: he had had other, more important things on his mind since Christmas.

"Close enough," Violet drawled. "We might have another new member in the family by Easter."

His mother's comment elicited speculation from the others at the table about whether the new arrival would be a boy or a girl. Brett, making a show of eating the fish stew Elania set before him, let the conversation swirl around him as he studied his wife's animated face. A new baby. One month ago, for one flashing moment, Brett's heart had leaped with joy at the idea of a new baby. His baby. From Brett out of Jo. The spoon paused halfway between his mouth and the bowl. On the night he'd returned from Pennsylvania his hopes had soared with the suspicion that Jo was pregnant. But, had he hoped for a child, or to use the child to keep Jo with him? Brett slowly lowered the spoon to the bowl, his eyes hungry on Jo's face. Maybe not that night, but now, at this moment, Brett knew he wanted the child. Jo's child. Brett was painfully aware of the fact that he would probably never see that child.

"Brett!"

The exasperation that tinged his mother's tone was a clear

indication that it was not the first time she'd said his name. Shifting his gaze to Violet's face, Brett smiled ruefully. "Yes, Mother?"

"Are you feeling all right?" Violet's exasperation was over-shadowed by concern. "You've barely touched your soup."

"I'm fine," Brett assured her quietly. "I was just wondering if the family conclave has been postponed . . . due to chicken pox and confinement."

"Not at all." Very motherlike, Violet searched Brett's face for telltale signs of illness.

"Brett's a big boy now, Mother. I'm sure he knows how to take care of himself," Wolf inserted dryly. "Even if handling both Atlanta and New York are too much for him."

Brett chose to ignore Wolf's taunt, which caused his mother's frown to darken. "How do you propose to have a family conclave with only half the family here?" In an effort to ease his mother's worry, Brett arched one pale brow exaggeratedly. Before his eyes, mother changed into Madam President.

"Have you ever heard of the conference line?"

Out of the corner of his eye, Brett caught the gleam of the appreciative grin that revealed Jo's even white teeth. Damn, she is beautiful! Dragging his concentration back to his mother, Brett nodded. "Yes, sir." His own grin wouldn't be denied when Brett heard Micki's soft laughter whisper down the length of the long, highly glossed table.

"That's more like it." Violet's expression of concern faded at Brett's apparent return to more normal behavior. "I've slated the conference for three o'clock. That will give you and JoAnne a chance to change clothes, or whatever."

Brett's inclination was to opt for the whatever but, for the moment, he focused his attention on getting through lunch with-out making a complete ass of himself. He'd already aroused his mother's concern and Wolf's taunting speculation. The last thing he needed was to create a scene at the lunch table. Elania would never forgive him!

270

Fortunately, Wolf chose to be briefed over the salad, and the remainder of the meal was consumed along with dry business details. By the time Brett and Jo went back upstairs to his bedroom less than forty-five minutes were left till conclave time.

Their cases were placed neatly side by side on the storage chest that ran the width of the bed at its base. Maintaining the cool silence that had enveloped them since leaving the dining room, Jo set to work immediately unpacking her case. Watching her from behind half-closed eyes Brett knew revealed both longing and desire, he shrugged out of his jacket, tossing it onto the foot of the bed as he strolled across the room. Dropping onto the padded chair, Brett sprawled with deceptive laziness, eyes now mere slits, watching her as she moved gracefully back and forth between suitcase and closet.

When her case was empty Jo closed the lid and snapped the locks. Would she, Brett mused, perform her wifely duty and unpack his case? She would. Brett felt a thrill shiver through his body at the sight of Jo's slim hands on his clothes.

You poor jerk! Brett sighed silently. You are positively besotted! When you can be turned on by observing a woman handling your faded Levis you have gone beyond the pale!

"Brett?" Jo's near whisper revealed the fact that she thought he was sleeping.

"Hmmm?" Brett raised his lids slightly, just enough to show her he was awake.

"Am I expected to attend this family conference?" Jo asked hesitantly.

"Are you a member of the family?" Brett laid the drawl on with a spade.

Jo responded indirectly. "I . . . I'm going to have a quick shower. I'll only be a moment."

"Take your time." Brett's smile mocked her. "We won't have to punch a time clock as we enter the boss's study." His smile disappeared as, with a toss of her head that betrayed her impatience with him, Jo strode into the bathroom.

Biting back a rather pungent, self-descriptive epithet, Brett jerked to his feet, crossing to the double dresser in four long strides to retrieve the shaving kit Jo had placed there. Tugging the zipper midway around the case, Brett inserted his fingers and withdrew a small velvet box. Flipping the lid, Brett stared down at the flawless, pear-shaped, three-carat diamond beautifully displayed in a delicate, intricately fashioned setting. Furs. Diamonds. The lid closed with a tiny snap. The Maserati was on order.

Sliding the top dresser drawer open, Brett dropped the box onto the neat pile of underwear inside, then slammed the drawer closed forcefully. Brett knew now that Jo could not be bought, either physically or emotionally. He had known it for some time. If Jo had been with Wolf, it had not been for the apartment, or the small car that was seldom moved out of the apartment parking area, or to advance herself in the company. If she had been with Wolf, it was because she had *wanted* to be with him.

Brett's body became absolutely still, while his mind pounced alertly on his last thought. Because she wanted to be with Wolf! Raising his head slowly, Brett stared into the wide, gray eyes reflected in the oversized mirror on the wall above the dresser. Because she *wanted* to be with Wolf!

She's with me now!

The gray eyes staring back at Brett suddenly glittered silver with hope. Could that mean . . . does Jo *want* to be with me? But Wolf's well now. A little thin, à little gaunt, but well! A shudder tore through Brett's slender frame.

Dear God! I have got to get her away from here!

There were twelve minutes left to go before the appointed hour of three when Jo rushed out of the bathroom. Clamping down on the urge to grab hold of her and run, Brett strode into the bathroom to replace her under a cold shower. When Brett walked back into the bedroom Jo was gone, as were the minutes till the hour of three. Pulling open the top dresser drawer, Brett smiled at the small velvet box before removing a pair of the silky navy very-brief briefs. Stepping into the faded Levis, Brett imagined he could feel the warmth of Jo's recent touch, smell her scent on the soft denim. A pale-blue chamois shirt, a double stamp into supple leather ankle boots, and Brett went striding out of the room, eight minutes late and primed to fight.

Four pairs of eyes swiveled to observe Brett's entrance into the study, and Eric's voice complained from the squawk box attached to the phone on Violet's desk.

"Hey! Where did everybody go?"

Sweeping a look over Brett that told him she was now "boss" not "Mother," Violet said crisply, "We are still here. And now your brother has condescended to join us." Brett met her drilling stare with calm detatchment.

"Congratulations, Brett." Eric's voice smiled. "You picked a winner this time."

Brett's eyes easily broke the hold of his mother's to stalk those of the "winner." "Thanks, Eric." Pride swelled inside Brett as Jo stared back at him serenely. It was as if she was saying, There's not a Renninger alive who can make me lose my composure. She is magnificent! The observation hardened Brett's determination to keep her. Refusing to release his visual hold on her, Brett added, "And how is your winner?"

"Doing fine," Eric assured. "You may be uncle again before the night is out."

"Then what the hell are you doing on this line?" Brett startled everyone, including himself, with his sudden harshness. "You should be with Doris, Eric." Brett felt the edge, of patience, of reason, of . . . whatever, looming closer. If he didn't do something soon to resolve this mess he'd created, Brett decided, he'd fall headfirst over that precarious edge.

A stunned silence held sway for an instant, then a soft voice issued from the squawk box. "Brett's right, you know." Di offered her opinion. "Eric should be with Doris, and I should be with Dirk. Mother, can we wind this meeting up fairly quickly?" Before Violet could respond, Di added, "Brett, Jo, I hope you'll

273

be very happy. I'm holding my gift to you until you have a permanent address."

At that point Jo stole the initiative from Brett. Maintaining his oddly intense stare, and wondering what the devil was going on in his head, Jo infused warmth into her voice. "Thank you, Di. And you too, Eric. I'm keeping my fingers crossed for a boy."

Eric's laughter, and possible reply, were cut short by Violet's brisk voice. "Of course, Brett and Di are both right. We can have an in-depth meeting when everyone is well again. But there is one consideration I'd like you all to think about. Eric and I have discussed this and we are in complete accord. It's time for the company to expand again. I want to open another region—the northwest region, from Colorado west, including Oregon and Washington." She glanced at Brett. "I had considered giving Richard Colby the mid-Atlantic region and, as he was a bachelor, asking Brett to take over the new region." A soft smile curved her lips as she shifted her gaze to Jo. "But as Brett is now married . . ."

"We'll take it."

Jo blinked, for a second stunned by Brett's hard, decisive tone. Then swift anger rushed through her. How dare he presume to make decisions for her? Not that she would object to going to the Northwest or, for that matter, hell, as long as she was with him, but she would appreciate being consulted first! Breathing deeply, Jo managed to keep her tone neutral.

"Brett, I think we should discuss this in private." Jo's tone was belied by the flash of amber in her hazel eyes. "I don't know if I . . ."

"You'll do as your told." Brett's eyes glinted a warning for her to be silent; his tone was thick with ice. "Mother, we will take it."

"Brett!"

A chorus of voices, in varying degrees of shock, cried his name. Jo's was not one of them. Without even being aware of having moved, Jo was on her feet, her body shaking with

274

humiliation and fury. Wolf was on his feet also, a protective alertness in his stance.

"Brett." The big prowler's voice commanded attention. "What in hell do you think you're doing? Apologize to Jo at once."

"Mind your own god-damned business, Wolf." Taut with anger, Brett ignored the collective gasp his snarling voice elicited. "Jo is *my* wife. I don't need you, or anyone else, to instruct me on how to handle her."

"Oh, sharp as a marble, you ass!" Eric's angry voice exploded from the squawk box.

There was more of the same, from Violet, from Di, from Micki, and from a now-incensed Wolf. Jo heard without hearing. Her eyes stinging with tears of shame, and hurt, and a jumbled mess of other emotions, she stared at the beauty of Brett's chiseled face until it blurred, then she ran, blocking out the angry voices that bounced off the paneled walls of Violet's study.

What had come over him? What had she done to turn Brett into a snarling dictator? Did he hate her so very much? The questions hammered in Jo's mind as she ran along the hall, through the spotless kitchen, and out the back door. Where could she go? Jo's tear-filled eyes swept the wide expanse of bricked courtyard behind the house, passing then slicing back to the two vehicles parked there. A jeep and a pickup truck, keys in the ignitions of each. If she could get to the airfield, or an airport . . .

No!

The protest was a rebellious scream inside Jo's mind. No, damn it! She would not run again! In effect, she had run from a bad situation—*not* of her making—when she'd left home at nineteen. If only in her mind, she had run from the pain and humiliation inflicted upon her by Gary. And, at least figuratively, she'd been running from a showdown with Brett since the first day she met him. How long could the mind employ evasive tactics? How many avenues of escape could her consciousness scurry along in avoidance of the truth? Besides, Jo had the uncomfortable feeling that if she ran now Brett would not follow her, and that would prove her mother's theory about love, and the relationships therein, correct. Sniffing, Jo shook her head in silent denial.

Ignoring the vehicles and the tears trickling down her face, Jo slid her fingers into the back pockets of her jeans and began pacing off the distance between the kitchen door and the four-car garage set to the right and rear of the house.

What the devil had come over Brett? Again. Jo came to an abrupt halt midway between house and garage, the single word repeating in her mind. Again? Yes, again. Even though there had been constraint between them since the night he'd returned from the Poconos, Brett had unfailingly treated her with polite consideration. What had caused his sudden harsh thoughtlessness? Jo raked her mind, examining every minute since their arrival at the house. A recent scene flashed into her memory, and, frowning, Jo relived it slowly.

"Are you as hungry as I am?"

The echo of Brett's sensuously warm voice tantalized her memory; he had certainly not been cold before lunch! But wait! Jo's frown deepened. Brett *had* turned cold before they'd gone down to join the family. What had she said to him? Something about the family waiting? No. That hadn't chilled his ardor. What then? Jo kicked at a tiny pebble in frustration; damn it, what else had she said? Memory clicked.

"But we haven't even seen Wolf yet!"

Wolf.

Wolf?

Jo went absolutely statue still. Brett had grown frigid at the mention of his brother's name . . . and not for the first time! It was almost as if Brett was jealous of Wolf, as if he believed . . . Oh my God! Could Brett really believe that she . . . and Wolf? Remembered images flashed through Jo's mind again, not entire

276

scenes, but small, isolated fragments, beginning with Brett refusing to let her see Wolf after the accident.

Brett, warning her not to call Wolf while he was in Vermont. Brett, oddly backing down the time in his office when she'd lifted the phone to call Wolf. Brett, telling her they'd probably both regret it but that he had to have her. Brett, suddenly coldly remote when they'd come to the farm at Christmas time. Brett, withdrawing from her on learning about a preexisting prescription for birth control pills. Brett, mentioning her previous affair in that odd, intensely accusatory manner.

Could it be . . . could it possibly be . . . Jo spun around at the sound of the kitchen door closing, breath catching in her throat at the sight of Brett's face. His expression austere with grim determination, Brett walked to her with slow, measured strides. In the seconds required for him to reach her, Jo tried, and failed, to suppress the wild hope rioting through her. As he drew close, Brett's eyelids narrowed over eyes gleaming silvery with intent, increasing her hope tenfold. Could it be that the fire raging inside Brett was caused by love for her? Was Brett jealous over her? All this time? All this long wasted time?

Brett had reached the very edge; it was either fish or cut bait, and he sure as hell was not about to cut bait at this stage of the game! Stalking his wife, Brett conceded that he might have gone about it with more tact, but, tactless or not, Jo was going with him to Colorado! And, after the way his family had ganged up on him when Jo had run from his mother's study, Brett was perfectly primed for an argument.

She is mine, and I will not give her up.

The avowal revolved in his mind as Brett studied Jo's face through the slits of lids narrowed against the glare of late-afternoon sunlight. The evidence of tears on her cheeks gave him momentary pause. It was the second time he'd made her cry. Brett felt a twist of pain in his chest. Damn fool! You've hurt her again! I'll make it up to her, he soothed his stinging conscience, but I cannot give her up!

277

Two steps from her, Brett hesitated; he could not talk, or argue, with Jo in the courtyard, not with his mother, Wolf, Micki, *and* Elania for an audience! One step from her Brett reached out, grasped her wrist firmly with his hand, then, pivoting, strode back to the house, a gasping Jo stumbling behind him.

"Brett!" Jo gave an ineffectual tug of her arm. "Have you gone mad?"

"Be quiet." Brett snapped the order without turning his head. "You'll have plenty of time to talk when we're alone in our room."

When he got to the kitchen door, Brett thrust it open and strode through, tugging firmly on a now angrily sputtering Jo to keep her following him. If nothing else, his precipitous action had one good result, Brett thought with a grimace; Jo was no longer crying.

His gait unchecked, Brett loped along the hall. He had made it to the bottom of the stairs when the door to his mother's study was flung open and Wolf, Violet and Micki at his heels, rushed into the hallway, only to come to a dead stop at the sight of Brett literally dragging Jo through the house.

"For Christ's sake, Brett!" Wolf's voice held a note of sheer disbelief. "What in hell are you doing? Let her go!" Snaking out a long arm, Wolf caught Jo's other, flailing wrist.

At the command "let her go" all the accumulated months of frustration exploded inside Brett's mind. When Wolf put his hand on Jo, anger exploded out through Brett's mouth.

"Don't touch her!"

For long seconds shocked silence smothered response, then bedlam took over as everyone protested at once. Even Elania, coming from the living room to investigate the cause of all the noise, added her two cent's worth of condemnation. Brett's voice, coldly, frighteningly savage, cut through the babble.

"I want silence." Brett knew his objective was achieved through shock; he knew it and used it. "I assure you all that I have no intention of harming my wife." His eyes dropped to rest deliberately on Wolf's fingers, curled around Jo's wrist. When he lifted his gaze, Brett's eyes had the look of opaque ice. "I told you not to touch her."

For whatever reason—curiosity, surprise, whatever—Wolf's hold on Jo's wrist relaxed, then fell away.

"Don't *ever* touch her again." Once again Brett spoke through an outburst of protest. "If you will all excuse us?" Tugging gently on Jo's arm, he started up the stairs. "Jo and I would like to have an argument in private."

Trailing Brett's anger-tightened body up the stairs and into their room, Jo felt excitement stir, then radiate through her system. Incredible, unbelievable as it seemed, Brett *was* jealous of Wolf. Why he was jealous of Wolf was the question Jo hoped soon to have the answer to. All these months! Why hadn't Brett simply asked her? Of all the lunkheads! Jo wasn't quite sure if she was referring to Brett or herself; they both fit the description! Hearing the door snap shut behind her, Jo spun to face her husband, trepidation closing her throat at the glittering glance he raked over her. Barely breathing, Jo watched his eyes until a flicker of movement caught her attention, drawing her gaze to his hands. The purposeful work of Brett's fingers as they unbuttoned his shirt opened Jo's throat enough to allow the passage of a startled squeak.

"What are you doing?"

His expression mocking her for asking the obvious, Brett yanked the shirt free of the jeans waistband and tossed it carelessly to the floor. His fingers found employment at his belt buckle as he began walking to her. Eyeing him warily, Jo edged toward the bathroom door.

"All right!" Jo felt rather proud of the steadiness of her tone; inside she was a jumbled bundle of excitement-tied nerve ends. "I know *what* you're doing. I thought we were going to talk."

His mocking smile deepening, Brett sauntered past her to drop onto the edge of the brightly colored chair. "I've changed my mind." His eyes laughed at her evasive edging toward the bathroom. Lifting one leg, he tugged at his boot; it landed on the floor with a soft thud. As he pulled at the other boot, Brett motioned at the bed with a brief nod of his head. "I've decided to give you a demonstration of the resiliency of the mattress after all."

"Brett . . ."

"You must admit," he went on, ignoring her attempt at protest, "the bed is the one place we communicate beautifully." The second boot plopped to the floor. "You had better get busy," he chided softly to the background sound of the descending zipper. "I'm way ahead of you."

Way ahead of you. Way ahead of you! A light clicked on in Jo's mind. Good grief! Had she left her reasoning power behind in the yard? Watching Brett's slim, muscularly corded length emerge from the jeans, Jo's adrenaline kicked all her senses into overtime. Brett may have been referring to her fully clothed state, but Jo interpreted his words in a different light. His cool detachment was nothing more than a facade! Introduce her to the bed's resiliency indeed! Brett was hell-bent on making a statement of ownership! He was not only jealous, he was running scared! Clamping her teeth together to contain a whoop of joy created by the wave of relief washing through her, Jo tore uncaringly at the buttons on her pure silk shirt. A raging fire? Jo's shirt landed unaimed on top of his. She'd show him an inferno!

Watching the play of emotions across her face, Brett knew the moment Jo reached a decision. When she began tearing at her clothes his already aroused manhood took on the quality of pure, painful iron. As her silky loveliness was exposed to his hungry stare an earlier thought reasserted itself.

She's with me now!

"Jo."

Brett wanted to say much more, so very much more, yet the only sound he could force through his constricted throat was the anguished whisper of her name. Consuming desire combined with a desperate need to claim erased all other consideration.

They both moved at the same instant.

There was no time for teasing kisses. There was no time for stroking caresses. There was no time for tiny erotic nuances. Mouths locked together in all-consuming need, they dropped to the bed, Brett thrusting into her on contact, Jo welcoming his invasion with a cry of exquisite pleasure. Never had their love-making been quite so fierce, or quite so savage, or quite so shatteringly satisfying.

The words that should have been said months before were purged from Brett's throat at the moment his life force erupted from his quivering body.

"I love you, Jo. Oh, God, how I love you!"

Sweet, sweet release. Release of tension. Release of fear. And, finally, unashamedly, release of long-pentup tears . . . both hers and his.

"Don't cry, darling!" Unmindful of her own wet cheeks, Jo brushed trembling fingertips over Brett's face. "It hurts me."

A tender smile softening his chiseled lips, Brett lowered his head to dry the salty moisture on her cheeks with his mouth. "You haven't said the words." Raising his head again, he gazed compellingly into her eyes. "Say it, Jo. Please. I need to hear it."

"I love you."

Jo felt the tremor that ripped through Brett's body in her palms still gripping his hips, in her body still pressed to his, and in her soul, now, at last, at one with his. Though complete, Jo was not so lost in euphoria she missed the significance of Brett's declaration without question. The significance thrilled her. Brett still labored under the illusion of a previous affair between her and his brother. What, Jo wondered mistily, had it cost Brett to make that declaration? Very likely a lot more than she'd ever know.

"You'll go to Colorado with me?" The uncertainty underlying Brett's tone drew Jo from speculation.

"I'd go to the moon with you." Jo's firm response brought a teasing gleam to his eyes.

"We've just been there."

Floating in contentment richer than whipped cream, Jo sighed as, levering his body a few inches from hers, Brett caressed her skin with his right hand. Long fingers drew a gasp of pleasure when they outlined the contour of one breast, the murmured confession that followed drew a gasp of dismay.

"I'd hate to have to admit the times I tormented myself with the thought of Wolf's hand stroking you like this."

"Brett—" Jo choked on the protest.

"Or," Brett continued raspily, "his mouth drinking from yours."

"Brett . . . please, listen."

"Or," Brett went on, unable to stop, "his body resting in the cradle of your thighs."

"Brett, stop this!" Releasing her hold on his hips, Jo brought her hands up to grasp his face, forcing him to look into her eyes. "There has never been anything personal between us. Never. *Ever.* Wolf has been my employer and my friend, nothing more." Jo sighed. "You should know better than I how very much Wolf adores Micki. I can't imagine where you ever got the idea that Wolf and I . . ."

Oh, God! Levering himself out of and off her completely, Brett lay beside Jo on his back, staring at the stark white ceiling. To believe the worse all these months, to live with the agony, day in, day out, only to find . . .

"He owns the apartment you live in." Started now, Brett had to have it all out.

"He does not own it!" Jo corrected, her tone revealing a hint of anger. "Wolf is holding the mortgage on it. Without his help I never could have managed it."

Brett turned his head to find Jo's eyes glaring at him. She was telling the truth and he knew it. Still he kept on, needing to hear it all. "He has a key to the place."

"Yes," Jo admitted readily on a sigh of exasperation. "He has a key. I gave it to him, but not, I assure you, for any unsavory purpose." Jo smiled wryly. "I have a bad habit, you see. I lock myself out on occasion."

Brett smiled, then laughed aloud as he gathered her close to his side. "Oh, hell, honey. I feel like such a jerk!"

"You should." Jo wasn't about to let him off the hook easily, not after the trauma of the last months. "Not for having the doubt in the first place, but for not asking me straight out if your suspicions were correct."

"Forgive me?" Brett hid his seriousness behind a grin. He'd take the rap, for there was no way he'd bring Micki's name into the discussion.

"Yes, of course." Jo snuggled closer to his warmth, shaking her head in wonder at her own obtuseness. "And here all the time I believed you were resenting Gary," she admitted in a murmur that turned to a yelp as Brett sat bolt upright.

"Who in the hell is Gary? And why in the hell didn't I know about him before now?" Brett asked angrily.

"Brett, you had to have realized there was someone before you," Jo said carefully.

"Yeah, sure, but I thought it was—"

"And now you know it wasn't," Jo interrupted gently. "Gary was the first, the only one before you." Praying that he wouldn't spoil what they had just found together, Jo explained her one disastrous affair in minute detail.

His expression contemplative, Brett stared down at Jo for long seconds when her recital was finished. He didn't like the idea of Gary Devlin, and not only for the hell he'd put Jo through. "Were you in love with him?" The question was a mild form of self-torture. Contrarily, he wanted her to say yes and no at the same time. Yes, because he couldn't abide the idea that Jo would live with a man she didn't love. And no, because he hated the mere thought that she'd loved a man before him. It was irrational. Brett knew it was irrational. Hadn't he thought himself in love with Sondra?

"I thought I was," Jo finally replied, unknowingly voicing

Brett's last consideration. "Of course I know now that I was merely infatuated with him. But it's too late to change things now, isn't it?"

"Yes." Bending to her, Brett brushed his lips over hers. "And it no longer matters." Surprisingly, it didn't, Brett realized in relief. Hell! Screw Devlin! "I don't mind not being first." His movement swift, Brett nipped gently at her lower lip. "As long as you make damned sure I'm the last."

"And what about you?" Jo arched a forbidding brow at him. "No more Marshas?"

"Jo, I told you . . ."

"What you told me, exactly, was 'Not for lack of trying on my part.'" Jo repeated his exact words. "I would like an explanation of that remark." The demand made, Jo held her breath. She knew she really had no right to an answer, but then, neither had he, and she'd been honest with him. Deep down, where she lived, Jo knew she was testing not only his love for her but his trust in her as well. When Brett smiled her personal world settled into place.

"The explanation is simple." Brett's hesitation was hardly noticable. Damn it, man, he scorned himself, she trusted you, it's your turn. "I meant exactly what I said. We were alone in Marsha's apartment in Vermont. We were undressed. We were in bed together." Brett paused as Jo's eyelids closed to conceal her pain. "Look at me, love." When her lashes lifted he stared into her eyes. "I was thinking about you, and I couldn't make it. Do you understand what I'm saying? I could not make it with another woman. I *wanted* you."

Jo blinked against a fresh swell of hot moisture and trembled with a fresh surge of hot response. Lord! Jo felt sure that if Brett touched her now he'd burn his hands! Lifting her hands, she grasped him around the waist to guide his body onto hers. "And now that you have me," she whispered, "what are you going to do with me?"

"I've been thinking about that," Brett answered solemnly, his eyes betraying his growing heat.

"And?" Jo prompted, moving against him sensuously to speed up his thinking process.

"I've decided to keep you." In retaliation, Brett angled his hips into hers, smiling at her gasp of pleasure. "And let the fire rage forever."

NIGHT STRIKER
AMII LORIN

Winner of two *Romantic Times* Reviewers' Choice Awards

"An unforgettable classic...a treasure to be read over and over again!"

—*Romantic Times*

From the ranches of the wealthiest Texas oil barons, to the estates of British nobility, Courtney Tremaine-Smythe searches for the one man who can free her from a past filled with danger. But soon she discovers that her fate rests in the hands of three desperate men: a brutal criminal who abducts her for her money, a brilliant Irish politician who needs her power, and an undercover agent who wants only her love.

___3187-6 $3.99 US/$4.99 CAN

COME HOME TO LOVE

AMII LORIN

Winner of two *Romantic Times* Reviewers' Choice Awards

"Amii Lorin always gives her readers something special!"

—*Romantic Times*

Ruthless, cold, and calculating—those are the words Katherine Acker uses to describe wealthy entrepreneur Matthew Martin. So the young widow is stunned when Matt offers to marry her if she will act as a hostess to his business associates. Little does Katherine realize that her marriage of convenience will be full of surprises—and one of them may be that her new husband loves her....

_3317-8 $3.99 US/$4.99 CAN